# ODYSSEYS OF THE SAINTS

# ODYSSEYS OF THE SAINTS

by

## Carol T.F. Bennett
## and
## Joseph Friedman

"You cannot therefore stand as idle and disinterested spectators of the scenes and events which are calculated in their very nature to reduce all nations and creeds to *one* political and religious *standard*, and thus put an end to Babel forms and names, and to strife and war. You will, therefore, either be led by the good Spirit to cast in your lot, and to take a lively interest with the Saints of the Most High, and the covenant people of the Lord, or on the other hand, you will become their inveterate enemy, and oppose them by every means in your power..."

The Church of Jesus Christ of Latter-day Saints,

"Proclamation to the Rulers and People of all Nations," 1845.

ISBN: 1-58500-994-6

1stBooks - rev. 03/21/00

# About the Book

*Odysseys of the Saints* is a fictional history of the Mormons. In it, five generations of one family experience the controversial and often bloody evolution of the Latter-day Saints from a persecuted cult to an affluent community with a mission to guide the world toward its own revelations.

The characters include Ted Bailey, a young newsman sent to Nauvoo, Illinois, in 1846 to report on the Mormon exodus to the West. He meets George Wood, a devout Mormon who has left his faith after many years of sacrifice for it. Amelia Carter ventures west to Utah with her family, but finds her community embattled by the U.S. Government, and her faith tested when her husband marries three other wives. Anders Erickson, a Norwegian convert, becomes a missionary on a tiny island near Tahiti. His son-in-law, Frank, Amelia's great-grandson, becomes an FBI agent after World War II. Frank is distraught when his son Joshua is excommunicated from the Church for being gay.

*For Dorothy Friedman*

*and Evelyn Jo Wilson*

# Contents

# Authors' Note

In its characters, this work is both fact and fiction. In every case, we have tried to portray historical people as they actually were. Especially on significant matters, quotations attributed to them are either actual quotes or consistent with their other words and deeds.

Every significant episode that appears in the book actually occurred in historical fact. At each event, historical figures appear only if they were there, and their actions are in character with their lives.

For the sake of clarity, characters with the following last names are fictional: Bailey, Rogers, Hendricks, White, Wood, Carter, Alderson, Erickson, MacGregor, Hall, McDonald, Molinari, Driscoll and Koenig. Characters identified by only one name are generally fictional, except for politicians, military officers and Indian leaders.

Because we are not Mormons or ex-Mormons, we have had to rely on knowledge and experience other than our own on matters of ritual and theology. Throughout the book, we have tried to represent these matters both accurately and fairly. If we have not succeeded in places, we apologize and would welcome corrections.

# BOOK ONE

## INVITATION TO ASSASSINATION

# Prologue

## September 1846

"I'll rent you nothing better than this chestnut gelding," the stable owner in Quincy warned Edward Bailey.

Bailey looked over the aging animal. "And why not? I'll pay your price."

"Because you're riding into real danger, and I don't want to risk losing a good horse."

Bailey handed him the money. "Danger isn't going to stop me," he said.

The stable owner appraised the young man. "Two pieces of advice, son. Don't let anyone in Warsaw know where you're headed. And if you hope to learn anything or just survive, you'd better lay low, or better yet, get rid of your high-and-mighty attitude. Folks here don't tolerate strangers who act like that."

Bailey nodded as he took the reins. "Thanks," he said.

"Well, this horse is sound enough to get you to Nauvoo and back," the man assured him. "But don't get him caught in the crossfire."

Bailey rode north all that day and the morning after, until the changes in terrain told him he was nearing his destination. Renewed excitement pounded in his chest as he felt his weariness recede. From where he rode, on the bluff above the Mississippi River, all to the west was frontier. Below him was the confluence of the meandering Des Moines River, which marked the border between Iowa Territory and Missouri. Fifteen miles ahead of him was Nauvoo, Illinois.

Bailey halted the horse at an opening in the woods, now turning yellow. His bones and muscles ached, and his thighs were chafed and raw. Bailey was a spirited man in his early twenties, but he was unaccustomed to riding on horseback so long. He had been struggling to control the animal, a wretched headstrong creature that was growing unaccountably jittery.

Down the bluff below him, Bailey saw the hazardous

Keokuk rapids of the Mississippi and the newly settled village of Keokuk across the river. Painfully, he dismounted and stretched his sore limbs. He pulled off his broad-brim hat and drew his hand through his brown hair, plastered to his scalp by perspiration. His clean-shaven face and well-tailored Eastern suit were layered with sweat-laden dust. His blue eyes were veined with blood-shot fatigue.

The humidity was oppressive where Bailey stood above the river, and he quickly remounted. He felt impatient to complete the final miles of his journey. Bailey had traveled four weeks, mostly in discomfort, to reach Quincy. For nine days, he was confined in crowded stagecoaches that pitched and swayed over miserable roads. After endless jostling all day, he slept poorly in vermin-infested inns, sharing rooms with foul-smelling strangers. From Toledo through Chicago and Springfield to Quincy, the food had been tasteless, overcooked or spoiled. Bailey smiled at the now distant memory of the pleasant steamboats up the Hudson River and across Lake Erie, and the excitement that surged through him as the rickety new railroad raced ten miles an hour along the route of the Erie Canal.

A month earlier, James Gordon Bennett, publisher of the *New York Herald*, had summoned Ted Bailey to his office.

"Get to Nauvoo, Illinois the fastest way you can," the publisher had told him gruffly. "Then report back here on the hostilities."

Ted could scarcely contain his elation. He had graduated just a year earlier from Harvard College and had never traveled farther west than New York City.

"The Mormons," he whispered.

"Yes. I expect you to uncover their plans for moving west."

Bennett handed Ted two yellowed clippings. "Here, read these editorials."

Ted looked at the dates on the columns from the *New York Herald*. They were published two years earlier, a few days apart, after Joseph Smith, President of the Church of Jesus Christ of Latter-day Saints, was shot to death by a mob in Carthage, Illinois.

4

In high spirits, the young reporter read Bennett's earlier editorial. He nodded in agreement as he read the last words aloud. "'The death of the modern Mohamet will seal the fate of Mormonism. They cannot get another Joe Smith. The holy city must tumble into ruins, and the 'latter day saints' have indeed come to the latter day.'"

"Read my second editorial, Ted."

Ted carefully unfolded the other column. But he felt more bewildered than enlightened as he reached the final paragraph.

"'Instead of sealing the fate of Mormonism, we are now rather inclined to believe that this revolting transaction will give additional and increased strength to that sect. Joe and his brother will be regarded as martyrs to their faith, and but little knowledge of human nature and the history of the past is necessary to inform us of the fact that violence, oppression, and bloodshed strengthen instead of subduing fanaticism.'"

Ted came from the ninth generation of a Massachusetts family, and was no stranger to religious dissenters.

"I'll find the truth among the contradictions," the young reporter vowed. "My family was once Puritans."

The publisher shook Ted's hand. "Good luck, then. If the Mormons resist answering your questions, remind them that Joseph Smith, himself, awarded me an honorary LL.D. from the University of Nauvoo."

Ted looked uncertainly at his employer.

Bennett smiled at the improbable fact. "Yes, and the rank of brigadier-general in the Nauvoo Legion."

The nervous horse suddenly whinnyed, then reared up, nearly bucking Ted out of the saddle. But as he cursed at the animal, Ted saw clouds of dust being kicked up by horses near a field of tall-standing wheat. He forced his mutinous horse toward the commotion.

"What is it?" Bailey asked a heavy-set man mounted on a large gray stallion.

"Mormons are harvesting wheat," the man answered with dispassion.

"Surely, that's no surprise. The grain is ripe."

5

"We warned the Mormons not to let themselves be seen outside Nauvoo. Except traveling west, away from Illinois. They promised they'd be gone four months ago."

Bailey watched in horror as half a dozen armed men seized a group of harvesters and began to beat them with musket stocks. He yanked on the reins and turned to ride toward the farmers, but halted when he heard a pistol cocked behind him.

"By what authority do you stop me?" Bailey demanded.

"Ours," the stranger said. "Men have been kidnapped and whipped for less."

"And their crime?"

"Being Mormons is crime enough, or their friends. What about you? Are you their friend?"

Ted fumed at his own helpnessness. "I've never met a Mormon in my life," he answered truthfully.

The man evaluated Bailey with suspicion, then he grinned as he responded. "I saw a Mormon near age sixty get carried away from his home, stripped of his clothing, and whipped until his back was cut up bad. His *crime* was being too old to resist."

The implied threat angered Bailey. "Can't you just let them leave?"

"Leave? We aren't fools enough to think they're about to abandon Nauvoo."

"Why not?"

"Answer me this," the man challenged. "If they're leaving, why'd they lavish so much money to finish that Temple of theirs? If you've seen it, you know it's the most beautiful building in western Illinois. Of course, only Mormons get to see the inside."

Bailey shrugged, unable to imagine why anyone would do so.

The man pointed to the north with his pistol. "Days ago, before we opened fire on Nauvoo, we gave the Mormons a chance to surrender peacefully. But they scorned our white flag of truce, so we hoisted the red flag instead."

"The red flag?" Ted asked warily.

"The red flag forewarns massacre. No quarter will be given,

6

and no mercy."

With helpless alarm, Bailey watched the ruffians chase and scatter the harvesters. But it seemed they were not interested in inflicting serious harm. Soon tiring of their game, the gang was content to watch the farmers flee on foot toward Nauvoo without stopping to gather their belongings.

Ted breathed easier when he saw the man holster his pistol and turn to ride off with the mob.

"You'd better choose your side well," the stranger warned him. "We have 800 armed men, not all of them gentlemen like me."

The man spat into the dust and galloped away.

Bailey's stomach was knotted with fear and excitement as he rode past the farmers toward Nauvoo. He heard the crack of occasional small arms fire and the boom of cannon, growing nearer. He remembered the warning at the stable and the vow he had made to his publisher.

"I've come twelve hundred miles," he swore aloud, "I will proceed, damn the consequences."

Ted rode onward for an hour, past fallow farmland, ungrazed pastures, and young orchards heavy with unpicked fruit. He rode past drainage ditches and saw the efforts that had channeled the flows of water and filled the ground. Then in wonder, Ted halted the horse. Half encircled by a bend in the Mississippi River, a substantial city rose before him. Its new brick and wooden buildings were surrounded by green gardens, spreading two miles east and west, and a mile north and south. Towering on a hill stood a tall, limestone Temple, its tapering spire resplendent with white and gold.

Nauvoo had recently been the most populous city in Illinois. But it stood almost deserted now, the new non-Mormon residents having fled in fear of unknown horrors by the mob. Abandoned and forlorn, the well-built brick houses waited in the silenced city. Fences had collapsed, windows were left broken, doors were open and sagging.

Unchallenged by any authority, Ted rode through the wide, empty streets. He rode past the library and university and

7

concert hall, all newly and solidly built, architecturally-impressive, but deserted. All around him were recent hallmarks of industry and enterprise and life. He dismounted and tied his horse to a hitching post by a water trough.

Curious to see more, Ted walked through abandoned workshops and smithies. He spun an idle spinning wheel and fingered a stray nail on a dusty workbench. No one called out to him as he walked. Dead ashes stood in fireplaces, and well laid-out gardens grew newly unkempt to weeds. Ted tried to peer inside the upper window of the Masonic Hall, but it had been whitewashed to be opaque. Why, he wondered, had the Mormons gone to such extravagant efforts to finish their Temple?

Ted stepped around a corner and was surprised to encounter a make-shift cannon, manned by several young soldiers. He approached them cautiously.

"I'm unarmed," he said.

"Then you're the only one in this city," a soldier replied.

With a grimace, Ted said, "I'm impressed to see that you have cannon."

"Some cannon!" scoffed the youngest soldier, a slender boy who could not have been older than fifteen. "Two of our cannon are old discarded steamboat shafts, cut and rebored, then mounted on wagon wheels. The other four were brought up from New Orleans, where they'd lain in sea water for years and grown rusty. We rebored them and fitted them into wagons."

A fusillade of gunshots rang out from the north and the soldiers answered with cannon fire. The cannonballs were lead and not iron, and Ted could see that the cannon bore was plugging up. From the small size of the cannonballs, he expected that the gun created more noise than did much damage.

"We've been under siege most of a week," the boy grimly told him. "The mob is growing larger, and outnumber us now four to one. Many non-Mormons are starting to fear that defense is hopeless. *They*'re giving up, but not Seth Rogers."

"Then you aren't a Mormon?" Ted asked.

Seth shook his head. "Not all the non-Mormons are

mobbers."

The smoke and smell of spent gunpowder made Ted's eyes water. "What about your fellow artillerymen here?"

The boy stared straight ahead, trying to find enemy positions. "They're a few of the ten Illinois militiamen still fighting alongside the defenders."

"But if you aren't a Mormon," Ted asked, "why are you fighting?"

"To protect our property. My mother bought an inn here in Nauvoo."

"Where is it?"

Seth pointed toward the southeast. "On Page Street, between Parley and Sidney."

Ted noted where the boy pointed. "Have there been many casualties?" he asked.

"Three Mormons have been killed, including the commanding officer and his son. We hear there are some deaths among the mob. The militiamen say the mob is drunken rabble, unable to organize a proper assault, though they've got us more-or-less surrounded."

The red flag of massacre, Ted uneasily recalled.

"We've repulsed the mob's advance four times," Seth said proudly. "Perhaps God has indeed cast His lot with the Saints."

"Where are they?" Ted asked.

Seth pointed to the Temple.

Ted retrieved his horse and rode up the bluff to the Temple. As he approached it, he saw that its steeple was transformed into a watchtower. A guard stood at the top with a rifle and spyglass, ready to ring a steamboat bell to warn of mass invasion by the mob. Two guards stood at the doors. Most windows were whitewashed so that anyone outside could not see what transpired inside it.

"Who are you?" the guards demanded.

"Edward Bailey, a reporter with the *New York Herald*."

The men stared incredulously and unresponsively at Ted.

"Could I meet with your commander, to ask him a few questions?"

9

"He's dead."

Ted hoped his Eastern clothing would convince them that he was not a scout for the mob.

"Someone must be in charge."

"You may not speak to him," a guard answered coldly.

"I'm unarmed," Ted insisted, holding open his coat to show he had no weapons.

Behind the two guards, a door opened, and a tall, bearded man emerged from the Temple.

"Leave immediately," he ordered.

Ted tried to peer inside the Temple, but the door was shut as quickly as it was opened. Hiding his disappointment, he argued, "From what I've witnessed here already, I'm sure to write a story favorable to your cause. You Mormons must be eager to win national public sympathy, so why not tell me what you see as the truth?"

"Because your newspaper is two-faced, at best, with its noblest ambition to sell more papers. The Church of Jesus Christ of Latter-day Saints, as we prefer you call our faith and our society, has been treated like a freak show by most newspapers, including yours."

An older man's voice came from inside the Temple. "William, it's foolhardy to let a reporter wander free, asking questions at will."

Ted spoke louder. "But Joseph Smith, himself, awarded special honors to my publisher!"

"Some stories in the *Herald* have been favorable," William admitted. "And our Prophet appreciated that. But even the *Herald* hasn't drawn a fair picture. Sarcasm and innuendo infuse your ink, not to mention the vilest sort of scandal-mongering."

"We've done nothing worse than report what eyewitnesses swear is true," Ted protested.

William shook his head in disgust. "And we're cursed that our apostates exhibit no shame in the falsehoods they swear against us. The decency and strength of our community, and our devoted faith, deserve more coverage than all those rumors, which we've repeatedly denied."

Below them in the streets, cannon boomed. At the door of the Temple, the men tensed.

"I can promise you a chance to publish the words you feel you merit!"

"William, tell him to get on his horse and leave Nauvoo."

William appraised Ted coolly, then spoke in a whispered voice. "You can surely understand why the Saints remaining here are frightened. All too well, they remember the suffering, illness and death when we ran for our lives during the terrible escape from Missouri. Our new exodus, to only God knows where, cannot help but be worse."

William pointed west toward the river. "How can we be sure that this bloodthirsty mob will not slaughter us if we agree to surrender? Then after we cross the Mississippi, the Missouri Pukes may find it sporting to bushwhack us. But rest assured that we don't despair. Our faith decries melancholy fatalism."

"You seem well-supplied with guns and ammunition," Ted remarked.

"True, but just a couple of hundred fighting men are still in Nauvoo. We had thousands of well-trained militiamen, but almost all went west with their families months ago. Everyone else here is too old to fight or too sick to travel, or too poor to buy provisions and be gone."

"Where are they going?" Ted asked.

The voice from inside the Temple spoke sharply. "William, you're giving him more knowledge than an outsider ought to possess."

William nodded and pushed open the Temple door, turning away from the reporter.

Ted tried to see inside again, but beyond a white wall, nothing was visible. Ted feared that he would have no other chance to get his story. After venturing 1,200 miles, he was distraught that he might fail in his mission and his promise to James Gordon Bennett.

"Tell me, sir," he blurted hurriedly, desperate not to lose his chance, "why did *you* become a Latter-day Saint?"

11

William turned to face him again. "'The glory of God is intelligence,' Mr. Bailey. That's what Joseph Smith teaches. Why should we suppose that God granted revelations only to certain ancient Jews a couple thousand years ago, then ceased?"

Ted shrugged, unable to think of an answer.

William smiled for the first time and spoke earnestly. "God loves us no less than those men! Why should we imagine that the saints all lived long ago? We are no lesser people than they! I was raised to think faith is enough, yet it was the saints' *deeds*, not beliefs, that made them saints. Now is hardly the most favorable time for you to join us, but in time..."

"William!" cried the voice from inside the Temple. "Now is hardly the time for missionary labors. Godspeed on your travels home, Mr. Bailey. Now leave us!"

William stepped into the Temple and pulled the door shut behind him. Ted stood alone in the silent afternoon. From the heights where the Temple rose, he looked down to the city. The guns, for the moment, were quiet.

"If I can't learn the truth from the Mormons, I'll ask it of their enemies," Ted grumbled as he mounted his horse.

He headed down the bluff and into the woods where he had seen puffs of smoke from attacking cannon fire. But a cannonball from a sudden artillery barrage toppled a nearby tree, and Ted leaped off the horse and into a ditch for shelter.

When the gunfire abated, Ted remounted and rode until he came to a grove of trees where he could watch from his horse under the shadows. Intermittently, the mob artillery fired from concealed positions, then the Mormons responded from their defenses in Nauvoo. Ted heard a brisk rifle fusillade, then the thunder of cannon from the town. He could see 300 mobbers waiting on the Mississippi riverbank, positioned to cut off reinforcement and retreat.

After fifteen minutes, the horse began to fidget and whinny. As Ted reached down to quiet the animal, three burly mobbers leaped from the bushes behind him. One yanked the reins from his hand, while another jabbed him hard below the ribs with the butt of a musket. Pointing a Colt pistol at Ted, the third man

12

shouted angrily, "You throw down your guns and dismount right now or my friend will bust your ribs if I don't decide to shoot you first."

Ted felt a sudden stabbing pain in his ribs. He fell heavily to the ground, pulled from the saddle when his leg was jerked sharply by the mobber with the musket. He landed awkwardly, bruising his hands and face, and the musket was thrust again into his side. The rocks jabbed into Ted's back as he looked helplessly up at his attackers. He heard the sound of a pistol being cocked against his ear.

Terrified, he stammered, "I'm not armed."

The three surly guards glowered down at Ted.

"Who the hell are you?" one demanded.

"Edward Bailey. I'm a reporter for the *New York Herald*."

"You're a spy for the Mormons," another man angrily accused.

"No, *no*," Ted pleaded. He knew that men had been kidnapped and whipped for less.

"Prove you're not a Mormon spy."

"Look at my clothing. It's English serge, tailored in New York City."

A mobber yanked Ted up by the neck of his coat, then threw him back against the rocky ground.

"Ain't no Mormon," the man said, disappointed. "You couldn't catch 'em dead wasting money on fancy clothes. What do you want?"

Two cocked muskets were still aimed at Ted. He sat up warily.

"I'd hoped to ask your commander a few questions."

"What for?"

"To learn your side of the story."

They regarded him with unallayed suspicion.

"He's busy," one spat. "How about if we ask *you* a question."

"What is it?"

"Have those Mormons got grape-shot to fire from their cannons?"

Ted trembled at the idea that they could think he held knowledge of their enemy. "I don't know," he answered as calmly as he could. "Why ask me?"

"We hate them, but not enough to die on their account."

"Can I get up?" Ted asked.

"No."

Ted sat on the ground, listening to the rattle of muskets, rifles and artillery. On both sides, the gunfire sounded desultory to him, as if neither side were fighting with passion.

Ted saw a burly man approaching. The other men stepped back in deference.

"Who's your prisoner?" the man demanded.

"Says he's a reporter named Bailey. From the *New York Herald*."

The large man looked at Ted's clothing. "He's no Mormon, that's for sure. What do you want, Bailey?"

Ted stood up without asking. "And your name, sir?"

"Thomas Brockman, commander of this Posse."

"And he's a Campbellite preacher," a guard added.

Despite his claim to authority, the commander seemed awkward and uncouth to Ted. But the young reporter was desperate not to enrage Brockman, and he tried to sound respectful. "I wonder, sir, if I might ask you a few questions."

"Nothing to say, Bailey. Go back to New York or wherever the hell you came from."

"Why can't you let the Mormons leave Illinois in peace?"

Brockman regarded Ted with contempt. "We made most of 'em leave all right. But everyone knows these new *citizens* of Nauvoo are secret Mormons. If we don't rout 'em out, they'll vote in our elections again."

"Isn't that a man's right in a democracy?"

"Democracy!" Brockman scoffed. "Mormons don't believe in democracy. Last election, *every* Mormon voted the straight Whig ticket. Except they *all* scratched Abe Lincoln's name and voted in a man who once did a political favor for Joseph Smith."

Brockman turned and strode away. "Turn him loose, boys. He can't do nothing against us."

14

Without looking behind him, Ted mounted his horse and sped back south to Nauvoo. Grateful for a lull in the gunfire, he galloped in the direction the young soldier, Seth Rogers, had pointed toward his mother's inn.

Ted left his horse in the care of the livery stable, then stepped inside the back door of the adjacent Rogers Inn. It looked cleaner and more hospitable than most inns where he had stayed in recent weeks.

Still breathless from his ordeal, Ted stood waiting in the hallway for someone to come and take his money. He could not help but overhear a loud conversation emanating from the dining room.

"I hope my steamboat isn't getting all shot full of holes," a man grumbled in a distinctly Southern drawl. "Battlefield or not, I had no choice but to dock here for repairs."

"It's an optimistic promise, Caleb," an older man said with a laugh. "Your claim to offer a 'regular schedule' north from St. Louis to Fort Snelling."

The older man noticed Ted in the hallway and beckoned him toward a chair beside them. About age sixty, the man was portly and well-dressed, with a stout cane lying on the floor. Grateful for a chance to rest, Ted accepted his invitation.

"Not that my boat is any floating palace," Caleb said. "Not like the boats that go south from St. Louis. But she's mine and everything I've got."

Caleb was middle-aged but trim, wearing a tobacco-stained white suit. His blue eyes shone brightly above a gray moustache that occupied much of his weatherbeaten face.

The older man introduced himself. "I am Franklin Hendricks, and this is Captain Caleb White. I'm a Quincy lawyer and former judge, here with a committee from Quincy that's trying to negotiate peace."

"My name is Edward Bailey," he said, shaking hands with each man.

A sudden flash of color caught Ted's attention, then he heard an exclamation in a female voice. He saw a woman run down the stairs, nearly tripping over them in her haste. She tried

15

to hide her disappointment at seeing he was only a guest.

"I'd hoped it was my son," she explained sadly. A gray-haired woman in her forties, Mrs. Rogers' pleasant face was etched with lines of worry.

Caleb said, as he and Ted stood up, "We would've called out, Mrs. Rogers, if it were Seth."

"I met your son not four hours ago," Ted told the innkeeper. "He was alive and quite well at his gun position then."

Mrs. Rogers exhaled with relief. "Room and board for tonight?" she asked Ted.

"Yes."

Mrs. Rogers counted his money and nodded.

"Dinner is at six o'clock," she told Ted as she turned to the kitchen. "The only meat I can offer you is mutton. The Mormons took west all the cattle and cured pork they could find."

"Tell me, Mr. Bailey," said Caleb. "What brings you to the siege of Nauvoo?"

"I'm a reporter for the *New York Herald*."

"The *Herald*!" the Judge exclaimed. "Your publisher certainly possesses some curious fascination with the Mormons. He's given them so much coverage over so many years."

"And so much of it favorable, too!" Caleb added.

"Is it perhaps because he's Scottish-born?" the Judge asked. "Or might his interest be heightened by the sensationalism that makes people eager to buy a newspaper?"

Ted grimaced as he sat down again. He was in no mood to defend against the often-heard accusation that the *New York Herald* sought less to inform the public than to entice them by stories designed to swell circulation.

Recognizing Ted's weariness, the Judge relented from his teasing. Ted was grateful when Mrs. Rogers brought coffee to the men.

"Coffee is ample," Mrs. Rogers said. "But the Mormons took away almost all the sugar, too."

She offered coffee to another man, sitting by himself at the farthest table. Wordlessly but politely he declined, and

16

continued to stare out the window.

"Are you a religious man, Mr. Bailey?" the Judge asked.

"Of course," Ted replied, surprised that the Judge might expect some other answer. "My family belongs to the Congregational Church. I am a believer."

Judge Hendricks shook his head. "No, Mr. Bailey, what I mean to ask is whether you've been touched by the religious fervor sweeping through this country. Do you believe in miracles, the End of Days?"

Ted answered with a smile, "Not more imminently than most men believe. I'm not a Millerite, surely, selling all my belongings and gathering with other Millerites in western New York to await the Second Coming of Christ."

"Or a Shaker?" Caleb said. "Surviving and repopulating despite a thorough dedication to celibacy."

Ted drank his coffee too quickly and burned his tongue.

"The religious and emotional passion of today is far more powerful than when I was young," the Judge lamented. "Intuition and genius are valued above logic and reason, and enthusiasm is cherished beyond knowledge. Look at Goethe, and Byron and Coleridge, even Emerson's enticement by Transcendentalism."

"I once heard Ralph Waldo Emerson speak at Harvard College," Ted recalled. "'Hitch your wagon to a star,' Mr. Emerson advised us. 'There is no doctrine of the Reason which will bear to be taught by the Understanding.'"

Sporadic gunfire sounded in the distance. Mrs. Rogers looked out the window, lost in worry.

"The Millerite movement alone touched 50,000 people," the Judge said. "And some were men with well-warranted prestige. But when the End of Days failed to appear, two years ago, they blamed the lateness on the curious idea that Christians don't celebrate the Sabbath on its proper day! Well, though there's doubtlessly a Supreme Architect, I remain unconvinced that Scriptural phrases are authentic, divine contracts."

"God's promises are certain," Caleb objected. "I suggest you read your Bible, Sir."

"Indeed! Is that how you justify slavery, Caleb?"

"Can you deny Genesis 9:25, the story of Noah and the Flood?"

"With ease," the Judge replied.

"In the South," Caleb said calmly, "we treat our slaves better than Northerners and Englishmen deal with their miners and factory workers. On the lower Mississippi steamboats, slaves are too valuable for their lives to be risked, so immigrant Irishmen and Germans perform the most dangerous tasks. Thousands of English immigrants have swelled the Mormon ranks because laborers are treated so cruelly there."

"Slaves are hardly free to emigrate," the Judge scoffed.

"The ancient Greeks proudly held slaves," Caleb argued. "And theirs was the most brilliant society the world has produced, until our own."

Hearing a noise outside, Mrs. Rogers ran hopefully to the window. She turned away, disappointed again.

"Brilliant?" protested the Judge. "Is that why your Southern politicians are now instigating outrageous violations of our Constitution? Petitions on slavery are forbidden from even being raised in Congress. Brilliant! Abolitionist mail cannot now be delivered in the South."

Ted tried to add a comment, but the men were arguing too heatedly to listen.

"A worse outrage," Caleb claimed, "is how those foolish Abolitionists diverted votes to their Liberty Party. They handed the Presidency to Polk and thereby brought about what they feared most, the annexation of pro-slavery Texas."

"All too true," the Judge grumbled. "And now Polk has the Army marching recklessly across Mexican territory, provoking war. They hope to grab all the land all the way to the Pacific Ocean."

"With particular greed to seize California," Caleb said.

"California is too distant to be ruled by Mexico City," Ted interjected. "It isn't Mexico's destiny but ours instead. The manifest design of Providence is to roll our population westward to the Pacific!"

Judge Hendricks waved his arms in the air. "This war with Mexico is immoral, unjust and unwise, Mr. Bailey. Our Army has only 5,300 men, scattered in a hundred posts. That's too few men to fight one war, let alone *two*. Thank God we settled our dispute with England over the boundaries of Oregon Country."

"A sailing ship around Cape Horn can take five months," Caleb added. "Let's hope news of the treaty reaches Oregon Country before the men there go to war."

They heard a rustling of small arms fire, then the boom of cannon.

"War seems to be the order of the day," Ted sighed.

The Judge nodded solemnly.

"This is violent country, Mr. Bailey," Caleb said. "Not many years ago, ruffians, including river pirates, inhabited both sides of the Mississippi. Men work hard on the boats and along the banks, then drink and fight hard for amusement."

"Many would cheerfully pay money to watch a hanging," the Judge added, "and they need little excuse to form mobs. It's even worse on the western edge of Missouri, which has gathered even more of the most fiercely individualistic Southern ruffians."

"It isn't only Southerners," Caleb protested. "Have you forgotten the murder of Elijah Lovejoy?"

"Who?" Ted asked.

Caleb stroked his moustache. "Lovejoy was a newspaper editor and minister in Missouri, whose inflammatory editorials condemned mobs that use lynch law against blacks. A Missouri mob merely destroyed his printing press and hounded him out of the state. But when Lovejoy crossed the river to Illinois and began publishing again, a mob in this *free* state riddled him with bullets before they demolished his press."

"To be fair, the East has had shameful murders, too," the Judge said. "It was in New York state that the most infamous and mysterious murder of the late 1820s occurred."

"Who was murdered?" Ted asked.

"Captain William Morgan," Caleb answered. "He was a Mason who quarreled with members of his lodge, and perhaps for revenge, tried to publish a book that revealed the secret rites and oaths of Masonry."

"What happened to him?"

"Late at night," Caleb continued, "a group of masked men seized the printing press. They set it on fire and beat its owner, then abducted Captain Morgan for a mockery of a trial. He was taken to Fort Niagara, on the Canadian border, never to be heard from again."

The Judge stiffened. "As a Mason, I can tell you it was a practical joke that tragically got out of hand. Masonic ritual oaths dictate some horrible penalties for violating secrecy, but no reasonable man could imagine taking them as orders. Murder is specifically not condoned."

"Were Morgan's abductors ever captured?" Ted asked.

"Five prominent Masons stood trial," the Judge said. "Three were acquitted and two were sentenced to less than a year."

"The public felt it was a travesty of justice," Caleb said. "Local residents demanded an investigation, but the Mason-dominated legislature refused. Throughout much of the country, newspapers and churches inflamed the public against the Masons."

The Judge winced at the memory. "There's even anti-Masonry in the *Book of Mormon*. Captain Morgan, you see, was abducted just nine miles away from Joseph Smith's home in western New York."

"I knew Mrs. Morgan."

The quiet voice startled Ted. He turned to face a man so small that Ted had forgotten he was sitting at the table in the corner.

"Who?" Ted asked.

"The wife of Captain Morgan."

The man who spoke was barely five feet tall and weighed no more than a hundred pounds. He wore a well-pressed gray broadcloth suit, and his pale, handsome face was graced by a trim, sandy-colored beard. He appeared to be about thirty-five years old.

"This is George Wood," the Judge introduced him to Ted.

"Edward Bailey, from New York City."

Ted shook his small hand.

"George is chief bookkeeper for a Quincy shipping line," Caleb said.

"My company bought some excellent property here," Wood explained. "At an exceptional price, 18 cents on the dollar to be exact. They sent me to check on its condition because I once lived in Nauvoo."

Ted was taken aback by his words. "Then you are a Mormon?" he asked.

"No longer," Wood answered softly.

"Can I ask you why you left the Church?"

Wood took a deep breath, then smiled sadly. "I suppose you could say I hitched my wagon to a star."

Ted leaned in closer so he could hear Wood's whispered voice.

"And I leaped off the wagon only when I saw the star hauling it recklessly over the side of a cliff."

From a few blocks away, the cannon boomed once, then twice. The men in the room fell silent for a moment as they awaited returning fire.

"How did you come to know Mrs. Morgan?" Caleb asked him.

"I knew her third husband well," Wood replied.

"And who was he?"

"Joseph Smith."

# Chapter 1

## 1830

"You're going *where*?" Thomas Wood asked.

"To Mayfield," George replied, finishing his breakfast.

"But that's a dozen miles away," his brother said. "Why must you travel so far on the Sabbath?"

George owned a modest farm in northern Ohio with his older brother, a man blessed with far greater appetite for farming than George.

"Sidney Rigdon is promised to be preaching this morning."

"Another of your Campbellite revivalists, I suppose," Thomas sighed. "How many of them does that make?"

"Sidney Rigdon is different, Tom. I've heard him preach before, and he has a sort of elegance in his manner."

"It seems like any man with a voice can call himself a Campbellite preacher."

"Sidney Rigdon has a first-rate religious education!" George objected.

"What's wrong with our church, a proper Calvinist tradition? No, our minister isn't thrilling like the *elegant* Mr. Rigdon. And yes, he'll exhort us again this morning about the *depravity* of man. Church on the Sabbath isn't *amusement*, George, but Christian duty."

George did not disagree, yet he felt certain that his destiny must be elsewhere.

"Can you even understand it, Tom? You've been blessed, not cursed, with how you stand in the world."

"Oh, the height business, again," Thomas said.

"No one's ever made you the butt of obscene and practical jokes. Over and over again! You have no fears that pretty women will disdain you if you even think to court them."

"Don't be so despondent. You're 21 years old and have your whole life in front of you."

"There are twelve-year-olds bigger than I am!"

"And you blame God for that?" Thomas said.

"Who should I blame? Our Presbyterian Church teaches that all matters in Heaven and Earth are predestined. If I believed that in my heart, I'd believe I am damned, despite whatever good I may do."

Thomas shook his head. "You have many God-given strengths far more noble than height. You're handsome enough and not awkward, and unafraid of hard work with your hands. And our farm has greatly profited from your record keeping, planning and calculations. You're graced with more intelligence and bookish skills than any other young man around here."

"Great good that did me when I tried to teach school," George reminded him. "I couldn't handle those taunting, boisterous boys any better than a woman could."

"And you're manly," Thomas added. "That whore in Cleveland swore it was true when Uncle Simon brought us to that brothel. She was surprised, she said, that you were so..."

Embarrassed, George interrupted, "That's enough." He left to get dressed in the inconspicuous clothes he always wore in the hope he could escape being noticed.

"So you're going?" Thomas sighed when he saw his brother standing at the door.

"Yes, Tom," he tried again to explain. "These new preachers, you see, inspire a man to believe that, with the Bible's guidance, he can determine his own acts and fate."

The road beside the Chagrin River was thick with other people, bound the same direction as George. With excitement, he wove his way through the crowd as they approached the town of Mayfield. George found a place to watch on horseback beneath the yellowing elms, where he could see above the standing men and women. Breathlessly, he waited as the revivalist rose to the pulpit, then looked out over the crowd.

"Brothers and sisters," Rigdon somberly began. His forceful voice reached across the expanse of listeners.

"In my religious yearnings, I have *never* been fully satisfied. I have walked many nights, unable to sleep, praying for light and comfort in my religion."

George nodded in understanding.

"Never, I tell you," said Rigdon, speaking louder. "Never. Not until that wondrous day when I first heard of the golden plates. That same day, I learned of the miraculous revelations from God to Joseph Smith. And that day, all at once, my soul found peace."

"Golden plates?" many voices in the crowd asked one another. George was silent, eager to hear what had caused such enlightenment for this admirable man.

"The golden plates? You may ask," Rigdon said. "These golden plates reveal the history of the Nephites. A wandering tribe of Israel, they journeyed to this continent 2,000 years ago. The Nephites prospered here, but alas, were annihilated by their brother Lamanites, who are the Indians.

"It was the Angel Moroni, himself a Nephite, who led Joseph Smith to the hidden plates, onto which are etched the *Book of Mormon*."

George heard the heightened passion in Rigdon's voice.

"Mormon was the father of the Angel Moroni, who first appeared to Joseph when he was quite a young man. Only years later was Joseph found worthy to unearth the golden plates from where they'd lain for centuries entombed in Hill Cumorah, near Palmyra in western New York."

George wondered to himself, Could such a thing be?

"'Golden plates, indeed!' the skeptics among you may doubt my words. But have you never heard of these tumuli, yourselves? They are not so uncommon. Hundreds of Indian burial mounds have been uncovered here in northern Ohio and in western New York. In them, we've found skeletons, implements of stone, copper, even beaten silver. Eight such Indian mounds were unearthed within a dozen miles of the farm where Joseph Smith was raised. We know such plates can exist!"

Perhaps, George thought in silence. But how could this man Joseph Smith know what the writings meant? Surely, he did not claim they were written in English!

Rigdon gazed into the crowd. "Then the Angel Moroni gave Joseph two transparent stones. You've heard of these very stones before, in the Bible. They're called the Urim and Thummin! With these seer stones, Joseph translated the holy words from the reformed Egyptian language."

Rigdon paused, breathed deeply, then challenged the crowd. "Who among you wishes to be baptized into the Church of Jesus Christ of Latter-day Saints!"

Bashfully, George looked around the crowd and saw that he was not the only skeptic. Relieved but disappointed, he saw only one person step forward, an aged man he knew to be a deadbeat. George tied his horse to a willow tree and joined along with many others who were walking to a nearby pool to watch the baptism.

Without hesitation, Rigdon strode into the pool fully clothed until he stood waist-deep in the water. Then he began the most powerful, arousing exhortation that George had ever heard in his life. Through Rigdon's words, he saw a glimmer of Joseph Smith's immense vision of what Eternity *must* be. Astonished, George watched as people in the throng, one after another, came forth to be immersed in the pool. Not once did Rigdon falter in his preaching. As George watched and listened, he felt his knees tremble and his head become light. For Rigdon's stirring words had illuminated to him Joseph Smith's revelation of what a godly community can be.

George Wood was a man who led a somber, unexceptional life, but all at once, he saw his life charged with meaning. Then he realized that he, too, had gone into the water.

George was baptized into the Mormon Church half a year after it was founded. With no regrets, he left his farm for Kirtland, Ohio, where Sidney Rigdon's followers were gathered. Joseph Smith was not yet among them.

In Kirtland, George met Parley Pratt, a man of about his own age.

"I left my farm when I was nineteen," Parley told him. "It was 70 acres in western New York, but I lost it when I could find no market for my crop."

George nodded sympathetically, knowing such failures were not uncommon, nor often the farmer's fault. Mortgage sales were frequent, putting bankrupt and brokenhearted families out of their homes.

"So I resolved to go west," Parley said, "and leave behind me the civilized world, which brought me only sorrow and unrewarded toil. But here in Ohio, I heard Sidney Rigdon preach. And I *knew* Sidney spoke the truth, so I joined his group. Yet I was troubled. He held no *authority* to minister in holy things."

"Sidney is an inspiring preacher," George agreed.

"Early this year," Parley said, "I returned to western New York. The *Book of Mormon* had just been published. That night, as I turned the pages, I *knew* it was that authority! I asked Oliver Cowdery to baptize me at once, and together we came west to bring Sidney the gospel."

George approached Oliver Cowdery, a thin man who had been a schoolteacher.

"What did the golden plates look like?" George asked him.

"I saw the golden plates only with my spiritual eyes," Cowdery answered. "No one but Joseph could look at them with natural eyesight and live."

Deeply disappointed, George protested, "But you were Joseph Smith's scribe. At the front of the *Book of Mormon,* you testify that you've 'seen the engravings which are upon the plates.'"

Oliver Cowdery explained, "As we testified, the plates were shown to David Whitmer, Martin Harris and me by the power of God and not of man. Joseph sat behind a curtain when he dictated the translations, at first to his wife Emma, then to Martin Harris, then to me."

"But how were you *sure*?" George pressed.

"Martin Harris resolved any doubt. He hefted the plates beneath a covering cloth, and judged them by their weight to be either lead or gold. Martin knew that Joseph could not afford so much lead, let alone gold, so he determined they *must* be from God. To pay for printing the *Book of Mormon,* Martin mortgaged his well-to-do farm. Of course, that was after his wife destroyed the first 116 pages Joseph had translated."

27

Taken aback, George asked him, "Why ever would Mrs. Harris do that?"

"I suppose she guessed that Joseph would talk Martin into mortgaging the farm. She knew that Joseph was a money digger and peepstone looker, as was his father before him. They tried other ways to make money, too, like when Joseph's father entered the ginseng trade, but only became poorer for his efforts."

"A money digger?" George asked.

"Money digging was not unusual there," Cowdery explained. "Joseph would put his seer stones into a hat and try to envision where hidden treasure could be found. Other people used divining rods instead, such as they might use to find water. Joseph's strength was in the seeing, not the digging. But four years ago, he was tried in court for being an unsuccessful glass-looker, and was fined a few dollars."

George said nothing as he listened to Cowdery's revelations. He had placed so much faith in this man he had never met. And what has a man got but his reputation?

"Joseph owns magic parchments, too," Cowdery said.

"Magic parchments?" George asked weakly.

Cowdery nodded. "They have magic symbols for protection and purification, and for conjuring spirits. 'Holiness to the Lord,' some of them say, or 'Saint Peter bind them,' and 'Jehovah, Jehovah, Jehovah.'"

Cowdery took an envelope out of his pocket and on it drew stars and astrological signs, angels and letters in Hebrew and Greek, and Maltese crosses. Some words and symbols looked familiar to George, who had joined the Freemasons that summer.

"'Holiness to the Lord' is from the Bible," Cowdery said. "But the words also invoke good spirits and defeat melancholy."

When he and Cowdery parted, George was left to face the alarming idea that Joseph Smith was known to conjure up magic. But as he pondered the facts late that night, George came to understand how the callings were not so dissimilar. A seer might see all manner of things, some of them not yet understood. After all, when Isaac Newton studied alchemy, gravity and

28

calculus were made no less real. And how far is seeking treasure from Calvinist faith, where finding it is surely proof of grace? Joseph Smith, to his credit, ceased digging for money as soon as he left Calvinism behind him. And God chose him to receive the golden plates, which explained so many things about their lives.

George waited to meet this remarkable man face-to-face. For whatever talent Joseph Smith possessed in seeing visions, his far greater genius lay in making others see his visions, too.

In January 1831, George stood among 150 other converts on the main street of Kirtland. In the frigid air, he waited, unaware of the cold, watching the condensation of his unsteady breath.

Through the Chagrin River valley, Joseph Smith and Sidney Rigdon traveled to Kirtland by sleigh. They stopped the horses in front of the General Store.

"You've prayed me here," Joseph proclaimed to the assembled throng. "Now what do you want of me?"

George and all the others cheered. Through him rushed a thrill that he had never felt before.

Joseph Smith was almost a very handsome man. Though his nose was somewhat coarse and his lips a shade thin, his smile was attractive and infectious. He had just turned 25.

The following day, George was brought to meet him. To a man of George's stature, Joseph Smith was a powerful presence. He stood over six feet tall and weighed 220 pounds.

"How can I help you in your mission?" George asked.

Joseph Smith replied, "He who waits to be commanded in all things is a slothful servant." His eyes were strikingly beautiful.

"I excel at making accurate records," George told him. "And interpreting the meaning of numbers."

Joseph spoke with a disarming cordiality. "I can certainly use a man like you. Though I can't promise to always heed your opinions."

To George, he seemed honest and benevolent, devoid of artifice, and he quickly dispelled any doubts about his character. Yet George knew that most men like Joseph Smith, men with huge imaginations and ambitions, are loath to be reminded of details and calculations. Cautious numbers cast shadows on their visions.

A few weeks later, George rode out to the farm to see his brother. The fertile fields lay blanketed in snow, though the day was not bitterly cold. Inside the warm farmhouse, Thomas ladled out for George a bowl of thick stew.

"I want to sell you my half of the farm," George told him.

"I have no cash," Thomas warned. "Nor the prospect of getting any."

The meaty stew warmed the younger man, chilled by the cold. "Then I'll have to deed my half over to the Church."

"What?" Thomas exclaimed. "Why?"

"To finance Joseph's revelation of our community. All converts must deed our property to the Church, though we retain possession as tenants. You could join us, Tom."

"Your *Church* is to be my business partner!"

"Well, yes."

"Then I'll buy you out," Thomas sighed, "and give you a promissory note."

"Fine. I'll assign it to the Church."

"But it's all the inheritance you'll ever have from our father and mother, God rest their souls. What's happened to you, George? You were such a cautious fellow!"

George ate another bite of stew, then tried to explain. "Joseph never lets me forget that he values me, Thomas. How *I*, better than anyone, inform him what the records mean and what numbers will arise from his plans. For a small man with bookish skills, his community is a fine place."

Thomas scoffed, "Like those other utopian colonies, Brook Farm and New Harmony. They *cherish* the romance of farming but feel themselves too *refined* to muck out their stinking communal stables and barns."

"We're a practical community, not foolish dreamers."

"They say your prayer meetings are pierced by fits and trances. Doesn't that make you shudder in pious disbelief of your fellows?"

"Well, before Joseph arrived," George admitted. "But he's denounced false spirits and tempered our excesses. When I hear Joseph speak of his revelations, both my reason and passion are reassured."

Thomas rolled his eyes upward to the heavens. "Tell me the truth, George. Don't you agree that continuing revelation is more than a little self-serving to a man like Joseph Smith?"

"I can't honestly swear otherwise," George allowed.

"Aha!" Thomas exclaimed.

"But more than the man, it's the gospel revealed to him that's made a convert of me. The Latter-day Saints are a thoroughly fresh version of Christianity."

"How?" demanded Thomas.

"Almost uniquely among Christian faiths, we pay scant heed to Original Sin. And we deny Justification by Faith, reprobation and election. We aren't priest-ridden, despite our hierarchy, since every adult man is called to be a priest."

"You, too?"

"Of course," George said. "Does that surprise you? And after death, a glorious Eternity is promised to us, far removed from our old Calvinist brimstone and hellfire. You should join us, Thomas."

"Never! I hear you can't use coffee and tea, let alone liquor and tobacco. How can *tea* be such a mortal threat?"

"Because we can't grow it on our farms," George explained. "If coffee and tea weren't forbidden, we'd spend precious money to get them. We believe, nonetheless, that God intends this life to be enjoyable."

George finished his stew and stood up to leave. "Have you read the *Book of Mormon* I sent you?"

Thomas shook his head with sad disbelief. "And I never will, George. But I wish you well. What should I tell your brother Masons?"

George shook Thomas' offered hand. "Tell them they should join us."

31

# Chapter 2

"Come on now, men!" Joseph called. "I challenge all comers to a wrestling match!"

Eight hundred miles west of home, George sat weary but contented at the campfire. He watched the easy comraderie of the men, glad for their fellowship. George felt grateful that no one would expect him to pick up the gauntlet. A few men did and were quickly pinned to the ground by Joseph Smith.

Curious behavior for a clergyman, George thought to himself as he watched. Joseph enjoys himself so thoroughly at sport and entertainment, and indulges, though moderately, with food and drink. He is no longer a Calvinist, George reminded himself, and has no calling to be pompous or dour.

George anticipated the next morning with great eagerness, and recalled his hesitation at the outset. He had waited quietly in the doorway in Kirtland, not wanting to interrupt the feverish writing that occupied the room.

"You asked to see me, Brother Joseph," he had finally said.

Joseph Smith looked up. He smiled at George as he set down his pen.

"As you know, I've received a vision of the New Jerusalem. Oliver Cowdery has been sent to western Missouri on a mission to explore a site for it."

George knew of these events. In the spring of 1831, the state of Missouri was selling large parcels of land at low prices.

"Oliver has bought land at the westernmost edge, near Independence on the Kansas River."

"The westernmost edge?" George replied. "That's 800 miles from here!"

"I've received a revelation calling thirty men to go there."

George performed a quick calculation. "Traveling from here to there will take *six weeks*."

"Sidney and I will go, too."

George found it almost frightening when Joseph spoke with intensity. The blood drained from his face and left a luminous

33

pallor.

"You are called to go with us," Joseph said. "Will you come?"

"Of course."

George suppressed a grin as he left to prepare for the journey. He harbored no delusions that it would be easily accomplished. But for him it was an unaccustomed joy to be chosen as a worthy companion of such remarkable men.

The first phases of their journey, on horseback and then by steamboat, had not been very difficult. But after the steamboat left them off at St. Louis, they had to walk the last 250 miles to Independence. Although the Missouri River was navigable, the population was too sparse for a steamboat. They had been walking ten days.

"Many thousands will follow us in a pilgrimage procession," Joseph said.

At the campfire, George listened to Joseph's bold plans, and wondered if the rigors of the journey would let them come to pass. But in the morning, he awoke with an enthusiasm he could barely contain. Soon, they would reach the land that Joseph had envisioned as New Jerusalem.

Late that afternoon, they finally walked into Independence. Aghast, George looked at the town. It was barely a village, just a dozen miserable log cabins, a few stores, a school and a courthouse.

"Worse, the people are so unlike us," Rigdon said.

George nodded in weary disappointment. The Mormons were Northerners, communal in commitment and belief, while their new neighbors were individualist, pro-slavery Southerners.

"Not to mention the violent border ruffians!" Rigdon added.

The American frontier had always been a refuge for fiercely independent, often half-barbarian men, steadily drifting westward. But in 1830, just a few months earlier, the Indian border was fixed at the western limit of Missouri. This border now fenced such men in.

"We'll call our colony Zion," Joseph said.

George and the others pitched their tents and held church

services. The next morning, they began working hard to clear land and plant crops, and build the colony into Joseph's vision. But some of the men quickly grew disaffected with the crude life in Missouri.

"We must return to Ohio," Rigdon said.

Joseph asked him why.

"Without us there," Rigdon warned, "some of our wealthy converts may apostasize and renounce their property deeds. They'll file suit if we don't return their property, and the courts will surely rule against the Church."

As he listened to the preacher, George knew that Sidney Rigdon's prestige was indispensable to them.

"Some of you will remain here," Joseph resolved, selecting certain men among the group.

George would have preferred to return to Ohio, but he did not question being called to stay in Zion. He and the other men continued to work hard, clearing land, planting crops and building houses. George kept records and helped with the plans. Within a year, 300 settlers had joined the colony. Their newspaper, the *Evening and Morning Star,* was the only printing press within 120 miles.

In the spring of 1832, a new settler brought news of Joseph Smith. A crowd quickly gathered around him.

"Joseph was living with his family in a town outside Kirtland," the man said. "He was revising the Bible and editing his revelations to be published."

A woman brought the new settler some water. He drank it thirstily.

"One Saturday night, a group of men smashed their way into the house where Joseph and his family lived."

"But why?" a man asked.

"Some apostates roused hostility in our neighbors. They say a mobber suspected Joseph of being too intimate with his sister."

The listeners looked at one another. "What happened?"

"The gang beat Joseph badly, then stripped him naked. They tarred him and poured feathers over him, and forced the tar-paddle into his mouth. Then they threatened Joseph with castration."

Stricken, George exclaimed, "They didn't do it!"

"No. But they beat Sidney Rigdon unconscious and dragged him across the frozen ground."

George shuddered at the thought of the dignified, eloquent preacher lying bloody in the snow.

"It took most of that night to scrape the tar off Joseph. But by Sunday morning, he'd regained his strength and will to preach. And when he looked out over the congregation, Joseph recognized several of the mobbers. They were no less astonished to see him. It seems they'd only come because of boasts and wagers that he'd be too weak or scared to appear."

"And Joseph denounced them from the pulpit?"

"No," the man said. "Not a word."

With the others, George cheered at Joseph's endurance, and with even higher spirits, they worked to make the Missouri colony thrive. With Joseph Smith and Sidney Rigdon, Kirtland remained the more prominent site, but they dedicated land for the primary Temple in Zion. Zion was the place where most of the poorer Saints were sent. Almost all of them were single men and married couples, and the dearth of young women saddened George.

One afternoon, George welcomed a newly baptized group of new arrivals. With them was a girl of seventeen who was standing modestly between her parents. She was uncomfortably aware that the eyes of all the nearby men had focused on her.

Like the other men, George admired the girl's pretty face, her brown eyes and hair, and attractive figure. But she stood four inches taller than George. And he knew that many men would soon be competing for her hand in marriage.

"What is your daughter's name?" George asked her father, after the women were brought into the houses.

Her father regarded George cautiously. The man is awfully short, he thought to himself, but handsome enough, and evidently important.

"Lily," he replied.

That Sunday, when George heard Lily's clear contralto

36

voice, he found himself suddenly enthralled. He was never unaware of her presence. He knew he should not imagine her lying with him, but her image came to him in his dreams. When they talked, George found her sensible and well-spoken, but so reserved that he was never sure what she was thinking.

As often as he dared, he asked Lily to dance at the frequent dances they held in the colony. All the men clamored to be her partner, but George was graceful on the dance floor and she never refused him. With Lily in his arms, he felt like the tallest man on Earth.

After three months, George could bear the uncertainty no longer. He approached her father.

"Please tell me," George asked. "Do I even stand a chance to marry Lily?"

"You are intelligent, kind and well-spoken, George. Those are rarer traits than height on the frontier."

The next day, his heart pounding, George called at her house. "Will you marry me, Lily?" he asked.

She smiled as she said, "Yes, George, I will."

Elated and astonished, George took a deep breath, then he promised, "I swear to you, Lily, I will never deny you anything you ever ask of me." He could not conceive of ever breaking that vow.

# Chapter 3

By July 1833, the Zion colony had grown to 1,200 settlers. George and Lily's new home had just been finished, and Lily was three months pregnant.

George read the headline in the *Evening and Morning Star*, the newpaper of the Zion colony, then grew pale.

"Lily, look at this," he said, aghast.

Lily put down her knitting. "What is it?"

"We've reprinted the Missouri law that prohibits entry by free blacks without a certificate of citizenship from another state!"

"Can that be so awful?" Lily asked.

George silently handed her the newspaper.

"'As to slaves we have nothing to say,'" Lily read aloud. "'In connection with the wonderful events of this age, much is doing toward abolishing slavery, and colonizing the blacks in Africa...'"

George interrupted, "Don't our men know how the Gentiles will interpret this?"

"How?"

"The Gentiles will think we're instructing free Negroes and mulattos from other states on how they can join the Mormon Church in the promised land of Jackson County, Missouri!"

"But Joseph has always been cautious. He's even *justified* slavery."

George sighed. "He's hoped to avoid conflict with other Missourians. But here in border states, slavery is never without passions. And as the old settlers here have watched our numbers double, then redouble, some of them have grown hostile against us."

"We've been good neighbors," Lily protested.

"Well, our Lieutenant Governor doesn't agree. A pro-slavery politician and landowner like Lilburn Boggs has nothing to gain from a large voting block of non-slaveholding Saints."

Suddenly, they heard a commotion in the streets.

"Wait here," George said to Lily.

George ran outside, joining about fifty other Mormons. As the disturbance grew louder and nearer, his heart sank. A furious mob of several hundred white Missourians, armed with guns and sacks of feathers, was riding up the street into Zion. Other men marched with a bucket of tar.

Stifling his fear, George took a deep breath and stepped into the street. The smell of hot tar was nauseating to him. With far greater calm than he felt, he addressed the men, "What are you doing here? What do you want?"

"*What do we want?*" their leader mocked. "We've got five demands for you Mormons."

"And what might they be?"

The mob leader counted them on his fingers as he spoke. "Halt your immigration. Close your shops, immediately leave Jackson County…"

George interrupted, "We can't abandon what we've worked so hard for!"

The leader looked down at George with contempt. "We don't *want* to talk to you. We're looking for your so-called Bishop."

Roughly, he shoved George aside as the mob moved onward, yelling angry curses about igniting slave rebellions. George and the small group of Mormons followed them at a safe distance. The gang halted at the door of the *Evening and Morning Star*, then forced their way into the two-story brick building.

Helplessly, George watched while the mob heaved the printing press from the upper story, then scattered the type, books and papers in the street. The Mormons dared not try to stop them, for fear of inciting them to murder.

George began to tremble when the gang seized the Bishop and another man. Boasting they would outdo one another, the mobbers stripped the two men, then plastered them with warm tar and then feathers. They tied ropes to the supports of the newspaper building and pulled it down to the ground.

George ran back to his house to find Lily. She stood on the

porch terrified but unharmed.

A passing mobber called to George, "You'd better get your pregnant wife away from that house."

George promptly complied. He and Lily fled to the outlying farm colony where her parents lived.

Incensed, George wanted to fight back.

"But how?" Lily asked.

George fumed with the knowledge that they could do little more than wait for State authorities to intervene, if they would. But the voters of Jackson County quickly organized and passed a more formal petition, ordering the Mormons to leave the county by the following spring.

Dismayed and demoralized, the Mormons dispatched a messenger to Kirtland to seek the counsel of Joseph Smith. He returned with the news that Joseph had received a revelation ordering forbearance, not retribution. So they publicized their tolerance of slavery and retained a lawyer, Alexander Doniphan, reputedly the best militia general in Missouri. They sued for damages to their property and petitioned the Governor for enough militia troops to keep order.

But order was not to be. On Halloween night, 1833, a mob of fifty men rode to the outlying colony where George and Lily lived with her parents.

"What is that, George?" Lily asked.

George and his father-in-law hurriedly grabbed their rifles and rushed outside. George stepped out into the open.

The older man gripped George's arm. "We can't stop them," he whispered. "There are too many. If we don't shoot, the mob will disarm us. And shooting will bring unbridled war."

George gave his gun to his father-in-law, who quickly took cover in the woods.

An enormous man on a very large stallion rode up close to George.

"Hey, look at this one," he called out. The light from the torch in his hand illuminated the anger in his eyes. Five other ruffians, all drunk, wheeled their horses and pulled them up surrounding George.

41

"Awfully tiny to be much of a threat," another laughed.

"What should we do with him?" the first one yelled. "He's too small to be sporting to whip."

As they laughed, George smelled the foul liquor on their breath.

"Let's cut off his little pecker!"

"Why not? Who's to stop us!"

George stood petrified with fear as the men stripped him naked and tied his arms and legs to a fence. One of the men unsheathed his knife.

"It isn't so little! Let him keep it."

The men roared with laughter, watching George cower in terror.

"Maybe he's got a little wife."

"I bet she'd like to find out how a big man feels."

"Or half a dozen of us!"

Two men stayed behind with their revolvers trained on George. Naked and tied to the fence, he could see that they hoped he would give them an excuse to open fire.

The other four men kicked the cabin door down. George's heart pounded in terror and wrath as he watched them force his wife and her mother out the door. The older woman was screaming and hitting at the mobbers, but they just laughed at the futile, feeble blows.

One of the men put his hand on Lily's belly. "Bad luck to stick it to pregnant women," he warned.

"How about from behind, like bulls do to cows?"

A gleeful mobber jabbed George with his gun. "How'd you like to watch us do that!"

Nearly blind with fear and rage, George dared not say a word.

"Still bad luck, boys."

"What about the older one, then? She's no worse than most whores in Independence."

A mobber held his torch close to Lily's mother's face. But as he did, from the woods came the cracking of a gunshot and a bullet that tore a hole in his hat. The men looked cautiously toward the woods, then toward the other houses in the settlement where their fellow mobbers had gone.

"Nah, there's lots of them Mormons. We'll find someone younger and prettier. Maybe a virgin."

Still clasping the women tight, the mobbers emptied the house of its belongings. They drove the livestock away, then set fire to the cabin and barn. When the property was burned too far to salvage, the men released their captives and climbed back onto their horses.

"Get out of Jackson County," they yelled as they rode away.

Shaking with fury, cold and relief, George thanked God that the encounter was no worse.

"How can we leave the county now?" he muttered as Lily untied him. "It's already November, and we'd die of the cold if we tried to leave in winter."

George and his family retreated to another settlement, where they quickly organized for their defense. Just a few days passed before suspicious sounds again disturbed the darkness.

"Wake up! Wake up!" a guard bellowed. "Mobbers are sacking our storehouse!"

George rushed outside to join the other men. Noise and dust from horses galloping in retreat filled the air.

"We've captured one of the robbers!"

"What should we do with him?"

"Take him to the Justice of the Peace," George advised. "They'll put him in jail."

Several men rode off with their captive. George stayed behind to guard against renewed assault by the mobbers.

By noon the next day, George was baffled. His friends should have returned hours earlier, and with mounting alarm, he waited for news.

Several days elapsed before they learned what had happened. A neighbor galloped into the settlement.

"The Justice of the Peace refuses to swear out a warrant for the robber's arrest. He's jailed our men instead for *false* arrest!"

Disgusted, George threw up his hands.

"But other news is worse," the neighbor said. "In a clash

43

last night at another settlement, a Saint and two Gentiles were killed. One of the dead was the Campbellite preacher who led the mob."

Still on his horse, the neighbor stopped to catch his breath.

"My God," George said, fearing to hear more.

"Now the mob is threatening to lynch our jailed men in revenge. And they've demanded militia troops to protect *them* from *our* vengeance! Lieutenant Governor Boggs has called out the militia, led by a Colonel who signed that damned petition against us."

The man turned to ride to the next settlement.

"What should we do?" George asked.

"Gather together west of Independence," he called.

West of Independence, where a large group of Mormons had assembled, George watched the hostile Colonel and his heavily armed escort ride up to them.

"Surrender all your weapons!" the Colonel ordered. "And the men who'll stand trial for the murders of proper Missourians."

George listened with the desperate knowledge that the jailed Mormons were likely to be lynched.

"Lieutenant Governor Boggs urges you Mormons to obey," the Colonel said. "He's ordered me to disarm the posse when you surrender your men and your guns."

With grave misgivings, George and the other men handed over their weapons to the militia.

That night, the mob systematically sacked every nearby Mormon community. By morning, they had set fire to 300 houses.

Helplessly, George and Lily stood among 1,200 Saints, herded into a weaponless mass. The biting north wind stung their cheeks, warning that winter would quickly be upon them.

"We must flee across the river," he told Lily. "They say that Clay County is more sympathetic to us."

Lily's face was drawn by anguish as she cried, "Where will my baby be born?"

"We will find shelter," he assured her. "Haven't saints in all

44

days been called upon to suffer for their faith?"

George and Lily, her parents, and ten other Mormons were grateful when they found an abandoned shanty on the other side of the Missouri River. The building was nothing more than one large room and a lean-to, which they found to be of scant use. Though little remained of the rat-infested floor, the one inhabitable room was warmed by a large fireplace. They hung blankets back a few feet from the fire, then spent the winter huddled there, all of them together inside the blankets to keep from freezing. Some nights were so cold that the ink froze in George's pen while he wrote his accounts. Lily suffered a miscarriage on one such night, and all of them shed bitter, angry tears.

In the early spring of 1834, a horseman rode up to the shanty. Everyone in the house ran out to greet him.

"Zion's Camp is on the way!" he announced.

"Zion's Camp?" they asked.

"Yes! Joseph has received a revelation that there must be an army of liberation. He's leading 200 men here to Zion."

Though most of the men cheered, George was perplexed by the news. "But the Governor has ordered the militia to be ready to escort us back to Jackson County," George said. "He's advised us to apply for public arms."

"Even armed, we'd still be badly outnumbered," his father-in-law argued. "Who went to Kirtland to tell Joseph?"

"Parley Pratt and Lyman Wight."

George shook his head with apprehension, imagining what they had said to Joseph. To him, Parley Pratt was an overly passionate man, and Lyman Wight was zealous and bellicose.

The messenger said, "When the men of Zion's Camp arrive…"

George interrupted, "When our enemies hear of this, the militiamen won't wait for orders. They'll muster themselves to fight us off!"

Soon, word of the approaching invasion reached Independence. Mobs stormed the jail and seized the stockpiled Mormon arms, then they methodically destroyed the few remaining homes and farms of the Saints.

Untrained, undisciplined, and with inadequate food, the men of Zion's Camp suffered in the rain and heat on their 800-mile march from northeastern Ohio to western Missouri.

As Zion's Camp drew nearer, the Jackson County Sheriff rode out to intercept them. He informed Joseph Smith that entering the county with arms was an act of insurrection, and he ordered the army to disperse. But cholera had already assaulted Zion's Camp. As fourteen men lay dying of cholera, and others were left too weak to fight, Joseph had no choice but to retreat back to Kirtland.

George and Lily managed to settle in Clay County, where they and other Mormons began to rebuild. As before, they built schoolhouses before they built cabins and granaries. But the anti-Mormons were not finished with their mischief. Two years later, in the summer of 1836, hostile Jackson County men began to ride across the Missouri River to Clay County. They resumed insulting and plundering Mormon victims.

George was riding home late one day, when he was startled by three horsemen galloping fast in his direction. George wheeled his horse and spurred it the opposite way at top speed.

Afraid to look back, George prayed his small size would let him outrace his pursuers. He left two of the men far behind him, but the third sprinted ahead and grabbed his reins. As George's horse slowed, the other two men pulled up beside him.

"Give us your horse," they demanded from George.

"Why can't you just leave us in peace?" he asked, panting.

"We don't like Mormons," one man said as he raised his whip above his head.

"I can see that," George said, refusing to dismount. "But none of you truly seem like church-going men. Surely, you can't hate us for our new Christianity."

"We don't like nobody who doesn't like slavery."

"We aren't abolitionists," George argued, hoping to talk them out of their intentions.

"Then why in hell don't you own slaves?"

"Is it wrong to do our own work? The *Book of Mormon*

46

says…"

The first man raised his whip again, while the other two looked at one another.

"And you're way too sweet on the Indians."

"Indians are our misguided brothers," George explained. "Not vermin to be exterminated, or even fools to be exploited."

"That's what we mean. Get off your horse!"

Furious, George walked the four miles to his house.

The old settlers of Clay County feared that worse assaults would come, and advised the Mormons to find a more distant home. So the Saints petitioned the Missouri legislature to assign them some sparsely-populated place. The legislature, showing some sympathy for their plight, designated Caldwell County, farther north. The Mormons harvested their crops and sold their property, bought out the claims of most Caldwell County residents, and laid out the town of Far West.

# Chapter 4

## March 1837

George looked over the rail of the steamboat as the fast-moving current carried debris down the Ohio River. Traveling overland would have been a shorter route, but the steamboat was quicker, safer and less wearing. George was pleased that Joseph Smith had called him back to Kirtland, to report in person on the progress in Missouri. He had not been back to Ohio since 1831. George observed the prosperity in the regions he crossed and welcomed in particular the improvements in transportation. He had traveled down the Missouri River to fast-growing St. Louis, now a city of 15,000 people, then down the Mississippi River to Cairo, Illinois. He had come up the Ohio River past bustling Cincinnati, toward Portsmouth, where a 300-mile canal now connected southern Ohio to Cleveland.

Still, the journey had taken three weeks, and George found himself lonely for Lily. He smiled at the thought of his sweet-tempered wife, who had grown even more attractive at 23 than she had been at seventeen. But he knew it saddened her that, after another miscarriage, they had no children. George asked for and respected her opinions, for they were sensible, but there were parts of Lily's personality that he never felt he fully understood.

Naturally, George expected to see progress in the six years since he had left Ohio. But he still gasped with awe as the carriage brought him from Cleveland into Kirtland. He stared at the massive three-story stone Temple, part Gothic, part colonial and part Greek. Throughout northern Ohio, the Temple of the Latter-day Saints was regarded with wonder. Even with donated materials and labor, the Temple cost $40,000, much of it borrowed.

Joseph Smith had spared no effort or expense in his plans to transform Kirtland into a handsome city of 15,000. About 1,000 Saints were living and working there, all of them laboring to

49

finish the Temple. George admired the improvements as he walked across Kirtland, pleased to know his own report would be favorable.

While George waited for his meeting with Joseph, he went to see an old friend, the chief bookkeeper.

"George!" the bookkeeper greeted him warmly. "We heard you were called back to Ohio."

They discussed the news of Kirtland and Far West, and their families.

"Have you heard, George?" the bookkeeper asked. "The Federal Government is now requiring gold or silver to pay for public land."

George had not heard of this change. "But we haven't got the hard cash to buy the land we need in Missouri!"

"We have found another way to finance our plans."

"How?"

"Joseph has received a revelation that the Church must enter the banking business. Several prominent men among us have been called to invest all their gold and silver into bank stock."

George inhaled deeply. In the mid-1830s, the nation was caught up in a mad financial boom, fed by easy credit and paper money issued by private banks. This paper money was notorious for having only questionable backing.

"Could I see the accounts?" George asked.

"Of course."

Cautiously, George examined the numbers. He quickly recognized that, even with the hard currency, nearly all the bank's capital lay in real estate.

"These real estate values must be exaggerated five-fold!" he exclaimed.

"Six-fold," the bookkeeper sighed. He handed George an elaborately engraved banknote from the Kirtland Safety Society Bank Company.

George glanced at the note. "What backs these up?"

"A few thousand dollars worth of gold and silver. Look closely at the word *Bank*."

George held the $3 banknote close to his eyes. In small

letters, the word *Anti-* was stamped before *Bank* and *ing* was stamped after it. Bewildered, he looked up again.

The bookkeeper hesitated, then he explained. "A few weeks ago, Joseph ordered these banknotes from an engraver. But the Ohio legislature refused to charter our bank, perhaps doubtful of its backing. Naturally, that did not stop Joseph. He organized it instead as the Kirtland Safety Society Anti-Banking Company. A bank might be illegal, he claims, but surely an anti-bank is not!"

George shook his head and waited to be summoned by Joseph Smith. It was clear to him that Kirtland's rapid growth was being fueled by Joseph's extensive borrowing for his family and Church purposes.

George was called an hour later. He reported on Missouri to Joseph, then abruptly halted.

"It's counterfeiting, Joseph!" he protested.

"You know that isn't my intention."

"Of course not! But these banknotes will very soon become worthless."

"These notes are for *exchange*," Joseph patiently explained. "Not to be *paid*."

"In our community, yes. But we'll be flooded with the banknotes, then they'll flow into the Gentile settlements."

"Times are prosperous. Haven't you seen that on your travels here?"

"The Gentiles will expect to be paid," George warned.

Joseph shrugged and said, "Come join us tonight at the Temple. Seventy Elders among us are learning Hebrew."

"Hebrew?" George asked with surprise.

"Yes. Our instructor is a Jewish rabbi. Often, we study until midnight."

"But why?" George asked.

"My soul delights in reading the word of God in the original."

Late that afternoon, George went into the vault and counted many boxes labeled $1,000. Reassured, he hefted one, then opened it, and saw a bright layer of fifty-cent silver coins. But as he tilted the box to replace it in the stack, he could feel shifting sand underneath the silver facade.

After two weeks, George returned to Missouri, worried about what might happen. His own brother had shown him Mormon banknotes he had willingly taken in trade for lumber. George had not known what to say to Thomas. He hoped the Gentile banks and merchants would not soon demand hard currency for the notes.

The Kirtland Safety Society Anti-Banking Company issued paper money until mid-year 1837. By then, its doubtful banknotes traded for 12½ cents on the dollar.

George found it a small comfort that the Saints were far from alone in the blame. Throughout the country, the financial bubble burst, and 800 banks failed in May 1837 alone. But Joseph Smith was arrested and released seven times in the course of four months.

On a wintry night, Joseph Smith and Sidney Rigdon fled westward from Ohio, hoping to escape yet another arrest for bank fraud. When they finally reached Far West in January 1838, the entire town came out to greet them in the snow.

"At last, we're united!" Lily cheered. "It's the answer to our prayers!"

George celebrated too, though he could not help but count the cost. The financial scandal had racked the Church and earned them a reputation for sharp practices, if not dishonesty. Hundreds of Saints had now become dissenters, including Cowdery, Harris and Whitmer, all three of the witnesses to the *Book of Mormon*. Some dissenters were loudly anti-Mormon, and deeply embarrassing to the community. To prevent their arrest or defection, Joseph Smith had sent Brigham Young and many other Elders to England on the first foreign mission of the Church. It seemed a wise step to George, preserving the loyalty of their leaders.

But all was well in Caldwell County, Missouri. In a year, the 1,500 Saints had developed Far West in accordance with Joseph's generous town plan. They had built many good houses, four dry goods stores, three groceries, half a dozen blacksmith shops, and two hotels. Now that Joseph Smith and Sidney Rigdon had arrived, they started excavating the basement for the Temple, 80 by 120 feet. Soon, 600 once-dissenting Saints, disgusted by the rantings of apostates in Ohio, began arriving in long trains of wagons. Kirtland, with its newly finished Temple, reverted back to the sleepy town it was before the Mormons came.

That spring, Joseph Smith and a party of men rowed up the Grand River to Lyman Wight's ferry, then crossed into Daviess County.

"Come look at these rocks!" one man called from a bluff that overlooked the river.

George and the other men climbed up the bluff behind him. The rocks formed curious formations, some resembling fantastic animals, while others seemed like stone structures built by men. One formation looked as if it were the ruins of some ancient altar.

Joseph gazed at the beauty of the springtime prairie and was silent for several minutes. George and the others waited to hear what he would say.

"*This*, indeed, is the very same altar where Adam offered sacrifices to Jehovah! It is here where Adam dwelt after he was cast from the Garden of Eden."

"What's this place called?" a man asked Joseph.

"Adam-Ondi-Ahman. Here, we will build a town!"

George hesitated only for a moment. Most of the other men had been in Kirtland while he and Lily faced their terrible trials in Jackson County.

"This land is in Daviess, not Caldwell County," George warned. "The Gentile town of Gallatin is just a few miles away."

Joseph stared past him at the stone altar. "Lyman Wight will be President of the Stake," he proclaimed.

When George went home that night, he told Lily, "We are called to live in Adam-Ondi-Ahman."

Lily looked up at him puzzled. "Where?"

George explained what had happened that day. "And what's

worse, the Stake President will be Lyman Wight. His belligerence led to the disastrous Zion's Camp, and his sermons trouble me deeply."

"How so?" Lily asked.

"Don't you remember Lyman's loud preaching? 'The Gentiles ought to be *damned*, and sent to *Hell* where they properly belong.'"

"Well, yes. But we must go where we are called."

George nodded but sighed, "Joseph is far too partial to the men who served with him in Zion's Camp. They're *nine* of the twelve Apostles, and *all* of those high ranking men called the Seventies."

"George, you mustn't appear jealous."

"Now Joseph has organized a secret, armed body of men for our defense. He's chosen Sampson Avard to lead these Danites."

"Why are they called Danites?" Lily asked.

"Sons of Dan, from the Bible. *Dan shall be a serpent by the way, an adder in the path, that biteth the horse's heels, so that his rider shall fall backward.*"

"Will you join them?"

"No."

"Why not?" she asked, disappointed in him.

"Because they're said to be the scourge of heretics," George replied. "And informers for unmasking dissenters. It's whispered that divulging Danite secrets can mean death."

In the spring and summer of 1838, the Mormon communities of western Missouri saw rapid progress. At their Fourth of July celebration, Joseph Smith laid the cornerstone for the Far West Temple. To make a bold statement, he organized a parade of the entire community, many of them marching as infantry or cavalry units.

Sidney Rigdon rose to speak in the bright sunshine. Again, he spoke in the same impassioned voice that George had found so compelling eight years earlier. But as the preacher went on, threatening reprisals, even extermination against attackers, George heard the rousing words as he feared the Gentiles would hear them.

"We this day then proclaim ourselves free," Rigdon vowed, "with a purpose and a determination, that can never be broken—no never! *no never!!* NO NEVER!!!"

The crowd of the faithful roared its approval, but the hair stood up on the back of George's neck.

Unconcerned about the rage of the Gentiles who heard it, Joseph Smith printed and circulated Rigdon's speech. Missouri newspapers answered with angry editorials denouncing the threats against non-Mormons.

All remained calm in Caldwell County. But that August, an anti-Mormon leader was running for the Missouri state senate in Daviess County, where George and Lily lived.

"We'll all vote against him," an Elder said at a prayer meeting.

There was no dissent.

"We have about as many men as the Gentiles," George told them. "He'll lose if his opponent gets any Gentile votes at all."

They all rode into Gallatin on election day. George was the first in line to vote, but three large men stepped in front of him to block his way.

"Daviess County don't allow Mormons to vote no more than niggers," one of them muttered.

George counted 200 Gentiles against thirty Saints. Then, without warning, George felt a blow to his head and found himself sprawled on the ground. From where he lay, he saw a neighbor flash a sign with his hand that could only be a Danite signal.

By chance, the Mormons were standing near a woodpile, and some of them grabbed oak hearts, each four feet long and weighing about seven pounds. George clambered to his feet and joined his fellows in a frenzy of clubbing. Within minutes, nine Gentiles were lying badly hurt on the ground, and though none were killed, many others were bruised.

A messenger leaped onto his horse and galloped off to Far West. Sampson Avard quickly mustered the Danite troops, who rode to Gallatin with Joseph Smith.

George waited, his wooden club gripped in his splintered, sweaty hand. As unaccustomed to victory as he was, he felt uneasy that he had enjoyed the battle. When Joseph Smith and Sampson Avard rode into Gallatin, they demanded that the Justice of the Peace sign a cease-fire treaty with the Saints. Then George voted, along with the other Daviess County men.

But their triumph was only short-lived. The anti-Mormon candidate secured a warrant for Joseph's arrest, calling his demands intimidation and threatened murder. Lilburn Boggs, now the Governor of Missouri, called up six militia companies to enforce the warrant.

"My God," Lily said, "it's like Jackson County all over again."

"I fear it will be worse," George replied.

In all the Mormon settlements except Far West, armed hostile gangs began setting fires to hayracks and granaries. They stole horses and cattle, beat men and terrorized women and children.

All autumn, the bitterness intensified. Millers refused to grind Mormon grain, leaving people without flour for bread. Along with hunger came panic at the impending winter, while more converts were arriving from the East, needing food. Soon, the towns of Adam-Ondi-Ahman and DeWitt were under siege, behind hastily-built barricades.

Along with all other able-bodied Mormon males, George joined the defensive force. Being small, he was chosen to spy on the movements of the raiders at close range. But George was untrained and quickly caught, then beaten so badly with a hickory withe that his back was ribboned with bloody welts.

"We'll let you go if you'll deliver a message," the gang told him when they grew bored.

"What is it?" George gasped.

"Surrender your leaders or die."

"I'll tell them," he promised.

George found his way back to Lily, and together they escaped in the dark to Far West. Grimly, he delivered the message.

In Far West, George was mortified to learn that a small force of Mormons had seized the offensive. Claiming that God stood on their side, they scattered the Gentiles in Gallatin, looted and burned down a store, then set fire to several cabins. George listened to their boasting and felt appalled that they were weak enough to believe that God would let them persist in their plunder. When the looters attacked two more settlements and brought the spoils to Far West, several Apostles abandoned the Church in horror.

Outside Far West, rumors quickly spread that a huge Mormon army was preparing to lay waste to that entire section of Missouri. A militiaman and three Mormons in fact died in a skirmish, but Governor Boggs believed a vicious lie that Mormons had massacred a whole militia company of fifty men. Two defecting Apostles gave Boggs affidavits exposing the Danites and admitting that Mormons had pillaged Gallatin. Within a week, every isolated Mormon cabin was burned down. Boggs called up more militia, and Far West prepared for a siege.

In late October, a poorly armed group of Mormon men, women and children sought shelter together at Haun's Mill, fifteen miles from Far West. Although 240 militiamen surrounded them, Haun would not surrender the new flouring mill. Unwilling to be denied, the mob fired 1,600 rounds of ammunition, massacring nineteen men and boys. One of the dead was Lily's father. A militiaman was heard to boast, after he murdered a nine-year-old boy cowering under the bellows of the blacksmith shop, "Nits will make lice, and if he had lived, he would have been a Mormon."

George and Lily watched with heavy hearts as the terrified Haun's Mill survivors straggled into Far West. Among them, a dozen were wounded and bloody.

"Is there nothing the Government won't do against us?" Lily's mother asked, bewildered, as Lily tried to comfort her.

"Militiamen outnumber our fighting men five to one already," George told Joseph. "Within two days, Boggs could set 10,000 men against us."

They stood in silence for awhile, all of them aware that their position was hopeless. Then Joseph sent out a group of men to negotiate the Mormon surrender.

When they returned, they announced with resignation, "The terms are harsh. We surrender our leaders to stand trial for treason. We pledge to depart, all of us and at once, from Missouri. And we give up all our property and arms."

George listened to the answer in silence.

The next morning, Alexander Doniphan, a militia general, solemnly rode into Far West. George had not seen him since 1834, when he had served as their attorney.

Doniphan held up an official-looking paper. "Governor Lilburn Boggs has issued an executive order," he announced.

Doniphan read from it aloud, "'The Mormons must be treated as enemies, and must be exterminated or driven from the state if necessary, for the public good.'"

George heard the words with disbelief. *Exterminated.*

"I was ordered to execute your leaders this morning," Doniphan told the stunned crowd. "But I refused to obey because it is cold-blooded murder. And I *vow* that any man who fulfills that order will face trial for murder, himself."

George watched as fifty of their leaders were bound over for trial. Then he, like the others, relinquished his gun to the militia.

"Six thousand militiamen know we are defenseless," George said grimly. "Lily, you must keep out of sight."

George and Lily quickly found a place where she and her mother could hide. Then, sick to his stomach, he helplessly stood by as hundreds of militiamen went berserk. They shot all the hogs and cattle for amusement, then came after unfortunate people.

"You let my daughter go!" one man shrieked.

But they bound her to a bench in the schoolhouse, there to be violated by a score of soldiers.

"I *will* take vengeance," the man vowed as the militiamen held him down. "From this moment on, I will fault *nothing* that we ever do to seize power and use it as we see fit."

When the Mormon leaders were arraigned at the Clay County courthouse, the main witness against them was Sampson

Avard, the man who had been chosen to lead the Danites. He falsely claimed Danite numbers in the thousands and withheld no secrets about their schemes. Denied bail, Joseph Smith, Sidney Rigdon and a few other men were imprisoned in the jailhouse in Liberty, Missouri.

George, Lily and her mother joined thousands of other Saints on a forlorn winter exodus.

As they walked, George said to Lily, "Surely, it is Providence that Brigham Young escaped. He's planned our route east and arranged for food along the way."

Lily said nothing as she labored through the snow.

"All is not lost," George told her. "Even *Missouri* newspapers are beginning to report on the travesties of justice we've suffered."

Lily stopped and turned to face her husband. "Boggs' extermination order still hangs over our heads!"

Bitterly, George agreed. "But the investigators *must* recognize that there's no evidence of treason by Joseph."

"Do you *actually* believe they can get a fair trial in western Missouri?"

"Not even the Gentiles believe that," George replied.

The small chance of acquittal made holding the Mormon prisoners an embarrassment to local officials. Joseph Smith and the other men endured four months in jail, then were taken to a different county. There, they bribed the sheriff, who allowed them to escape and join a straggling group of Latter-day Saints moving east, across the Mississippi River to Illinois.

# Chapter 5

Destitute and exhausted, George and Lily Wood reached Quincy, Illinois with the first group of Mormons in February 1839.

Quincy was a prosperous river port city for the steamboats that headed up and down the Mississippi River. The city had developed road connections to settlements in the East, and the men of vision there hoped to soon establish railroad links.

When the first Mormons arrived, Judge Franklin Hendricks, a wealthy railroad attorney, called a meeting of the Whigs in Quincy.

"We must establish a committee to investigate the facts," Judge Hendricks urged. "And we must get the Mormons food and clothing, and do our best to find housing."

Another man spoke up. "Remember, Judge, it's an election year. The Democrats control Quincy, and they'll be more than pleased to welcome such a large block of voters."

"Indeed," the Judge grumbled, absently stroking his crippled leg. "They'll be quick to distinguish themselves from those Missouri border ruffians."

A merchant added, "Our workingmen fear that the Mormons will lower the wages of the working class."

"They must take jobs to keep from starving!" a woman said.

"Yes, but there are so many..."

"And many new ones will soon be following on their heels."

The Judge held up his hand and said calmly, "As victims of injustice, the Mormons merit our sympathy and aid. The laws of humanity require us to observe decorum and not wound their feelings in any way."

Soon after he arrived, Joseph Smith re-established his newspaper, the *Times and Seasons,* and published the story of the massacre at Haun's Mill. Then he forwarded copies to all leading newspapers, winning nationwide publicity and sympathy for Mormon suffering at the hands of the Missourians. But when Joseph traveled to Washington to request Federal help with reparations, he returned empty-handed.

"President Van Buren said he could do *nothing*!" George told Lily. "Or rather, *would* do nothing. He won't risk a bill in Congress to compensate us."

"But why not?" Lily asked.

"In the balance of free and slave states, Missouri wields too much power."

"Then *we* must obtain power, too!"

"Yes, of course," George agreed, distracted by the other news he had to tell her. "Would you help me pack a few things?"

"Where are you going?" Lily asked.

"Fifty miles upriver. A new convert is arranging to sell Joseph a large tract of land."

Lily folded a spare set of clothes for George. "Who is this new convert?"

"His name is Isaac Galland."

George and the other men rode for two days until they reached a swampy forest, where a high bluff overlooked a hamlet called Commerce. Across the Mississippi River stood the ghost town of Montrose and an abandoned military barracks in Iowa Territory.

"This swampy area may be sickly," George warned Joseph. "The residents of Commerce are suspiciously eager to sell out."

Joseph looked out from the bluff. "We'll rename the town Nauvoo, old Hebrew for the beautiful place that we will make it."

"I mistrust these purchase contracts," George told him. "They're complicated exchanges that will soon require large payments."

"We'll buy that land we passed, fifteen miles south of here, across the river near Keokuk, Iowa. We must build a settlement there, too."

"They say that land titles here are prone to false documentation," George said. "Deeds can date from French or British, Canadian or American rule. How well do we know this Isaac Galland?"

"Our city will be built with wide streets and blocks, centered around an immense Temple."

"Transportation to and from here is difficult," George added. "It's upriver from the Keokuk rapids. During low water, they could be impassable."

"Our efforts will overcome such hindrances. And if it can't be done, there's a good steamboat landing just south of Warsaw. We'll buy it, then build a railroad to connect it to Nauvoo."

George could not agree. "Five thousand people live in Warsaw, and their harbor is silting up. We'll threaten their prosperity if we own that landing."

"We'll *double* their numbers within three years."

"Yes, but they despise us already. The *Warsaw Signal* is the only newspaper in Illinois that didn't welcome us. They fear we'll dominate the political offices in the county."

Joseph pointed toward the green forest as if it were already cleared. "Nauvoo will have no saloons, only one single shop licensed to sell liquor that men can take home. Vagrancy and indecent language will be punished by six months in jail and a $500 fine."

"Six months in jail!" George exclaimed. "Gentiles will feel unwelcome in Nauvoo."

Joseph looked past George and said nothing.

Within a few weeks, George and Lily bought a parcel of land for their home from Joseph Smith. The price was reasonable, he felt, though George knew it gave Joseph a good profit. But as he feared, the swamps of Nauvoo were unhealthy, and many people caught malaria and died. If they had not had quinine, the Mormons might have had to move onward. Like other men, George had pledged to donate every tenth day to work for the Church, and they labored hard and fast to drain the swamps.

As he had for so many years, George resumed the work of constructing a community. He never lost the vision, instilled in him by Sidney Rigdon's words, of what a faithful community can be. Though there were far stronger men, few worked with greater dedication to build for the present, and for Eternity.

Frequent social occasions rewarded their hard work. George would dance with Lily, or listen to her singing, and know that God had blessed every sacrifice and labor by giving him his lovely, pious wife. Soon, they were delighted to find that Lily was pregnant again.

But Joseph's conflicts with the Missourians remained unresolved. In September 1840, a Missouri sheriff appeared in Nauvoo with a warrant, signed by Illinois Governor Carlin, to arrest Joseph as a fugitive from justice. Unable to find him anywhere, the Missourians soon gave up and went home. But the following year, a Missouri posse ambushed Joseph as he rode back from a meeting with Carlin, who knew of the plan. Though he was freed on a defect in the warrant, Joseph Smith never knew when the Missouri sheriffs might reappear.

And there were other troubles with the law. Since the earliest white settlement, many river bandits had lived along the Mississippi, and a few joined the Church to gain the unwitting protection of the Mormons. One day, a Gentile posse seized four recent converts and exposed a warehouse full of stolen property. Thievery then became another ready accusation to cast against the Saints.

But a greater thief lay in their midst. In 1841, Isaac Galland absconded with the money Joseph had given him to pay for the Illinois land. That year, they also learned that their Iowa land titles were forgeries. After a year of labor on improvements, 250 families were forced penniless across the Mississippi once again.

George and Lily were more fortunate than many. But when the time came for Lily to deliver, they were devastated that their baby girl was stillborn.

Gently, George took Lily's hand. "Perhaps our new convert can help."

"Who?" she asked weakly from her bed.

"Dr. John Cook Bennett. He's a specialist in female ailments. Maybe he can give you medicines when you become pregnant again."

Lily looked up hopefully at George. "Could you arrange to

have him see me?"

"Of course," George said as he stroked Lily's hair. "Joseph is quite impressed by Dr. Bennett's many talents. He's also Quartermaster General of the Illinois Militia."

Bennett soon demonstrated his political talents by securing extraordinary charter laws for Nauvoo from the Illinois legislature. The charters exempted Nauvoo from the usual state laws controlling the city council, local government and courts. The charters authorized a university and a militia, the Nauvoo Legion, answerable only to the Governor. To gain these benefits, Bennett promised both the Whigs and Democrats favor by Mormon voters, now numerous enough to swing elections.

In appreciation, Joseph Smith appointed Bennett as the Mayor of Nauvoo, Chancellor of the University of Nauvoo, Brigadier-general of the Nauvoo Legion, and Assistant President of the Church.

"That's second in power to Joseph, himself!" George complained to Lily.

"He's a very fine doctor," she replied. "His manner was most reassuring."

George smiled hopefully at his wife. "Yes, as a doctor. But in our Church, Bennett now outranks Sidney Rigdon."

George did not divulge to Lily a new concern about Bennett. In his travels East, Hyrum Smith had uncovered proof that Bennett had deserted a wife and two children in Ohio, and had been expelled by a Masonic lodge. But Joseph ignored his brother's news.

Loath to worry Lily with the rumors, he told her, instead, "Dr. Bennett is forming our own Masonic Lodge. When I was 21, I joined the Masons. Uncle Simon sponsored my application, then a committee of members investigated me thoroughly. Still, I feared that a single, secret vote against me, a blackball, would reject me."

"I thought the *Book of Mormon* opposed Freemasonry," Lily said.

The *Book of Mormon* tells the story of the Gadianton robbers. *And it came to pass that they did have their signs, yea, their secret signs, and their secret words; and this that they might distinguish a brother who had entered into the covenant, that whatsoever wickedness his brother should do, he should not be injured by his brother...thus they might murder, and plunder, and steal, and commit whoredoms, and all manner of wickedness, contrary to the laws of their country, and also the laws of their God.*

"That's why I left my lodge in 1830," George said. "But Joseph must've had a new revelation."

Lily looked perplexed.

"You see," George explained, "Masons value personal honor and respectability regardless of religion or politics, rank or wealth. George Washington, Benjamin Franklin and James Monroe were Masons. Andrew Jackson and Henry Clay were once Grand Masters."

"But what do Masons do?" she asked.

"I can't divulge that, Lily. All I can say is that I had to memorize large parts of the three degrees, a series of dramatic morality plays. And I felt proud that illiterate, stupid or lazy men could not accomplish it. But when Dr. Bennett asked the lodge in Quincy, the closest to us, to sponsor a lodge here in Nauvoo, Judge Hendricks and the other Masons there refused."

"I thought the people of Quincy were kind," Lily said.

"They may be suspicious of how we got our city charter," George admitted. "Or they may wonder about that banking scandal in Kirtland, or question that we'll treat them as brothers. But the Illinois Grand Master has promised to grant a charter to Nauvoo Lodge, and make Joseph Smith and Sidney Rigdon Masons-at-sight. That's a rarely-used prerogative of a Grand Master, when a busy, prominent man will bring honor to Freemasonry."

"Then he must recognize the stature of our leaders!" Lily exclaimed.

"Or perhaps he has political ambitions," George allowed. "He hopes to be elected to the legislature, though I doubt that an English-born Jew aspires to high political office."

"A Jew is Masonic Grand Master?" Lily asked.

"Yes, and in Kentucky before Illinois."

George was pleased to rejoin the worldwide brotherhood. Brother Masons were obliged not to cheat or wrong him, but treat him as an equal and try to help him if he were in distress, or aid his widow or orphan if in need. Although inactive at the time, George was dismayed when the Anti-Masons ran a national presidential campaign in 1832. But he had understood the animosity. Masons often favored fellow Masons, and seemed too privileged and controlling for a presumably democratic society. Most newspaper owners, bankers, leading businessmen, landowners and politicians were Masons, as were many clergymen. Anti-Masonic newspapers made that appear dangerous and evil, implying that Masons put fraternal loyalty above state and society. Rabble-rousers fanned the flames lit by Captain Morgan's abduction and seized on Masonry as the focus of lower-class resentments.

Like George himself, so many men quit their lodges that Masonry nearly vanished over much of the country, except the South, for many years. In 1840, just one year earlier, the leaders of the National Republican Party joined forces with the Anti-Masonic Party to form the Whigs.

George was warmly welcomed into Nauvoo Lodge. But as the weeks passed, he watched with alarm as his lodge overturned crucial rules. Six days a week, morning, afternoon and evening, they held meetings to give new Mormon Masons the insignia and benefits without the patient effort demanded of regular candidates. Without investigation or proper ceremony, Nauvoo Lodge granted Masonic degrees to 1,400 of their men. In all of Illinois the year before, all Masonic lodges had 230 members altogether.

When he could restrain himself no longer, George complained to the Secretary of the Lodge. "Degrees that should take months are granted in days!"

"Why does that matter? Aren't they worthy men?"

"Yes, of course," George agreed. "But men can't absorb the meaning of our rituals so fast. And the Gentiles will surely question the worthiness of their new brothers. They'll fear a quick Mormon takeover of Illinois Grand Lodge."

"Nauvoo Lodge was told to confer degrees on all worthy men who want them," the Secretary said. "And the new Grand Master has granted us charters for *four* more lodges. Soon we'll have 600 *more* members."

"The lodge in Quincy will expose these outrageous improprieties," George warned him. "It can only lead to suspension!"

"Joseph doesn't agree," the Secretary said. "Nor does John Cook Bennett."

In silence, George wondered what Bennett had done to earn expulsion from his lodge in Ohio. Masons were quick to expel or suspend a man for unmasonic behavior.

In Warsaw, too, a lodge was organized, and the new Grand Master chose Mormon Masons to assist at installing Warsaw officers. George stood warily at their first meeting, helping to install Mark Aldrich, Warsaw postmaster and militia captain, as Secretary of Warsaw Lodge. George feared that their presence was unwise. With the blood already bad between Warsaw and Nauvoo, the new Warsaw Masons would suspect that Mormons already dominated Illinois Freemasonry.

George recognized that newly settled Nauvoo was dominating more than Freemasonry. He had compiled a list of applicants to Nauvoo Lodge, and counted skilled men more numerous than could be found in established cities like St. Louis, let alone Quincy or Warsaw. He proudly showed the listing to Joseph Smith, whose own occupation appeared as Merchant.

| | | | |
|---|---|---|---|
| Accountant | 2 City marshals | Innkeeper | 2 Reed makers |
| Agent | 10 Clerks | 17 Joiners | 2 Rope makers |
| Artist | Coach driver | Justice of the peace | 2 Sadlers |
| Agriculturalist | Cobbler | 40 Laborers | Sailor |
| 4 Attorneys | 2 Confectioners | Landlord | 13 School teachers |
| 4 Bakers | Constable | Malting manufacturer | Seaman |
| 2 Barbers | 35 Coopers | 10 Masons | Shepherd |
| 46 Blacksmiths | 9 Cordwainers | Matmaker | 2 Ship carpenters |
| Bishop | Coroner | Mechanic | 2 Shopkeepers |
| 2 Bookbinders | 2 Cotton spinners | 23 Merchants | Silversmith |
| 2 Bookkeepers | Cradlemaker | 7 Millers | 2 Spinners |
| Boot caulker | Cutler | 5 Millwrights | Steamboat pilot |
| 43 Boot and Shoe makers | Dentist | Miner | 30 Stone cutters |
| 24 Bricklayers | 12 Doctors | 17 Ministers | 24 Stone masons |
| 7 Brickmakers | Driver | Overseer | Student |
| 4 Brickmasons | Editor | 12 Painters | Surveyor |
| Brick-molder | 3 Engineers | Pattern maker | 18 Tailors |
| Broker | Engraver | Peddler | 6 Tanners |
| 5 Cabin makers | 489 Farmers | 4 Plasterers | 4 Tinmen-tinkers |
| 8 Cabinet makers | Grinder | Plumber and glazier | 2 Traders |
| Captain | Grocer | Policeman | 5 Turners |
| 90 Carpenters | 7 Gunsmiths | 2 Portrait painters | 5 Wagon makers |
| 18 Carpenter Joiners | Harness maker | 2 Potters | Watchmaker |
| Carpet weaver | 8 Hatters | 4 Printers | 6 Weavers |
| Carriage maker | Horse doctor | Professor | 7 Wheelwrights |

| 9 Chairmakers | House carpenter | Pump maker | Wool carder |
| Chemist | House joiner | Recorder and postmaster | Yeoman |

They, and 196 others, were indeed worthy men. But in early 1842, the Illinois Grand Master learned of the outrageous granting of degrees, and he revoked the charters for all five Mormon lodges. Insolently, they continued to hold meetings and add members, becoming clandestine lodges which other Masons were forbidden to recognize. But clandestine or expelled, the former Masons knew the rituals, symbols and secrets.

By then, Nauvoo had become the most populous city in Illinois. Among its 12,000 residents were many immigrants from England, where Brigham Young had established an office to charter ships and organize provisions. Converts were charged only four English pounds for their passage to New Orleans, then Joseph Smith's steamboat picked them up and brought them upriver to Nauvoo. Two hundred Mormon converts left England in 1840, 1,200 in 1841, and 1,600 in 1842. Within two years, 8,000 Saints were waiting to emigrate.

By the spring of 1842, the national publicity about the Mormons had grown favorable. Many prosperous American and Canadian converts had invested their capital into factories. Nauvoo quickly boasted two large steam sawmills, a steam flour mill, a tool factory, and a foundry. For awhile, the town even had a brothel, fronted by a grocery store, until some militiamen tipped it backward over a gully and let it crash to the bottom. As much as possible, the community kept their trade and business to themselves.

That spring, the *New York Herald* printed an editorial, praising Nauvoo's improvements and its militia of well-disciplined troops. All able-bodied Mormon males from age 18 to 45 belonged to the Nauvoo Legion, and they faced heavy fines for failing to appear at their regular and strenuous drills.

Lily dried the sweat from George's forehead after a parade.

"Bennett keeps our Legion very well supplied," George admitted. "I'll give him credit for that."

"We're blessed to have among us the Quartermaster General for the entire Illinois militia."

"I suppose so," he sighed.

"Do you dislike Dr. Bennett, George?"

George shrugged. "Joseph favors him more than worthier men. He grants Bennett more intimacy and privileges."

"Might you be jealous?" Lily asked as she helped him take off his boots.

Unable to deny it, George said nothing.

"At your parade today," Lily said, "I stood alongside a steamboat captain. His boat was taking on supplies at our landing."

"Do I know him?" George asked.

"I don't think so. His name is Captain White. He said our military band is excellent, and he admired Joseph's fine uniform."

George nodded as he unbuttoned his collar. Joseph wore a blue coat with ample braid, buff trousers and high military boots. His large hat was embellished with stars and ostrich feathers, and a sword and two pistols were attached to his belt.

"Captain White stared in surprise at the parade ground," Lily said. "'Those are rifles!' he exclaimed. So I told him, 'Dr. Bennett has organized companies of riflemen, with rifles belonging to us, not the State.' He seemed quite flustered at that."

"Rifles are effective at 300 yards," George explained, "*three times* as far as muskets. And like other militias, we also have 350 muskets and three cannon furnished to us by the State."

Lily brushed some dust from George's hair. "Then the captain said, 'The *New York Herald* claims that your militia has 1,500 troops. That's as many as in twenty towns, where the typical militia is 60 to 100 men. Even regiments have only 300 to 600.'

"'Well, that's not precisely true,' I explained. 'The Nauvoo Legion has 4,000 men.'

"'Four thousand men!' the captain shouted. 'That's far more than all the other militia companies in Hancock County combined.'

"Then Captain White pointed to another field, where the younger boys were drilling with great enthusiasm. 'There must be 500 boys out there, and they, too, seem infected with military fervor.'

"'After our suffering in Missouri,' I told him, 'many of them feel that it's them and their fellows against the world.'

"'I was an Infantry sergeant, Madam, in 1812,' the captain said, 'and I believe I'm a good judge of soldiers. Your Legion looks excellent, man-for-man even better, brighter and more serious than Regular Army enlisted men.'"

"He said that?" George asked, pleased.

"Yes, so I said, 'And we don't rely on the State for our weapons. We have a tool factory and foundry, and at least seven gunsmiths.'"

"What did Captain White say about that?" George asked Lily.

"He watched for another few minutes, then he whispered, 'Well, Joseph Smith can surely boast a dedicated and well-equipped private army. And from Nauvoo, it's just a few hours march to either Warsaw or Carthage. Wouldn't *that* be a nasty civil war!'"

# Chapter 6

One afternoon in April 1842, Lily hurriedly entered the house and shut the door. She immediately approached George where he was working at the dining room table.

"Have you heard about the scandal?" she confronted him.

George looked up blankly from his accounts. "What scandal?"

"George!" she said angrily. "Have you heard of celestial marriage?"

He hesitated before he cautiously answered, "Yes."

"Why didn't you tell me?" Lily asked, sitting down at the table.

"I could not explain it."

Lily glared at him with impatience.

George inhaled deeply, then exhaled slowly. "Joseph has confided to a few of the Elders that he's received a divine revelation sanctifying plural marriages."

"Plural marriages!" Lily cried. "Then the scandal is true!"

"What scandal?" George asked again.

Lily took off her bonnet and set it down on the table. "It seems that Dr. Bennett warned Nancy Rigdon, Sidney's daughter, that Joseph planned to propose marriage to her. Naturally, Nancy was astounded since he's a married man. And when Joseph did propose, she refused him at once. So Joseph wrote Nancy an elaborate justification of his celestial marriage idea. Nancy immediately showed it to her father, who is simply furious with Joseph. Sidney knew nothing at all of this sacred polygamy."

"What did Joseph do then?"

"He tried to dispel Sidney's anger by claiming he was only testing Nancy's virtue. But no one seems to believe it. Her rejection is the talk of Nauvoo."

George sighed, then gently took Lily's hands into his own. Knowing he could not explain it, he knew he must try. "In Joseph's revelation, those who practice celestial marriage will gain rewards throughout Eternity we've never known before."

"What sort of rewards?" Lily asked.

"Marriage and procreation throughout Eternity. But a man with only one wife will not be married to even her in Eternity. He will be forced to spend Eternity as a ministering angel, not as a god with many wives."

Dumbfounded, Lily sat in silence.

"When I first heard of celestial marriage," George said, "I felt fascinated and chilled by the boldness of it. Christians have always insisted on monogamy. But when Joseph reinterpreted the Bible for our new gospel, he recognized how the Old Testament never forbade taking plural wives."

"Harems," Lily whispered. "In Illinois."

George answered his wife softly. "Joseph believes that the sin of adultery lies in abandonment, not in sexual union. If there is no abandonment, there is no sin. He's devised special rites for these celestial marriages so they cannot be seen as adultery."

Lily shook her head in disbelief. "What does Emma Smith say?"

"I can't imagine she's pleased," George disclaimed. "Joseph's plural wives are all attractive women. Do you remember that rumor a newspaper in St. Louis reported, about a woman who spurned Brigham Young's proposal?"

"I thought it was nothing but hateful libel."

"It was in fact the truth. Now Joseph can't afford another public scandal. He threatens to excommunicate any man who preaches or engages in plural marriage without his sanction."

With deep concern, Lily looked at her husband. "Do you have his sanction, George? The rewards our Prophet envisions, a woman younger than me, a woman who can give you children…"

George interrupted her, "I did not and will not ask. You're the only woman I want as my wife."

Lily smiled at his unhesitant reply, then she asked, "But why did Dr. Bennett forewarn Nancy?"

"I don't know," George answered honestly.

During the spring of 1842, the community discovered just

how eagerly John Cook Bennett had taken personal advantage of the bold new ideas about marriage. At first, Joseph Smith merely rebuked the doctor for preaching promiscuous intercourse. Then Joseph learned that Bennett was using his name to seduce innocent women. The doctor promised not only marriage, but abortions if the girls became pregnant. Disgusted, Joseph finally confronted Bennett with the evidence and the charges that Hyrum Smith had uncovered earlier, that Bennett had abandoned his family in Ohio.

"Dr. Bennett swallowed a vial of poison," Lily said. "Surely, he has repented!"

"He's a doctor," George reminded her. "He knew the dose wouldn't kill him."

"Then why doesn't Joseph excommunicate him?"

"Bennett has too much intimate knowledge about us. That's why Joseph let him resign amicably, with a public vote of thanks for serving as Mayor of Nauvoo. But Bennett refuses to leave the city."

At the Masonic Hall, George sat in discomfort among a hundred brethren at a public hearing on the matter of Dr. Bennett. He listened aghast as Bennett wept like a child and confessed to numerous misdeeds. It had come as no surprise to George that a handsome, tall and charming man like Joseph Smith would earn a reputation as a womanizer. But Joseph, George believed, was sincere about celestial marriage, while to Bennett, it was nothing more than sham. And in the doctor's confession, some women required little more persuasion than most men!

Then Brigham Young and William Law, two of Joseph's closest advisers and friends, stood up to plead that Bennett should be forgiven. George realized that Joseph faced a difficult decision. If he was loyal to his friends and forgave Bennett, he would stand accused of tolerating seduction, prostitution and abortion. But how could he permit such immorality? George was angered and astonished when Joseph chose mercy for Bennett.

A month later, Joseph Smith recognized his error. George

75

felt vindicated at the doctor's excommunication and he was hopeful that the scandal would now subside.

George brought home a stack of newspapers some weeks later.

"Why so many?" Lily asked.

"A Springfield newspaper has been publishing a series of letters from John Cook Bennett."

Lily took a deep breath. "What do they say?"

George sadly replied, "The letters accuse Joseph of the most vicious crimes, ranging from libertinism to murder. Bennett claims that Joseph seeks to establish a despotic empire, hoping to overthrow the Western states. He says Joseph has organized religious orders of prostitutes for the basest pleasures of Church leaders!"

"But those are out-and-out *lies*," Lily said. "Reasonable readers will surely see that he's an unreliable opportunist."

"Perhaps," George sighed. "But newspapers throughout the country can't resist the temptation to reprint the Springfield letters."

He held open a copy of the *New York Herald.* "Even the *Herald,* unable to verify the reports, has republished the letters as Bennett wrote them."

Lily read a few paragraphs. "Why is he so venomous against us?"

"I don't know," George said. "But his overzealousness doesn't serve him well. Joseph might contain the scandal by counter-accusations."

"Such as what?" Lily asked.

Embarrassed, George hesitated, then opened the *Nauvoo Wasp* to an article written by William Smith, Joseph's brother. "Here, Lily, see for yourself."

Lily read it, then gasped, "Is it true? Bennett stands accused of 'adultery, fornication, and ... *Buggery.*'"

"Apparently so," George replied.

"Perhaps he'll be quiet now," Lily said.

"But as long as we're amusement, the storm won't blow over. Now they're ridiculing us in 13-stanza poems."

George read aloud from a column in the *Warsaw Message.*

"I once thought I had knowledge great,
But now I find 'tis small.
I once thought I'd religion too,
But now I find I've none at all--
For I can have but *one lone wife*,
And can obtain no more;
And the doctrine is I can't be saved,
Until I've *half a score.*"

Lily smiled uneasily at George. "Are you sure that isn't your ambition?"

"Not now or ever," he vowed. "Shall I read you the other twelve stanzas?"

George was distraught to learn another reason for the growing Mormon notoriety. That summer, an assassin in St. Louis shot at Lilburn Boggs, former Governor of Missouri, through a window. Hit three times in the back of his head, Boggs narrowly escaped being murdered. The prime suspect was Orrin Porter Rockwell, personal bodyguard to Joseph Smith.

"Do you suppose the accusation is true?" Lily asked George.

"I don't believe it was Joseph's idea."

"Does Orrin have an alibi?"

"No," said George. "He's been away for weeks and only reappeared in Nauvoo two days after we heard news of the shooting. He told friends he's been in Missouri."

A worried look crossed Lily's face.

"It's new fodder for Bennett," George said. "In the *Quincy Wasp,* he claims he heard Joseph prophesizing Bogg's violent death, even offering a $500 reward for the deed. Bennett has gone to Missouri to personally tell Boggs what he knows and suspects."

Boggs soon brought charges against Joseph Smith as a fugitive from justice and accessory before attempted murder. He persuaded the Missouri Governor to request Joseph's extradition, and Illinois Governor Carlin agreed. The Missouri sheriffs quickly arrested Smith and Rockwell. But under the powers of their extraordinary charters, the Nauvoo court released them.  Orrin Rockwell left the state, and Joseph Smith went into hiding in a secret bricked-in vault inside his home.

Baffled by the questionable legal obstructions, the Missouri sheriffs left to get new orders.  They soon returned, but Joseph, certain that extradition to Missouri would be his death, had gone into hiding on a farm two days north of Nauvoo.  While the sheriffs made repeated visits to the city, Joseph lived four months as a fugitive, terrified by the knowledge that a handsome bounty was offered for his capture.

"Joseph has come out of hiding at last," George told Lily.

"Why now?" she asked.

"Our new Governor, Thomas Ford, has agreed to hold an extradition hearing in Illinois, not Missouri, if Joseph will go to Springfield to give himself up.  I'm riding with him to deal with some business there."

"Won't that be dangerous?" Lily asked.

"The Nauvoo Legion will escort him with forty of its best and fully-armed men."

Despite a prairie gale that raged after Christmas, Joseph Smith and the escort party rode the hundred miles to the capital.  To George's amazement when they arrived, Joseph moved about Springfield freely and was regarded like a celebrity, although he was under arrest.

"Smith impresses me, I must admit," one legislator told another loudly enough for George to overhear.

"And he controls so many votes," the second legislator smiled.

The first one nodded.  "Have you heard?  We've agreed to let them preach a sermon on Mormonism in our House of Representatives on New Years Day."

The Springfield court quickly declared the Missouri warrant invalid, and Joseph, a free man, rode home in triumph.  Then he had the City Council pass a law forbidding any law officer from serving a warrant in Nauvoo without the signature of the Mayor, who was now Joseph Smith himself.  And any sheriff who presented a writ based on the Missouri controversies now faced life imprisonment in Nauvoo.

78

Despite these laws, in June of 1843, Joseph Smith was arrested again. Disguised as Mormon Elders, the Missouri sheriffs crossed into Illinois. They caught Joseph unescorted on a preaching tour, then forced him into a wagon at gunpoint.

When word reached Nauvoo, 140 armed men from the Legion galloped out to intercept his captors.

"What are the charges this time?" Lily cried.

"Bennett persuaded the Missouri Governor to have Joseph arrested on the treason charge he fled in '39."

Tearfully, Lily looked at George. "Have they abducted him to Missouri, then?"

"We don't know. Let's pray our men reach Joseph before he's kidnapped across the Mississippi River."

In the town where Joseph Smith was captured, the citizens refused to let the sheriffs carry him away without a lawyer and a trial. Joseph quickly engaged the leader of the Illinois Whig Party, who was there by chance, campaigning for the Senate. The attorney immediately charged the Missouri sheriffs with assault and false imprisonment. He and the Democratic candidate for Senator, also courting favor with the Mormons, agreed that the case should be tried in Nauvoo. To no one's surprise, Joseph Smith was promptly freed.

At Christmastime that year, George and Lily were dressing for a dance at Joseph and Emma Smith's newly-finished home. George helped Lily fasten the back of her dress.

"I think it's blasphemous," he said.

"What is, George?"

"Hyrum Smith's claim to have received a *divine* revelation saying the Democratic candidate must have our vote. Hyrum endorsed him to advance his own political ambitions. But Joseph didn't disavow his brother's 'revelation,' so almost every man among us voted Democrat."

Lily examined her reflection in the mirror. "Wasn't it the *Whig* candidate who kept the sheriffs from taking Joseph away to Missouri?"

"Yes, but when the Missouri Governor issued still *another* warrant, the Democrats promised that if we voted the

Democratic ticket, Governor Ford wouldn't call out the militia to arrest Joseph."

"If the Prophet tells you to vote Democratic, then you must," Lily said. "Would they have won without our vote?"

George shook his head. "They would've lost. And the Whigs, I fear, won't forget this betrayal."

The guests were already dancing when George and Lily arrived at Joseph and Emma's home. The icy wind blew off the river as they stepped from the carriage into the house, cheered by holiday warmth and lively music. While they danced, George smiled at the beautiful woman in his arms. With the latest legal victory against the Missouri sheriffs, they held real hope for a peaceful new year of 1844.

All of a sudden, a large man noisily forced his way through the front door. His clothing and shoes were in tatters, and his black, stringy hair hung down to his shoulders. He lunged for Joseph Smith while George and Lily gasped in alarm.

Just as abruptly, Joseph burst out laughing.

"Orrin Porter Rockwell!" he exclaimed, embracing the disheveled man. "We thought you were locked up in a St. Louis jail."

"For nine months, I was," Rockwell said. "But they had no proof at all I shot Boggs, and let me go. I was so eager to quit Missouri, I rowed across the river at night."

Joseph fondly touched the bodyguard's long hair, then proclaimed, "I prophesize that if you keep your hair long like Samson, your enemies will forever be powerless against you!"

Across the room, George observed the warm interchange. Rockwell may require such power, he thought to himself, for rumor said the bodyguard had boasted of the deed.

# Chapter 7

"Are the rumors true?" Lily asked. "Joseph is running for President?"

By the spring of 1844, the campaign was heating up between James Polk and Henry Clay. The abolitionists were also fielding a candidate.

"Yes," George replied. "He wants to show the Gentiles that our political force must be respected. But Joseph harbors no delusions of defeating the Democrats and Whigs."

"Perhaps it is no delusion," Lily said.

George looked uneasily at his wife. Since her third miscarriage, Lily had grown ever more passionate in her faith.

"As you'd expect, Joseph's platform is quite imaginative. He proposes to eliminate two-thirds of Congress, cut their wages to $2 per day, then use those savings and funds from selling public land to buy freedom for the slaves over six years."

"What wonderful ideas!" Lily said. "When might Joseph achieve them, do you suppose?"

Uncertain how to answer, George looked quizzically at Lily. "Joseph is dispatching every man who can be spared to campaign for him in the Eastern cities. All twelve Apostles and 250 missionaries."

"Will you be going with them?"

Hesitantly, he replied, "No."

"Why not?" Lily asked softly.

In her voice, George heard disappointment in him, so he tried to explain. "I cannot wholeheartedly campaign for Joseph when he proclaims, 'I go emphatically, virtuously, and humanely, for a Theodemocracy, where God and the people hold the power to conduct the affairs of men in righteousness.'"

"And why not?" Lily asked.

"It flies in the face of the First Amendment!" George complained. "And Joseph has now petitioned Congress to form an independent Federal territory in Nauvoo, with our Mayor empowered to call out Federal troops whenever necessary."

"If our Prophet has seen it, it must be so. If not in Nauvoo, then somewhere else."

"The petition will not only be rejected," George said, "but we'll lose our few remaining friends in Illinois."

George withheld from Lily another, deeper concern. That March, with great secrecy, Joseph had chosen members of a Council of Fifty 'princes' to form what he proclaimed to be the highest court on Earth. Then that court ordained and crowned Joseph Smith as King of the Kingdom of God. George had not been there, but when he heard of it, he felt the chill of blasphemy.

Despite their differences over the years, George could never manage to stay disenchanted with Joseph for very long. A few weeks later, George stood next to Lily in a crowd of 10,000 at a funeral, as Joseph Smith spoke from the pulpit.

"You don't know me," Joseph told them, "you never knew my heart. No man knows my history. I cannot tell it; I shall never understand it. I don't blame anyone for not believing my history. If I had not experienced what I have, I would not have believed it myself."

George was struck by the truth in the words. He glanced in all directions at the fine-looking Latter-day Saints who surrounded him, in the excellent city they had built from a swamp. Surely, nothing less than divine revelation could have brought it all into being.

Joseph Smith was in his prime, 38 years old, and powerful politically, militarily and economically. His followers numbered 16,000, though he boasted of 100,000, believed by some people to be true. There was little open hatred of the Mormons, except among some Gentiles living not far from Nauvoo.

That spring in Nauvoo was particularly pleasant, with lushness in the gardens and forests, and wildflowers in bloom in the meadows. George worked in his trade as a bookkeeper, drilled with the Nauvoo Legion, and tithed to the Church in cash and labor, working every tenth day to build the Temple. Lily helped the teachers in the school and sewed for the Female Relief Society. Their only cause for sadness was their childlessness.

In May, George was asked to appear before a high ranking member of the priesthood.

The man looked down solemnly at George. "Do you fully understand the concept of celestial marriage, Elder Wood?"

"I believe I do," George replied.

"Then you'll understand when I tell you that your wife Lily has agreed to become the celestial wife of one of our Apostles."

George stared at him stunned and speechless. It was not possible. Lily, the woman by his side through ten years of misfortune and rejoicing, could not become the polygamous wife of another man.

"Of course you know, Elder Wood, that celestial marriage can embrace plural husbands as well as plural wives."

George felt light-headed, almost faint, his arms and legs growing weak.

"It isn't so uncommon, Elder Wood. Captain Morgan's widow, for instance, had remarried years before she became a celestial wife of Joseph Smith."

George stammered, "Just how many wives *does* Joseph have?"

"To my knowledge, forty-nine, a dozen of them already wed to other men. Lily says you have vowed never to deny her anything. She has asked that you stand as witness at her celestial wedding."

George felt the veins in his neck swelling as if they would burst. "I'll be damned in Hell before I do."

"I know this is a surprise," the man said gently. "Take some time to think over your refusal."

"I don't need any time!" George exploded with rage. "At least King David had the decency to have Bathsheba's husband slain!"

"Perhaps you don't fully understand our theology, Elder Wood."

"I wish I could believe it was *theology*!" George shouted. "Theology revealed and fervently resisted until Joseph could deny it no longer. Or that he, as a seer, knew we *must* have

83

polygamy to establish Zion on Earth. I wish I could believe it was so innocent! But his *theology* lets his officers steal from his men, not only their daughters but their wives."

Devastated, George returned to his home. Lily did not notice him as he entered. For a moment, he watched her sewing, still pretty in face and figure, always pleasant if not cheerful, and happy with him, he believed.

"For God's sake, Lily, *why?*" he cried in anguish. "You know I love you more than life itself."

"Because our Prophet says it is ordained by God."

For the first time in fifteen years, George drank whiskey. He drank glass after glass into insensibility, while Lily was being ceremoniously sealed to another man for Eternity. George felt enraged, insulted and humiliated that a man deemed more worthy had coveted his wife and now had her for his company and pleasure. Body and soul, he felt betrayed. He had loved Joseph Smith, labored and suffered for him, and followed him loyally! Inspired by and eager to please him, George demanded and brought forth more good work from himself than he still believed possible. But he loved his wife. It was no consolation to him that, in the eyes of the Church, Lily's chastity was not violated and her moral reputation was unsullied.

Without success, George tried not to imagine this man taking his pleasure with Lily.

"Joseph Smith's vision of Eternity be *damned*," he cursed aloud.

George was not the only one to abandon the Church for the sake of his wife and his manhood. That May, he felt morally bound to join a small but ominous schism, a group inside the Mormon faith who were respected for their integrity and competence. They were led by William Law, a wealthy Canadian. Law had been profoundly moved by Joseph Smith's gospel message, and had served for two years as Second Counselor to him.

"If they persist in this wickedness," George said to Law, "they must cease taking married women, or their cause is doomed!"

William Law and Robert Foster were the leading industrialists and builders in Nauvoo. But Law had angered Joseph by refusing to pay for publishing his revised version of the Bible.

"What do you think of Joseph's financial arrangements?" Law asked George.

"In financial matters," George replied, "I've never had cause to doubt the honor of his intentions."

"Never?"

"Well, I've been troubled that he fails to properly distinguish between Church interests and Smith family finances."

"What about his real estate monopoly?" Law asked. "It's unseemly for a man of God to threaten *excommunication* against men whose only sin is buying land in Nauvoo without his counsel! Don't you suspect that he's diverting money to buy land for himself, so he can sell it to newcomers at a profit?"

George was not sure he agreed. "It's true that you and Foster anger Joseph by paying cash wages and drawing workmen away from building the Temple, where they can earn only goods and city scrip."

"How much money he demands for the Temple! Public buildings should wait until our new converts have housing."

That spring, Joseph Smith attempted to entice Jane Law into his gathering of celestial wives. When his wife was the next to be approached, Foster filed a legal suit.

Joseph Smith did not bother to deny the charges. He publicized the complaints in his newspaper, the *Times and Seasons,* to embarrass the Fosters and persuade the community that they were lying. If he expected the suit to be withdrawn, they disappointed him by persisting. But along with the other men and women in the schism, George Wood was excommunicated.

Distraught and exhausted from the struggle, George sighed, "Why don't we simply leave Nauvoo? We're no longer Latter-day Saints and have no *calling* to endure so much abuse."

"Joseph is a fallen prophet, not a false one," Law said. "We must reform, not abandon, the Church."

"But how?" George asked.

"By establishing a church with a similar gospel."

"William Law will be president," Foster proposed. "We'll finance a newspaper to expose the truth."

"Let's call it the *Nauvoo Expositor*."

"A printing press can be shipped here within weeks," George said.

Law nodded in agreement. "We'll go to Carthage in the meantime and persuade the Hancock County Grand Jury to indict Joseph for adultery and polygamy."

"Those charges won't intimidate him," George said. "His plural marriage ideas are masked in arcane words. Only the initiated know what they mean."

As the dissidents pressed legal action, Joseph answered with violent vilification in the *Times and Seasons*. The perpetrators of the schism had so recently been respected leaders of the faith that the community of Saints was left bewildered.

On June 7, 1844, the first and only edition of the *Nauvoo Expositor* appeared. At the newspaper office, George read the printed pages as they came off the press.

"Your editorial shows admirable restraint," he said to Law.

George read a few sentences of Law's simple story aloud. An unnamed English girl arrives alone in Nauvoo and soon receives a proposal for plural marriage.

"'She was thunderstruck, faints, recovers and refuses. The Prophet damns her if she rejects. She thinks of the great sacrifice, and the many thousands of miles she has traveled over land and sea, that she might save her soul from impending ruin, and replies, 'God's will be done and not mine.'"

George reached the end of the story, then fell silent, thinking of the sacrifices and the thousands of miles he had traveled.

George carefully picked up another newly-printed page. He read affidavits from William and Jane Law, then his own, swearing to what they knew of plural marriage and its promises for Eternity. In other columns, the *Expositor* condemned Joseph Smith's attempts to unite church and state, his political manipulations, financial maneuverings and land speculations, and his "moral imperfections."

With mounting alarm, George read the printed sheets. The newspaper censured the abuse of privilege in the special Nauvoo charters, urged their repeal, and denounced politically-ambitious revelations. Without mentioning the March coronation, the *Expositor* proclaimed, "We will not acknowledge any man as king or lawgiver to the Church: for Christ is our only king and lawgiver." Warily, George looked across the room at the editor.

When the *Nauvoo Expositor* hit the streets, Joseph Smith immediately convened the City Council. Without a jury, or lawyers or witnesses for the defense, the Council conducted a speedy trial of the *Expositor.* Joseph accused its editors of seduction, pandering, counterfeiting and thievery, and he denied again that polygamy existed in Nauvoo. The City Council decreed that the newspaper was a libelous civic nuisance, then sentenced it to a quick execution. Members of the Nauvoo Legion carried out the sentence, invading the *Expositor* office, smashing the press, scattering the type in the street, and burning every copy of the newspaper they could find.

George sighed in weary resignation. "Smashing opposition presses isn't so uncommon on the frontier. Men were tarred and feathered when it was done to us in Missouri."

"It's unconstitutional!" Law thundered.

Not to mention unwise, George thought to himself. A leader of a despised minority should never hand his enemies a strong moral issue.

With the other dissidents, George rode to Warsaw, a dozen miles away, to the office of the rabidly anti-Mormon *Warsaw Signal*. He listened to Foster recount the wrecking of the *Expositor*, then accuse Joseph Smith of seducing numerous women and encouraging his bodyguard to assassinate Boggs.

The *Warsaw Signal* published a gleeful editorial. "War and extermination is inevitable! CITIZENS ARISE, ONE AND ALL!!! Can you *stand* by and suffer such INFERNAL DEVILS! to ROB men of their property and Rights, without avenging them? We have no time for comments; every man will make his own. LET it be made with POWDER and BALLS!!!"

Saddened and heartsick, George read the *Warsaw Signal.* He could not dispel a foreboding of disaster. He declined to go with Law and Foster to Carthage, the county seat, where they sought a warrant for Joseph's arrest on the charge of riot. Unable to stop loving Lily, George was too fearful for her safety.

Too restless to stay home, George wandered through the streets of Nauvoo, listening to rumors. For once, he was grateful to be inconspicuous.

"Governor Ford has gone directly to Carthage to investigate," a man reported. "They say he's ready to call out the militia to enforce the law."

"Call out the militia!" another man scoffed. "They're surely mustered already and preparing their attack on Nauvoo!"

"But Joseph has sent the Governor a long letter and *explained* what he did."

"Great good that'll do if the militia is assembled. We'll face devastation if Ford orders them into action."

The crowd gathered closer to debate what might happen.

"Governor Ford has no choice. He must demand that the despoilers of the *Expositor* submit promptly to Carthage for trial."

"Joseph will be lynched if he does! He mustn't agree to appear unless the Nauvoo Legion escorts him."

"Yes! The Legion has 4,000 men, and we're better armed than all the other militias in Hancock County combined."

"Ford can't allow *that.* He'll fear civil war if the Legion were to march into Carthage. He'll order the Legion to disband instead, and surrender all our State-owned arms."

"Don't forget Far West!"

"And Zion!"

"As if I could! I'd fight to the death before I'd ever repeat that catastrophe."

George shuddered at the memory of Far West, the helpless terror he felt when he was disarmed and unable to defend his wife.

"Joseph has ordered the Apostles back here at once," the first man said. "They're to bring arms and ammunition in their luggage."

"Good! And we own thousands of rifles and muskets that don't belong to the State. It'll only take a moment's notice to get them to our fighting men!"

George stood by himself at the far edge of the parade ground, watching the Legion men fall into orderly ranks. Numbly, he listened as Joseph Smith gave them orders on their defense of Nauvoo. George pondered over what he should do.

After sunset, George quietly rode away from the city, afraid of what the men loyal to Joseph Smith might do to him. Among the Danites, divulging a secret could mean death, and George knew many secrets.

# Chapter 8

Joseph Smith was well aware of the risk of massacre. Hoping to spare the others, Joseph and his brother Hyrum tried to flee Illinois, but weeks of soaking rains had left the Mississippi River in a raging flood. For miles both above and below Nauvoo, the river was filled with loosened trees that were now battering rams and farmland that had washed into mud. Unable to cross the river, Joseph and Hyrum retreated to Nauvoo to face whatever destiny brought.

Later, when the news reached Quincy, George wondered whether they were forced back, or whether Joseph had resolved not to abandon his flock.

Joseph and Hyrum Smith, along with a few other men, rode the fifteen miles to Carthage to submit to the Governor's demand for their surrender. They were escorted by disciplined, orderly troops from the McDonough County militia. But when they reached the county seat, the Warsaw and Carthage militiamen jeered.

"Stand away, you McDonough boys, and let us shoot the damned Mormons!"

The other defendants were released on bail, but Joseph and Hyrum Smith were locked up in a spacious second-story room in the Carthage jail. Joseph spoke at length with Governor Ford.

"I'm riding to Nauvoo in the morning," Ford said, "along with the McDonough County troops. I want to speak to the people of Nauvoo."

"May we come with you?" Joseph asked.

The Governor agreed to let them come, but the next morning, June 27, he reconsidered. He spoke with the commander of the McDonough militia.

"The Nauvoo Legion boasts 4,000 men, and they might easily overwhelm your troops."

The commander nodded. "They might be tempted to try if their 'Prophet' and his brother are in our custody."

"We'll ride to Nauvoo without them," the Governor ordered.

"Three militia companies will stay on duty in Carthage. The others will disband and go home, in particular, the Warsaw company, the most belligerent against the Mormons."

"The Carthage Greys are scarcely less hostile," the McDonough commander warned.

"They live here," Ford said. "They're the logical men to remain."

"Even if ordered to disband, the Warsaw company could be plotting to ride back to Carthage."

"The Carthage jail is strongly built," the Governor shrugged. "It'll withstand an attack."

When they learned of these new plans, two Mormon messengers galloped off at the speed of their horses toward Nauvoo.

At five o'clock that hot and sultry afternoon, a mob of 150 men attacked the jail. Armed with guns and knives, their faces blackened, the assassins scaled the small fence and forced their way into the building. The outnumbered guards pretended with good nature to resist the lynch mob and fired over their heads.

At the sound of nearby gunfire, Joseph grabbed a six-shooter from his coat. Hyrum had only a single-shot pistol. The guns had been smuggled to them earlier.

The assassins rushed up the stairs to the second-story room and burst open the door. They fired a barrage of gunshots inside, instantly killing Hyrum Smith. Without doubt, the shots were fired by the Carthage Greys, men who were posted there for protection. Two other Mormons were visiting the Smiths, and one was wounded, but they were not the targets of the assassins.

Witnesses swear that Joseph Smith gave a Masonic distress signal, but no man responded to help him. Then he was hit by a musket ball fired from inside the jail. Joseph emptied his gun at his assailants, wounding at least three, two of whom later died. He threw down his gun and grabbed the window.

"Oh Lord My God," he groaned, falling two stories to the ground.

"Shoot him! God damn him! Shoot the damned rascal!"

shouted Levi Williams, the Warsaw militia colonel.

Joseph Smith was killed by the fusillade that followed Williams' order. A witness said that Joseph was set up against a well curb, where his body was riddled with bullets. Perhaps fearing civil war, the Nauvoo Legion did not come.

In Quincy, George sadly shook his head as he read about the murders of Joseph and Hyrum Smith. The newspapers named nine men indicted for the murders, and four of them had Masonic affiliations. George himself had helped install Mark Aldrich as Secretary of Warsaw Lodge, where Levi Williams was voted in, *after* being indicted for the murders. Unlike the shameless rabble who assaulted them in Missouri, Masons were reputed to be honorable men. But Brothers in the mob had the blood of Brothers on their hands.

The shocked Mormon community resisted the temptation to retaliate. Sidney Rigdon tried to assume the presidency of the Church, but Brigham Young was chosen instead. A few dissident groups splintered off, some of them disavowing polygamy.

George struggled to rebuild his devastated life. He joined the Methodist Church, worked as a bookkeeper for a steamboat company, and tried to put his role in the Mormon controversies behind him. George felt no interest in remarriage, since under law and in his heart, Lily was still his wife. Wanting to belong to a larger institution, he applied to join the Quincy Masonic Lodge, but he was blackballed. Though the nine men on trial for the lynchings were acquitted, George felt some satisfaction when the charter of Warsaw Lodge was suspended.

A year passed, and in September 1845, a meeting took place in the settlement of Morley, twenty miles south of Nauvoo.

"The thefts in Hancock County have gotten out of hand," the leader said. "We *must* find some way to stop them."

Around the circle, the other men nodded.

"I'll wager that those robberies can be traced to desperados from Nauvoo," a man muttered. "It's happened before."

"When?"

"Remember back in '41? The Mormons have been known to

harbor criminals."

As the men talked, the crimes of the entire county were laid at the door of the Mormons.

Suddenly, they heard a few scattered gunshots.

"It must be the Mormons!" a man called.

From neighboring settlements, volunteers rushed to aid the men of Morley. Determined to expel the Mormons, they banded into mobs and burned down dozens of dwellings, driving the residents into the bushes. Rumors quickly spread that a force of armed men was on the march south from Nauvoo. A Mormon-owned flouring mill and carding machine were reduced to ashes. Buildings and stacks of grain were set ablaze.

For ten days, the burnings spread from settlement to settlement without any Mormon resistance. Not only their own property, but that of their defenders was destroyed. Governor Ford did not dare to call up the militia, fearing that a muster would bring friends and enemies alike. On both sides, people were killed. Even the non-Mormon sheriff, whose posse tried but could not restore order, sent his own family to Nauvoo. Nowhere else in Hancock County was safe.

George approached the men who led Quincy. "You must do something to stop this violence!" he begged them. Despite all efforts, he could not help worrying about Lily's safety.

Judge Hendricks threw up his hands. "What can we do? In the course of six years, the people of Quincy have lost patience with the Mormons."

"Perhaps with good reason," George allowed. "Still, the people of Quincy don't feel the deadly hatred that's feeding this persecution."

"Further efforts to live in peace with them are fruitless," the Judge warned.

"I suspect the Mormons have reached the same conclusion."

"We'll establish a committee," the Judge mumbled as he limped away.

In late September 1845, the Quincy Committee issued a resolution, urging the Mormons to leave Illinois in six months, to prevent further bloodshed and sacrifice of lives.

Judge Hendricks sighed with relief when he received a message a few days later. The Saints agreed to depart, though they argued that March was too soon for them to stockpile enough provisions. They proposed to leave in May if the anti-Mormons would not molest them, but assist them instead to sell their property.

With the consent of the Quincy Committee, the promise to depart was sealed in writing. To keep the peace, the Governor dispatched a small military force to Nauvoo. That autumn, the Mormons did not plant crops, but gathered supplies and built wagons.

# Chapter 9

## September 1846

The door to the inn opened softly and Seth Rogers stepped inside. With tears in her eyes, Mrs. Rogers ran to embrace him.

"The rabble is winning, Mother," Seth said. "But except for a few scratches, I am well."

Ted Bailey watched Mrs. Rogers and the boy climb the stairs. She sighed as she came down alone.

"Seth wanted to rest," she explained.

Overwrought, Mrs. Rogers sat down with the men.

"Thank God he's all right," said Caleb White, taking her hand.

Mrs. Rogers smiled wanly at the men. "I confess that I've doubted my wisdom in buying this inn."

Ted glanced around the pleasant, well-built inn. "When did you buy it?" he asked her.

"This past February. My late husband left me only a small sum, not near the full value of the inn. I paid 25 cents on the dollar."

A cannon boomed again, and the people in the room looked apprehensively at one another.

"Such terrorizing gets the Saints to sell their property even cheaper," Mrs. Rogers said. "And to the very men who covet the land the Mormons worked so hard to improve. All their haste to leave isn't quick enough for the ruffians who take pleasure in threatening annihilation."

"Annihilation is precisely what our Quincy Committee is trying to prevent," Judge Hendricks said.

"Since February, Seth and I have watched the Mormon emigration," Mrs. Rogers said. "At the peak of it, five ferryboats carried wagons across the Mississippi River, day and night."

Caleb shook his head. "Yet their show of good faith and the Governor's promise of security haven't stopped the mobs from raiding outlying farms."

"The Mormons are no less stubborn men," the Judge said. "How can they justify more loss of life defending a city their leaders have left?"

"Have there been no Mormon reprisals?" Ted asked.

"A few," the Judge admitted. "But they've forborne until forbearance is no longer a virtue."

"Not from weakness, either," Caleb added. "The Mormons are exceedingly well armed."

The Judge nodded. "The best gunsmith in western Illinois was Jonathan Browning, an old friend of mine who joined the Mormons here. He was always tinkering with new ideas for guns."

"Browning has invented a four-shot repeating rifle," George told them. "He manufactured a number of them here."

"A repeating rifle?" the Judge looked cautiously at George. "If the Mormons ever decide to avenge what they've suffered, they'd be dangerous enemies. And they will be wherever they go."

From the distance came another rattle of small arms fire.

"As for your mission, Mr. Bailey," the Judge continued, "I personally doubt that your publisher wishes to abandon the romantic image of a religious martyr that he has helped to create."

"A newspaper doesn't *create* news," Ted objected.

"I disagree, Mr. Bailey. Why else have we witnessed so many instances of scattering type in the streets?"

All eyes were on Ted, but he could think of no answer to that question.

The Judge sighed. "In spite of all his charm and imagination, Joseph Smith was ignorant of shameful English and European history that made America's founders demand a free press and separation of church and state. Still, what's the *Herald* to gain by telling the whole truth of what transpired here and at Carthage?"

"The whole truth?" George turned to confront him. "Can a skeptic like you, Judge Hendricks, possibly *understand* the whole truth? Lacking strong faith, can you fathom the people who have it? Your cherished *reason* is little more than orderly presentation, not necessarily wisdom or truth. And it can readily decay into rationalization for whatever ends are desired. As you know well, sophistry is a vice of the educated."

Judge Hendricks coughed loudly. "I apologize, George. Diplomacy was always my downfall, which is why I became a one-term judge. My opinionated passions, like my gimpy leg, are my mementos of war."

The clock ticked loudly above the fireplace as they all sat in silence. Impatiently, Ted wondered how much longer the siege of Nauvoo could persist. He listened intently for gunshots, but heard nothing.

"How were you wounded?" Ted asked.

"It was the War of 1812," the Judge answered, "when we thought we could take Canada by bluff and bluster. We declared war on England, but we weren't prepared to fight, and came close to military disaster both on the Great Lakes and near Washington. I was an Infantry lieutenant, but due to casualties and illness, I was soon promoted to captain. Then at Lundy's Lane, I became a casualty, myself."

"How did it happen?" Mrs. Rogers asked.

"A damned foolish order for a frontal attack cost us half of my company. I would've bled to death on the battlefield, but I was captured. A British captain brought me to his military surgeon when I gave a Masonic distress sign."

Ted looked skeptically at the Judge. "Might you not have been rescued as a courtesy to your rank?"

"I was treated as a brother Mason by the British."

"I heard a story like that," Caleb said, "but I thought it was a Texas tall tale. It was the *last* time we fought with Mexico, ten years ago. Sam Houston's army, reduced to a demoralized remnant, was being hunted down by General Santa Anna's 1,500-man brigade, part of his 6,000-man army. But the Mexicans took an arrogant, unguarded siesta, camped against a narrow bend in a river. Houston saw the opportunity and ordered an attack. Enraged by recent massacres at the Alamo and Goliad, the Texans annihilated the Mexicans in a very bloody close-quarters battle. In fifteen minutes, they killed 625 men. Santa Anna, too, surely would've been killed, but he gave a Masonic distress sign. They brought him unharmed to General Houston, likewise a Mason, where he promised independence to Texas if they spared his life. The Texas soldier who recognized the sign is said to have Santa Anna's Masonic apron as a trophy of war."

Judge Hendricks smiled at the story. "Tell me, George, isn't it true that Joseph Smith took Masonic rituals and symbols and put them into his own Mormon ceremonies?"

"Joseph wouldn't state it like that," George replied.

"Well, how would he put it?"

"He'd explain that it's all the same mysteries, divinely revealed and ritually passed down across the ages. He'd say the Masons have it slightly imperfect."

"Indeed!" the Judge grumbled.

George looked at the faces of the people in the room before he spoke. "Since all of you seem honorable, I will divulge a portion of the secrets. Shared by Mormons and Masons are group prayers, the use of a drama, the apron, certain tokens, penalties and signs. The subject of the drama, the covenants and anointings are not alike."

"If you'd been there at Carthage," Ted asked the Judge, "would you have tried to aid the Smiths as the enemy British officers helped you?"

"The question is moot," the older man sighed. "Even if they'd wanted to do it, the Masons there were far too few to resist the mob. Besides, a Mason isn't obligated to respond to a distress sign given by a man from a clandestine lodge."

The Judge stopped speaking for a moment, and silence permeated the inn.

"But that isn't why the killings leave a feeling of ashes in my mouth. I saw Joseph Smith as a dangerous despot and subverter, not only of conventional Christianity, but of forms of government I deeply cherish. Joseph Smith invited assassination. He made us look like gullible fools, and I, too,

100

shared in the anger."

"As did I," George agreed. "Still, I assure you, Gentlemen and Mrs. Rogers, if Joseph Smith were to step into this inn this very moment, I would bet my good money that whatever prophecy he made would come to pass."

Ted felt his eyes drawn toward the door of the inn, as if the Prophet, or his ghost, stood just outside it. Perhaps George is right, Ted thought to himself. Through his vision and will, all of this was brought about.

"Can you answer me this, Mr. Wood," Ted asked. "Why did the Mormons lavish so much effort on finishing their Temple, *after* they agreed to leave Nauvoo?"

George smiled. "Even though I'm excommunicate, I won't divulge the answer to that."

A flurry of gunshots rang out, rapid-fired as if triumphant, and rattled the windows of the inn. Mrs. Rogers and the men looked at one another, then out the window. No motion was visible in the darkening street.

Ted asked as he stared out the window, "Do you believe the Mormons will all really leave?"

"Who knows what they'll do?" the Judge disclaimed. "Everything the Mormons do defies logic."

"But they're industrious and cooperative," Mrs. Rogers said. "With God's help, they could create a successful colony somewhere."

"Where can they go and be welcome?" Caleb asked. "Both Oregon and Texas are being settled by the same sort of people who fought them so bitterly in Missouri. Their reputation for sharp practices precedes them from Ohio and Illinois."

"And after our embezzlement of Texas," the Judge added, "Mexico won't welcome another armed immigration of non-Catholic Americans."

Ted was startled when the door of the inn flew open. A well-dressed man rushed inside and called out to Judge Hendricks.

"Brockman has accepted the settlement!"

"Then the siege is over?" the Judge asked.

"Yes," the man answered breathlessly. "The Mormons will surrender Nauvoo. They've pledged to deliver all their weapons to our Quincy Committee at three o'clock tomorrow, to be returned at the crossing of the river."

"What terms has Brockman offered in exchange?" the Judge asked.

"He agrees to let them go in peace."

The Judge nodded in satisfaction.

George Wood turned to face Ted. Ted could see a fierceness in his eyes, despite tears, and a remnant of the passion that had led him to immerse everything he possessed in the community. And Ted could see the hollowness that remained when his faith left him behind. But Ted saw no defeat. George spoke with a pride and a strength in his voice that he earned from having accomplished remarkable deeds.

"*Hundreds* of people have emigrated west on this continent, Mr. Bailey. But *nobody* has even *thought* of moving *12,000* men, women and children, healthy and sick, and all of their livestock and belongings. Each and every day, they must have adequate food and water. Forage for livestock, wood for fuel, places to repair wagons, and defenders to protect them against ruffians and hostile Indians. *And they do not know where they are going!*"

"I wonder," Ted asked, "can it even be done?"

"I imagine it can," Judge Hendricks said. "But what I *cannot* imagine is possessing that degree of faith."

# Chapter 10

Polygamy, thought Ted as he tried to sleep. How astounding to encounter it in these United States in these times! The *New York Herald* had reported the rumors, of course, since scandalous sexuality raises newspaper sales. But no one in the East had actually believed it was true. And this polygamy was not merely justified, but sanctified by a Christian religion! Uneasy himself, Ted knew his employer would be pleased.

In the cool September morning, Ted stepped out of the inn, his back aching from when he was knocked off his horse. He walked through the streets of Nauvoo as a witness to the last, desperate preparations of the people who must embark on their journey. In the seven years since it arose from a malarial swamp, Nauvoo had been a theater for their times. He wondered how the drama would end.

At three o'clock that afternoon, Ted watched the triumphant mob boisterously ride into Nauvoo. Behind Brockman came 800 armed men and 700 unarmed ones, all curious to see the once-proud city humbled at last. Brockman wasted no time in setting himself up as a tribunal, judging which residents could stay and which were to be forced away. Non-Mormons, too, risked expulsion, and Ted hoped Brockman would not learn that Seth Rogers had fought among the defenders. At the point of bayonets, the Latter-day Saints were ordered across the wide river before dark.

With rising alarm, Ted realized that the mob had quickly violated its treaty. From house to house they ran, plundering pig-pens, cow corrals, beehives and hen-roosts. Gangs burst open trunks, looting property regardless of its ownership by Mormons or those who bought them out. They searched wagons that were waiting to be ferried across the river. They stole firearms and scattered goods to the ground. They taunted people who were burying their dead.

The pillagers clambered inside the newly-finished Temple, ringing the bells, shouting and hallooing. Then the gang seized several people, men and women, and forced them down the bluff to the river. Throwing them backwards in the water in mock baptism, they held their victims immersed until the people gasped for mercy. Only Ted's Eastern clothing confounded the mob and kept him safe.

With accustomed reverence, Ted stepped inside the doors of the massive, now desecrated Temple. He walked through several unremarkable chambers, then came abruptly to a halt in one that was wholly unfamiliar. In it was a large, deep-chiseled marble basin, supported by a dozen life-size white wooden oxen. Ted wondered what mystic, unhallowed rites had occurred in this basin and Temple. Celestial marriage, he supposed. And what else? The mob had wasted no time in defiling the Temple, as if they acted in some dispassionate and half-understood crusade. They turned the Temple floors into vomitories and latrines.

With almost superstitious relief, Ted stepped out into the daylight. He gazed up at the sculptured outside walls of the Temple, built as it appeared in a vision to Joseph Smith. Curious stone depictions of suns and moons and stars illustrated the exterior walls. He found the sunstones to be particularly inscrutable. Each bore a broad-nosed human face, flattened almost to an oval and haloed by a pointed and radiating corona. Above the finely-chiseled lips, the eyes stared down as if bemused. To Ted, they seemed like ancient artifacts, not stonework carved only months earlier. The stone hands held what appeared to be trumpets, and he wondered what Joseph Smith could have meant.

Ted retrieved his horse from the stable, then rode down the hill to the banks of the Mississippi River. He looked westward across the river to the Poor Camp, as he heard it called, where 600 Mormons were huddled in a mass. Forced out unprepared for their journey, they could do little more than pitch tents on the far riverbank and wait for help. These were the sick and wounded, the halt and blind, the old and poor, whose shelter and food were inadequate to endure the impending winter. Ted hoped the decent citizens of Illinois and the Mormons already further west could get them aid before the snow fell.

With the ghost town of Nauvoo at his back, Ted gazed across the wide Mississippi. Through the chill autumn wind that gusted from the north, he could feel the unstilled pulsebeat of the now departed faith. Looking westward, Ted tried to compose the words of the story he would write. But the future of the Mormons was too cloudy for the young reporter to predict.

Reluctantly, Ted turned his horse southward to Quincy, where the road would take him back east. But as he looked west one last time, Ted felt a pang of envy for the adventure and quest that lay ahead of the Saints in the unknown.

# BOOK TWO

# VENTURES OF FAITH

Dear Franny,

This letter, if it reaches you, will be the last you will receive for many months. For with certainty of little other than our faith, we are emigrating at once to the West.

I, for one, am eager to depart. After leaving you and Father in Pennsylvania, and journeying to Ohio with John, then on to Zion and Far West in Missouri, and then fleeing to Illinois where we had hoped to live in peace, I feel a deep desire for a permanent home. It matters not at all how far I must venture to reach it. I have faith that Brigham Young will lead us on to such a place, outside these United States if need be, where we can live our religion with the freedom that is the birthright of all Americans.

I know that Father, and perhaps secretly you too, holds contempt for my feelings of faith. More than once he has intimated that it was only the zealotry and handsome countenance of my husband that led me to be baptized as a Latter-day Saint. Father would prefer me to be a Shaker, I suppose, and pledge myself celibate and childless, or that I marry a Mennonite neighbor and remain near home. Granted, no man wishes to see his daughter run off, and John *is* handsome. Yet the words of my missionary husband, not his face, made me ask him to immerse me in the cold Susquehanna.

Don't you see, Franny? The miraculous power of the gospel lives here and now with us, not in that pale Christianity in which you and I were raised. Why should we imagine that revelation was confined to the Biblical ages alone? Negation abdicates our rights and responsibilities! We ask, indeed expect, to experience signs of divine power, to feel the faith that overcomes all things and gave those prior saints powers over the elements, rebuking sickness and even death, and making visible to all the presence of the living God.

Father, being a man of letters as you well know, and not

entirely despairing of me, has examined every word about our controversies. To me, these writings signify little, scribbled as they generally are by apostates, several of whom I have had the displeasure to know. Some were penned by opportunists with perverse and vain ambitions, and others by mere fallen mortals whose own vision has sadly failed. I know that Father read the *Book of Mormon* I gave him, yet he chooses to believe that old story about a Reverend Spaulding who wrote a clever novel and whose lost manuscript was allegedly found by Joseph Smith and hastily plagiarized into theology. Father scoffed that such a long and tedious book could not have been created inside six months. I assured him it was not. Father is free to believe what he chooses; his disparagement does not matter to me. It fades to nothing amidst the power of God and the Holy Ghost and the vision of sainted men in this century, on this continent, to bring the Kingdom of God forth throughout the Earth.

Never doubt that I am grateful, Franny, that you remain in Gettysburg to look after our aging Father. One of my very few regrets is that I could not attend you at your wedding. Charles was an outstanding lad when I last saw him, and I am certain that a Princeton education has shaped him into a man of fine character. I can envision Father's overflowing pride as he escorted you down the aisle, then wholeheartedly gave you away to Charles.

We have sworn that we shall depart when grass grows and water runs, but we will in fact leave at our soonest opportunity. Nauvoo resembles a vast mechanic shop, where everything is humming with industry. John is absorbed in building wagons despite a sore shoulder that has ached since a heavy timber fell on it in December. He will not sit still and let it heal, with so many tasks to be fulfilled. It is only his left shoulder, John insists. For a millwright by trade, he has become an accomplished wagonwright. But naturally, we are not building mills in Nauvoo anymore.

Despite our covenant to evacuate, we did complete our Temple, to the amazement of the Gentiles. The workmen kept their guns always ready to fire, knowing that a persecuting mob could ride through our streets at any moment. The first ceremonies were held in the Temple in October, and since then, Brigham Young has administered the Endowments to more than 1,000 Saints. I can divulge nothing further about it, Franny, other than to say it was very inspirational.

When they witnessed our devotion to the Temple, the Gentiles started to suspect that we might recant our pledge to abandon the city. So they redoubled their persecutions against us. Here in Nauvoo, our own numbers and the Illinois state militia keep us safe, but in isolated villages and farms, mobs are ruthlessly burning Mormon homes and barns. There can be no looking back as we leave, all 16,000 among us. John has been scouring the countryside, trying to buy cattle and wagons and horses. All we have to trade are our personal effects, land and buildings, and those at a fraction of their worth. Since all our property was thrown onto the market at once, we are lucky to get half or quarter value. And the burnings ensure that prices stay low. Payment is not made in scarce money, since it is mostly furs and skins that circulate as currency this far West. So we barter our labor and trade our goods for portable property in any form.

Sad to say, some of our property has not sold at any price. John could find no buyer for Mother's chinaware, so we will leave it for sale by brethren who are not yet prepared to go West. I must leave behind most of our furniture, and the books that you and Father have so generously sent us all these years. We cannot spare the money to return the books to you, so I hope some new resident will be glad to have them. I wish I could read them once again, but I am kept thoroughly busy sewing wagon covers, tents and clothes, and muslin sacks for flour and crackers. We are preserving as much food as we can carry, corned and dried beef, pickled pork, salt bacon, preserved fruit and parched corn, and dried potatoes, pumpkins and squash. With grand expectations, I have gathered garden seeds, cuttings and seedlings, and carefully bound their roots in sacking, to plant at our distant home.

Today, after all the wheat was ground, John carefully

111

disassembled the flour mill machinery. He loaded it onto the sturdiest wagon, to be hauled by the strongest team of oxen. Thousands of wagons have been built altogether, first from seasoned timber, then from wood hastily dried in kilns or pickled in brine. The blacksmiths have forged tons of ironwork fittings and wagon tires. Our gunsmiths have made or reconditioned thousands of rifles and pistols, revolvers, shotguns and muskets. As thoroughly prepared as we can be, we are ready for our Exodus to begin.

You may wonder why we must gather in some isolated place, instead of scattering all over like most Christians. Ever since Roman times, Israel has been dispersed among the nations. But now the time has come for us, as heirs to Israel, to claim our landed inheritance in Zion. It is surely the prelude to the Kingdom of God.

Pray for John and me, Sister, and for Joshua, Ann and Paul. They are all vigorous children, and at ages 6, 4 and 3, undaunted by the dangers of our adventure. Do not despair if you hear nothing from me the rest of this year or even next, until we reach the place ordained by destiny. Some say it will be Texas, or Vancouver Island or even Mexico, though all of these places are under dispute. I only hope those sabres rattling over Oregon and Mexico are merely noise, not beginnings of wars into which we are marching headlong.

I will miss your fond letters, Franny, and the pleasure of writing to you. For that comfort, I will only have my journal. But for me, the die was cast the moment I was baptized a Latter-day Saint, and with high spirits, I will go where I am led.

Your Affectionate Sister,
Amelia

*** 

Shivering in the icy wind, Amelia held Ann and Paul by the hand as they walked down the bluff toward the Mississippi River. Joshua, the oldest at age six, strode ahead.

"Look, Mama! The ferryboats!" the boy called.

Heavy snows had fallen in recent days and Amelia had planned to keep the children indoors, hoping they would remain healthy. They would have ample outdoor living soon enough! But none of them, Amelia least of all, was able to stay quietly in one place.

Amelia and the younger children soon reached the spot where Joshua stood gazing at the commotion. The men were absorbed in a wet and cold, muscle-wrenching job, loading all the goods, then the wagons, onto the flatboats. The ferries, jammed with men, women and children, wagons, livestock and furniture, were then pulled to the Iowa shore, unloaded, then rapidly returned for another load.

"Look, Mama! The oxen are trying to kick holes in the boats."

The north wind tossed the boats about, but as long as the weather allowed it, the ferryboats operated all day. Large floes of ice, floating thickly in the river, hindered their passage.

Amelia shivered, aware that this perilous crossing was to be the first step in their journey. Despite it, she knew they were ready. She had married John a decade earlier in Kirtland, but now they and the children had been blessed with the ordinance of sealing in the Temple. It was their first opportunity, just after the attic story of the Temple was completed.

Amelia listened to the conversations of other onlookers.

"Nine babies were born on the Iowa side last night," a man said, pointing across the Mississippi. "In wagons and tents in the snowstorm."

Amelia thought to herself, if I were with child and near my time, I would beg to stay behind a few days and bring my child into this world in the sheltering warmth of a house.

"Mama!" Joshua called.

Amelia looked to the river where the boy pointed. A flatboat was sinking in the frigid water.

A man standing alongside Amelia rushed into the river to help pull out the distressed passengers. Other onlookers salvaged the soaked goods.

Paul, just three years old, broke free of his mother's grasp and ran toward the icy river.

"Paul!" she yelled, grabbing him with a panicked sweep of her arm.

The boy looked up guilelessly at Amelia.

"I want to help, Mama," he said.


February 17, 1846

As miraculously as the Red Sea parted for Israel, the Mississippi River has frozen solid for us to cross in our own Exodus. Quickly, before the ice could thaw again, we drove our wagons and livestock across it. Then we traveled nine miles to our first camp at Sugar Creek.

It saddens me that Sugar Creek lies just beyond sight of the Temple high on the bluff in Nauvoo. As I took one final look at it, I committed our Temple to memory. I do not mourn the precious labor and money we poured in it, for that and more was recouped in our Endowments. But existence of the Temple was ordained by the Prophet Joseph, and many years will elapse before we see its equal again.

For many days, wagonloads of families have swollen our ranks, all of us buffetted by icy wind as we impatiently wait to move onward. This morning, President Young stood up in his wagon to address us. "The Lord's empire is established," he proclaimed, "and the powers of Hell shall not prevail against it." All who heard him cheered, inspired and comforted at once.

Except that it is westward, I am wholly uncertain of our earthly destination. Some remote and isolated place is our aim, and to it, every step is one step away from the merciless persecution that lies behind us. Despite the driving sleet and rain and blasting winter wind, I feel little cause for complaint. Even if my heart is not carefree, I try to waste no time in fruitless remorse. Instead, the children and I gather wild onions, chipping them out of the frozen soil.


March 22, 1846

It is now three weeks since our wagons began rolling out of

our camp at Sugar Creek. Our procession has swollen to 3,000 wagons, stretching in a line from horizon to horizon. Some 30,000 cattle are plodding alongside us, plus uncountable mules, horses and sheep.

Our emigration, cruelly pressed by our enemies, left too early in the year to expect generous weather. While the snows appear to be past, we suffer sudden whirlwinds of sleet, and rain falls almost every day. The chill and steady downpour soaks our clothes and tents, and creates muddy quagmires, then shallow lakes. The rain has left no wood dry enough for a fire, and it mildews even goods well-packed in crates. We wasted several days encamped in circled wagons before we could press onward again. But the wagons sink to their hubs, or even deeper, mired in mud churned by livestock hooves and wagon wheels. As the oxen pull and flinch and stall, we must all help push at the spokes and lift the wagons, with our feet massed in mud boot-top deep. On good days, we accomplish six miles.

It is curious what one misses on such travels. For not one instant have I forsaken faith, yet how eagerly I would violate the Word of Wisdom for a steaming cup of fragrant, sweetened tea!

Every morning, I pry myself out of my rain-soaked bed, underneath the leaky wagon covers. Then I force each chilled foot into a stiff and sodden shoe. Each morning, I remind myself how much more comfortable we are than we were during our Exodus from Missouri. Then, our food was seldom better than a piece of frozen bread, broken into milk still warm from the cow. Now our food is abundant, and our clothing, when dry, is more than adequate.

The few residents of Iowa we meet must wonder how such outcasts can pray with such devotion, let alone dance with so much merriment. Every company among us boasts brass or stringed instruments, fiddles, guitars and harmonicas. Buglers call us to prayer, held separately by each family, morning and night. At campfires after our labors, there is singing and dancing and storytelling. Captain William Pitt's Brass Band, baptized together in England, plays for us often, and for Gentiles wherever they will pay in corn or honey or cash.

115

As the weather slowly gets warmer, our men find occasional work along the way, at decent wages paid in goods. Feed for the livestock remains sparse, with the grass not yet up on the trail. Cottonwood bark is often their only fodder, and the springtime is too young to hunt for game. But the swaying of the wagon churns our cream into nice butter, and we have cool buttermilk to drink at our noon meal. Thus, we journey on day after day, ever mindful that the Kingdom of the Lord rolls forth with us.

April 21, 1846

By now we have progressed 150 miles away from our home in Nauvoo. John and I remain well, but the children have suffered relapses of the ague that plagued them all so fiercely last autumn. Ann burned with a nervous, bilious fever on Sunday, and her chest was racked with a hollow cough. I first feared that it might be that terrible threat called lung fever. But Ann has since recovered her strength, as has Paul. Joshua was able to do some of his chores, though he is still too weak to carry a full pail of water. Many others among our company are sick with chills and fevers, rheumatism and other ailments common in cold and wet weather.

We were thankful to arrive in Garden Grove, where we will remain several days. On this tract of once burned-over timbered land, we are planting some 700 acres of grain to be harvested by Saints who will come through in summer and fall. This morning when the trumpet sounded, I counted 100 men felling trees and splitting rails, and 10 more men building fences. A dozen men were digging wells, while 48 built houses and 10 built bridges. Some 180 men were plowing and planting grain or herding cattle. John is helping the blacksmiths forge horseshoes and wagon fittings, so all are prepared to resume the trail. Other men have crossed the river into Missouri, trading our surplus horses for oxen, and hoping to barter heavy featherbeds and dishes for fresh food and supplies.

At night, the fiddlers play and choirs sing under the brush arbor and stars. The priests exhort us to live our religion. The guards protect us from raiders and try to keep order among ourselves. Last week, they had to force a man from camp for challenging another to a duel.

May 14, 1846

The trail is drier now and springtime is beginning to flower. Fording of the streams is quicker, the wagons mire less in mud, and each day brings our livestock better graze. Where we can find them, the children and I gather wild strawberries to serve with cream, and I make spiced pickles from the prairie peas. If I could only overcome my continual terror of the rattlesnakes!

Mercifully, my family is well, suffering little from either flux or constipation. But many other people are sick. Supplies of medicine are dwindling, with no prospect for obtaining more.

We have heard some recent news that makes me heartsick. Instead of gathering westward with us, some Saints have followed Sidney Rigdon to Pennsylvania. They went to Chambersburg of all places, just 25 miles away from Gettysburg! Hearing of Sidney's arrival, Father can only be disappointed to learn that his grandchildren and I did not join this faction. And Emma Smith and the Prophet's three sons, who deny that Brigham Young is rightful President, chose to remain in Nauvoo, to a fate that only God knows.

And there are likewise schisms in our ranks. Apostle Page, disfellowshipped soon after we left Nauvoo, departed with his followers for Wisconsin where Apostle Strang has established a church. The Prophet's brother, William Smith, is there with Strang, along with, of all men, the infamous Dr. John Cook Bennett. We hear that several eastern stakes ally with Strang, although the missions in England are loyal to us. And yet another group apostasized this week and left for Texas, where Apostle Lyman Wight has led his followers.

In communities across Iowa Territory, illness and exhaustion have made stragglers of many Saints. Some of them claim to have had revelations that the Apostles have strayed from the true faith. I sympathize and understand their weariness, yet I fear for the apostates and Saints who wander from us. How can they possibly believe they have reached Zion?

117

June 10, 1846

Though it is not yet summer, we are already preparing for the winter. Here at Mt. Pisgah, 40 miles beyond Garden Grove, we are spending several weeks in planting 1,400 acres, fencing fields and building cabins. Emigrants who start too late or find themselves too sick or ill-provisioned to go farther may winter here, along with residents who will stay to tend the crops, resupply and repair late-arriving wagons.

Today the children helped with the washing, the task I most dread. Joshua fetched the water, then built the fire to boil it. Bravely, he endured the smoke in his eyes while he stirred lye soap into the kettle. Before I could finish scrubbing all the dirty spots against the washboard, we had yet another of those drenching thunder squalls. I took shelter for half an hour until it passed, relit the fire, then boiled and rinsed the clothes, and pulled them from the kettle with a broomstick. After they cooled, Ann laid the wet clothes over the bushes to dry. Even Paul helped to wring the excess water from the clothing. But I had to watch him closely when he tried to put soapy water into the drinking water pail. All any of us needs is the flux!

Every day, I am thankful that Paul no longer requires diapers. On the trail, where water is scarce, the overwhelmed mothers of infants frequently resort to drying and scraping the diapers, airing them, then putting them back on their babies. But keeping clothing clean is far from easy, so none of us has cause to fault another.

Last night, we held a dance in one of the log cabins, with speeches, songs and recitations into the night. The men spread the dirt floor with clean straw, then draped the cabin walls with sheets. The women scooped out the insides of fresh turnips and placed candles inside them. When these were fastened on the walls and lighted, the image was very picturesque.

\*\*\*

"Brother Brigham has called me to a meeting tonight," John

118

said somberly.

"But it's the Fourth of July," Amelia protested. "The festivities are about to begin."

"You and the children go without me."

With a sinking feeling in her stomach, Amelia asked, "What is the meeting about?"

"I don't know," John replied.

"Has it anything to do with that group of Army officers who came into camp three days ago? From the look of their horses, they'd been riding hard to find us."

"I don't know," he repeated.

"When I saw the soldiers' uniforms, I rounded up the children," Amelia said. "And you reached for your rifle."

Fearfully, Amelia watched the Independence Day celebration. When she and the children came back to the wagon, John was not there. Her hands were too shaky to sew as she awaited his return.

"What is it?" she asked when John appeared, unsmiling and silent.

He inhaled deeply before he spoke. "Brigham Young has asked me to enlist for a year in the infantry of the United States Army. He's pledged 500 of us to be organized as the Mormon Battalion for the war with Mexico."

"But why?" Amelia asked in disbelief. "Is this not just a further attempt by the Gentiles to keep our people from gathering in Zion?"

"No, Amelia. Brother Brigham sent word to Washington that we are willing to work, opening roads, transporting military goods, or if necessary, fighting battles."

"But don't we have enough to accomplish already?"

John shook his head. "We're desperate for money, and the pay is in cash, the scarcest of all commodities we lack. And who knows what other benefits it might bring?"

Amelia felt the panic rising in her chest. "But the Mexicans proved repeatedly in Texas that they take no prisoners!"

"The Army will furnish my rations all the way to the West," John said calmly. "The soldiers' pay will not go to their families, but to President Young to use as he sees fit."

With grief, Amelia stared at her husband. "More than a common soldier, you're an uncommon millwright, not to mention husband to me! If volunteers are so necessary, surely Brigham Young can send another man."

"Other men will help you with the wagons," John said gently, "as I would gladly help if another husband were called instead of me."

"Who will help me with the children?" Amelia asked.

"You will not complain," John rebuked her.

Amelia felt stung and chastened. She bit her tongue so she could not give voice to the words that arose in her mind. Did Pharoh ask the Israelites to leave their Exodus so they could help them to fight some ancient war?

July 9, 1846

These endless, treeless plains, drowned so recently in mud, are now instead shrouded in dust. Though ample away from the trail, the graze along it has all been devoured by cattle from prior companies, leaving it barren and laden with dust. While the path is not so difficult, the air we must breathe remains full of dust raised by thousands of hooves and wheels that go before us. The grit conspires with the scorching sun to swell and redden our eyes and burn our skin. The wind blows without relenting, filling my mouth, nose, ears, lungs and hair with dust. The prairie mosquitoes plague us, while the rattlesnakes threaten our cattle. The only fuel we can find is dessicated buffalo dung.

John is still with us as we follow the trail to Council Bluffs. For myself, I feel only the aching unfairness of it all. With every blistered step, I must force myself to cast aside doubt that the priesthood possesses the authority to act for God.

July 20, 1846

John left for Fort Leavenworth today, marching in formation as a foot soldier in the United States Army. Last night, Brigham Young gave the soldiers his blessing and promised they will all return alive if they obey the counsel of the priesthood among them. He cautioned them to wear their Endowment undergarments, which render them invulnerable to hostile weapons. Then he warned them not to preach in public unless people show desire to hear them. Apostle Parley Pratt advised the soldiers to treat the Mexicans as fellow human beings to whom the gospel is yet to be preached.

There followed lively dancing until dark, but I, for one, did not enjoy it. And later, I felt bereft of passion as John and I lay together as husband and wife one last time. I do not want to bear a child on this trail.

***

Winter Quarters, Camp of Israel<br>Omaha Nation<br>August 29, 1846

Dear Franny,

Yesterday we arrived at Winter Quarters, where the Platte and Missouri Rivers meet. Considering the trials we have encountered, the children and I are faring remarkably well. From Nauvoo, we have traveled 400 miles and six months, and for now, we are content to rest.

If I know Father, he owns a copy of Fremont's map, which shows the nearest settlement to us, Pointe aux Poules, an American Fur Company trading post. We are surrounded here by Indians on every side, but there are almost no Gentiles for 100 miles. Missionaries are departing tomorrow for England, and they will carry this letter on their journey East.

How I wish I had some news from you, Franny! Even the promise of news at some certain date. After so many months of patience, waiting is a burdensome task.

You may wonder why I tell you nothing about John, and the reason is I have no news of him. A month ago, he enlisted in the Army to fight in the Mexican War. I pray that Charles is there with you and did not volunteer to fight this war! Of comfort is the fact that John is serving in a battalion of fellow Saints, not tossed among a rabble of mobocratic men. The rumor circulates here that a regiment of Missourians is on the march to Mexico, too. They are commanded by our old benefactor, Alexander Doniphan, who nobly defended us when Governor Boggs ordered our extermination. But even Doniphan might be powerless to hold back bloody vengeance if the two forces should meet before being sobered by their common enemy.

Still, fretting is needless and futile. As all else, what will happen to my husband rests with a beneficent Providence.

Yesterday, as we crossed the Missouri River on a flat-bottomed ferry, this great camp appeared, bright with white canvas in the sun. Winter Quarters is humming with industrious arrivals who are constructing nothing less than a city. Hundreds of log cabins and dirt-roofed shacks are being built, along with many dugouts that are half underground. Before Christmas, we hope to build 700 log homes to shelter 3,500 people. Scattered in such communities behind us on the trail are perhaps 7,000 more Saints.

At Winter Quarters, we are sowing immense quantities of grass for hay, and assembling a flouring mill for wheat. We must be frugal with food, but it is adequate, supplied in part from the Battalion's wages, which are paid to the Church, not to the families. Along the riverbanks, we gather the abundant black walnuts, and wild grapes and plums which I am drying and preserving for the winter ahead. Horses and mules, oxen and cattle, sheep and goats graze by the thousands on the Missouri River bluffs. When the children and I climb those bluffs and look out, I feel a proper pride to witness what God has led us to accomplish in this great cause.

You would be astonished, Franny, as I was, watching our men build a bridge over the Elk Horn tributary of the Platte River. There they worked in the searing sun, in water up to their necks, floating along with the logs that were destined to become the piers and abutments of the bridge. The men dove down to plunge the logs under water, then in an amazingly short span of time, they secured them into precise positions.

Who can doubt that our American fate is to tame this savage wilderness all the way west to the Pacific? If John must fight this war with Mexico to prove it true, then it can only be a worthy sacrifice.

Who can doubt that our American institutions are superior to any the world has known? Our democracy, religious freedom, and inventions of our countrymen, are destined to spread by inspiration and imitation to all the less fortunate, less happy peoples. When our missionaries go abroad, many thousands of converts seek to join us. And why? In England, a woman born into the lower classes must not expect to be unchained from the toilsome drudgery of her existence. But here, she can advance toward equality with any woman, even our poetess Eliza Snow, who conducts blessing meetings almost every night. True, the work is hard, but there is fellowship in it, and among us there is none who idly waits to be served. A democracy of the Holy Spirit underlies our faith. As Brigham Young asks, "What is there to prevent any person in this congregation from being so blessed, and becoming a holy temple fit for the in-dwelling of the Holy Ghost?"

If you examine Father's atlas, you will see that we sit squarely mid-continent, in the heart of this immense empire. Behind us to the east are the free states, and just to the north are free territories. The slave states are immediately south and east. To the west for many hundreds of miles stretches Indian Country, as far as the crest of the Rocky Mountains. Northwest of that lies Oregon Country, whose sovereignty is disputed between America and England. All the land southwest of that is Mexico, with whom we now find ourselves at war. If the Apostles indeed know where we are going, they have not confided it to me.

In truth, our months of labor have not advanced us very far. Though somewhat farther north, Winter Quarters is little west of Independence, our home seven ancient years ago. We are just within Indian Country, in a favorable location for defense against mobs. While we are numerous here, a mindless attack is not impossible by the reckless and barbarian fanatics who are proud to call themselves our old enemies.

Of course, we fear violence from the Indians, but we do not count them among our foes. The Lamanites, as we call them, are descended from a wandering tribe of Israel who, with their brother Nephites, found their way to the New World 600 years before Christ. Jesus preached to them after his resurrection, and the Nephites, a delightsome people, accepted him as their savior. But the Lamanites, a lesser people, rejected Jesus. Over time, bitter war ensued and the Nephites were annihilated. But just before it, a Nephite whose name was Mormon recorded their history on golden plates and buried them in a hill in western New York. There, the golden plates lay for many centuries. At last, guided by the angel Moroni, the son of Mormon, Joseph Smith unearthed these plates. He was given the seerstones Urim and Thummin to translate the *Book of Mormon* into English.

Thus, the Lamanites are not our enemies but our misguided brothers who have woefully forgotten their own past. When we obtain the chance, we remind them. The Lamanites here, of the Omaha nation, listen to our sermons but still steal our cattle, then run to us for help against the Sioux.

Newly-written maps and books feed my desire to see for myself the phenomenal natural features of the West. And they describe a grand adventure that, with the help of God, will be fulfilled. But for now, we must remain in Winter Quarters until the growing grass again nurtures our livestock and allows us to resume our westward march. Within a year, I believe, we shall reach Zion.

My best love and constant thoughts to you and Charles and Father,

Amelia

January 9, 1847

Men will be men, I suppose, and despite being Saints, they have infected Winter Quarters with their sinfulness. Liquor is smuggled in when it is found, or they distill it from scarce grain, claiming they need whiskey to ward off the chill while guarding us at night. Bound up here together, we may indeed be fortunate that women and children outnumber men four to one. More than once, a man has allowed his hand to wander toward the bodice or rear of my dress as he was helping me with the wagons. Several men have been properly flogged after being tried and found guilty of adultery or carnal communication with girls.

With good cause, Brigham Young has rebuked us again, exhorting us to find righteousness here. Unless we desist from covetousness and disobedience, he warns, we will "all be destroyed by the Lamanites as were the Nephites of old." A few repentant sinners have been rebaptized in the icy Missouri River. I am thankful that my boys are too young to get entangled in anything more sinful than the occasional childish mischief.

February 27, 1847

Time is passing ever more slowly here, as each day brings a greater longing to be traveling. Twelve months have elapsed since we ventured away, and it is now half a year since John departed. The children and I have heard no news, but at least we have heard no bad news.

We are blessed to sojourn at the same winter camp as Brigham Young. He zealously preaches his sermons with a strong and sonorous voice, and when I hear how deeply he feels his words, I cannot help but feel them, too. He is an excellent bass singer and fine mimic, and when he speaks, his manner is pleasing and unaffected.

While we are well, many others are not. Brother Brigham and the Apostles lay their hands on the afflicted and speak holy words, and sometimes the devils are cast out. But burial parties are constantly at work. Many families have sacrificed half their members, mostly from the cursed Black Canker. And babies often die within hours of their birth. For good reason, these Missouri Bottoms have been called the 'Misery Bottoms.' Deaths along the trail now number close to 600.

Yet why should we expect Zion to be easily reached? It is my complete conviction that the path we are pursuing is but a test of ourselves and our faith. Far from fearing the wilderness before us, I welcome its immensity of adventures.

We hear that other camps are more impaired than ours, so we have sent them supplies from Winter Quarters. Every day, I give the children a few dried grapes or a prune, and they are not troubled by scurvy. Other people, I hear, take a teaspoon of wine for this purpose. I do not believe that God would fault them for it.

Bishop Miller, reproached by Brigham Young for endangering a wagon train, has apostasized and departed from us.

May 20, 1847

Once again, we are on our grand march! The children are equally joyful, all of us feeling strengthened and grateful to leave our idle sojourn behind. The days have quickly settled into regular, familiar form. Bugle at 5:00, breakfast and feeding livestock until 7:00, traveling until 8:30 at night. Then we circle the wagons, eat and pray, sing hymns by the fire, and often dance. On the Sabbath we rest, all of us, man and beast.

Brigham Young and the Apostles left Winter Quarters on April 16, a month before our wagons set out. I had asked if I and the children might go with them, but they explained that they must travel swiftly and unencumbered to pass ahead of the Gentile emigrations. Through science and revelation, this Pioneer Company will determine the best path to our promised place. Just before they departed, a missionary brought them a full set of navigational instruments from England, to accurately locate our latitude and longitude.

Among their party of 70 wagons are only three women and two children. Since 500 men are in the Battalion with John, and 143 men proceed us on the trail, our own wagon train is comprised chiefly of women and children.

June 19, 1847

The rains came down powerfully this morning, with dreadful lightning and thunder, and hailstones near the size of eggs. The wagon masters thought it best to remain in camp. All our fellow-emigrants kept busy, bathing and baking, then a public prayer meeting was held. About noon, the storm relented so we broke camp and traveled nine miles.

For a month now, we have been traveling along the northern bank of the Platte River. The plains are treeless here, except a narrow band of cottonwoods along the riverbank. From time to time, we observe Gentile wagon trains on the trail along the southern bank. Joshua, Ann and Paul always wave and call out gaily to the children they see across the river. Their track may be harder packed than ours and their river crossings less hazardous. But graze on this side is more abundant and we need not risk camping next to men who may plot to do us harm. The travel is steadier along the Platte, and if a day presents good weather, we frequently accomplish 15 miles. To do so, we must accept shortened rests for body functions, and the wagon masters yell insults at malingerers.

We are fortunate to know our progress with such certainty because the Pioneer Party has invented a sort of roadometer. They added cogs on the wagonwheel axle to count rotations that measure the miles. Every 10 miles, they leave us messages in prairie post offices, which are sometimes slotted boards or dried buffalo skulls, or mileposts made of wood. We anticipate these messages eagerly. Today we passed a sign that read, "From Winter Quarters 300 miles, May 9, 1847, Pioneer Camp All Well."

* * *

"Mama!" Ann shrieked in panic.

Amelia spun around beside the oxen where she was walking. She saw a small body fall to the ground in front of the wagon.

"Paul!" she screamed, jerking the oxen to a halt. Amelia prayed as she ran back to the wagon. The few seconds seemed an eternity.

Bravely, Paul tried to crawl away. But he could not escape the deadly rear wheels, which lumbered over his small body.

Amelia knelt by the boy. He was still breathing, but she knew that the wagon's crushing weight had left his body bleeding inside.

"A herd of antelope was running by," Ann explained.

"He stood up in the wagon," Joshua said. "He lost his balance."

Paul offered his family a look of loving farewell. He did not suffer long.

Amelia stroked his cool hand, then she said softly, "Your brother has been called on a mission to our Heavenly Father."

"Father..." Ann said.

Joshua looked up at his mother.

If he indeed lives, Amelia thought grimly. Once the bitter tears started, she could not stop them. She felt unable to go on or turn back.

At last, Amelia recalled some words of comfort.

"Children," she whispered, "Paul died too young to be capable of sin. He is exalted for Eternity in the highest degree of the Celestial Kingdom."

Amelia knelt on the ground, stroking the smooth, still cheek.

"Ann," she said, "please get his clean suit of clothes from the wagon. Joshua, empty a dry goods box."

Amelia sat with the small, lifeless body while the children did as they were told. With a shaking hand, she wrote on the simple coffin, "Paul Carter, 1843-1847. Holiness to the Lord, Our Salvation."

Desperately, Amelia prayed that the wolves would not unearth her son's grave.


July 10, 1847

It has now been 10 days since Paul departed this life, and a year since John marched off to war. Soon, his enlistment will be fulfilled, but how will John know where to find us?

How frequently I must remind myself to trust in all-seeing Providence!

Today we traveled 15 miles and camped where the Pioneers did. They left a guide board here, saying they had killed 11 buffalo. At dusk tonight, I met with some girls as they spoke in tongues, and I listened while the Lord poured out His spirit to them. His presence made my heart glad.

We have entered the foothills of the Rocky Mountains, and the landscape is transforming before our eyes. In this drier climate, 425 miles from Winter Quarters, the rocks sometimes take on fantastical shapes. For three days, we approached Chimney Rock and watched it loom in unearthly splendor on the western horizon. This massive inverted stone funnel appears in the distance like a shot tower or cathedral spire, or even as the work of a mad sculptor. From far away, the strange colored rocks of Scott's Bluff appear as a castle of decayed magnificence. Here, the land is so alive with buffalo that our livestock wander and commingle with them. But it is dangerous for those who must collect our animals in the morning to drive them westward.

Out of necessity, I have become a fair teamster. Hunting down straying oxen is no easy task, nor is yoking them up or walking alongside them 15 miles. But I find that hard work, my family and faith help to heal the heartbreak of Paul's death. At noon today, I climbed a small hill and watched with satisfaction the long and twisting column of white-top wagons. At my feet lay a lovely valley, thick with wildflowers, through which I could trace our progress for many miles.

This evening, after Joshua and Ann collected buffalo chips for the fires, they eagerly scaled the bluffs and tried to catch coyote pups and prairie dogs. A prairie dog will sit erect on the mouth of its burrow, and when a child gets too near, it will chirp a sharp hissing alarm then dart into its hole. The children are charmed, though I cannot help but worry about snakes.

July 24, 1847

We are now in the vicinity of Fort Laramie, 530 miles from Winter Quarters. We will rest here several days, camping by the adobe ruins of Fort Platte.

A few men who rode ahead to Fort Laramie brought us back tremendous news. When the Pioneer Party arrived there on June 1, they were met by several members of the Mormon Battalion, just mustered out. These soldiers reported that the Battalion suffered only four deaths. And John Carter was not among the four!

With lightened hearts, Joshua, Ann and I washed the clothes, then hung them up to dry in the cottonwood trees. The white muslins and red flannels fluttered cheerfully, along with the multicolored but faded calicoes. Then I baked pies and bread, while the children searched for edible greens. We are in better health than when we started, for which we are extravagantly grateful.

Feeling no need to meet with Gentiles, I did not go on to Fort Laramie. But this morning as I awoke, I watched the sun reflecting a luminous pink against Laramie Peak. The sight was beautiful, the first of what will surely be numerous mountains before us. The mountains are obstacles we must conquer, I know, but I could only feel their awesome grandeur. They tell us we have reached the end of the relatively easy Platte River road.


August 12, 1847

For an interminable 70 miles, our trail leaves the Platte Valley and cuts across rough country, where fording streams is difficult and oversized cobblestones hinder our way. But the fishing is good, and Joshua has grown adept at it, and when we traveled by one creek, the smell of crushed mint was like perfume.

As we plodded toward the last crossing of the Platte, a splendid recognition came upon us. Ferrymen were there, and they are our own fellow Saints! Equally delighted to see us, they told us they have been ferrying Gentile wagons for a month, paid in cash or foodstuffs at Independence prices. Even deep into this wilderness, the Oregon Trail is amazingly well traveled.

Onward through the Rocky Mountain passes, the route has grown very steep. Every day, we send work parties ahead of the wagons to improve the trail. But gullies and canyons cut every which way through this land, so the wagons must often be lowered by ropes. In the blinding sun and dust, it is a painfully slow enterprise. All of us must help to hold the wagons back on steep downgrades, or lift them over immovable boulders.

Our wagons are growing ever worse from the wear. Dry air shrinks the wood away from its fittings, so spokes pull out of wheels, or iron tires roll away, or wagon tongues break under the strain. The dry axles make an alarming shriek. All the animals are thinner and weaker from fatigue and sparser pasture. In some places there are alkali sinks and poisonous-smelling creeks, and mosquitoes by the millions in the mud. When our cattle drink the foul water, they bloat into a loathsome death.

Wear among our travel party is growing worse. We are becoming short-tempered, tired of the ordeal, the lack of privacy and fresh food. Impatient with those whose malingering or ineptitude delays us, we are shouting more, and there is an occasional fight. A few women whose husbands help me regard me with suspicion, and I, too, suspect some men of dishonorable thoughts.

Finally, today we reached Independence Rock, named for the belief that travelers to Oregon must get to it by Independence Day, or risk being caught by the snows. We were greeted by two more Latter-day Saints, who are engaged in a prosperous trade. For a fee, they will chisel the names of Gentile emigrants into the gray granite dome. Many names and messages grace the fissured rock, not only from this summer but years past.

Wherever we are going, I hope we are not too late.

* * *

"Look, Mama!" Joshua called out from where he rode up in the wagon. He pointed toward the west.

Amelia saw a tall column of dust rising on the distant horizon. Indians, she thought with alarm.

"Maybe buffaloes," Joshua said. "I wish I was big enough to go with the hunters."

Hoping for barter or hunting, a group of men rode out with their guns. But they galloped back at the speed of their horses, shouting tremendous news.

"That dust was raised by Ezra Benson and the others riding east to find us," they yelled.

Bursting with excitement, Amelia waited for the eastbound riders to catch up. The company gathered close around the small group of men.

"Zion is established!" Benson proclaimed.

The crowd cheered with loud passion, and Amelia hugged Joshua and Ann. Ebullience quickly replaced the tiresome complaining.

"Where?" a man asked.

"Beyond the mountains, in a valley on the shore of the Great Salt Lake, just as Brigham Young saw it in a vision."

"Is this valley nearby?" the weary travelers asked.

"About 300 miles farther."

Amelia and the children looked at one another. "Three hundred miles!"

"Yes," Benson said. He read them a letter bidding them to travel on with a lighter step.

"You'll soon reach Devil's Gate," he explained, "where the Sweetwater River cuts through the Rattlesnake Range. Fort Bridger is 180 miles beyond that. Then, as you venture onward to the valley, you will encounter Brigham Young and some others, who are on their way back to Winter Quarters."

September 19, 1847

Of our entire undertaking--400 miles to Winter Quarters and 1,000 miles beyond it--it is fated that these final 40 miles are the ones most demanding of our dedication and faith. We are stuck at the very gates of this Valley.

Surely, this strange and spectacular mountain pass cannot be recommended on any proper map. It is grand, to be sure, but not much of a wagon route. In all our journey, the gorges here are the steepest, the passageways narrowest, the torrents maddest and deepest, and the boulders largest to block the way. We can see where the Pioneer Party, and perhaps another before them, hacked away the brush and felled trees, pried boulders out, and leveled and graded the trail. We have had to do much more of the same. But even if all passing parties improve the road a bit, it will still be a difficult route.

Like many others, Ann and I are sick with mountain fever. Joshua, though not yet eight, is taking zealous care of us both. It is a small comfort to know that Brother Brigham suffered this same illness in these mountains. So while my body burns with fever, and the bouncing, springless wagon multiplies the nausea and aches, my spirit gently rejoices. Mountain fever is rarely fatal, and we have almost arrived home.

September 24, 1847

With mounting excitement today, we ascended the ridge of Little Mountain, which would bring our first sight of the Great Salt Lake Valley. Through the virgin forest, I urged the oxen faster, eager as I was to view this Great Salt Lake and the vast desert beyond it. My breath caught in my chest as we reached the summit.

But nothing had forewarned me of the ruinous effect on my spirits as I gazed out beyond the mountains. The view was so desolate, barren and parched, and so isolated from all I have ever known. What I saw was the end of the inhabitable land, for the alkalai desert is as cruel to life as the briny sea. After venturing so far, I felt myself imprisoned within a narrow band of earth, confined by twin devastations of searing sun and impassable snow.

For the children's sake, I tried to hide my anguish but could not. Heartsick, I stood beside the wagon, the salty tears rolling down my face. Joshua and Ann stood by my side, but they knew no words that might console me.

With a resigned and heavy step, I began our descent through Emigration Canyon, when a light, fresh rain began to fall. All at once, the truth of our remoteness overwhelmed me, and a new joy came to replace my tears. Whatever else befalls us in this unfamiliar place, there is no one to persecute us here.

And when the clouds parted, I looked again at the landscape that had inspired such melancholy in me. Underneath the gray clouds, the Great Salt Lake waters were glistening with sunbeams of gold.

\*\*\*

Dear Franny,

There is grand news!  John has returned to us safely.  He arrived here today with a group of men, tired but otherwise well.

But amid the rejoicing at our reunion, I knew I faced the devastating duty of telling John how our little son Paul fell to his death from the wagon.  John and I both wept as I relived the bitter story, then he regarded me in weary silence.  John insists he does not hold me at fault.  If he had been there, the tragedy would not have happened, he said, so I cannot be blamed.  I felt comforted when he reminded me how constantly I cautioned the children to take care.  John was so glad to see Joshua and Ann growing strong.

Despite the approaching winter, some veterans of the Battalion are heading east tomorrow, hoping to join their families on the trail or at Winter Quarters.  This letter will travel east with them, though I expect you will not get it until spring.

But when will your letters begin to come west?  I am so desperate to hear news of you.

John tells me that the Mormon Battalion earned an excellent reputation with the regular Army.  They marched a nearly endless 3,000 miles but found almost no combat.  They had no casualties in their only battle, since they persuaded a Mexican garrison at Tucson to withdraw.  The shortage of food and water was their cruelest hardship, and in the trackless desert tablelands, they suffered without water for several days.  In parched desperation, John and the others dug wells down 20 feet and at last discovered sweet water.  Those wells will long benefit future travelers along the route.  For hundreds of miles, they improved the trail by hewing passages through rock with crowbars, picks and axes, and widening the way for their wagons.  The Battalion marched past ruins of several grand and ancient Nephite cities, which John says can only verify the *Book of Mormon*.

Fifty veterans of the Battalion remained in California, but John was eager to rejoin the children and me. Brigham Young sent a guide who brought them east on the trail across the Sierra Nevada Mountains. John was disappointed to learn that President Young has returned to Winter Quarters and will not come west before next summer.

John tells us they saw a ghastly scene when the men passed the summit of the Sierras. They found the scattered and putrefying remains from an emigrant party who left in '46 as we did, but were trapped by early mountain snows. While death is common on the trail, and scavenging animals might unearth any burial, John swears that these remains were not natural. It was cannibalism! Some people had been cooked and then eaten by their own fellow travelers! It was this party, the Donners, who built at fatal cost some of the improvements that eased our way on that last brutal route into this Valley. The Donners were the second party ever on that trail, and our own wagon train was the fourth.

The Donner Party, it is said, included a Mormon woman, an apostate no doubt, or she would have been with us. But even an apostate does not merit that fate! I am far less convinced about Lilburn Boggs, former governor of Missouri and our sworn enemy, who traveled for awhile with the Donners but split off before this abomination. Again, that blackguard Boggs has cheated the ignoble death he deserves.

Our site here at Great Salt Lake City is on a gently sloping bench at the foot of the Wasatch Mountains, 17 miles from the shore of the lake. The soil is excellent, but vegetation dies quickly from lack of rainfall, so we devised an irrigation system. Crops are watered from a bright mountain stream of clear water, called City Creek, which pours forth from Parley's Canyon. Our larger community is called Deseret, named for the honeybee, for everything is industry here. Deseret has a census of some 1,700 Saints this autumn.

When we began our journey before the war, this land all the way from the Rockies to the Pacific belonged to Mexico. It will not become American until the treaty of peace is signed and ratified. But here, we can afford to be patient. Insulated on the east by 1,000 miles of prairies and mountains, and on the west by 500 miles of mountains and deserts, we are safe from American mobs. We have bought out the only Gentile landowner, so we have no competitors in Deseret. Far removed from any semblance of our past civilization, we will innovate our own.

In the meantime, we are living in our wagons until John can erect an adobe cabin. But I expect he will soon be too busy constructing the badly-needed mills, while other men build bridges, roads and stone fences. The Ute Indians living nearby appear unfriendly, so we are building a fort of logs and adobe with walls nine feet high and 27 inches thick. These walls enclose 10 acres and have no openings except slits for guns and a gate that is open by day and shut at night. Until the mill is finished, we have only rough bread of unground wheat. Food will be in short supply until we harvest our first crop.

As Brigham Young says, "I have Zion in my view constantly. We are not going to wait for angels, or for Enoch and his company to come and build up Zion, but we are going to build it."

Franny, I must rejoin John, so I must force myself away from this letter. I think of you and Father daily, and I pray that you and Charles will someday join me.

Your Loving Sister,
Amelia


March 27, 1848

It is a struggle to keep my faith that this is indeed the Promised Land. While winter was not horribly cold, the rains have now come in torrents, pouring through the roof and melting the adobe bricks that comprise our home. Bedbugs crawl out from the exposed logs to torment us, and mice burrow under the house and weaken it. Though we catch a dozen or more mice every night, the house trembles at the slightest provocation. Wolf packs hunt through the city at night, undeterred by the poison we leave as bait to kill them. Still, the rains have been favorable for the crops, more essential to us than the houses. In summer, we will build sturdier homes.

Day by day, the provisions are growing poorer. Joshua and Ann gather thistle roots, sego lilies and cow cabbage, and I boil these greens into a soup made from cow hides, all that remains of our slaughtered cattle. Every night, we ask the Lord to bless our humble meal, and it needs His blessing, for it contains too little nutriment to bless itself.

May 30, 1848

Evidently, God has not wearied of sending us extravagant trials. Last fall, we plowed and planted 2,000 acres of wheat, then 3,000 acres of corn in the spring. Our crops were green and thriving and they gladdened the eye, making us more thankful every day. Then a late killing frost devastated both the corn and the wheat. In my garden, the cucumbers, beans and melons, pumpkins and squash are all ruined.

As if that affliction were too mild, crickets are now swarming across the land. By the millions in black clouds they arrived, multiplying and devouring everything spared by the frost. Each of these black and voracious creatures exceeds one inch in length, and after gorging on our crops, can bloat up to three horrid inches. Massed together, they can fell fullgrown cornstalks and consume them without leaving a trace. Today I saw a swarm of them eat a rattlesnake.

In desperation, we are sparing no weapon against this scourge, burning them and crushing them and drowning them. They are said to dislike certain noises, so the children and I bang on bells and sticks and pans in the fields to harass them. Some say that the crickets are cannibalistic, so we kill large numbers at the borders of the fields and hope they will eat their fill on one another. So far, all our remedies have failed.

I try not to despair, but we find ourselves disarmed, and the insect invaders show no sign of relinquishing their upper hand. Every hour, I remind myself that saints of God in all ages have suffered. Why should we be more indulged than they?

June 21, 1848

These latter days have witnessed nothing less triumphant than God's miracle! He has not suffered His people to journey to this faraway place, only to let us starve in the wilderness.

After weeks of ravaging plunder by the crickets, our community was facing the specter of starvation. We fasted and prayed for an end to this plague, or for some revelation of what God expected us to do. Still, no revelation came, and Brother Brigham had not returned to Deseret.

But our Heavenly Father heard our prayers and sent deliverance. Last week, a flock of white seagulls appeared high in the skies over the Great Salt Lake. At once, the gulls swooped down and began to feast on the crickets. Then came a larger flock of the miraculous birds, then an even larger one. By the thousands, seagulls were dispatched to devour the vermin laying waste to our crops.

Ann and Joshua and I never tire of watching these angel-winged messengers. The seagulls gorge themselves on crickets until full, drink some water, then regurgitate the villainous insects. Then they resume their consumption of more crickets. It is as though their entire mission is to deliver us from this pestilence and siege.


August 10, 1848

Today, beneath a large awning, our community celebrated a Thanksgiving no less momentous than the one first held by the Pilgrims. Amid spirited shouts of Hosanna to God and the Lamb, we feasted on foods produced in the Valley, under the dominion of our plows. Joshua particularly enjoyed the firing of the cannon, and I, the lively music and dancing.

Many Saints have been arriving here this summer, residing in their wagons or in brush sheds until cabins or dugouts can be built. Every day but the Sabbath, three sawmills are abuzz, producing lumber. A temporary gristmill is at work, and John is constructing an even better one. On City Creek, a water powered threshing machine can thrash 200 bushels of grain daily. Inside the fort walls, 440 log or adobe homes are completed, and land in town will soon be allocated among the settlers. Unmarried men will not be eligible to buy these lots.

Anticipating winter, most people are already living on short rations, and we are sending wagonloads of grain east to relieve incoming parties. On their return, the drivers recover metal abandoned on the trail, to be reworked by our smiths into tools. We have timber for corrals but no fodder, so we turn the livestock loose on the range and entrust them to a generous Providence.

Some skeptics believe we may be moving west again, so they have not planted their precious fruit tree cuttings. But my fruit trees, roses and geraniums are thriving, at least so far. Since our corn and wheat was devastated by the crickets and frost, the harvest was only adequate instead of bountiful. Still, every bushel and stem of it dispels a doubt by a skeptic about the site of our Prophet's revelation.

***

"Come, look who's arrived," John called to Amelia on an afternoon in late September, 1848.

"Who is it?" Amelia asked, untying her apron.

"James Brown, a fellow veteran of the Battalion," John said. "And there's an even more distant surprise."

"Who?" Amelia asked.

"You will see."

Amelia and John joined the people surrounding the new arrivals.

"Where've you been, James?" one of them called.

"In the California foothills," the young man replied. "Orrin Hatch and several dozen of us spent the winter at a place called Sutter's Fort. It's really more like a town, with a trading post and living quarters, a flour mill, gunsmith and carpenter shop, a brewery, tannery and shoemaker. You should've come with us, John."

"Why?" John asked.

"We were building Mr. Sutter a sawmill along the river. But the men who started it set the millwheel too low for the tail race, so we had to deepen the channel. As we dug down to the bedrock, suddenly we saw something shiny in the water. One by one, we realized it was gold."

Gold, Amelia pondered as she listened.

"We kept working to finish the sawmill, but in our off hours, we prospected for gold. In the river, there's a sandbar they call Mormon Island, where gold can be dug with just a penknife. This summer, we left California and came to Deseret as we were counseled."

"Weren't you tempted to stay in California?" a man asked.

"It's been two years since we saw our families."

Amelia stared in disbelief when she saw a familiar man walking toward them.

"Addison Pratt!" Amelia exclaimed. "We last saw you in Nauvoo five years ago. I didn't dare imagine you were still among us."

"You were headed to Hawaii," John recalled.

"I've been baptizing natives on the islands of Tahiti," Pratt replied. "I'll share my adventures later, but not until I spend some time with Louisa and our daughters. They arrived only eight days ago from Winter Quarters, as if we had a pact to meet here today!"

Amelia smiled at her old friend.

"We've also seen Sam Brannan," James said.

"Didn't he lead a party by sailing ship to California?" John asked.

"Yes," the young man said. "They left New York City about the same time as we left Nauvoo in our wagons. But their passage was so much easier! They sailed around Cape Horn, then lingered in the Hawaiian Islands, and they still landed in California in July '46."

"That's a full year before the Pioneers reached the Salt Lake Valley," Amelia said.

The young man nodded. "When they landed, the 238 of them outnumbered the residents of the village that's now called

San Francisco. Sam established a farming settlement fifty miles inland, and a newspaper, *The California Star*."

"Sam tried to persuade Brigham Young that we should all settle there," Pratt told them. "Instead, Brother Brigham insists that Sam bring his colony to Utah. But he won't do it. Now Sam is urging Mormon miners, perhaps 150 in all, to give up 30 percent of their gold."

"He proposes to hold it for the Church," James explained.

Addison Pratt shook his head. "I doubt the Church will ever see any of that gold. Brannan is accused of worse abuses, like excommunicating people for small offenses. And he's the very man who first rode his horse through the San Francisco streets, crying, 'Gold! Gold!'"

James held open a small leather pouch, and Amelia touched a few shining gold flakes with her finger. She could not help but wonder what the discovery would mean for Deseret.

***

Great Salt Lake City<br>September 12, 1849

Dear Franny,

I was astonished when your letter arrived in barely six weeks from Pennsylvania. They used to take almost that long to reach Nauvoo! But the miners traveling to California have left our small community far less alone than we could have imagined just two years ago. The wiser ones carry the *Latter-Day Saints' Emigrants' Guide*, which the Church published in 5,000 copies last year. It sells for $5, though we have heard of some desperate men who gladly pay $25 when they cannot obtain one for less.

To us, the endless stream of miners can only be accounted a mixed blessing. They do indeed bring us mail and things we cannot readily get, like metals, tools and mechanical equipment. And they pay us well for repairs and provisions they need for their journey ahead. Our men will drive a team of fattened oxen to the miners' camps and exhange it for three exhausted teams. Then we feed and rest those worn-out oxen and trade them to later wagon trains. But scoundrels among the gold-seekers make traveling dangerous for our community. Recently, a pack of vagabonds from Missouri murdered some Indian women to get their horses, and now some Indians are attacking all whites. And the miners' drunken brawling so fouls our city that we are grateful for their haste to reach the goldfields.

While the miners bring us fond letters, like yours, they also spread hearsay about us. I could imagine the horror in Father's face as I read with amazement the article you enclosed from your newspaper in Gettysburg. These rumors have been unleashed on us before by apostates, then circulated by newspapers greedy to capitalize on the prurience of the public. The alleged polygamy of the Saints is a favorite old tale among our enemies and others who would profit from our persecution.

The simple explanation is that emigrants often lodge here temporarily in family homes, since we have not yet built hotels. Naturally, they are surprised to see so many women and children, unheard of in the wilderness this far away. From that, they infer we are polygamous. It is true that certain men, in particular the Apostles, have taken unmarried women into their homes. But this is only under the supervision of their wives. How else could we provide for numerous young unmarried women, unfortunate widows, and their children? I assure you and Father that no marriages here go unblessed by God. Please be reassured that taking multiple wives is the farthest thing from John's mind.

When I observe the uncouth miners in the streets, I am reminded how blessed I am to be with John. The prospectors scorn our men for their disinterest in gold, but mining can only weaken men's faith. Like gambling, its ambition is sloth, whose favorite pastimes are drunkenness, whoring and fighting. When we mint the miners' gold into coins, we stamp the words in a circle around an all-seeing eye, "Holiness to the Lord."

Some Saints who have been to California suggest that we

prospect here in Deseret. But Brigham Young forbids it, though he believes that gold and silver could be found. "We are a thousand miles from any bases of supply," he says, "and the people would rush in here in such great numbers that they would breed a famine. They would be willing to give a barrel of gold for a barrel of flour rather than starve to death."

When we first arrived, we could make only knitted clothing, but the miners have brought us woven fabric and even ready-made clothing. Household utensils and some furniture are now available, along with sugar, which we cannot otherwise get. A year ago, Ann and Joshua went barefoot most of the summer because their shoes were worn and outgrown, and their moccasins were for special occasions. Today I bought us each a pair of factory-made shoes at prices lower than in Illinois.

Two years ago, here in the Great Salt Lake Valley, fewer than a dozen whites lived under Mexican rule. Our population now exceeds 11,000, and we have just petitioned Congress to become a state. Imagine, Franny, establishing our own state in so little time! Naturally, we have civil government and religious freedom. Some may claim that our institutions are undemocratic, but survival here requires that each man not be ruled only by what is best for himself. Each man must be ruled by what advances God's kingdom, which is best understood by our Prophet. Unfortunately, Gentiles in the West are far from predisposed to agree. They are therefore not encouraged to settle here.

With constant love to you and all our family,

Amelia

\*\*\*

June 10, 1850

Many domestic improvements are appearing in Deseret this summer. A well-graded road, called the Golden Pass, will soon connect Echo Canyon with the Valley. It is far less hazardous than the route we battled through Emigration Pass, so we will charge the Gentiles a dollar per wagon to take it.

Today, the *Deseret News* published its premier edition. Hungry for the printed word, I read each precious line on every page. So much is happening in Deseret!

The *Deseret News* wonders, as I have, how long our prices will stay so topsy-turvy. Yesterday, John bought a full set of joiners' tools for $25, which he said would cost $150 in the East. Contrariwise, pack mules and horses, generally worth $25, now trade for $200 worth of manufactured goods. John and two friends from the Nauvoo Legion are eagerly establishing a stock farm.

It is now more than a year since President Young reconvened the Nauvoo Legion, manned by all able-bodied adult males. That morning, the whole militia assembled with their weapons, then laid them down as ordered and picked up tools and posts and boards to build the Bowery. At almost 50 yards square, the Bowery can hold 8,000 for open-air worship on the Sabbath. It is only used in summer because its roof is just a yearly replenishment of brush for shade.

How I wish Brother Brigham would reconvene the Female Relief Society! In Nauvoo, we boasted 1,400 members, each admitted only with a recommendation as to her worthiness. With spirit, we advanced the building of the Temple, each of us donating a penny a week for glass and nails. It is not that our work here is undervalued, but only that we are not organized. Naturally, women are ordained to perform Endowment rites for other females, and even if subordinate to male teachers, our gifts of healing, prophesying and speaking in tongues were blessed by the Prophet Joseph, himself.

The season is bringing a resurgence of miners tramping off to the goldfields. Men who once scorned Joseph Smith for money digging are mindlessly venturing west. Brother Brigham warns, "Gold is a good servant, but a miserable, blind, and helpless god, and at last will have to be purified by fire, with all its followers."

September 8, 1850

Today, John and I attended a meeting in the Bowery, along with 2,500 other Saints. Afterwards, Joshua, Ann and I climbed the mountainside above the city and looked down to take stock of our progress. From there, the town appears as an immense arrangement of gardens, with a house standing in the middle of each one. Almost everyone lives in houses in town, even farmers who go out to their fields every day outside the city. This strengthens our defenses, uses irrigation well, and brings us nearer to our Church and civic callings.

We looked down to the wide streets and blocks, and identified our own thriving garden. This summer, it is yielding beets, turnips, melons and potatoes in abundance. The cherry and apple, peach and apricot trees appear promising, although still too young to bear fruit. Ann and Joshua and I enjoy our work in the garden, savoring the independence of it as much as the diversity of flavors.

Brigham Young insists that no one should own more of Mother Earth than he can properly use. So farms in Deseret are much smaller than the average in the States. We also use farm machinery more extensively. When new machinery saves labor for our farmers, it frees them up to go on missions and preach the gospel.


November 1, 1850

Congress has callously denied our appeal for statehood. Refusing to admit the State of Deseret into the Union, they established the Territory of Utah instead, with a far smaller area than we rightfully claim. Fortunately, President Young is named Governor, and we will have a delegate in Congress. But we will have no vote. Judges and Federal officials will be imposed on us, so we fear that being a Territory will leave us worse off than we have been as an unsupervised region. California, settled no earlier than Deseret, has been admitted as a State!

I fear that our admission will require more than simply gaining population. In front of 20 members of Congress, President Zachary Taylor vowed he will veto any bill that grants

145

us statehood, calling us a pack of outlaws not fit for self-government. It is horribly unjust that our enemies wield such powers over us.

Our exertions to build Zion are not deterring our missionary duties. Hundreds of missionaries have been dispatched in recent months to England, France, Switzerland, Italy and Scandinavia, South and Central America, India and Australia, and the Hawaiian and Tahitian Islands.

September 28, 1851

The scoundrels imposed on us by Washington have left us disheartened and bewildered. How graciously we invited Judge Brocchus to address our Conference in the Bowery! How patiently we listened, all 2,500 of us, while he droned on for two hours, obstensibly to request that we contribute a block of marble for the Washington Monument, which we had already arranged to do. Then, having squatted here just a month, Judge Brocchus dared to scold us for immoral behavior, and demand that Mormon women return to lives of virtue! As if womanhood could possibly be more virtuous! Does the Judge imagine that the father of the baby in my womb is any man other than my husband?

Now, terrified by our just indignation, Judge Brocchus and two other Federal officials have run away, seizing the Territorial seal and records and $24,000 of Federal money, which is desperately needed here. He dares to charge that we threatened him with assassination! A vain, ambitious man, corrupt and fond of intrigues, Judge Brocchus is, I hope, being ridiculed in Eastern newspapers as a fool and coward for deserting his post without cause.

January 5, 1852

None of my prior three confinements was halfway as difficult as this one. I was grateful to be attended by our best midwife, whose blessings and anointings gave me much strength.

"We anoint your spinal column," she said to me, "that you

might be strong and healthy, no disease fasten upon it, no accident befall you, and your kidneys that they might be active and healthy and perform their proper functions, your bladder that it might be strong and protected from accident, your hips that your system might relax and give way for the birth of your child, your sides that your liver, your lungs and spleen might be strong and perform their proper functions, your breasts that your milk may come freely and you be unafflicted with sore nipples as many are, and your heart that it might be comforted."

Then she requested blessings from the Lord for the health of my child, and her prayers were granted. As painful as my labor was, it is all worth it. Molly is a beautiful baby, and John is delighted with her.

***

With a somber look in his eyes, John Carter approached Amelia in the spring of 1852. Haltingly, he said, "You know that I have always entertained strict notions of virtue."

"Yes, John, of course," Amelia said.

He hesitated. "Outside this principle, as a married man, I feel it is an appalling thing to do."

Amelia felt the breath catch in her chest. She listened in apprehensive silence.

John looked at his wife. "Nothing but a knowledge of God, and the revelations of God, and the truth of them, could induce me to embrace such a principle!"

Amelia's heart sank as she witnessed her husband's disquiet. She knew it could mean nothing else than her deepest secret fear had come to pass. For a decade, Amelia had been aware of their peculiar institution, though it was still unpublished for the world to observe and condemn.

"It's the third time I've been so ordered!" John demurred. "Our leaders counseled me again to live up to my privileges and take what is mine by revelation."

Amelia wondered whether John was begging her to refuse. Despite her terror, his anguish inspired in her a deep affection

147

for her husband.

"I have prayed on this for weeks," John insisted. "My reluctance is as much for myself as for you."

Amelia looked downward and stroked his arm. "How readily you otherwise always obey counsel. Missionary duties and marching off to war…"

"How can we refuse?" John interrupted. "We are told that innumerable spirits await human bodies to occupy on Earth in their progression to the worlds of Eternal bliss. It is the duty of men and women to procreate tabernacles of flesh for these spirits."

"Who is she?" Amelia asked.

John looked up. "Margaret Hill, an English immigrant who arrived last year."

"The pretty girl with lively blue eyes and brown hair?"

"Yes."

"She is perhaps 20 and I am over 30," Amelia said

"A woman can be saved only through marriage," John whispered.

Amelia took a deep breath and exhaled slowly. She spoke with more conviction than she felt. "Then is it not part of my commitment to help bring the Kingdom of Heaven to Earth?"

John smiled weakly, more with relief than anticipation.

"And I could never bear as many children as you deserve throughout Eternity."

John gratefully embraced Amelia. She looked up into his eyes.

"Yet to share you with another woman you might prefer to me!"

"That will never happen," John promised.

Amelia felt numb and alone after he left. She longed to discuss it with Franny, or even some friend within the Church. But how could she appear to doubt the revelations granted to the prophets? All she could do was pray that she possessed enough faith to endure it.

June 4, 1852

John has been called away to our new settlement at San Bernardino, California. He had asked that his family come with him, and Margaret of course, but his request was denied. It seems too many Saints are tempted by the fertile soil and pleasant climate, not to mention the seduction of gold. Last year, when Brother Brigham sought 25 Saints to settle there, more than 500 volunteered.

I feel heartsick at the thought of John's departing again, leaving me to care for his new bride. But the colony needs a grist mill and sawmill, and San Bernardino will be a useful way-station in the Pacific region. A hundred miles beyond it is the port of San Diego, where our immigrants who sail directly from Europe can land, and missionaries to the Pacific Islands can embark. Though 700 miles through the desert, the Old Spanish Trail to San Bernardino is said to be comparatively safe. And it is passable in fall and winter, unlike the snowy paths through the Sierra Nevada Mountains.


February 21, 1853

Yesterday, Margaret gave birth to a healthy baby girl. She is recovering well, and I have sent the news to John in California. Molly, barely one year old herself, is fascinated with the new arrival.

Over the months, Margaret and I have evolved into friends. At first, I perceived her as a rival, even after our husband left us both for California. But one day I forgot my prior claim and admired her fine needlework aloud. She smiled in surprise, then complimented my garden. Then we both confessed how glad we are that we have someone to share in the tedious chores of the laundry. With John away, I find Margaret to be a sympathetic listener. When he left, she did not know she was pregnant! At her confinement, Margaret thanked me for my anointings and blessings. She whispered, "The curse that women must bring forth children in sorrow almost felt lifted away."

As I attended the miracle of birth, I was reminded of Brother Brigham's discourse in the Tabernacle last month. "How difficult would be the task to make the philosopher, who, for many years, has argued himself into the belief that his spirit is no more after his body sleeps in the grave, believe that his intelligence came from eternity, and is as eternal, in its nature, as the elements, or as the Gods. Such doctrine by him would be considered vanity and foolishness, it would be entirely beyond his comprehension."

Paper being in perennially short supply, I donated several bundles of rags to be milled for the *Deseret News*. Mail is also sparse here. It has been three months since we heard any news from east of the Great Basin.

April 6, 1853

Amid lively martial music and singing by the choir, President Young today laid the southeastern cornerstone of the Temple. With Margaret and the children, I watched the stirring ceremony underneath the flags that floated in the breeze and a banner celebrating "Zion's Workmen." The granite foundations of the Temple rest 16 feet below the ground, beneath the reach of our mountain floods, and are built of rock 16 feet broad at the base. Mobs and robbers will thus find the Temple too laborious to raze to its foundations, leaving not one stone upon another, as they did to the Temple in Jerusalem. As they did to the Temple in Nauvoo.

Margaret does not appear half as lonesome for our husband as I am. She feels tenderness for John, I know, but it seems more domestic attachment and rather unimpassioned, I think.

January 9, 1854

John has returned from California! Naturally, Ann and Joshua and I rejoiced to see him, but Molly regarded her bearded father with curiosity. He looks well but thin, so Margaret and I shared a vow to fatten him up.

John reports that our settlement at San Bernardino is well underway, with the mills completed, a school established and vineyards planted. But he fears that the California outpost is a magnet, drawing undesirable elements to our society. The evils of private interest, worldliness and materialism have reared up their heads among the Saints. There are land distribution disputes and heavy debts, and a sizable Gentile minority that chafes at Church rule. John was astonished to witness apostasy by some high churchmen who labored zealously for Zion for years, but now turn against the brethren and abuse the authorities.

John tells me that Addison and Louisa Pratt, and their daughters, are now living in San Bernardino, after all of them returning from a mission to the Islands of Tahiti. Joshua's eyes and mine, I confess, lit up at the chance of such adventures.

John also brings news of Sam Brannan, now excommunicated for the second time. Sam has become a wealthy land developer in San Francisco and president of its Vigilance Committee. Appalled by the lawlessness of gunfighters and miners there, the Vigilance Committee organizes arrests and hangings, if need be, to preserve order.

***

Amelia sat next to John at a meeting of the Polysophical Society. She listened with interest for an hour, but after awhile, the discourse grew arcane and dry. Amelia found herself listening instead to the rumors that buzzed behind them.

"The controversies with the Gentiles are worsening," one man whispered. "It's hard to believe we once wanted that Federal land survey. It could be used to evict the Church from land in the public domain."

"We've been hobbling the survey," another man boasted. "Last week, we removed some corner stakes and ran off a few of the surveyors' mules."

"Did you hear how some men seized a Federal clerk? They made him answer questions about the Government's intentions."

"Yes, with a noose around his neck!"

"Another survey clerk leaped half-dressed from the window and escaped, but one man fell and was crippled."

John turned to the men. "We've denounced these acts from

151

the pulpit," he said softly. "But we haven't prosecuted them in our courts."

The first man nodded. "The Indians think the survey is part of a plot to seize their lands, too."

"The Indians! Even with their trouble-making, Jim Bridger refuses to stop selling them ammunition."

At the front of the hall, the speaker glared at the people talking in the back.

"Now Bridger is accusing us of stealing Fort Bridger from him," a man whispered.

Amelia spoke softly to her husband. "You never saw Fort Bridger, did you, John? We passed by it without you, 120 miles east of here."

"What does it look like?" John asked her.

"Fort Bridger is really more an Indian trading post than a fort, though it's built in the usual form, of pickets. It's ringed by cottonwood thickets on a large island formed by a tributary of the Green River. Strong timber gates around a large yard protect livestock from Indian attack."

Another man nodded at Amelia. "Last year, when the troubles started, Governor Young rescinded all licenses to trade with Indians inside Utah Territory. But Jim Bridger flagrantly ignored the order and sold them guns and powder and lead."

"And some Mormons were killed. When a posse was sent to arrest him, Bridger fled in the night. Then we caught him, and negotiated, and paid him $8,000 for his fort."

"But now Bridger claims that we stole it."

May 14, 1855

The jury reached a verdict of manslaughter today, the only possible verdict against the Indians who ambushed Mr. Gunnison and the seven other railroad surveyors. If we hope to survive here among the Indians, how can we convict them of murder? The Gentiles may think us weak on justice, but our fears of warfare by the Lamanites are not unreasonable. So we postpone prosecuting the culprits, then convict them of nothing worse than manslaughter.

In fairness to the Indians, recent travelers have committed many cruel, outrageous acts and enraged them to understandable vengeance. How can we expect the Lamanites to discern the difference between friendly and hostile Gentiles if we cannot? Yet every time an official dies in Utah, we stand accused of aiding and abetting his murder. The same is true for three apostates who died under unexplained circumstances last year.

Brother Brigham has again warned Mormon women not to be excessively friendly to the Gentiles who stop here on their travels. "If any wish to go to California to whore it, we will send a company of them off; that is my mind, and perhaps some few ought to go for they are indeed bad enough."

He has urged all women to use our industry and skills to produce from local sources every article of food and clothing our families need. Margaret and I are trying faithfully to comply in this enterprise.

March 12, 1856

Thank God this winter has nearly passed. It has been thoroughly severe, ruinous for our winter wheat and orchards. Horses and cattle have starved, with countless people not far behind them. After last year's drought, our own stock of food remains low, so I have rationed the family to a half-pound of breadstuffs per day. Few families are any better off, and many are faring far worse. We need a bountiful harvest to replenish our stores, and we pray that the crickets do not swarm as voraciously this year as last. On this cold afternoon, I daydream of planting walnut and cherry and quince trees, if I can find any seedlings.

In his sermon on Sunday, Brother Brigham proclaimed that all whining wives are to be set free of their marriages in two weeks. But if any wives choose not to go, he will hear no more of their complaining. I have tried to take his message to heart.

April 9, 1856

Yet again, John is being called away, this time to the Salmon River Mission to the Lamanites. It is 380 miles northwest, he says, at Fort Lemhi in Idaho Territory, where he will build a gristmill and preach to the Bannocks and Shoshones. Last year, at the Salmon River Mission, two dozen Elders planted crops on irrigated land and built barns and corrals for the horses and hogs. A similar number are called this year, plus some women.

John is very eager to go. Ever since he saw the ancient stone cities of the Nephites when he marched with the Battalion, John has been convinced that the Lamanites are truly our lost relations. And some of them have the same understanding, he insists.

"Twenty-five years ago," John said, "when Apostle Parley Pratt first gave the *Book of Mormon* to the Indians in Ohio, they thanked him for 'this news concerning the book of our forefathers.'"

"But you'll be in danger!" I said to John.

He quoted me a prophecy of Joseph Smith. "'Also I saw Elder Brigham Young standing in a strange land, in the far south and west, in a desert place, upon a rock in the midst of about a dozen men of color, who appeared hostile. He was preaching to them in their own tongue, and the angel of God standing above his head with a drawn sword in his hand, protecting him, but he did not see it.'"

Nonetheless, Margaret and I are worried. As the Lamanites watch our farms and towns emerge on land they consider theirs, they do not always peacefully acquiesce.

***

Great Salt Lake City
May 31, 1856

Dear Franny,

We have just now heard of the violence in Bloody Kansas, and how Missouri mobs crossed into Kansas to cast votes for proslavery men. It sounded sadly familiar to me, how the free-staters petitioned Congress for statehood only to be attacked by a posse of Missourians, who sacked their city! Then John Brown and his men hacked five proslavery settlers to death and escaped. Mr. Brown calls himself an instrument of God, and I do not doubt that he personally believes it. But our own bitter encounters have persuaded me that such belligerent acts can only raise the stakes that must, in time, be repaid in blood.

A few nights ago, John and I saw a drama of *Uncle Tom's Cabin*. As I watched the play unfold, I felt a poignant sympathy for the slaves as they fled for their freedom. But accusing us of immorality, Congress has once again rejected our petition for Utah to be admitted as a free state. As if slavery were not immeasurably more immoral.

Franny, I may as well divulge it. Four years ago, John took a second wife and we became a polygamous family. Yes, it is true! Please do not tell Father. Nothing good would come of that.

Why am I telling you now, instead of then? Because, I suppose, I have found it to be not so bad. Before, you would have offered me the pity I asked of you, and its bitter taste might have flavored my perceptions. I cannot say what polygamy is like for a man, but for a woman, it can be at once a severe trial and a blessing.

Soon after his second marriage, which I attended, John was called away to our settlement in San Bernardino, California. Having traveled near there with the Mormon Battalion, he was eager for all of us to go, but he was ordered there alone. The night he left, I wept, recalling that lonely year I spent on the trail without John. And I had seen the gleam put in his eye by his new marriage, and I feared losing John altogether. I was desperately afraid that Father might be right about the wellspring of my faith.

But in between sobs, I heard my rival for John's favor in the upstairs room, weeping too. Then I realized her situation is far more desperate than my own. I could retreat to you and Father, who would embrace me as his beloved, prodigal daughter. But Margaret has no home beside mine, and allowing her to feel unwelcome in it is indecent.

So I went upstairs to Margaret, knocked softly on her door, then comforted her as best I could. When I asked, she told me her history.

Margaret's mother died when she was four, and her father, unable to care for five children, parceled them out to different families until he could afford to reunite them. Alas, he never could afford it. So she lived for 12 years with a miserly foster family who permitted her no education and valued her only as a household drudge. Margaret eavesdropped on the other children's lessons, and she secretly read the Bible and the children's adventure books. One day, at the market, she bought some fish wrapped in a copy of our *Millennial Star*. From it, she learned that Mormon missionaries were coming to her Lancashire town, near Liverpool.

That night, Margaret slipped out of the house to hear them preach. With fresh hopes and a spirit of rebellion, she asked them to baptize her. But when the family found out, they imprisoned her in the cellar with only bread and water, demanding that Margaret recant. For many days, she defiantly refused, until they angrily ordered her out of their home. There were, after all, thousands of young servant girls who would not dare be insubordinate. Gratefully, Margaret left, then the Perpetual Emigration Fund, established for this cause, helped her to travel here. Such a grant is a loan and not a gift, and repaying it is the first lien on an immigrant's industy and income.

As I listened to her story, I was aware that Margaret and I have more in common than either one of us will ever have with the husband we share. And if our custom is truly God's will, then she and I are bound not only for time, but for Eternity. As we make the best of our curious situation, we find ourselves less alone than most frontier wives, even when their husbands are not away.

Compared to what I hope is your romantic marriage with Charles, mine must seem quite peculiar. But I can bear witness that it is no abomination. Here, most affluent men have plural wives. And John has gone to some expense to provide us an architecture of equal comforts in one home. If she were not a plural wife, Margaret would likely be a childless servant in a house such as yours, or a toilsome single wife married to an impecunious man.

Certain women, of course, find themselves unsuited to polygamy. Unhappy plural wives must find their comfort entirely from their children, and avoid thoughts of what their husbands might be doing in their absence. Such wives may be pleased to see their husbands the same as they are pleased by a visit from any friend. In the '40s, plural wives were often already married to other men, but that is no longer our practice.

Utah civil law allows for this institution by granting divorce for a wide range of causes. And the Church readily grants divorce when requested by a woman, but only with difficulty when asked for by a man. Brigham Young says that no man should ever put away a wife, except for adultery, and not even always for that. So little shame is laid on women who divorce and then remarry, that some women almost seem engaged in a sequence of polygamy themselves!

I suspect you find it hard to imagine my life, Franny, let alone understand my faith. But next to you, Margaret is the closest I have known to a sister. Our enemies accuse Mormon converts of coming from the degraded and ignorant classes of Europe, but that is rarely true, and least of all with my sister wife.

Love to you, your family, and Father,

Amelia

P.S. Mail delivery is still erratic to and from Deseret. I hope this letter reaches you more speedily than the last one I sent. And please thank Father for the books he sent the children. I wish he would enclose a word to me, but I am resigned that he will not.

\*\*\*

Joshua rushed into the garden where Amelia was picking autumn squash. It was late September 1856.

"Mother, the handcart expeditions are arriving!"

Amelia took Molly's hand and followed Joshua and a long train of people heading toward Emigration Canyon. Ann quickly joined them, then Margaret and her daughter followed closely behind.

Amelia heard the music of William Pitt's brass band before they reached Emigration Canyon. There, the newest immigrants, pushing and pulling their handcarts, were escorted by a long line of carriages bearing Church officials and their wives.

"They've all come from England and Europe," Margaret said, "where so many ardent hearts for Zion were born. Indeed, nearly half the population of Deseret."

"Let's go look at the handcarts, Mother," Joshua suggested.

Margaret took Molly by the hand, while Amelia walked to where Joshua stood examining the handcarts.

"What curious vehicles," Amelia said.

As wide as normal wagons, the handcarts were only about six feet long, some open and others covered. When loaded with provisions, bedding, extra clothing and a tent, they could carry 500 pounds. They were built with few or no iron fittings, many having axles that were a single hickory pole without iron skeins. Some of the wheels were hooped with thin iron tires, while some were not. Men, women and boys had pushed and pulled these carts for 1,300 miles.

"Some of the wood must've been green," Joshua said. "Look how badly it's shrunk and warped in the dryness of the plains this summer."

Amelia nodded, touching a badly cracked wagon. "How different their journey must've been from ours! All those hours we wasted chasing after straying cattle and worrying about poisonous water."

"I've heard that the handcarts traveled faster than any other party," Joshua said. "A hundred days from Iowa City, without livestock to tend. And the Indians didn't bother to attack because there was so little to steal."

158

Amelia and Joshua walked back to Margaret, who was welcoming the English immigrants.

"An immigrant can come all the way from Liverpool to Salt Lake City for only $45," Margaret said.

"That's very little," Amelia replied.

"Yes. And another handcart company should be here soon, with two more expected next month."

Amelia looked back to the carts. "Well, I hope they arrive in such good condition and spirits."


October 19, 1856

Everywhere in Deseret, the great cause of religious revival is bursting out, and I, too, feel it stirring fresh within. Last week, the Home Missionaries stopped by for their regular visit. When they asked me, "Do you enjoy the spirit of our religion?" I answered with a resounding "Yes!"

In a splendid two-day conference, we heard 21 sermons and speeches to help dispel the "evil ways, fog and darkness." We heard warnings against greed and forsaking the Sabbath, and denunciations of our brethren who sell grain to Gentile emigrants when any among us are hungry.

It is beyond dispute that we are in need of such awakening. At one meeting, Brother Brigham asked every man to stand up if he had committed adultery. All of us were astonished when so many men hesitated, then reluctantly rose to their feet. "No, I mean since you have become Mormons, come to Salt Lake," he explained. Still, the men remained standing, their faces ashamed.

Our southern settlements have been enduring floods, diseases and Indian troubles, thought to be none other than the wages of evil ways. But strong countermeasures have been taken. These settlements, they say, have sprung into revivalist camps, with whole communities on their knees praying and crying out their repentance.

We have just learned that Apostle Strang, who apostasized after Joseph's death and led some former Saints up to Wisconsin, has been murdered by a mob of Gentiles and apostates from his own group. The last we heard, Strang had been called a "third-rate infidel" for instituting bizarre ceremonies, covenants, oaths and blood rituals.

November 10, 1856

Last night, another handcart expedition straggled into Salt Lake City. But it carried tragedy, not celebration.

Delayed in Liverpool until May, this company did not reach Winter Quarters until late August. All the seasoned lumber was used up in earlier carts, so their handcarts were frail and hurriedly-built, and they wasted precious time in repairs. Then an early snowstorm caught the emigrants in the unforgiving heart of the Rocky Mountains. Pushing their carts across the snow, the 400 of them could advance just a few miles a day on frozen feet. Exhausting their food supplies, they forged ahead in misery, many dying from illness or cold.

When the Church learned of their plight, we rushed relief provisions to them, reaching them near Devil's Gate, 300 miles to the east. Quickened by the mules and nourished by the flour and meat, they were able to speed up their progress. Still, 70 people died on the trail and others struggled to get here only to die. Some survivors face cruel amputations of their toes and feet. This morning, I had to tell Molly not to stare at the injured children in the company.

President Young has rebuked the wagon masters for departing so late in the season. They could, after all, have stayed in Iowa City or Winter Quarters. But the emigrants, unaware of the severity of our winters, put their trust in a generous Providence, and the wagon masters let their faith override their judgment.

More disheartening to us is the knowledge that a final handcart company is still wandering somewhere out in the wilderness. They left Winter Quarters two weeks later and can only be suffering a horrible fate. Nearly 600 people started, and we fear we will find 150 dead.

December 29, 1856

The Home Missionaries came by our house again this afternoon. I was happy to see them, but Margaret was not, though she smiled modestly and they did not know it.

In separate rooms, the confessors asked Margaret and me a long series of questions, urging us to admit to past offenses. We knew these sins would be reported at the public congregation, as others have been all autumn. I readily answered most questions "Yes" or "No," though I admitted I had not fully taught Molly the gospel of salvation. Margaret looked flushed as she closed the door behind them when they left. If she is withholding some confession from them, she has not confided it to me.

The *Deseret News* is publishing a new series of stories about our persecutions in Missouri, Ohio and Illinois. As I read the sad histories and wept, Molly came to comfort me, so I recounted to her the extraordinary events as I remembered them. Retelling these bitter memories has aroused me from my lethargy and inflamed my passions. Nor am I alone in this. There have been frequent rebaptisms in the cold this winter.

Last month, the *Deseret News* printed a song that I have often heard sung in ward festivals.

> "Now sisters, list to what I say,
> With trial this world is rife
> You can't expect to miss them all,
> Help Husband get a Wife!
> Now this advice I freely give,
> If exalted you would be,
> Remember that your husband must
> Be blessed with more than thee."

I confess, it is only half-heartedly that I join the chorus:

> "Then, O, let us say
> God bless the wife that strives
> And helps her husband all she can
> To obtain a dozen wives."

The Church has openly warned Gentile men that by marrying Mormon women, they are inviting trouble. And they are warned that any man who corrupts and pollutes our community should only expect bloody death.

February 8, 1857

Brother Brigham preached a rousing sermon in the Tabernacle today, condemning Saints who fall into sin.

"Suppose that he is overtaken in a gross fault, that he has committed a sin that he knows will deprive him of the exaltation which he desires, and that he cannot attain to it without the shedding of his blood, and also knows that by having his blood shed he will atone for that sin and be saved and exalted with the Gods, is there a man or woman in this house but would say, 'shed my blood that I may be saved and exalted with the Gods?'"

We all said it was right and raised our hands. Brother Brigham decries that too many in the fold are willing to black the boots of the Devil.

April 14, 1857

A year has now elapsed since John left for Idaho Territory, to reside among the Bannocks and Shoshones. The news we hear is favorable, that the Salmon River Mission is thriving.

Relations with the Indians are improving in our southern settlements, too. We now believe they would ally with us in any conflict, a fact I find immensely comforting. It has indeed proved wiser to feed and trade with the Lamanites than to fight them. Still, Indians are reputed to have murdered a Gentile man married to a Mormon woman. I suppose we will never know for certain, nor about the murders of two former neighbors, the Parrish brothers, and a man named Potter. They were apostates, so I expect there will be scant investigation.

Our religious revival has lost no momentum with the coming of spring. Today we heard more preaching against licentiousness and theft, blackguardism, lying, swindling, cheating, hypocrisy, and lukewarmness in religion. When the Home Missionaries come to our door, asking about adultery, drinking and tithing, I feel I should confess my suspicions that

Margaret is not being fully honest. I have not done so because her actions are entirely above reproach.

This week, I planted six more peach trees, some of the 5,000 that Heber Kimball is offering for sale at low prices. I also bought currant bushes and apricot trees. As it is said, "The individuals who believed that it was not possible to raise fruit here have no currant bushes, no apple trees, no peach trees, no plum trees."

While fruit grows in lush abundance, we are having no success with sugar beets. It seems our soil is too alkaline to make them sweet. Sugar is nearly impossible to find, since it costs so much to transport here. But mail from the East has speeded up since delivery was taken over by President Young. A beautiful letter from Franny arrived here in just 30 days.

April 20, 1857

With great anticipation, Margaret and I awaited John's return home from his mission. We thought we would rejoice, and naturally we do, that our husband has arrived safely. But John has brought with him a young Shoshone girl, who is called Fawn, whom he proposes to marry!

Margaret and I sat side-by-side, listening numbly while John explained how it came about. Many Lamanites, he told us, are baptized without understanding much of our doctrine. But Fawn is altogether different, he believes. She was sick and he healed her with prayer and consecrated oil, then he explained the gospels, then she asked him to baptize her in a nearby stream.

Margaret and I looked at one another. I forced down a sigh and asked John to bring her by in the morning so we could meet her. Knowing we would consent to the marriage, he agreed.

It is part of the times, I am afraid. Last week, I watched the men's eager eyes as they listened to Apostle Heber Kimball preach a sermon. Most men of age 60 will wither and dry up, Brother Heber said, while a man with plural wives looks fresh and spritely. God loves that man who has many wives to help him carry his burdens, Brother Heber claims. Of all men, he should know. In all Mormondom, he remains the most married and divorced man, whose wives I lost count of when they summed to 45. I pray that John does not aspire to that!

Our religious re-awakening has led to an epidemic of marrying. I am grateful that Ann is still too young, though girls years below her age of 15 are being sought after as wives. I consider this practice barbaric, even though girls that young are supposed to be left intact until they are mature. But who will know when a man takes his conjugal rights with his young bride? If Ann's father is approached by some Mormon who feels he must marry, I pray that John will defer to me in this, if nothing else.

I comfort myself with the thought that my husband does not possess so many wives. Today I walked through the Salt Lake City streets, amusing myself by counting plural wives. A pretty house on the east side was occupied by the late J.M. Grant and his five wives. On the corner, a barracks-like house is the dwelling of Ezra Benson and his four wives. A large, unattractive house on the west side is the residence of Parley Pratt and eleven wives. Half-hidden in a beautiful orchard and garden is a long ill-kept row of single rooms, home to Dr. Richards and his eleven wives. Wilford Woodruff and five wives live in a large house farther west. Orson Pratt and four or five wives, I have lost count how many, occupy an adjacent home. To the north, an entire block is covered with the houses and barns, gardens and orchards that are the home of Heber Kimball and eighteen or twenty of his wives.

May 25, 1857

Tragic news reached us today. A few days ago, in Arkansas, our poet and Apostle, Parley Pratt, was savagely murdered. He was not only a missionary and theologian, but a man who influenced our destiny by introducing Sidney Rigdon to Joseph Smith.

Brother Parley, it seems, had converted a woman, the wife of an official in San Francisco. Then he married her as his twelfth wife. But her previous husband tracked them down while Brother Parley was escorting her and her children to New

Orleans. Not content to shoot him six times, the assassin mortally stabbed our poet and left him to die. This faithful wife will join us soon in Deseret.

In Deseret each year, more and more Gentile merchants are establishing shops. Despite Indian attacks on wagon trains, these enterprises are prospering due to high prices on goods freighted 1,000 miles. Though he does not forbid it like mining, Brother Brigham does not encourage us in mercantile trade. And our own merchants are disadvantaged when people ask for credit, though we would not expect it from the Gentiles. I hope these new merchants will give us favorable reports to the world outside the Great Basin.

\*\*\*

Amelia looked up and to the east from where she sat in the wagon. She saw the Stars and Stripes flying high from two of the tallest Wasatch Mountain peaks. A band was playing and the Nauvoo Legion paraded in uniform.

Amelia was glad to have arrived in Big Cottonwood Canyon. She and John, Joshua, Ann and Molly, Margaret and Fawn and their children had ridden two days and 25 miles in the wagon.

"It's such a beautiful spot," Margaret said.

Joshua was driving the wagon. "Look how many people have come all this way. There must be two or three thousand."

"We have much to celebrate," John said. "Precisely ten years ago today, the Pioneers first entered the Great Salt Lake Valley."

Another group of musicians took the bandstand, then there were speeches. Amelia listened, looking forward to the dancing in the evening.

Suddenly, in the midst of the festivities, four men raced up on horseback. Breathlessly, one of them spoke.

"A new Governor...escorted by a large force of regular Army..has left Fort Leavenworth, Kansas. He has orders...to enforce Gentile rule in Deseret."

"We've ridden 20 days..." another said. "From the Missouri River...1,000 miles."

"Thousands of soldiers...here in Deseret...by September."

The riders sped away to meet with Brigham Young and other leaders. Bewildered, Amelia and John looked at one another.

"How can this be, after a decade of peace and hard labor?" John asked.

"Thousands of soldiers don't scare me," Joshua scoffed. "We'll be ready for them by September."

John looked at Margaret, then at Fawn, his wives who would be judged concubines in the States.

"We've built a hundred towns in Deseret," Margaret said.

Molly took Amelia's cold hand.

"Our trees bear fruit in such abundance," Fawn said. "We have to thin out the ripening plums and peaches, or the tree limbs break from the weight."

Amelia shuddered, able to think of nothing but the military force marching toward them. They had built, then fled Zion, Far West and Nauvoo. But it had always been mobs, not the United States Army, that forced them out. How could it be that Utah was next?

September 25, 1857

John has confided to me a rumor so horrid that I cannot bring myself to imagine it is true. Two weeks ago, at a place called Mountain Meadows, far to the south, an entire wagon train of 120 emigrants from Arkansas were massacred, men, women and children, with just a few babies surviving. Of course, John was not there, but other Mormons were, and some witnesses say our men were responsible. That idea is so senseless that it can only be slander propounded by the most malevolent of our enemies. Hundreds of emigrant wagon trains have passed through Deseret without incident! No one has divulged how it happened, only that the Indians are to blame.

\*\*\*

Dear Franny,

After those few precious months of faster mail delivery, we are now informed why our contract for the mails was summarily cancelled this summer. A disgruntled Gentile, whose mail contract we underbid, wrote a libelous letter to the United States President.

This man claims that Mormons are "in an uncontrolled state of lawlessness, in which murder, rapine and terrorism flourished and which had been superimposed upon a helpless society by a vicious, despotic, self-constituted theocracy at the head of which was Brigham Young." He urges that "speedy and powerful preventatives" be applied.

It is surely disappointing to lose a contract, but was his malicious letter the driving force behind this mindless military invasion? He contends that our tardiness in starting mail delivery breached the contract, but the contract itself was held up at Devil's Gate all winter by this same rival!

We need services that only the Federal Government can provide us, such as legal titles to our land and disposal of Indian rights. These are not merely legalistic niceties, as your lawyer husband surely knows. Lacking deeds, we might all be evicted as squatters. But the Federal Government, either in retribution for imagined past insults, or to simply rid itself of feeble and venal yet influential men, has foisted upon us judges who detest us. Inept officials are swept in our direction to pay political debts, or so they can escape honest business debts at home.

Let me give you two examples, Judges Drummond and Stiles, both of the Utah Supreme Court. Judge Drummond is a known Washington libertine who deserted his wife and children and instead came to Utah with a prostitute, who flagrantly sits with him at court! Drummond stood accused of perjury, assault and fraud before he came here. Judge Stiles is no better, an apostate and excommunicated Mormon.

True, some of us may have acted with excessive zealotry. Last year, a group of our lawyers found it necessary to seize Stiles' records for safekeeping, and in their haste, they seem to have set afire some of his law books and papers in a backyard privy! But these Judges have outraged our community by their behavior, and far worse, their court decisions. Yes, we have some Gentiles here, and in disputes with us, they do confront all-Mormon juries. But since Gentile judges are imposed upon Utah, our sermons on the duties of jurors merely balance the powers against us. For this reason, our legislature has granted jurisdiction to probate courts with Mormon judges, who apply the common law as they see it.

In the meantime, our enemies outdo themselves in thinking up absurd new accusations. We stand accused of enticing Indians into our Church so we can rouse them to attack the Gentiles. We are said to seek an empire on the Overland Trail to monopolize transportation east and west. It is alleged that proper actions of the courts are nullified by dictate of the Church. And that our population is perilously swollen with immigrants, whom we illegally naturalize. That our empire secretly plans to secede and create a Mormon theocracy!

For some curious reason, the Gentile public seems eager to believe that Mormon women are held in Utah against our will. Franny, nothing could be farther from the truth. It was with my consent that John married a third wife. While I admit I do not love her as I love Margaret, if it is the way of God, then I rejoice in it. Margaret, Fawn and I have turned the making of clothing into a cooperative enterprise. Fawn spins and I loom while Margaret sews. Fawn knows much about the local plants that yield the most colorful dyes.

I hope Father is not reading those scurrilous new anti-Mormon novels. You have seen them, I suppose, like *Martyrs of the Latter Days*, *Female Life Among the Mormons*, and dozens of dreadful others. In case you have not, I will share with you a passage from a book that has somehow wormed its way into our presence.

"She was taken one night when she stepped out for water, gagged, carried a mile into the woods, stripped nude, tied to a tree, and scourged till the blood ran from her wounds to the ground, in which condition she was left till the next night."

This novel, purported written by a woman, contains *30 more* examples of Mormon females being tortured with red-hot irons, tomahawks, whips and ice. I can only wonder if such prurient lies are what is feeding this belligerence against us.

To be sure, the Federal Government must find it more agreeable to challenge us than the true burning controversy, which is slavery. We do distract men's minds away from Bloody Kansas and proper outrage over the Dred Scott decision. But when you weigh the cost of this campaign against us, you might question what your taxes are buying. Army contractors, speculators and politicians are the only beneficiaries of these wasted public funds. Surely, there is no dispute that the U.S. Constitution is silent on the number of wives a man may have, while it loudly shouts the freedom of religion.

The Army General in command against us has already earned the title "Squaw Killer" for defeating a group of Sioux and murdering a number of their women and children. Help me pray that he knows where to draw the line.

Love to Father, Charles and your children,

Amelia

***

October 3, 1857

The Army of the West seems to merit less respect than raw fear. Soldiers paid so poorly must be runaways from civilian life, John says, or depraved or incapable of useful work, or inclined to sell everything for liquor. And the 500 teamsters, not under military discipline, may be even more reckless, though more intelligent. We fear the Army's mission is to capture and execute our leaders, impose cruel oppression, and enjoy a winter warm in our Endowment House.

To a man, our officials have sworn loyalty oaths, and we have fervently petitioned to become a state. Yet here we are preparing for war. Governor Young has prohibited the Army from entering Utah, and he has placed us under martial law. All of us are making voluntary contributions of wheat and corn, livestock, hats and shoes.

In the public square, 1,400 militiaman are camped, with older and younger men like Joshua in reserve. The youngest and ablest men among the Silver Greys have been alerted to be ready. We could easily field 5,000 soldiers. When I watch the young boys marching, proud members of the Juvenile Rifles, I cannot help but think of Paul, who would now be 14 and as eager as the others to join the men.

John believes that, if it comes to war, the Indians will ally with us by the tens of thousands. But would the Lamanites obey our orders not to draw the first blood?


October 10, 1857

This morning, John and Joshua rode away among the Nauvoo Legion to reinforce our troops in the mountains. As I embraced them, I was grateful that Joshua had received his Endowments this summer, so his garments will protect him from harm.

I felt chilled on the porch as I watched them ride off. Winter, it appears, is coming early. There are already eight-foot snowdrifts on Big Mountain.

Last night, John confided to me about his raiding adventures.

"A few dozen of us attacked three Army wagon trains," he told me. "We found the supply trains undefended in advance of the main Army units, and scattered across miles along the Green River and Big Sandy. The teamsters were all civilians who showed no desire to interfere. 'We came out here to whack bulls, not to fight,' one teamster shrugged. Another driver implored, 'For God's sake don't burn the trains.' So I assured him that it was for His sake they were being burned.

"Altogether, we set 72 wagons ablaze, with about 150 tons

of food and supplies. From the smell of one, we must've burned a wagonload of winter boots. Then we drove more than 1,000 captured cattle to Salt Lake City. I was relieved not to find any more unprotected wagons to burn. We would've been morally bound to feed the soldiers all winter if we did."

John's look showed his determination. "Then we burned all the forage on the road into Echo Canyon, the shortest route to the Valley. We've built fortifications along narrow points in the ravine, where their artillery won't be effective against us. We've set up stone walls and dug trenches to protect our snipers, and we've built dams that can be opened to flood water into the pathway of the soldiers. We have balanced boulders to be hurtled down."

Then John grimly shook his head. "We're ready to resist the Army," he said. "But our fortifications are still no match for howitzers."

October 17, 1857

Margaret, Fawn, Ann and I have joined with other women to harvest crops for our neighbors who are in the mountains with the Legion. Even Molly tries to help, though she is only five. Few able-bodied men can be found in Salt Lake City, so we women cut and haul the wood and do all the outdoor work the best we can. Mercifully, the weather has favored us this year, and our crops are large. The prospects would be excellent for replenishing our depleted stores, were it not for this impending war. As I gather in the wheat, I cannot help but wonder what we will be harvesting next year.

From the pulpit, Brother Brigham assails the spouters and scribblers, the "howling editors" of the East, who foment "mobocratic tyranny" against us. "Now the faint-hearted can go in peace," he warns us, "but should that time come, they must not interfere."

As I looked around the Bowery, I saw no one who appeared to be faint-hearted. As Apostle Heber Kimball has promised, "I have enough wives to whip out the United States, for they will whip themselves: Amen."

November 16, 1857

Nature is proving to be our finest ally, our scouts report. The Army advanced within 90 miles of Salt Lake City when it suddenly became aware of its peril. Perhaps they forgot, as I never will, that the final 40 miles through the mountains are the most treacherous, even when unguarded by an enemy. By November, their livestock were starting to lack fodder, with just sagebrush and cottonwood bark. And their oxen that survived were too weak and too few to pull the supply trains into the Valley. Then our merciless temperatures fell below zero.

So the Army retreated to Fort Bridger, which our men had burned to the ground last month. We also burned Fort Supply.

Set against us is an Army of 2,500 soldiers, whose every movement is watched from the hills by militiamen like Joshua and John. We have scattered circulars among the soldiers, informing them of the harshness of the Wasatch Mountain winters and offering them inducements to come join us. And since their cattle will surely die of cold and starvation this winter, it is a kindness to encourage them to run off.

\*\*\*

Amelia rushed from the kitchen into the parlor, hoping that the sound of the opening door meant John and Joshua had come home. It was early December and the mountains were already thick with snow.

Amelia hid her disappointment when she saw Margaret speaking to a middle-aged widow with brown hair and eyes.

"Lily?" she asked in surprise. "When did you return to Salt Lake City?"

"Just yesterday," the woman said in a pleasant voice. "Brother Brigham ordered all of us back from our outpost in San Bernardino. We came at once, bringing all the weapons, ammunition and supplies we could find."

"All 2,000 of you?" Amelia asked.

"Nearly all of us," Lily said. "Some refused, like Addison

Pratt, so Louisa came without him. I didn't hesitate for an instant, though I hated to abandon my home in the warm, fertile California valley. President Young also closed our outposts in Nevada and Hawaii, and he ordered the foreign missionaries to come home."

Lily brought out a box of sweet dates from California, and Margaret arranged them on a plate.

"Thank you, Lily," Amelia said, pleased at the gift.

Margaret tasted the unfamiliar fruit, then smiled and confessed as she left the room, "Don't you wish we had some tea to go with them!"

Lily regarded her suspiciously. "Last year in California, 500 true-hearted Mormons were rebaptized," she whispered. "And those who refused were not considered members of the Church. I think it was doing great good."

"Molly, you must save some dates for Joshua and Ann."

"On our travels back to Utah," Lily said, "we rested awhile at the Mormon settlement at Las Vegas. It's mostly a fort with thick adobe walls to protect immigrants and mail from the Indians. But it would be of little use if an invasion were launched from California. Our best defense on our southwestern border is the Great Salt Desert itself."

"Molly..." Amelia warned.

"In hopes of making bullets, our missionaries in Nevada tried to mine what they thought might be lead. But the metal was too brittle for bullets. Perhaps it's silver, instead."

Amelia sighed in distraction. "We could use it," she said. "The war has halted all travel by Gentiles, and very little money is circulating. So we've reverted to barter and printing scrip on the press of the *Deseret News*."

Suddenly, the front door opened, then Joshua and John stepped inside. Molly ran to embrace her father and brother, with Amelia not far behind.

"You feel so chilled," Amelia said.

"Some men had only old bed quilts to serve as overcoats," Joshua said. "We were better provisioned than most."

John went to stand by the fire. "Except for a handful of

173

scouts, our militiamen in Echo Canyon have gone home. The Army cannot possibly mount an attack until spring."

March 21, 1858

Our fears and deprivations notwithstanding, this has been a rather pleasant social winter. At Christmastime, many dances were held, where all were invited except the disfellowshipped and excommunicated, and those who sell liquor for gain. Even friendly Gentiles were asked to join us. All our schoolhouses, it seems, have dancing classes.

The *Deseret News* printed a hymn this winter:

> "We thank thee for the deserts
> And for the canyons bold,
> For all our rocky bulwarks
> And for the piercing cold,
> And that thou doest surround us
> With heavy mantling snows,
> For these are our defenses
> Against our Christian foes."

But the first hint of spring sounds the alarm to wake us up from our peaceful hibernation. Not much longer will our severe winter protect us from the hostile Army at our gates.

Today, in special Conference, President Young announced that we will undertake yet another migration. Women and children will move south, taking stores of food, in preparation for laying waste to Salt Lake City and the other towns in the Valley. I listened without surprise, having feared this all winter, but my breath still caught in my chest as I heard the grim reality of the words. A few people warily objected, but were met with the cheerful prediction that we will live in even better homes in a dozen years.

But *where*? I wondered in weary silence. Where can we go that is any more remote than Deseret? Oregon and California are now states, equally foreclosed to a gathering such as ours. Texas, where two of our Apostles went last decade, is an unrepentant slavery state. Perhaps Canada, needing industrious settlers, might welcome us.

As we await the day of our new Exodus, disturbing reports fill the air. It is rumored that the Army is enticing the Indians with presents, and has put a bounty on Mormons. Sadly, we have reason to believe it may be true. Bannocks and Shoshones have attacked the Salmon River Mission where John was, killing two Saints and wounding five others, and stealing hundreds of oxen and cattle. Federal soldiers are just 100 miles from there, and troops were spied in the vicinity. All of a sudden, the Utes have launched raids in northern and central Utah Territory. Fawn is sick to death with worry about her family. All the Indians at Fort Lemhi have been excommunicated.

April 15, 1858

Three days ago, the man who purports to be our new Governor arrived in Salt Lake City, escorted by a small, friendly party. Mr. Cumming was ushered into town by a distinguished delegation of Saints, then greeted with a faultless reception. Governors Cumming and Young seem to have formed a rather favorable opinion of one another.

Despite signs of goodwill, plans for our Exodus continue unabated. As advised, we have boarded up our windows and piled our possessions in our wagons. The sight of it inspires an odd familiar feeling in me. This is, after all, my fifth exodus. I am grimly determined that, if the Army advances, all of our improvements must be burned. Yet again, I would follow Brigham Young away from despicable thralldom. In this, I have heard no dissenting voice.

We know from our scouts that we must be away within two months. The harsh winter and our raids against their livestock will immobilize the Army only until oxen, mules and horses can be driven from Santa Fe, the nearest point of resupply in this season. The soldiers have endured an ill-provisioned winter, thanks to us, and may be spoiling for revenge. Governor Young sent them a gift of salt, which they angrily refused as an insult, although they doubtlessly need it.

May 4, 1858

Not having driven oxen for a decade, I was pleased to still remember how to yoke them properly and drive a wagon. Ann and Molly and I, Margaret and Fawn and their children traveled 50 miles in three days, among 30,000 of us moving south in what seemed to be a never-ending line.

On a treeless expanse west of Provo, here we are living in our wagons. Others have built board or log huts, or made tents, or shelters from willow branches and twigs. There is a scarcity of forage, but abundant rain and sometimes snow. Somewhere in the eastern hills, John and Joshua are off with the Legion.

How long must we live in such squalor and frustration here in these Provo bottoms? We are told that just a handful of guards remain in Salt Lake City, ready to burn it down if the controversy is not resolved. Homes of the Gentiles are also marked for demolition, but since they have nowhere else to go, they take their meals at the Globe Saloon and sleep on its porch.

Last month, when Governor Cumming addressed us in the Tabernacle, he urged all disaffected men and women to come forward, promising safe conduct out of the Territory. He evidently thought there must be thousands. But just 160 people asked to leave, English immigrants mostly, hoping to better their circumstances elsewhere. Then Governor Cumming pledged that he had no intention of quartering the Army within our settlements. He seems to find it repugnant, being foisted on us at the points of 2,000 bayonets.

But does this reasonable gentleman truly wield much influence in Washington? It is sobering to think how few hours would be needed to leave this Territory as desolate as we found it. And if the Army is bent on extermination, then John and Joshua and other men may have to sell their lives dearly from ambush.


June 12, 1858

At long last, the Federal Government has returned to the senses it took leave of last year. We are granted a free and full pardon, although from God knows what, I am unsure. All the Army demands is a triumphal march through Salt Lake City on its way to a permanant camp some miles further. They do not seem concerned that no one will be there to watch it.

We are impatiently awaiting word that we can return to our homes in Salt Lake City. The flies and dirt are worsening with summer here, as are the shortages of water and food. Joshua has joined us and is cutting and hauling wild hay, the only employment he can find.

July 7, 1858

As our wagons traveled north on the Provo Road, we encountered a long column of soldiers marching south to their new garrison. Warily, we regarded one another in the swirling dust, as the soldiers became entangled in the miles-long line of returning Saints.

Deseret is to be occupied by 2,400 Gentile troops. Halfway between Provo and Salt Lake City, 36 miles from each, the soldiers of Camp Floyd will keep their watchful eyes ever on us. What they hope to impress upon us, I suspect, is that we are nothing more than a Territory of these United States.

***

"Have you seen this?" Margaret asked, holding up a four-page newspaper. "It's called the *Valley Tan,* and it is scurrilous. It's designed to bedevil the Church."

"As one might guess from its name," Amelia said.

Margaret glanced down at the large boldface letters on the top of the sheet. "What does the name mean?"

Amelia set down her knitting. "'Valley tan' is what we called our locally tanned leather, inferior, we all knew, to leather found in the East. Soon, that epithet was used for anything of doubtful quality manufactured in the Salt Lake Valley. In particular, some virulent and abominable local whiskey."

"Then this libelous newspaper is honestly named," Margaret said. "Look at this! It accuses Mormons of trying to pack juries

177

and refusing to testify against one another in court."

"Would you expect anything else?" Amelia sighed. "How can they otherwise justify imposing *3,000* soldiers upon us?"

"It isn't all bad, Amelia. Our carpenters and masons are paid well to build Camp Floyd, and the Army pays us cash for food and timber. And they bring supplies of things we can't make for ourselves, like sugar."

"But what about that new settlement Camp Floyd has spawned across the creek? Frogtown, I've heard it called. It's said to be teeming with gamblers, prostitutes and saloons to serve the drunken soldiers."

"Not all the soldiers are drunken, Amelia. Discipline is generally good, and Governor and Mrs. Cumming seem personally rather agreeable when they accept our social invitations. The Walker Brothers are opening a branch of their store at Camp Floyd."

Amelia looked up at her sister wife. "But it's the largest military force *ever* concentrated in our nation in times of peace. To defend the country against *us*!"

Margaret handed the newspaper to Amelia. "Well," she said, "I hope and trust the *Valley Tan* will meet the speedy demise it deserves."

As Amelia glanced at the hostile headlines, a new thought came to her. "Perhaps, if we entertain the soldiers in our homes, some of them will be persuaded to join us."

\*\*\*

Salt Lake City
November 12, 1859

Dear Franny,

I was delighted to find your letter on the Overland Mail, which we are now receiving weekly. But the news you relate is so alarming! From Gettysburg, Harpers Ferry is only 50 miles, and by railroad, it must be just a few hours.

178

Surely, a man like John Brown would be tempted by Harpers Ferry, an arsenal town on Southern soil. And only three years after he and his zealots massacred five men in Kansas over slavery! But Harpers Ferry as a base for a slave insurrection? He must have known that Federal troops would immediately retake the town. It was suicide surely, or martyrdom, especially for the Negroes who fought alongside the whites and now must be made into examples for their fellows. They will, I expect, all be hanged.

In your letter, Franny, you asked to know our stance on slavery. I will give you President Young's opinion, not my own. "We consider it of divine institution, and not to be abolished until the curse pronounced on Ham shall have been removed from his descendants."

As you know from the Bible, Noah's son Ham saw his father's drunken nakedness and was cursed, "a slave of slaves shall he be to his brothers."

For this reason, our theology holds that Negroes, even if free, are not the equals of white men in this lifetime or Eternity. If brought by their owners, slaves may be held here in Utah, and President Young does not favor their escape. But Utah will become a free state--when our petitions for statehood are no longer denied--since it is unadaptable to slave labor. Slavery is useless and unprofitable, and slaves are a curse to their masters. There are few Negroes here, slave or free, and we send no missionaries to Africa.

The Lamanites are different, however. President Young has always urged us to treat Indians with absolute justice, and teach them farming, smithing and domestic arts. John was a missionary to the Indians in Idaho Territory, and Fawn, his third wife, is a Lamanite girl. Please do not reveal this to Father! Naturally, their twins are half-breeds, though fully Latter-day Saints. Fawn is little older than my son. When John asked for my consent, I could only sigh and remember myself as a girl, entranced by the passionate words of a handsome man from faraway.

By the way, I am pregnant again. I confess it gives me

pleasure to prove to all who may be wondering that, even with his two younger wives, my husband still finds me desirable.

With constant thoughts and love,

Amelia

\*\*\*

March 9, 1860

Fawn is a blessing to me, I admit, in helping me care for the new baby. She knows much about wild medicinal herbs, and can quiet a colicky infant. Her children, and John's, are so placid.

Yesterday, as she nursed her newborn son and mine slept, I asked Fawn a question I had long suppressed, fearing to offend her.

"Why did the Indians attack the mission at Fort Lemhi?"

Fawn offered the boy her other breast, then she answered me with her story.

"I was only 15 when the missionaries came, bringing seeds and tools, and instructing the people how to grow crops and raise cattle. I went to their settlement only because I liked the dried fruit they gave the children. Mormon women were called as missionaries, too, and I would play with their daughters. Some among us were willing to husk corn, chop wood and do chores, as I did, but others just waited to receive food. A few joined the Church and were baptized in the stream, but many more just wintered at Fort Lemhi.

"The spring before John came, Brother Brigham traveled to the mission. He spoke before 500 of us, and he counseled the missionary men to form strong bonds of matrimony with the Lamanites. But I was just a young girl and not interested in marrying or converting.

"Our own Shoshone leaders spoke to us, too, like Chief Washakie, a fine orator. 'This country was once covered with buffalo, elk, deer and antelope,' Washakie told us, 'and we had plenty to eat, and also robes for bedding and to make lodges.

But now, since the white man has made a road across our land, and has killed off our game, we are hungry. The time was when our Father who lives above the clouds loved our fathers who lived long ago, and He talked with our fathers. But after a while our people would not hear Him, and they quarreled and fought and stole, and He turned his back to us. But after a while the Great Father will quit being mad, and will turn His face toward us.'

"When John arrived, he did not speak Shoshone well, but he knew how to make people understand him. He climbed up to a plateau and gathered some pieces of slate, then put them together like a stone box. He set the *Book of Mormon* into the box and placed it inside a hill of sand. John did not know the word for gold, but I helped him, because I understood what he was trying to tell us. And I knew that what he said was true, for the traditions of our old men, who never told a lie, agree with this story. Our forefathers talked with God, and they wrote. And when they became wicked and went to war, they hid their records, and we did not know where they went. But *this* was the record, John explained, revealed to the Prophet Joseph by an angel."

Fawn looked up at me as if I was truly a sister wife. "Tears came to my eyes while he spoke. The Mormons say God talks to men, while the Americans say He does not. I whispered to my father, and he brought me up to John and asked if he would like to marry me."

I did not know what to say, for I knew beyond doubt that Fawn's story was more true than what John had said, about healing her with consecrated oil.

"But why did they attack the mission?" I asked again.

"My brothers were very angry," Fawn replied, "because Mormons claimed their sisters as wives, but wouldn't let their women marry Indians. Then, after the hunts failed and they lost their freedom to roam, the Lamanite men felt like squaws."

\*\*\*

Dear Franny,

Imagine my amazement when your letter arrived here in just twelve days! I wish I could reply as rapidly, but at $5 per sheet, the Pony Express is far too costly for us.

I know you must be proud of Charles, now commissioned as a Major in the Union Cavalry. Every day, I pray for Charles, and for the early surrender of the Rebels. I know you must be desperate about this War.

Joshua, now 20, asked his father and me, and the Bishop, for permission to enlist in the Union Army. John and I reluctantly agreed, but the Bishop sought counsel for several days, then sent Joshua on a mission to England. We gave a fine dance in his honor before he headed off to Liverpool last week. It is a solemn enterprise to go abroad in the world without money or scrip, bearing only the gospel and faith.

By the way, Joshua is quite unlike the Mormon children described in that article you sent from *DeBow's Review*. In fact, nowhere in Deseret have I seen children like it depicts as the offspring of the Mormon system of marriage: "Physical and mental defectives with yellow, sunken, cadaverous visages; greenish colored eyes; thick, protuberant lips; low foreheads and lank, angular bodies." Indeed! Joshua, Ann, Molly, and your new nephew Harold are all well-proportioned and handsome. Please reassure Father for me.

You will be pleased to know, I am sure, that Utah has rejected an invitation from the Confederate States of America to join them as a State on our own terms. Does it not seem ironic that polygamy, our own peculiar institution, has exempted us from fighting this war over theirs?

I expect you do not know that Joseph Smith prophesized this War. Nearly 30 years ago, he foresaw that the millennial war will begin with a rebellion in South Carolina. In the ensuing war, he wrote, the Southern States will call for aid from Great Britain, and war will be spread to all the nations. "Wherefore, stand ye in holy places, and be not moved, until the day of the Lord come; for behold, it cometh quickly, saith the Lord."

Could it be, Franny, that we are witnessing the beginning of the Final Days?

I confess to being skeptical, for it is difficult to believe that dire prophecy from here. While we sit out the War, life in Utah feels quite normal. The telegraph line to the East will be finished this fall, and we are building a new theater in Salt Lake City. The theater will be the largest west of Chicago, they say, with opulence unsurpassed in New York and Paris. We have recently had a famous visitor, the explorer Captain Richard Burton of England. After traveling widely in Asia, he seems to have been curious to compare the harems of the sultans with our own plural marriages. He actually asked to be baptized as a Saint, so he could witness for himself our Endowment House rites! Well, President Young refused, suspecting that Captain Burton has greater passion for prurience than for the Lord. The explorer's ardor also dampened when Brother Brigham informed him about the duty to tithe.

Even though we are far from likely combat, we are not fully detached from War endeavors. Utah is a vital link in a secure supply line from the West, whose ports are harder to blockade than eastern ports. And our pro-Union sentiments should discourage any Rebels who may want to cross our Territory to attack California. Farms in Utah are supplying provisions to the Union Army. This letter, for instance, will travel east with a Church train comprised of 200 wagons, bringing 72 tons of flour. If all goes as planned, the wagons will return west this fall, carrying immigrant Saints. We now have 40,000 residents, a third of them foreign-born.

It is not that Deseret has no troubles. An apostasy is emerging in an isolated canyon, led by a British convert, Joseph Morris, who claims to be receiving revelations. We hope this heresy will be speedily resolved.

Your letters, Franny, are a source of much delight and comfort. I hope mine are such to you in these troubled times, and that the War does not hinder them much. I still mourn about your letter that never did reach me last year. I suspect it was on the St. Joseph & Great Salt Lake mail coach that was robbed by Shoshones and its drivers killed.

Love and prayers to you and Charles, Father, and your children,

Amelia

\*\*\*

January 12, 1862

Quietly, John approached me yesterday. "How would you feel if I were to take another wife?" he asked.

"Who is it?" I sighed.

"An Englishwoman named Emmeline, who arrived as a girl with the fourth handcart emigration. Her family was quite poor. After their first few weeks of travel, she had only little cakes of flour and water to eat. Emmeline had only summer clothes to wear and no shelter from the snow and sleet. As they crossed the mountains, her feet froze so badly that all of her toenails fell out."

Suddenly, I felt very weary.

"But she isn't one of the crippled," John added.

I met Emmeline today, and she is 19 and very beautiful. This year, I will be 41.

Our third Governor, who repeatedly castigated us for insufficient loyalty to the Union, has resigned from his post. Before he could leave Utah, he was beaten by a gang of ruffians, who surely could not have been Mormons.

March 7, 1862

With high spirits, we dedicated our new theater last night, and it is splendid! The proscenium arch is 60 feet deep, and the galleries seat 2,500 people in comfort. Above the stage are gilt and painted decorations, and others grace the cornices and mouldings over the elaborate boxes. The central chandelier is richly carved with vines, leaves and tendrils, all gilted and suspended by a massive gilted chain. All of it was fabricated here in Salt Lake City.

When the opening ceremonies began, Brother Brigham explained his philosophy about it. Some people think of theater as the pit of Satan, he told us, but only the frailties of men can make it so. We can keep it as pure as a tabernacle. Thus, he believes it fully honorable for women to act in the theater. But not every sort of drama will be produced. Brother Brigham does not favor tragedy, nor sentimental romances about monogamy.

Liquor, tobacco, firearms and infant children are banned from the theater, but for the price of admission, home manufactures are accepted, also grain or livestock, delivered to the box office.

\*\*\*

Amelia stepped down from the buggy on a summer afternoon in 1862. She hitched the horse's reins to a post outside the office of the Overland Mail.

The proprietor stood in the street, looking east, his hand held above his eyes. A crowd of other people stood nearby.

"What is all the commotion?" Amelia asked him.

"The Morrisites," he replied. "They're marching the survivors here to Salt Lake City to stand trial."

"The survivors?" Amelia asked. "There were 500 apostates among them."

"My brother Luke was one of them," the man said. "Yesterday, it all ended in bloodshed."

"Is there news of your brother?"

"No," he sighed. "For years, Luke begged me to come along with him, to their settlement at Kingston Fort, up near the mouth of Weber Canyon. He said they always kept the fort very clean because they expected Christ daily. Still, fearing trouble, they fortified the walls six feet high and 18 inches thick. I was tempted to join them."

Amelia stared at him in disbelief. "But why?"

The proprietor answered in a whisper. "Joseph Morris had

300 revelations! He believed that our 1856 revival could begin the great cleansing before the dawning of the millennial day. He saw the destruction of the wicked, the imminent appearance of Christ, and the wrongfulness of the disparity between the city rich and rural poor."

Amelia strained to see what was happening down the street.

"Morris taught that polygamy was sinful, and that Brigham Young had lost the spirit and authority of the priesthood. Naturally, the Church refused to acknowledge him as a prophet. Still, Morris had his revelations transcribed, then translated into Danish. The Bishop of his ward became his convert, and 500 former Saints."

"What led to the bloodshed?" Amelia asked.

The proprietor watched as the survivors marched into view.

"Three dissident members tried to leave Kingston Fort without settling some claims against them. They were detained, then word leaked out that they were being held prisoner in the stronghold. A Mormon judge issued a writ for their release, but the Morrisites wouldn't comply. So 250 militia troops rode out to arrest Morris for holding the dissidents against their will. Morris, a zealot, would not surrender. The militia opened fire with cannon, then laid siege to the fortress for three days, then attacked again. Luke!"

A bandaged man, bloodsoaked and limping, looked up and waved grimly to his brother. He turned and faced forward again, marching with determination.

The proprietor smiled, despite the events. "In the fighting, ten or more people were killed, including Morris, two other ringleaders, six women and one militiaman. The survivors quickly surrendered, and most of them have been pardoned. But Luke seems to be among the hundred indicted for resisting arrest and murdering the militiaman."

Amelia watched the faces of the survivors. "The Morrisites are our largest apostasy in Utah. I fear they won't be our last."

After the men marched away, the proprietor turned back toward Amelia. "I'm sorry, Mrs. Carter. Did you have business with the Overland Mail?"

Amelia returned to her purpose. "I hear that your men recovered 36 sacks of mail at one station. And at others, they found ransacked mail pouches, their contents scattered. Is it possible you have a letter for me?"

Amelia followed the proprietor into the office.

"Our operations have suffered heavily from Indian attacks in recent months," he explained. "Envelopes that once held money were ripped open."

The man searched among the torn papers as he spoke. "Camp Floyd, abandoned when the War began, will soon reopen as a post for troops defending the Overland Mail. Naturally, it will have a new name, since Mr. Floyd has become a Confederate General. And President Lincoln has telegraphed President Young to ask that he muster into service a unit of volunteer cavalry to protect the mail and telegraph lines to the East. Ah, here's a letter. 'Mrs. John (Amelia) Carter.'"

Amelia quickly opened the long-delayed letter from Franny. All was well, she reported, at least all was well three months earlier.

\*\*\*

Salt Lake City
July 6, 1863

Dear Franny,

The telegraph has just conveyed the grand news about the two resounding victories at Gettysburg and Vicksburg! Our hopes are lifted high for a speedy deliverance from this War. After such disastrous defeats, the South must surely realize it cannot win, and that further bloodshed is abominable sacrilege. Has thirty months of war not been bloodbath enough?

Gettysburg, of all places! I cannot imagine what carnage you must have witnessed out your window, Sister. I pray the news we hear is true, that few bullets strayed to wound women and children, and that the Rebel troops behaved like gentlemen.

We grew up so close to Virginia that I cannot fully think of Southerners as enemies. I know many must feel as I do.

How hard it is to envision men charging through those familiar wooded hills, seeking cover in the rocks that you and I imagined were castles when we played there as girls. The wounded men clutching their arms and legs, bleeding from the bullets, while grape-shot and shrapnel flew across those fields and grassy meadows of our youth! How much rain will it take for the blood to be cleansed from that land?

The battle was almost lost, they say, and if it were, our father's house would be in the hands of the enemy. But if I know you and Father, the house is now a hospital, and you a nurse. They say that Vicksburg, Mississippi, surrendered to the Union after a horrible long siege, then short battle. All the while, here in Utah, we celebrated July Fourth with picnic suppers. You may be nearer than I am to believing the Final Days are at hand.

I pray that Charles is well and safe, wherever his Army duties have taken him, and that you are not too forlorn without him. Strange as it may sound, I would miss the companionship of my sister wives if John were away and I had none. I do not envy your witnessing the bloody combat, but my heart aches from wanting to be with you.

Since autumn we have had a new military post called Fort Douglas, situated in the foothills above us, three miles away. It is a commanding location, and the tensions it brings can be illustrated by a single example. To celebrate Colonel Conner's promotion to Brigadier General, earned by victory in their sole important battle with some Indians, the Army fired an early morning cannon salute at Fort Douglas. Instantly, an alarm was sounded throughout Salt Lake City, and a thousand Mormon militiamen assembled to defend President Young. Whatever the Army is doing in Utah, the soldiers are enjoying gentler duty than you and Charles.

With constant thoughts and prayers,

Amelia

188

P.S. There is talk that Nevada, severed off from Deseret, may soon be admitted as a state, despite a population one-sixth of ours. Though statehood would require us to send soldiers, that is a price we are willing to pay. Our newest plea for statehood is now rejected, though we insist, "We show our loyalty by trying to get in while others are trying to get out."

***

September 24, 1863

Ann, no longer young at age 22, has at last become engaged to Frederick Gray. He has long monopolized her time at all the dances, but Frederick is not wealthy, or they would have married years ago. But now the War has brought his farm enough prosperity that he can marry. When Freddy came by today, his whole bearing seemed lighter and he did not stop smiling for an instant. At long last he is sure that no graybeard polygamist is able to steal Ann away. Before leaving on his mission, Joshua likewise grumbled that all the young girls are quickly claimed as wives by older men. Freddy, of course, is not a polygamist, at least not yet.

In recent days, Deseret has been visited by missionaries from the Reorganized Church of Jesus Christ of Latter-Day Saints. Its leader is Joseph Smith III, the now grown-up son of our Prophet. The Josephites, as we call them, contend that he and not Brigham Young is the legitimate successor to the Presidency. The logic of this argument escapes me, since America has no hereditary monarchy. And they disavow polygamy, insisting that Joseph never practiced it. I wish I could believe that were true, but I have known too many women eager to swear solemn oaths that they are Joseph Smith's wives for Eternity. Despite these differences, the Josephites agree with us on most matters.

Margaret has told me a curious story about a small trade war going on. Her friends, the Walker Brothers, are four English converts who have prospered as merchants in recent years.

When the Army abandoned Camp Floyd, the Walkers shrewdly bought up a large share of the $4 million worth of surplus goods the Army auctioned off, paying about 3 cents on the dollar. Reselling these goods at reasonable prices, the Walker Brothers' profits have been extraordinary. Soldiers at Fort Douglas are particularly good customers, since they spend more freely than frugal Saints.

Now the Walker Brothers are refusing to pay their tithing to the Church. It is not miserliness, Margaret insists, since they are entirely willing to pay their 10 percent directly to the poor. They simply disagree with the authorities. So President Young has excommunicated them and ordered us to stay out of their stores. Their trade has surely plummeted as nearly all of us have obeyed.

But immediately after their excommunication, Margaret says, the Walker Brothers gave $1,000 cash to the Perpetual Emigration Fund to bring poor Saints across from England!

And they were not the only merchants to take advantage of low prices when Camp Floyd closed. President Young bought Army pork at a penny per pound, paying for it with $30,000 borrowed from Ransohoff & Co., a Jewish Gentile firm. All large payments in Deseret are made with our $5 pieces, minted by the Church and containing $4.30 worth of gold.

July 13, 1864

Lacking any combat duties, the soldiers in our garrisons are busily prospecting for gold. They are exploring the Big and Little Cottonwood Canyons, and in Bingham Canyon they have used blasting powder to tunnel open a mine.

But greed is merely the first of their motivating passions. General Conner has long cherished a scheme of diluting our majority through Gentile immigration, and gold is doubtlessly the quickest way to accomplish it. The soldiers have no intention of keeping to themselves the secrets of our mineral wealth. Still, we trust that our isolation, the steep cost of transport, and high prices for our labor and necessities, will frustrate his ambition for at least awhile. As Brother Brigham tells us, "Prosperity and riches blunt the feelings of man."

Molly and I have been gathering up rags to be milled into paper for the *Deseret News*. They say the War has finally made cotton growing profitable in southern Utah.

April 8, 1865

How can I feel other than self-indulgent, enjoying the theater with my husband in a safe and peaceful Territory, while this War between the States is still raging? Naturally, our programs begin with prayers for peace, but afterwards, all is entertainment. Tonight we saw *Camille* with Julia Dean Hayne.

I felt the same uneasy pleasure last week, when John and I attended a dance at the Salt Lake City Social Hall. Margaret and Fawn chose to stay home with the children, but Emmeline asked to come with us. I was displeased, but John was not. "It costs $5 for a man, and $5 for his first wife," he told us. "But only $2 for each additional wife." The dance pavilion was lovely. The orchestra performed beneath a bust of Shakespeare at the opposite end of the hall from where evergreens are woven to spell "Our Mountain Home."

Brigham Young, escorting several wives, is still sprightly at age 64. His dancing is more vigorous than graceful, as he has always promoted dancing as exercise for the body so the mind can rest. Far more singing and dancing occur in Heaven than in Hell, he insists, so why should we mimic the hot place? But polkas and waltzes are banned as indecent, while he favors cotillions and reels. John's favorite dance is the Mormon Quadrille, where each man leads out two partners. All around the floor, hands were clapping and feet were tapping.

Although the evening was delightful, I felt troubled watching John speaking softly to the silly young girls. I do not enjoy wondering if he intends to marry again.

April 10, 1865

Thank God, the War is over at last! There is rejoicing in the streets.

April 15, 1865

We learned the tragic news of President Lincoln's assassination within a few minutes by the telegraph. For the nation and for ourselves, I feel heartsick. Lincoln was a rare politician who never courted public favor by abusing us.

The President once likened the Latter-day Saints to the tree stumps in the fields of his farm. They were too wet to burn, too hard to split, and too heavy to move, so all he could do was plow around them. Lincoln said, "Tell Brigham Young I will let him alone."

How much more arduous will be the task of rebuilding without a man like Lincoln to lead us! Just last month, in his inaugural address, he pledged, "With malice toward none, with charity for all, with firmness in the right, as God gives us to see the right, let us strive on to finish the work we are in, to bind up the nation's wounds."

But malice is inevitable now. Here in Deseret, we know only too well the vindictive, venal and incompetent men that the Government can foist on those it rules. The South will surely reap the whirlwind that the War and their assassin have sowed.

August 14, 1865

Joshua is so much like his father. He returned from his mission to England, bringing Sally, a newly-baptized girl he plans to marry.

Sally is a pretty girl and seems pleasant. But as I watched her with my son, I realized that she made vastly different impressions on Joshua's two English "aunts." Margaret welcomed her warmly, while Emmeline appraised her critically and did not approve. I like the girl better for that.

Today, I brought Sally shopping for some things she will need as a wife. Until I showed her Main Street, I had taken little notice of the changes in the Salt Lake City landscape. Before the War, businesses were already crowding Main Street. The western block, opposite the hotel, was filled by some twenty small business buildings of irregular sizes and shapes. The bakery, butchery and blacksmith were there, as were hardware and crockery shops, the paint and whip warehouses, a tailor, shoe shop and tannery, the dry goods, grocery, liquor and furniture shops. There were saddlers, a watchmaker, a gunsmith, a candle and soap maker, dealers in hats and clothing, and a restaurant selling ice cream. The same goods were sold on the eastern side of Main Street, but in larger establishments. This was where the Gentile merchants lived.

But since the War began, stone business buildings have arisen. Throughout the War, business was brisk in Utah and prices high, so the profits seem to have solidified into structures. In early '64, the Mormon stores, such as the Eagle Emporium and Mr. Godbe's Exchange Building, started to rise up in stone. The Gentile stores began building soon thereafter, Walker Brothers and Ransohoff & Co. The construction of City Hall began at that time.

I imagine that Sally, anticipating a rough frontier town, was pleased to find our Main Street looking like an imposing merchant street in an English or Eastern city, or San Francisco.

***

Grimly, John entered the parlor. Amelia looked up from the book she was teaching Harold to read.

"There's new reason for alarm about the Gentiles," John said.

"What is it?" Amelia asked.

"Do you remember Dr. Robinson, the Gentile doctor who attended Brother James Brown when a camp-mate mistook him for a bear and shot him in the leg?"

"Yes, of course. He's married to the daughter of an Elder."

John sat down. "Last night at midnight, Dr. Robinson was called out on a medical emergency. A block away from his home, the doctor was attacked by a mob, beaten over the head, then killed by a bullet through his brain."

Amelia gasped and Harold looked up in concern.

"No one has been arrested yet. But this murder is suspiciously like the one last spring. Both victims had lawsuits

193

pending before our courts."

"I remember the murder," Amelia said. "But not the lawsuit."

"The victim was a newly-arrived Gentile," John said. "He persuaded a plural wife of an Elder that she wasn't legally married, and so she married him instead. Then she sued for custody of her children, fathered by the Elder, who was serving on a mission abroad. But while the suit was pending, a gunshot was fired from a dark alleyway and killed the Gentile. To this day, his assassin has not been caught."

"Dr. Robinson also had a lawsuit?" Amelia asked.

"He claimed ownership of 80 acres of land two miles north of Salt Lake City. The land includes the Warm Springs site."

"The City owns that site!" Amelia protested. "The water is sulphury, but a delightful 95 degrees."

"Dr. Robinson disputed the City's prior claim."

"But just last year," Amelia said, "the City opened the Warm Springs public bathing resort, with a bathhouse, tubs, a shower and a plunge."

John shook his head. "We've lived here 19 years and wrested all improvements from the land, but legally we're only squatters on it. Without proper titles to our land, we can't be sure that newcoming Gentiles won't contest our claims with the Federal authorities. I've heard that proper titles aren't being issued because no surveys have been completed here since '57."

Harold looked up in bewilderment at his father.

"But features of natural beauty properly belong to the community," Amelia argued.

"Dr. Robinson built a shanty on the Warm Springs land," John explained. "When the City Council ordered it destroyed, the case was tried in court. Gentile lawyers tried to fan the flames, but three days ago, the judge ruled in our favor."

"Then why was Dr. Robinson murdered?"

"One can only guess why," John replied. "And why Utah, *alone* among the Territories and States, is not covered by the homesteading laws that benefit the rest of the nation."

John picked up the six-year-old boy. "I only pray that Harold and Molly aren't tempted to marry Gentiles.  Unless, of course, they vow to join the Church."

July 5, 1867

We had a most delightful evening, the Fourth of July Ball, held at the theater last night.  I had only to share John with Emmeline.  As always, bald-headed Heber Kimball was one of the most constant dancers, and had to be, because he brought so many wives.  Our more respected Gentiles were invited to attend, but few came.

Before the dance, Fawn and I climbed the hill in back of Brigham Young's house to gather wild medicinal herbs.  From there, we looked out over the straight, wide streets, the irrigation canals running alongside them.  The canals reflected golden light from the setting sun as they watered the shady maple and cottonwood trees.  We could see the River Jordan, two miles away, and the wide basin spreading out for nearly fifty square miles before it reaches the Great Salt Lake.  The gardens around the homes are all in fruit, the summer vegetables are ripe, and the view in all directions is lovely.

It makes me heartsick that the end of the War has brought renewed violence against the Indians.  In the decade since John brought a Lamanite wife into our home, I have grown to love Fawn and admire her quiet knowledge.  Yet some people in our community whisper contempt behind her back.  Fawn pretends she does not hear them, especially their disparaging words about our husband's half-breed children.

Sad to say, most Indians who come to us do not stay long.  They listen to the stories from the *Book of Mormon*, then ask eager questions about the garments that are said to protect us from harm.  But liquor is killing the Lamanite men, who care nothing for the truth in the Word of Wisdom.  With particular exceptions such as Fawn, our efforts with them are futile or worse, for they feed a native tendency toward superstition.

October 6, 1867

After twenty years, I had given up hope that Brother

Brigham would ever reestablish the Female Relief Society, such as we enjoyed it in Nauvoo. He has always urged us to expand home manufacturing and buy local products, but we women have not been organized, and I have missed it.

But now, the Female Relief Society is to be newly reorganized! And it will be led by our poetess, Eliza Snow. She has written one of my favorite hymns of all:

> "In the heavens are parents single?
> No; the thought makes reason stare!
> Truth is reason, truth eternal,
> Tells me I've a Mother there.
> When I leave this frail existence,
> When I lay this mortal by,
> Father, Mother, may I meet you
> In your royal courts on high?"

We already have numerous ideas for reaching into every settlement, with charities, home industries, trading ventures, educational and public health programs, and prayer meetings. Through the Female Relief Society, we can enhance our self-sufficiency without abandoning proper female obedience.

Molly, who is now 15, sat beside me today in the magnificent new Tabernacle. I watched her face as she earnestly listened to Brother Brigham's pronouncement.

"I want our girls taught that they may be in all mental acquirements the equals of the women of the world whom they may meet...I want the young women to learn business. I want them to be our telegraphers and clerks. Why, go into a store now for a yard of ribbon, and a great lazy, lubberly fellow comes rolling up like a hogshead of molasses and cuts off the ribbon for you. Now that fellow we want out in the fields, up in the canyon, at work, and we want his and his fellows' places supplied by the young women."

Another new development brings a mixed blessing to our family. Sugar always being scarce in Deseret, the Church has bought a sugar cane plantation in Hawaii. We plan to ship sugar across the Pacific, then here to Utah. But John has been called to the island of Oahu to construct a sugar mill there.

December 8, 1867

The Home Missionaries, an Elder and a very young Deacon, came for their monthly visit today. Margaret, Fawn, Emmeline and I assembled in the parlor and listened to their message from the Bishop. He requested a special assessment, which I was able to pay from the household money. They seemed particularly concerned that no ill feelings exist in our house with John away. Fawn asked for instruction on some question of religion, but I listened only absently, I confess. Then Emmeline asked their counsel about the weakness of faith of her sister, who lives in a different ward. The teachers made a note of it, saying that our Bishop would inform her Bishop. Margaret mentioned that the widow behind us is sick, so they promised to send a young Deacon to chop wood for her and milk her cows.

Later, when I was with them alone, the Home Missionaries asked me about the spirit of my faith. Without hesitation, I responded as always. But when they questioned me farther, I felt compelled to confess that I do not love Emmeline. They asked why, and I said she is lazy and vain, and John indulges her. Emmeline does not always tell the truth or keep the Sabbath with good faith. She takes her advantage wherever she sees it, for herself and her children, so we other wives must keep up our guard. I sometimes suspect that her family joined the Church only so we would bring them away from that dreary mill town near Sheffield. The Perpetual Emigration Fund paid to bring Emmeline to Utah, so it seems we all must pay for the hardships she suffered on the way.

Now the missionaries will approach Emmeline and point out her failings to her. But even if they do so in a spirit of meekness and brotherly love, she will hate me all the more and not repent. Her wrongs are too trifling to warrant severe discipline, so I suppose I will be labeled a backbiter and jealous woman. I wish I had said nothing, as Margaret always does.

January 3, 1868

Today is the day of Molly's confirmation at the Endowment House. I imagine it will not be long until she goes there again to be sealed in marriage. And then again, I suppose, to witness the plural marriages of her husband.

It has been 16 years since our peculiar institution entered my life. Of my three sister wives, I love two dearly, but can abide the third only through the strong force of faith. Between us, we have borne 14 children, 12 of whom survive, and every child among them is a joy. I am more blessed than many plural wives. John has never proposed anything I find abominable, such as marrying both a mother and her daughter on the same day! And in our family, sister wives have not grown fond beyond decency, as I have heard whispered of elsewhere.

And John has not proposed to marry sisters, a common enough practice in Deseret. Heber Kimball, for one, is married to five pairs of sisters. How trying our lives would be if John were also sealed to one or more sisters of Emmeline! But how would I feel if Charles had been killed instead of wounded and Franny, miraculously converted, appeared in Salt Lake City and John suggested marrying her? I can almost see the mirth in Franny's blue eyes if she were here to join me in the whimsy of it.

Still, polygamy for my daughters? Naturally, Ann will agree as soon as her husband determines the time is ripe. But Molly, I fear, would apostasize before she would acquiesce. She complains, "The old polygamists interfere with courting by young men because they covet the young women for themselves." I can see that Molly suffers the same romantic notions that her mother entertained as a girl.

John plans to build a house for Emmeline and her children, and I am glad for it.

\*\*\*

Amelia was aware of being watched by a policeman as she entered the dry goods shop on Main Street.

198

"My husband ordered some shoes from you two months ago," she said to the proprietor. "I wondered if they've arrived."

The Jewish Gentile merchant smiled wanly. "Just yesterday, Mrs. Carter."

While the proprietor stepped into the storeroom, Amelia glanced around the well-stocked shop. Four days before Christmas, 1868, the shop was entirely deserted. Amelia resisted the impulse to look for any last presents for the children.

The merchant returned with the shoes. "Can I interest you in something else?" he asked.

Amelia shook her head.

"I know, I know," he sighed. "I'd hoped for more customers in this prosperous season. But ever since your Church bought out the businesses of six Mormons and a Jewish merchant, and combined them into ZCMI, what can I do?"

"Naturally, the Church expects us to buy exclusively from Zion's Cooperative Mercantile Institution," Amelia said.

The man showed Amelia the shoes. They had been sent from Cincinnati and were very well made.

"It's the first department store west of the Mississippi," Amelia said. "My husband is buying a number of shares of ZCMI stock."

"Who wouldn't if he could?" the man asked. "But Mr. Young will sell stock only to people whose tithing is paid. Now he tells us to take the capital from our stores and use it to build factories instead. But how can I be sure that, in time, he won't refuse to buy our products from those? Mr. Young used to say, 'To be adverse to Gentiles because they are Gentiles, or Jews because they are Jews, is in direct opposition to the genius of our religion.'"

The proprietor waved his arms around the empty shop. "Two years ago, fearing this, a dozen of us non-Mormon merchants went to Mr. Young and offered to sell him our businesses."

"What did he say?"

"He wouldn't buy them. Mr. Young used to say, 'Let the Saints spend their money with those merchants who pay their taxes and seek to build up this place and develop the country. Let our enemies alone.' Someone asked him, 'What, all the outsiders?' 'Not by any means,' Mr. Young replied. 'I trade with outsiders all the time.'"

Amelia paid the man for the shoes. "Some Gentile merchants are indeed our enemies. They conspire with anti-Mormon politicians and editors, miners and soldiers, to thwart our attempts to gain statehood."

"Have I ever been your enemy?" the merchant asked.

"Of course not," she assured him. "On the contrary. But merchants are growing rich in Utah. You can see that from the palaces they build. We've always paid high prices here, except when miners or the Army brought in goods."

"Freighting costs are very high," the merchant shrugged. "And we lose wagon trains to Indian attacks. Your apothecary, Mr. Godbe, has tried to lower those prices by taking orders, buying the goods in the East, then freighting them here at a reasonable commission. I've seen the crowds that throng around Mr. Godbe's wagons when the oxen pull them into Salt Lake City."

"I've ordered goods from Mr. Godbe, myself," Amelia said. "But ever since we arrived, I've tried to do as President Young has urged us, and manufacture as much as I possibly can at home. I've always been proud of our frugality."

"You have reason to be proud, Mrs. Carter. Didn't our last Governor boast that Utah stands alone among the Territories and States as being entirely free from indebtedness?"

Amelia leaned in closer to the merchant, although no one was present to hear her. "But my sister wife Emmeline," she whispered, "insists her dresses must be sewn of fancy imported fabrics, and John indulges her vanity. When the new railroad arrives next year, he'll find it even harder to resist her expensive whims."

"Ah," said the merchant knowingly. "Your Mr. Young fears he'll be unable to keep you from spending money on luxuries. So he hopes instead to capture the profits for your Church."

Amelia smiled weakly. She shook the Jewish merchant's

hand and wished him well for the new year.

"I can offer you a good price on shoes," he said hopefully.

Amelia shook her head. "What the Spirit of the Lord directs through our Prophet, I will try to do to the best of my ability."

But as she stepped again into the street, Amelia felt the eyes of the policeman upon her.

\*\*\*

Salt Lake City
May 10, 1869

Dear Franny,

Excitement is sweeping through every mile of Deseret! Not far from here today, the last spike in the railroad track was driven, linking the country from the Atlantic to the Pacific, and us to all.

I had hoped to give you a first-hand report of the celebrated event, but I cannot. Outraged at the drunken railroad crews and the company that owes our contractors so much money, President Young refuses to attend the festivities. Among us, only Joshua made the journey to Promontory. Indeed, he could not stay away, yearning for the adventures of traveling he enjoyed on his mission. And I confess, after constant travel in my youth and none since, I am also eager to see what lies beyond the Great Basin again.

For better or worse, the railroad will surely change our lives. That may sound curious to you, since the East has known railroads for decades. But ours is the last large community in America to be linked with either one coast or the other. Brigham Young frets aloud about keeping our society pure under an influx of Gentiles. Still, he says, "I wouldn't give much for a religion which could not withstand the coming of a railroad."

You must come visit me, now that the journey is just nine days. Twenty-two years ago, we traveled over 500 days!

You will find much to impress you here, Franny. Our

Tabernacle is a wonder of construction, oval in shape and supported by huge sandstone pillars, and able to hold 10,000 people at one time. There is even talk of granting women the right to vote in Utah. Oh, it is not that our leaders are so mindful of our opinions, but rather as a way to more than double our voting ranks. As the *Deseret News* wrote, "Our ladies can prove to the world that in a society where men are worthy of the name, women can be enfranchised without running wild or becoming unsexed." Our Church leaders trust that we women will not vote to end polygamy.

But if you come, I fear you will laugh at our Deseret Costume, designed for women by President Young himself. It is an unlovely three-piece garment with bloomer-like trousers, covered by a baggy short skirt that falls to the calves and a long loose jacket of antelope skin, worn with an eight-inch-high military hat. I predict it will not be in fashion for long. Few men throughout history have ever had as many wives and daughters to clothe as Brigham Young. In past years, he has accused us of wearing hoop skirts only because the "whores" do. As you can see, he does not mince words.

So while the blessings are not unmixed, I am immensely willing to relinquish our cherished isolation. And with us now in the midst of the nation, no longer on its farthest frontier, who can imagine what unknown visitor might appear without warning on our doorstep?

With love forever to you and Charles, Father, and your family,

Amelia

# BOOK THREE

## AN AMERICAN THEOCRACY

# Chapter 1

The graying man, well-dressed in a dark blue broadcloth suit and wearing a black broad-rimmed hat, looked disgruntled and felt close to queasy.   The railroad car he rode in was overcrowded with men, returning the 53 miles east from Promontory Summit to Ogden, Utah.  Most of them were sweaty and boisterously drunk, some still damp from the rain and the mud.  Their tobacco smoke crowded the air as the train lurched and pitched along the tracks, hastily laid down to meet the deadline.

No one noticed as the man muttered angrily to himself. "Dammit, Ted Bailey, did you think you'd escape a roily stomach and sick headache?  You had to sample all five make-shift saloons in Promontory, so you'd know which one boasted the greasiest pork and most execrable whiskey!  And with your stomach ulcer.  But that damned ceremony would inspire even a healthy man to be sick.  Truly pompous, all the while devoid of real awareness of what this momentous occasion means.  The Chinamen who laid the Central Pacific tracks seemed honorable, true, but the Union Pacific's Irishmen, almost all disgustingly drunk!  And that windbag Leland Stanford, president of the Central Pacific..."

Feeling another wave of nausea, Bailey rose unsteadily and walked to the end of the car.  He forced open the door and stepped outside, cautiously gripping the railing to keep from falling from the swaying train.  He breathed in deeply, savoring the fresh cold air mingled with the honest smell of coal fire blowing back from the engine.

Bailey frowned, anticipating the tasks that awaited him. Lawrence, his editor, expected him to write a dignified, laudatory article for the *Empire Monthly Review*.

"A landmark in American history and all that," Lawrence stressed.  "The truth is less crucial than the myths the future will know as facts."

Ted sighed, knowing Lawrence was right.  "I'll cultivate you some myths," he promised.

"Like how, in only four years, we've transformed Abe Lincoln from a man the press disrespected and constantly abused into a demigod."

Ted was more dismayed that he could not honorably forget the promise he had reluctantly made to Frances Alderson. On his way west from New York City, he had stopped in Gettysburg to visit Charles Alderson, an Army friend. When he said that Lawrence was sending him to Utah, Frances' eyes lit up with hope.

"Can I ask you an enormous favor, Ted?"

Ted had smiled. "I would be pleased to fulfill any request from a lady who always makes me feel so welcome in her home."

"Could you possibly look in on my sister? I haven't seen her in 25 years."

"But Frances," Charles said, "Salt Lake City is a two-day detour for Ted. There are no rails south of Ogden."

"The two towns seem so close on the map," Frances begged. "All I need is a candid report on how my sister is faring."

Ted swallowed hard, knowing he might have to lie. "Of course I will," he replied.

Bailey felt dismal, sure he would be wretched company when he called on the sister. "I imagine Salt Lake City is just another dusty Western town, unrefined and provincial and full of its own little self. With least delay, I must get back East!"

The habit of talking to himself arose from his profession, Bailey knew, his thoughts tried out aloud for his readers. But indulging in it, he also knew, came from his marriage.

Ted spoke with the conductor about the schedule and learned he could catch a stagecoach to Salt Lake City that night. His head pounded when he realized what that meant. To be fresh when he called on the sister in the morning, he must write the story now, on the pitching train. He inhaled one more breath of cool air, then reluctantly went back to his seat to write his story for the next issue of the *Empire Monthly Review*.

# AT LONG LAST, LINKED COAST TO COAST

by
**Edward Bailey**
May 1869

The final spike driven today into the transcontinental railroad tracks will long live as a magnificent symbol for the *United* States. Only four years after the horrible late War ended, Americans have transformed an ambitious dream into reality of steel. We accomplished it despite nearly unconquerable terrain, two exceedingly high mountain ranges and vast deserts, adverse weather, and 1,800 miles largely inhabited not by civilized men but by hostile Indians. Only recently, traversing the 3,000 miles from New York to San Francisco demanded six months of extreme and danger-laden effort. This new railroad compresses the time to one short week. We extend our utmost praise for the organization, engineering, and mobilization of resources, and the sustained human effort by the workmen to overcome all obstacles.

The significance of this achievement far transcends the ceremonies and celebrations that marked it at Promontory Summit, Utah Territory on May 10, 1869. The linking was symbolized by driving commemorative spikes into a pre-bored railroad tie of laurel wood. One spike was forged of California gold, another of Nevada silver, and a third of Arizona gold, silver and iron. Naturally, all precious metals were replaced by normal spikes before trains actually ran over the tracks. The maul to drive these spikes was made of hickory with a silver hammerhead. Most of the crowd of 500 was comprised of Chinese and Irish workers from the railroads, troops from the 21st Infantry and its regimental band, dignitaries and reporters.

Conspicuously absent were ranking dignitaries of the newly inaugurated Grant administration. The Mormons, disappointed that the route did not go through Salt Lake City, not to mention one million dollars of unpaid bills owed to them by the Union

Pacific, were represented only by a Scottish Bishop and construction supervisor, plus the Tenth Ward Band from Ogden.

At the appointed time, the dignitaries assumed their ceremonious positions. Governor Leland Stanford, president of the Central Pacific, was there, but not Crocker, its builder, or Huntington, its brain and political manipulator. General Dodge and the Casement brothers led a highly esteemed corps of field officers who performed an exceptional job as builders for the Union Pacific.

Mightily, Stanford swung the silver-headed maul. With a loud, resounding noise, he pounded the rail and missed the spike. Then Thomas Durant, vice-president of the Union Pacific, did the same.

Durant had more success in nailing down his personal ambitions while the railroad was being built. As the late War wound down, Durant and his associates acquired controlling interest of a company that became Credit Mobilier of America, the contractor for the Union Pacific.

At last, General Dodge and Samuel Montague cleanly drove the spikes home. Telegrams flew to both coasts that the deed was done, and the boisterous celebrations began.

Completing the transcontinental tracks is only the first step for the two railroads. The Union Pacific faces the greater financial challenge, already being delinquent in paying its bills. Between Federal money and the first mortgage bonds, funds should have been ample to build their tracks. But excessive fees paid at the start to Credit Mobilier might explain why they ran out of money.

Fortunately for the financially troubled Union Pacific, its surveyors discovered immense beds of coal in Wyoming. But in the near future, its operations will require a large infusion of cash. In particular, it must rework a considerable length of track, shoddily prepared in its race with the Central Pacific over where the tracks should meet. Both companies sent work crews laying track too far, trying to justify claims for more Federal money and land.

In this reporter's view, the allegations of wastefulness,

mismanagement and political corruption are troubling indeed. Nonetheless, even the severest charges of greedy practices do not diminish this extraordinary achievement. As it promises great wealth from speedy commerce with our Great Plains and Intermountain West, the railroad swells our feelings of national unity and pride.

\*\*\*

"Hail to the Highway of Nations! Utah bids you Welcome!" a banner greeted the train as it hissed and clattered into Ogden.

Bailey asked the conductor where he could find the telegraph office. He quickly walked the short distance and telegraphed the story to his editor in New York, then booked a seat on the afternoon stagecoach to Salt Lake City.

With several hours to spare, Bailey decided to walk down Main Street. Ogden was on the Overland Trail to Oregon, and also on routes to the Idaho and Montana mines, so many of the busy stores and offices resupplied and refit wagon trains. Among the bustling foot traffic were a number of fashionably dressed men, evidently from the East and California. Their clothing identified certain men as miners, teamsters or soldiers, railroad employees or construction workers, but most were Mormon residents in commonplace garb. Ted saw very few women.

Drawn by the sound of men's laughter, Ted stopped to listen to a loud conversation. The Irish brogues were familiar to him, and unmistakable. Both men were muscular, tanned and handsome, one of them still in his teens.

The younger man downed a long swallow from a bottle of whiskey, then spoke. "Didn't you hear about some local fellows who sawed ties for the last section of track before Promontory? They taught the UP bosses a fine lesson. 'Pay us cash now,' they demanded, 'or no ties.' Somehow or other, the UP scared up the money. When our pay was slow, I wish we'd thought up that same trick."

"What man isn't swindled every now and then?" the other

man said. "Even old Brigham Young, himself. He swallowed the blarney of the UP bosses and bet on the wrong horse."

"How is that, Gerry?"

"Both railroads were hoping to lay all the track they could, to get more government money and land. The CP was asking the Mormons to work for them, but the Mormons figured their freight and immigration is mostly East, so they went with the UP instead. Still the bosses worried, being in such a hurry, since the 'Saints' scrupulously keep the Sabbath. Truth be known, they finish more good work in six days than normal men do in seven. That terrain is so bloody rough through the Weber and Echo Canyons, it would've taken us a devilish lot longer to build the tracks."

The younger man passed him the whiskey bottle. "I'll bet Brigham Young was glad to be hired, and not only for the money. He's kept us ever-loving Irishmen out of reach of his 'Saints' and all their lonely wives and pretty daughters. Aren't you wondering about all those girlish wives, who want it more often than their turn?"

Both men laughed at the secret desires of the modestly dressed women who regarded them so warily in the streets.

"God knows what malarkey they've been hearing preached against you and me," the young man chuckled. "I'd sure welcome a chance to earn such a proper damnation. But I suppose there aren't many virgins here. In Utah, they say, all girls marry young. Brigham Young!"

Ted found himself smiling at the lusty humor of the Irishmen.

"Brigham Young isn't any fool," the older Irishman said. "He's a match for the UP's shenanigans. They reneged on their promise to route the tracks through Salt Lake City, after he subscribed to their bonds. So he's starting right away to build his own railroad. The UP paid part of what they owe him in rolling stock and wares to lay track from Salt Lake City to Ogden."

"He's welcome to both Mormon towns as far as I care," the young man scoffed. "When I got here in early spring, Ogden wasn't much of anything, maybe 1,500 or 2,000 people. And it's sure no fine place for any helling around. Corinne, the next stop west on the tracks, is more my liking. Have you not been there, Gerry? It's a true non-Mormon town, built by the General of the soldiers who garrisoned here during the War. Corinne is mostly built of tents, with establishments of pleasure galore, saloons and gambling houses and whorehouses. I'll bet a pretty penny of the Union Pacific payroll goes squandering away there tonight. I'm not stingy about the price for a loving woman!"

Ted listened awhile longer, then resumed walking among the wide streets. Along the streets, canals irrigated the trees, flowers and vegetable gardens that adjoined the houses. Only once before had Ted seen a town laid out with such wide streets in grid squares, with such generously-sized lots. It was Nauvoo, Illinois, in 1846.

Ted's articles for the *New York Herald* were very well-received as the only impartial eyewitness accounts. His candid and impassioned reporting advanced his career, bringing him to the attention of several wealthy New York businessmen. One of them arranged for Ted to meet his daughter, an attractive and well-educated girl of age 20. In wealth and social status in New York City, Lydia was well beyond his class.

Bailey tried to divert his mind from the bitter memories of his marriage. Unsuccessful, he was aware of talking aloud to himself. How frequently had Lydia brought that fault to his attention!

"Wouldn't Lawrence be surprised to learn the truth?" he muttered. "He sent me here out of compassion, hoping the journey would help me recover from what he thought was my despair over Lydia's death."

Ted was unable to confess that his grief was abiding remorse over his marriage. In good faith, he and Lydia were drawn to one another, and her father was pleased that Ted's family, if not wealthy, was among the first settlers in New England.

"As if family prestige ever mattered to me! But our desires were so divergent. How quickly I came to detest the bustling social life that she loved."

211

The early years of their marriage were pleasant enough, and Ted, for one, enjoyed both their daughters when they were small. At first, Lydia was charmed by his informal ways, the freedom and adventures of newspapermen and their stories. But she soon found it distasteful to be surrounded by people who possessed neither wealth nor social status. Worse, Ted wanted nothing to do with banking and insurance, the businesses that paid for her parties and clothes. The year after they were married, he realized that she expected him to go to work for her father and brothers.

Ted sighed in weary distraction. Lydia professed high moral standards, fashionable at the time, and she eloquently criticized social evils. Yet she thought it only right that she be spared the inconvenience of personally taking action to reform them. Though indignant at the gall of the Secessionists, Lydia never forgave Ted when he applied for a commission in the Cavalry the day the War began.

"It's romantic foolishness," she insisted. "You could've hired a substitute like my brothers. And you're too old."

To her friends, Lydia proudly displayed his handsome photographs in uniform, first as a major and then as a lieutenant colonel. But how deeply she resented Ted's absence from New York City, unavailable to escort her to lavish parties. Far from using the War as a personal opportunity to make money, like so many husbands of her friends, he was even in danger at times. The War took its toll, physically and emotionally, and not only on his marriage. Ted had seen too much in war to believe in a noble society or a benevolent God.

"Dammit, stop feeling sorry for yourself," he admonished aloud. "Four years of war left you nothing worse than piles, an ulcer and a few fully-healed minor wounds. You paid a far lower price than many comrades in arms, who died or were maimed like Charles."

Only one price felt truly unjust to Ted. Poisoned by four years of daily, undefended disdain for him by Lydia and her family, his daughters were now estranged from him.

That disdain was not entirely unjustified, Ted knew. His

212

present financial comfort and independence was due to their skill, not his, in investing his modest inheritance. He had in fact nearly squandered it on speculative enthusiasms, for which Lydia's family despised him as a naive fool. Far from being proud, his daughters seemed embarrassed by his articles in the *Empire Monthly Review*.

Despite everything, Ted and Lydia remained cordial in public, so their friends like Lawrence never knew. But his daughters' husbands and their families patronized him as an aging veteran unable to adapt to modern life. Ted could barely disguise his contempt for the wealth they had accumulated during the War. And the new business practices after the War presented so much temptation toward questionable ethics.

"I must get back to New York City," Ted said aloud. "So much is going on for an honest journalist to report!"

New York City was much changed since the War. Rapid population growth meant that countless unhealthy and disorderly immigrants were living in overcrowded tenements. And the politics were corrupted with graft. But New York had grown to be the center of the country, and it enjoyed tremendous vitality in commerce and theater and music. Ted was sure that someday it would be the center of the world.

Ted knew that if he dropped the slightest hint, Lawrence and other friends would make nuisances of themselves introducing him to attractive single women. Four years of bloody warfare had left women with a scarcity of eligible men.

"If only I could learn to care for one of them," he sighed.

As Bailey waited to board the stagecoach, the familiar smell of horse manure reminded him of home. The New York City air had grown befouled with smells and dust and unrelenting smoke. Summer and winter were unpleasant enough without the teeming streets being so unsanitary.

Ted felt fatigue far beyond his age of 45 as he climbed into the crowded Concord coach. Although stoutly built, the coach jerked and bounced on the roughly made roads, tossing the passengers against its walls or one another. Each jolt thrust a stranger's shoulder or knee into Ted, and after an hour, his body ached. Heading south, his seat by the open window got the full, intense heat of the afternoon sun, while the dust from sixteen hooves blew in the window. A fellow passenger offered Ted a drink from a bottle of whiskey, and he took a swallow gratefully.

"I've been spoiled by trains and boats, and carriages on macadamized pavements," he shouted to his benefactor over the clatter. "I surely hope this journey can be accomplished in its scheduled four hours."

Darkness descended on the swaying coach, and the temperature mercifully cooled. Bailey listened idly to the other passengers' conversations, but they held no interest for him. He tried to sleep, but the stagecoach kept jerking him awake on the rutted road. He was grateful when the lights they passed grew closer together, a sign that they were nearing Salt Lake City.

His limbs aching, Ted climbed out of the coach and retrieved his bag from the driver. He wearily entered the Salt Lake House, the first hotel he saw near Temple Square. He hoped that somewhere in the city, someone would sell him a drink.

In distraction, Ted searched his pockets for the letter of introduction.

"The woman I'm to visit is named Amelia," he muttered. "One of four women, at least that Frances is aware of, who are known as Mrs. John Carter. I hope Charles has telegraphed her that I'll be calling."

# Chapter 2

Bailey left his hotel room in the morning, surprised to be feeling so much at ease. He had slept well, bathed and shaved, and his suit had been brushed and pressed. He enjoyed a hearty breakfast, excellent except for the watery coffee. The desk clerk informed him that John Carter owned a couple of lots at 24th South and Fourth East Streets. The young man suggested hiring a horse and buggy because Salt Lake City was very spread out.

The air felt warm and clean as Ted stepped outdoors, and the view of nearby snow-topped mountains pleased him. On his way to the livery stable, he paced off the streets and found them 44 yards wide. Each oversized block contained 10 acres. Most streets were planted with tall, uniform rows of Lombardy poplars.

Breathless from the altitude, Ted walked onward, enjoying the clear air and open spaces. At Temple Square, he inspected the oval-shaped Tabernacle and the granite foundations for the Temple. The Tithing House and Endowment House stood nearby. A passerby informed him that the houses across the Southeast corner were the homes of Brigham Young's families. To Ted, they looked less like a harem than sturdy Yankee homesteads from New England.

At the livery stable, he hired a horse and buggy for the day, then drove it south on State Street. A system of irrigation canals, like those he had seen in Ogden, lined the streets. The houses were set back 25 feet from the street, some of two stories, others one story. Most were surrounded by small orchards of apple, cherry, peach and apricot trees in spring leaf, with well-tended kitchen gardens and banks of flowers. He saw some carriage houses, but no barns or large stables. Away from the city center, many of the eight lots in each block were undeveloped.

Ted turned east at 24th Street and drove the buggy onward until he reached Fourth East Street. As he had hoped, he saw a small wooden sign neatly labeled "John Carter." Behind the sign stood an elongated, two-story brick house with a gabled roof and a porch on each level. A smaller one-story wooden house stood on the adjacent lot. It was also labeled John Carter.

Amused by the dilemma, Ted guessed that Amelia might be favored as the first of the wives, and he decided to call at the smaller house. But as he approached the driveway, he saw a tall, middle-aged man descending the steps from the porch of the larger home. He stopped the horse and called out, "Mr. Carter?"

"I'm John Carter. What can I do for you, Sir?"

"Pardon me if I'm intruding, but I've been asked to call on you, or to be more precise, on your wife Amelia. Perhaps her brother-in-law, Charles Alderson, sent her a telegram about my visit? Charles and I served together during the War and he's become a close friend. When I told Frances that I was coming out to Utah Territory, to report on the transcontinental railroad, she suggested I pay a call on you and your wife. Amelia, that is."

Carter silently scrutinized him. Ted feared the polygamist would deny him entry and Frances would infer the worst. He reached into his coat pocket.

"My name is Edward Bailey. Here's my letter of introduction and my card. I write for the *Empire Monthly Review*, perhaps you've heard of it."

Carter glanced at the letter without reading it. "So Franny expects an eyewitness report, and from a veteran reporter, no less."

Sitting in the buggy, Ted flinched when the unfamiliar horse whinnied and thrust its head from side to side. Carter fingered Ted's calling card.

"Pardon me, please, Mr. Bailey, for my lapse from civility and hospitality. But Franny has always harbored doubts about the man who carried off her elder sister. I'm pleased you've come, for my sake as well as Amelia's. I enjoy talking with visitors from the East, we don't have many, or didn't. We've been warned the railroad will bring changes, but I didn't expect them the day after the last spike."

Ted climbed down from the buggy, relieved that Carter

216

understood his mission. He did not insult Carter by denying why Frances sent him.

"Amelia has gone into town to see her doctor," Carter said. "Our daughter Molly drove her, and they should be back shortly. Amelia has not been feeling well, I'm afraid. Hopefully, it's nothing worse than the normal female problems that bother most women of her age."

Ted acknowledged that Carter must know more about women than he did. He had never met a polygamist before. With a neatly trimmed beard but no mustache, Carter looked to be in his early fifties. He was huskier and stood a few inches taller than Ted.

"How long do you plan to stay in Salt Lake City?" Carter asked.

"I have a stagecoach ticket to Ogden in the morning, and a ticket on the train to New York tomorrow evening."

"Then you must stay for dinner, that's what we call our noon meal here. Amelia will want to hear all the news from home, information that letters can't convey."

"I'd be honored, Mr. Carter," Ted replied. "Tell me, was I about to call at the wrong home?"

Carter nodded. "Besides Amelia, I'm married to Margaret and Emmeline, both immigrants from England, and Fawn. Amelia, Margaret and Fawn get along well among themselves, but there are some antagonisms with Emmeline. Since I have to bear the lack of peace, Emmeline lives with her children in the smaller house. Are you married, Mr. Bailey?"

"I'm a widower. My wife died suddenly four months ago of pneumonia."

"I'm sorry to hear that," Carter said. "You must feel lonesome and lost. But we believe that marriages exist beyond this lifetime. You may find her again and be sealed to her for Eternity."

Ted shuddered involuntarily at the thought.

"Do you have children?" John asked.

"Our two daughters, ages 20 and 19, were recently married," Ted replied. "Sad to say, we are not close, and I have no other family."

"Perhaps you'd let me tell you about the Latter-day Saints, Mr. Bailey. I can see you're the kind of man who'd thrive in our community."

Ted smiled wanly. Frances had warned him that John Carter was a zealous missionary, who would try to proselytize him. Ted had not expected it so quickly.

"Perhaps some other time, Mr. Carter. Tell me, what kind of work do you do?"

Carter smiled patiently and shrugged. "I'm a millwright, though I've worked in related trades, particularly building structures and handling heavy machinery. I've been blessed with financial success, though the Union Pacific owes me substantial sums I may never collect. I also own a third of a stock farm just outside town. My daughter Molly helps care for the animals there, and keeps the records on the breeding. She's seventeen, and next year, when the Territorial University opens, I expect she'll take the qualifying examinations."

"They'll accept female students?" Ted asked.

"Why does that surprise you, Mr. Bailey? For all the Gentile charges that polygamy abuses our women, I believe we treat them more respectfully than you do. Very soon, we'll grant our women the right to vote. I'm proud of all my 16 children, but Molly is likely the brightest. I fear she takes after Amelia's father. Have you met him?"

"Yes, in Pennsylvania."

Sixteen children! Ted thought to himself. He had been unable to cope with two.

Ted heard a horse's hooves and the clatter of a buggy turning in from the street. He watched from the porch as Carter ran down the stairs and helped Amelia step down from the buggy. While the girl drove the horse into the carriage house, the Carters exchanged a few words that Ted could not hear.

In a louder voice, Carter said, "Amelia, we have a visitor you will surely welcome, a close friend of your brother-in-law Charles. Mr. Bailey is a magazine reporter from New York, and he's traveled here to witness the railroad high jinks at

Promontory. Franny proposed that he visit you while he's so near."

Amelia's smile showed genuine pleasure. "What a marvelous surprise!" she said. "The telegram about your visit arrived at Western Union just an hour ago."

Bailey looked at Amelia while they shook hands. She looked pale to him, though her hand was warm. About his own age, Amelia was of medium height, with a somewhat matronly figure. She wore a modest dress of dark blue patterned cotton, a shawl around her shoulders and a straw bonnet, but no gloves. As she took off her hat, he saw that her dark brown hair was streaked with gray, and her face was attractive but lined. Ted could see her resemblance to her sister, who shared a similar broad smile, though Frances had not begun to show her age.

"Please, Mr. Bailey," Amelia said, "tell me honestly how Franny and Charles are faring."

Ted described as best he could their appearance and general state of happiness.

"Charles rarely admits it, but the stump of his arm often pains him," Ted reported. "Fortunately, his war disability doesn't hinder his practice of law."

A young woman stepped gracefully up the stairs to the porch. She was slightly taller than her mother, her features and slim figure attractive but not dazzling.

Carter made the introductions. "Mr. Bailey, this is our daughter Mary, who's seldom called anything but Molly."

"How do you do, Mr. Bailey."

Ted glanced only briefly at Molly as she removed her straw bonnet. He noticed her fair skin and straight auburn hair, and that she wore a light green cotton dress. His own daughters had been more striking at 17, trained well by their mother and grandmother to be elaborately groomed and fashionably dressed. Even when performing daytime errands, they were corseted to show their narrow waists and generous bosoms and hips, wearing crinolines or many petticoats beneath their dresses.

"And I prefer you call me Ted. Calling me Mr. Bailey reminds me that my two married daughters are older than you

219

are."

Molly smiled modestly but said nothing.

"Molly, would you get some cool lemonade," Amelia asked, "and be sure Margaret knows to set an extra place for dinner. John, can you postpone going off to work until afterwards?"

"Yes, but then I must leave directly," John said. "Tell us, Ted, because he refuses to speak of it. How did Charles lose his arm?"

Ted shook his head. "I had to tell Frances, too. As you know, Charles was a major in the Pennsylvania 17th Cavalry. He was wounded at Gettysburg, which I understand is your hometown, Amelia."

"Many years ago," Amelia said.

"Were you a Cavalryman, too?" Molly asked, offering him a glass of lemonade.

Ted thanked her and sipped it. It was too sweet for his taste.

"Yes," he said. "When the war started, I received a commission as a major and was later promoted to lieutenant colonel. I met Charles when his regiment was attached to my division. I was used as a staff officer because I wasn't fit for combat command, too old and physically unable to take the punishment of hours of hard riding, saddle soreness, and piles, the all-too-common Cavalryman's complaint. That disabled some Generals too, like Stoneman, when I was on his staff."

"I knew Stoneman when he was a lieutenant, a company commander with the Mormon Battalion," John said. "A good man."

"Were you in Gettysburg, too?" Molly asked.

"Yes."

"But why Gettysburg, of all places?" Amelia asked.

"Well," Ted replied, "by summer 1863, the Confederate leaders concluded that the South must make a spectacular attack in the East and win a decisive victory because the battles on the Mississippi were going so badly. So General Lee quietly moved his Army of Northern Virginia north through the Shenandoah and Cumberland valleys into Pennsylvania, an easy route with many paved roads.

"It was a strong army, over 75,000 men, so powerful that it could easily chew up and spit out small Union formations that stood in its path. They could live off the land, with food, clothing and forage plentiful in Pennsylvania and Maryland, as it always was in the Shenandoah Valley of Virginia. Still, an army that large must keep moving because its men and horses quickly devour local stocks of food and forage. But before Jeb Stuart's highly-acclaimed cavalry could move out of Virginia, a Union cavalry division made a damaging surprise attack at dawn, almost literally catching them with their pants down."

Ted blushed when he heard his own words.

Amelia smiled and said, "Those of us who came west on the migration from Nauvoo aren't so delicate about body functions. Please go on, Ted."

Ted took a sip of sweet lemonade. "Stuart's cavalry were lucky to have time to mount their horses and fight at all. And when the Southern press lashed out at him for being taken by surprise, Stuart zealously wanted his division to accomplish some spectacular feat to restore his reputation. But by a series of fights, the Union cavalry kept Stuart's men from the vital mission of scouting the Union Army, which Lee thought was too far south to interfere with his offensive. Stuart was pleased when his men captured a Union supply train of 125 wagons, and brought it with them as booty."

Molly poured Ted another glass of lemonade. Unaccustomed to the dry air, he drank it thirstily.

"Lee did not know that large Union formations were nearby, and he ordered his scattered units, other than Stuart's cavalry, to concentrate a dozen miles northwest of Gettysburg. Stuart, slowed by the captured wagon train, moved north to York, because he mistakenly thought another Southern corps was still there."

"York is at least a day away from Gettysburg," Amelia told Molly.

"And from York, Stuart headed northwest, even farther away."

"But where was Uncle Charles?" Molly asked.

"Charles was with General Buford of the Union Cavalry. Knowing how the roads and terrain made Gettysburg a key point, Buford sent patrols north and west, then prepared to hold the town.

"Early on July 1, after marching three hours toward Gettysburg, a column of Southern infantry came under fire from Buford's cavalry. Though badly outnumbered, the men in Charles' unit had favorable position and firepower from their repeating carbines. Along with an artillery battery, Charles' cavalry held off the attack for a critical three hours, which let Union infantry and artillery begin fortifying Cemetery Ridge, Cemetery Hill and Culp's Hill."

"It's a beautiful place," Amelia sighed. "Franny and I used to play there as girls. The wooded hills rise abruptly about eighty feet above the open fields."

Ted nodded. "That was the Union defensive position that ruined Lee's Army then, and hindered its offensive capability for the rest of the War. But as they held off the attack, Charles' arm was shattered by a Minie ball."

Amelia looked sadly at Ted. "I've known Charles since he was a boy."

"Other men died of such wounds, Amelia, but your father stubbornly refused to let Charles die. He insisted the arm be removed at once, before gangrene could set in. He would hear of nothing else."

"That sounds like my father," Amelia said grimly.

# Chapter 3

A dark-skinned woman, many years younger than Amelia, stepped out the front door.

"Sister Amelia," she said softly, "all the small children have been fed, and dinner for the family and your guest is on the table."

"Thank you, Fawn. Please come inside, Ted."

The woman helped Molly gather the lemonade pitcher and glasses. "Thanks, Aunt Fawn," Molly said.

Ted choked on the last swallow of lemonade in surprise. Frances had not told him that one of the four Mrs. Carters was an Indian, if indeed she knew. He was grateful he had not treated her as a hired servant.

The house that they entered was large, with a common vestibule, parlor, dining room and kitchen. The rest of it was arranged in three sections, two upstairs and one downstairs, designed for each of three wives and her children. In the dining room, Ted observed that the furniture, though well crafted, was only common pine, undoubtedly of local origin.

Carter noticed Ted's appraisal. "When the Utah Central brings freight costs down, the first order I plan to make is for some good hardwood furniture. None of ours survived farther than Iowa."

"John," a woman with an English accent said laughingly, "you promised me the first order by railroad would be a Howe or Singer sewing machine."

Amelia smiled, then turned to Ted. "May I introduce my sister wives, Margaret and Fawn? Our guest is Edward Bailey, a dear friend of my sister Franny and brother-in-law Charles. Margaret is our treasured seamstress, who we all agree is rightfully entitled to the finest sewing machine John can afford."

As they sat down at the table, Ted saw that one place was still unoccupied. He turned when the front door opened noisily.

"I'm sorry I'm late, John, but I could see we had a guest, and I wanted to wear that new dress you gave me."

John smiled. "That's all right, Emmeline."

The woman offered her hand to Ted. "I'm Mrs. Carter."

"How do you do? I'm Ted Bailey."

Facing his first encounter with plural marriage, Ted felt at a loss for words. He wondered what it must feel like to John. God knew he found it trying enough to please Lydia, his only wife.

"I'm delighted to meet all of you," Ted stammered.

John recited Grace with somber care. Then the women passed the heavy plates of food to Ted. The food was plentiful, he noted, but bland. They offered him more sweet lemonade.

"If you'd come next month," Amelia said, "we'd have corn and fresh vegetables from our garden. Even better, come back in two months when the peaches are ripe."

Ted felt uneasy as he glanced among John's wives. Like Amelia, Margaret, Emmeline and Fawn were all attractive women, though Amelia seemed to enjoy a certain deference among them. Margaret wore her brown hair loose, while Emmeline's was blonde and set in a stylish chignon. Both had the fair and pretty complexions typical of many Englishwomen. But Emmeline's dress, cut noticeably lower in the front and worn over many petticoats, was obviously made of more expensive fabric. Fawn was the tallest and most modestly dressed, except for Molly.

Ted turned to Margaret and Emmeline. "I traveled widely in Great Britain in '47," he said, "a wedding gift from the parents of my late wife. It's a magnificent country."

"A magnificent country for the wealthy," Margaret said.

"Yes, I suppose so," he agreed.

"A great many English, Welsh and Scots have come here, Mr. Bailey," Emmeline said. "Many of them, like Margaret here, are very good workers, with useful and skillful hands. Better than mine, I confess. Which is why she is *our* seamstress, well, for most of our dresses..."

John interrupted. "A member of the English House of Commons praised Brigham Young for our efficient emigration system. Joshua, our son, also married an Englishwoman he met

224

on his mission during the War. Utah Territory has more British-born than most of the populous states in the East."

"Only if you don't count the Irish," Ted said. "There must be 200,000 Irish in New York City alone."

"We have many Scandinavian converts," Amelia added, passing him a plate of cheese. "Here, try some of our excellent Danish cheese from the Cache Valley."

"Mr. Bailey was telling us about the Battle of Gettysburg," Molly said.

"War isn't fit conversation for dinnertime, Molly," John said.

"True," Ted agreed heartily. "But the repairs are progressing well in Gettysburg. Your father, Amelia, is a prime mover in the efforts to have the battlefield recognized as a national monument. He was among the few people who noted or remembered Lincoln's words at the cemetery dedication, four months after the battle."

"Franny told me that Father disdained Lincoln."

"He did, at first. He saw Lincoln only as an odd-looking, self-educated Westerner who lacked an orator's impressive voice, resorted to barnyard stories to win arguments, and only won the 1860 election because the Democrats split their vote three ways. But your father confessed that Lincoln's speech at Gettysburg brought him to tears."

Amelia carried the cake and the plates from the sideboard.

"And how is my father?" she asked coolly.

"Remarkably well, given his age." Ted felt taken aback by Amelia's aloofness toward her father, and he wondered why Frances had not warned him. "He is worried about you, naturally."

"Naturally," she smiled wryly. "As is Franny."

"He is also worried for himself."

Amelia looked up, unable to hide her concern. "Is there something wrong, Mr. Bailey?"

"Oh, I suppose not," Ted replied. "But he worries that he'll soon die, and says you'll have him baptized into the Mormon Church! Frances assures him you'd do no such thing. But he

225

insists, 'That's precisely what Amelia intends to do.' He says a German pietist group, the Ephrata Cloister, near Lancaster, not far from Gettysburg, began baptizing the dead over 100 years ago. He says the Mormons have adopted this practice, too. Frances is quite afraid that he's started showing symptoms of senile dementia."

Amelia shook her head, then said finally, "Well, that's Father for you."

Ted continued, feeling awkward at bearing unpleasant news. "He told me he'd been astonished when he opened the *Book of Mormon* you gave him and read the Testimony of the Witnesses about the golden plates. Five of the twelve witnesses were named Whitmer, he said, and Cowdery and Page were married to women whose maiden names were Whitmer. 'I knew the Whitmers,' your father claimed. 'They're Pennsylvania Germans who once lived just a few miles away from the Ephrata Cloister. I don't know Harris, or the four witnesses named Smith, but the Ephrata believed in modern-day revelation."

Amelia offered Ted a slice of cake. "I love my father dearly, Mr. Bailey, but he lacks any sense of the miraculous. He is the poorer for it, I believe."

Perhaps we all are, Ted thought to himself. "Your father said the sect died out about the time he was born, but their curious beliefs lingered in the vicinity. He showed me many books published by the Ephrata Cloister, *Pilgrim's Progress* in German and the Mennonites' *Martyr's Mirror*. They even owned a bark mill for making paper. He spoke of mystic rites of the Zionitic Brotherhood, even more esoteric than the Angelic Brethren. And the Order of the Spiritual Virgins, since the Ephrata Cloister was celibate."

Amelia stiffened. "I assure you, Ted, we believe in no such nonsense. Celibacy is no virtue here."

"I can see that," Ted smiled, glancing around the large dining room. "Then your father mumbled some things that made no sense. About Jesus being the bridegroom at the marriage in Cana, and how his intimacy with Mary Magdalene and Martha, and the other Mary, would've been highly unbecoming and improper if they weren't his wives, but they were, and that's why he appeared to them first, after the resurrection. Well, Frances and Charles exchanged looks across the table, but of course, nothing can be done about senile dementia."

From the corner of his eye, Ted noticed that Molly suppressed a snicker.

Margaret asked, "Mr. Bailey, do you know much about the Church of Jesus Christ of Latter-day Saints? That is, other than scandal-mongering nonsense rampant in the press and countless books?"

"I know little of your history after you came to Utah," Ted replied, "but quite a lot of what happened before then. I was a reporter for the *New York Herald* in September '46, and was sent to western Illinois to cover the violence between the Mormons and their neighbors. By chance, I became an eyewitness to the final battle of Nauvoo. I met a short man there named George Wood, whose wife was..."

"Lily," Amelia said. "She died last year. Her husband had 11 wives."

"I also met a Judge Hendricks," Ted recalled.

"Hendricks!" John said. "That son of a...that hypocrite. He was one of the Quincy Masons who tried to keep us from forming our own lodge in Nauvoo. Maybe even one of those Masons who incited the Warsaw river rats to lynch Joseph and Hyrum! I know Hendricks was among the fine citizens of Quincy who forced us to abandon Nauvoo."

Amelia spoke softly amid Carter's surge of temper. "John, I know you must leave shortly to attend to some business in town."

Carter checked his pocketwatch and stood up abruptly. "You're right, Amelia, I must go. I'm sorry you're leaving tomorrow, Ted, and I can't spare more time today. Come back to see us again, now that the railroad makes it so quick. Amelia, suppose you and Molly drive Ted around, perhaps along Parley's Creek to the stock farm I was telling him about. Please excuse me, my Dears."

Carter hurriedly left the house and his other three wives

227

returned to the kitchen or their own quarters.

Amelia looked at Molly with concern. "I didn't have a chance to tell your father, but the doctor insisted that I rest quietly this afternoon. I'd be very pleased to go along, but I cannot, so we must bid farewell to Mr. Bailey."

"Oh Mother, I'll take Mr. Bailey by myself. After all, he's been Uncle Charles and Aunt Franny's very dear friend for many years. And he's leaving the Territory tomorrow, so there won't be any silly talk about my reputation, if anybody even notices us. Besides, he's commissioned as a spy for Aunt Franny, so we must use all our powers to keep Mr. Bailey on our good side."

Ted grinned at Molly's appraisal of him as though he were not standing in the room. He nodded his head slightly to reassure Amelia.

Amelia frowned at her daughter to show disapproval of such impudence in the presence of a stranger. Then she took a careful look at Ted.

"Very well," she sighed, "but stay out of Emmeline's sight. If your father finds out, we'll both be rebuked for risking your good name with everyone in the Stake."

# Chapter 4

Ted waited as Molly stepped up into the livery stable buggy, then he climbed up, took the reins, and urged the reluctant horse down the street. Casually, she directed him to go east and then south. Ted glanced at her again, noticing for the first time that her eyes were green and that her nose showed a few freckles. He could not help but compare her to his daughters when they were 17. Molly was less affected, less alluring.

Ted found himself pleased and amused by the circumstances of their clandestine outing. Underneath the bright sun, the May afternoon air was warm and clear. The view of the mountains nearby above the creek, the clattering rhythms of the horse and buggy, and the company of the attractive young woman, all combined to lighten his mood to unaccustomed good spirits.

"Before you conclude that I'm a thoroughly proper young lady, would you mind if I took the reins? The men around here bristle when I ask to drive the horses, even though many women, like Mother, drove ox teams for months during the emigration west. I love handling horses, and Father has given me a fine filly. I'll show her to you at the farm."

Ted's amusement with Molly grew as he handed over the reins. She did not seem to notice.

"We do that, you know," Molly said.

"You do what?" Ted replied, distracted by the speed of the unfamiliar horse. But Molly seemed well in control, so he said nothing.

"Baptize the dead. My grandfather is right, though it wasn't thought up in Pennsylvania. It's in 1 Corinthians 15:29, if you care to look it up. 'Otherwise, what do people mean by being baptized on behalf of the dead? If the dead are not raised at all, why are people baptized on their behalf?'"

"You baptize the dead against their will?" Ted asked, amazed.

"Well, not physically, of course. Since we can't ask them, we stand as proxies for them, but their spirits, like ours, remain free *not* to accept our faith.  We believe they'll come around to it in time."

"Do you believe all that?" Ted asked her.

"Of course," Molly answered in a pleasant voice.

"And do you believe in plural marriage?"

Molly hesitated, glancing around the buggy as if someone besides Ted could be listening.

He laughed aloud.  "But hasn't it prospered your large family?"

"I suppose," she admitted.  "And Mother isn't often unhappy, especially now that Aunt Emmeline has moved into her own house with all her spoiled children.  Still, happiness seems beside the point."

"How?"

Molly stared straight ahead, watching the horse.  "I was born and raised in Salt Lake City, but my favorite place is always the stock farm.  I don't know about your Eastern city girls, Mr. Bailey, but I understand how all creatures produce their young.  My body and spirit are proudly female, and I'll bring forth children willingly, in pain if need be.  But I can't acquiesce to being one among a stable of brood mares.  I'll die a celibate old maid before I'll agree to it."

"Surely, you don't see your mother as a brood mare."

"Of course not," Molly said.  "And I never knew her before polygamy.  Still, I cannot help but sense that Mother isn't all that she once was."

Are any of us? Ted wondered in silence.  "And you think polygamy is to blame?" he asked.

Molly shrugged.  "I feel sadness for my mother, who knows that my father prefers to mate with beautiful young Aunt Fawn, of whom she's very fond, or particularly with selfish, too-clever-by-half Aunt Emmeline.  It isn't a question of morality.  Even Aunt Emmeline possesses high moral standards.  All I know, at age 17, is that the world has opened up opportunities as numerous as the stars.  I won't be saddled with a man who won't let me have at least a few of them."

Ted smiled at her youthful enthusiasms.  "I hear most

Mormon men aren't polygamists."

"Ah, but they aspire to be," Molly said. "The more successful any man is, the more likely he is to be much-married. And any man I marry will be a successful man."

"Ha!" Ted teased her. "You're confident of your charms."

His interpretation of her words surprised Molly. "It isn't vanity, I assure you, nor vain ambition. And I wouldn't only accept a wealthy suitor. But I'd only consider a man who showed promise, and any man can be nurtured toward his highest potential. Yet if, by so enhancing him, I impel him toward making a brood mare of me, I'd surely defeat my own purpose."

Ted was taken aback by her candor. "But wouldn't such a husband feel too loyal to you to marry again against your wishes? And wouldn't you have any say in the matter?"

Molly shook her head at the dilemma. "Our men generally do what they're counseled, and that is our greatest strength. My brother Joshua can't yet afford a second wife, but I see him regarding my classmates with an acquisitive eye. With the means to support plural wives, men will marry them. So you see, there's no hope for girls like me."

Ted thought about his own daughters, ages 19 and 20. He had not seen them since the lavish church wedding of the younger girl. No, he reminded himself, they were all at Lydia's funeral.

"Well, can't you marry a promising fellow and have children, then divorce him if he takes another wife? Your Aunt Frances tells me that Mormon women can divorce their husbands far more readily than men can divorce their wives."

"You're a clever man, Mr. Bailey, but unsealing a marriage for all Eternity can never be quite so simple. I suppose reporters must be clever, and well educated. Did you attend college?"

"Harvard," Ted nodded casually. "Class of '45."

With excitement, Molly interrupted him. "Were you a classmate of Francis Parkman, who came West the year before Mother and wrote *On the Oregon Trail*? Did you know Richard Henry Dana, whose *Two Years Before the Mast* told about

California when it was part of Mexico, before men like Father helped win it away? Did you ever hear Ralph Waldo Emerson?"

"Yes, to all three questions, Molly. How have you come by such books?"

"My grandfather won't write letters, but he often sends us books. Mother thinks that, having given up on her, he's hoping to subvert his grandchildren."

Ted smiled, remembering the opinionated old man. "Well, I must say you show more interest in such things than either of my daughters, who were educated in costly finishing schools. Even the War seemed merely to annoy them, so many boys being away, interfering with their parties and all that."

Molly hesitated for a moment, cautioned by the sarcasm in his voice. "What happened after Uncle Charles was wounded?"

Ted shrugged, reluctant to answer her question. It was, after all, a springtime afternoon four years and 2,000 miles removed.

"You have a very pleasant voice," he remarked. "Do you sing?"

"I'm a contralto in the Tabernacle Choir. Not the lead, though I hope to be, someday. If you weren't leaving tomorrow, I'd ask you to come Wednesday night, if not on Sunday. I think you might enjoy our religion."

Ted looked away, so Molly continued. "Sometimes I practice by singing for the horses. They particularly like the laments about how cruelly we've been treated and how we've survived."

"As I would," Ted smiled at her. "Would you sing one for me?"

"Not now," Molly said. "If I did, you'd have tears in your eyes."

"Do the horses?"

"No, but they become calmed."

Molly's candor made Ted feel younger than he had felt since the War. "I'm not surprised," he said. "In fact, this horse could use some calming, himself."

Ted watched the passing scenery, so removed from bloody battle. He debated whether or not to answer her question, then

232

with mixed emotions, resumed the story.

"In the hours after Charles was wounded, both armies massed around Gettysburg. Cemetery Ridge and Cemetery Hill now bristled with Union guns. The fighting the next day was furious, fought with bayonets when ammunition ran out. There was widespread hand-to-hand combat. But as darkness fell on July 2, only the dead remained of the Southerners who reached or broke the Union lines.

"The defensively superior Union position held, while the Rebels' ammunition and manpower was rapidly diminishing. When the Southerners attacked the next morning, they were repelled and lost ground, leaving Union manpower and position far superior. Lee's last uncommitted forces were Pickett's excellent 15,000-man division and Stuart's now exhausted 10,000-man Cavalry, which finally arrived late the previous day. Lee had already lost the battle. Yet despite protest, he ordered Pickett's divison to attack the Union center from the west, while Stuart struck the Union rear from the east."

"Where were you, Ted?"

"On duty as a liaison officer with the observation group. Another liaison officer saw Stuart's division and quickly signaled orders. Then a Union Cavalry brigade intercepted Stuart and kept the Rebel Cavalry out of the main battle for Cemetery Hill."

Ted breathed deeply as he relived the somber memory. "The Confederate artillery opened fire on the Union defenses on Cemetery Hill. For an hour, the Union artillery answered, until its commander ordered a cease-fire to conserve ammunition. Rebel artillery ammunition was almost exhausted, so their artillery commander urged Pickett to advance while they could still give supporting fire. Through my field glasses, I watched Pickett's charge in disbelief. His infantry had to cross *three-quarters of a mile* of open ground, moving uphill. In plain view and converging on one point, the soldiers were exposed for almost 30 minutes to mass rifle and anti-personnel artillery fire."

Molly had been listening closely. "It sounds like *The Charge of the Light Brigade.* 'Half a league, half a league, half a league onward, into the valley of death rode the six hundred.'"

"Except there were 15,000," Ted sighed. "As exhilarated as I was by our triumph, I also thought of Tennyson's words. 'Not though the soldier knew--Someone had blundered.' But Lee's blunder was far worse than the Light Brigade.

"Pickett's division moved forward, men marching in straight lines, as if on parade. When they got into close range, they were mown down by devastating fire from Union artillery and from infantry behind breastworks. Some of our regiments maneuvered to positions at right angles and shot at Pickett's division from the side. I was aghast to see so many men die before *any* Southerners ran away or surrendered."

Molly shuddered, imagining the blood-chilling sights and sounds.

"What could've been in Lee's mind," Ted asked, "except arrogance and some sense he was infallible, like a god? Even if the attack succeeded, Lee had too few men left to defeat us, and we could've easily retreated, our forces intact. In history, Pickett's charge will be deemed glorious and heroic, but it was mindless militarily."

Ted knew he should revert to a more pleasant subject. But through the floodgates of memory flowed the words.

"I sometimes still feel shame, thinking as we did of men and animals only as things to be expended in battle, not living beings. I felt sick reading casualty reports and watching the dying and wounded men, and the horses, whose screams are horrible before they're taken out of misery. You Mormons were fortunate to be spared combat in the War Between the States. Not only that your men weren't casualties, but also that they weren't made coarse and casual about killing others.

"The senseless leadership in the South kept the war going on much too long, even though defeat was clearly inevitable. What could've been in their minds after the Union Army took Atlanta in '64? They harassed Union garrisons and threatened Washington, which could not affect the outcome, only provoke our decision to lay waste to the Shenandoah Valley and bring terrible retaliation on their civilians.

"I was one of Sheridan's operations officers who saw to it that those orders to devastate the Shenandoah Valley were obeyed. It was just about the richest farming country around, furnishing Southern forces with food and forage, and a well-paved corridor for attacking the North. When we were through, no food or forage remained to support any Southern force, nor any food for civilians that fall and winter.

"Now, even some Northern writers express sympathy for the romantic nonsense of the Southerners' 'Lost Cause.' What cause? Was it honorable to stubbornly persist with real misery, death and destruction for such an abstraction as states' rights? Or the way of life dependent on slavery? If the South hadn't started the war, existing slavery would not have been disturbed. Is it honor to start and sustain a terrible civil war because of literal belief in a Biblical curse? Does it 'sanctify' black slavery that Ham, the alleged ancestor of all Negroes, and all of his descendants, are to be slaves forever because he didn't avert his eyes from his father Noah when the old man was naked and drunk?"

Molly weighed the question for a moment. "Surely, that cannot sanctify slavery. But we believe that Negroes are cursed for some wickedness committed in their past by their spirits."

Ted looked quizzically toward the girl. "Please forgive an old veteran for his war stories, Molly, but it's made me cynical about many things. Not to mention melancholy and angry, and fearful of the moral callousness of our leaders."

Molly guided the horse down a narrow road. "I'm glad to listen, Ted. You've seen many places I've only imagined, reading books."

"Your father tells me you hope to enter the University of Deseret when it opens next year. I encouraged my daughters to get more education, but my wife and her mother dissuaded them. Higher education is uncommon for women in the East, though some colleges admit females, and some only females."

Molly smiled uneasily. "Though I'm good enough at book-learning, the entrance examination worries me. I suffered whooping cough while my classmates were taught geometry, and

I still have difficulty with mathematics. And I once found myself in trouble at school, when I felt compelled to challenge a teacher."

"Whatever about?" Ted asked, amused.

"Genesis 30: 37," she said. "Do you know it? The Bible says Jacob got Laban's sheep and goats to give birth to striped, speckled and spotted lambs and kids because they looked at multi-colored bark of trees while they were conceiving. The Elder, our teacher, rebuked me for questioning our faith, but I only spoke out because he taught it as fact and I know breeding does not work that way. I keep records of the bloodlines for horses at the stock farm because the man who runs it hates keeping books. Of course, I watch the breeding and foaling, when I can, and births of animals other than horses."

"Well, you're in good company, Molly. An Austrian monk named Mendel and an English naturalist named Darwin agree with you."

Ted lurched in his seat as Molly swerved the horse into the barnyard. Behind a grassy meadow, full of wildflowers, stood a large stable and barn, several corrals and a work shed.

"No one seems to be here," Ted remarked.

"True, the wagon and team of big horses aren't here. Most likely, the men have gone to get hay, but it doesn't matter. My filly is in the corral behind the barn."

"Do you always wear such clothes out to the stock farm?"

"I feared that Mother would reconsider letting us go," Molly said. "So I didn't stop to put on something more suitable for wandering in a barnyard full of animal droppings. Well, my clothes aren't so fancy."

Unconcerned, Molly jumped down just as the livery stable horse jerked the buggy forward. Her long skirt tangled in the moving wheel spokes, pulling Molly off balance and throwing her upended to the ground. Ted watched helplessly as she landed hard, soiled by the mud and the muck.

Molly cried out in pain, then bit her lip. Ted leaped from the buggy and stood beside where she sat holding her ankle. She did not curse or cry as she whispered, "I seem to have hurt my ankle badly."

"I've seen soldiers disabled by falls like that," Ted said.

"I don't suppose they were wearing dresses," Molly said through gritted teeth. Her skirt and the bodice of her dress were torn. Her clothing, arms and shoes were caked with mud and muck, already starting to dry.

Ted smiled, distracted, inspecting her ankle. "I hope it's nothing worse than a sprain. But we must put a cold compress on your ankle. Go ahead and raise your foot, and get your stocking off before the ankle swells. I'll get some water from the trough over there by the barn. Are there some clean cloths I can soak in the water to make a compress?"

Wincing, Molly replied, "No, not clean ones. But if you turn around and face away, I'll take off my stocking and a petticoat that you can use."

Ted turned away as Molly asked, then took the petticoat she handed him and soaked it in the cold water of the trough. Behind his back, he heard a loud neighing and hoofbeats muted by mud. The disregarded horse had chosen that moment to wander.

Ted ran to the buggy and seized the horse's reins. "I'm not an old calvary officer for nothing," he muttered. He tied the reins firmly to the nearest fencepost, some 30 yards from where Molly sat.

"As you can imagine," she sighed, "the best horses are not consigned to the livery stable for hire."

Ted removed his coat and folded it, then laid it on the buggy seat as a cushion for her foot. As he moved around the barnyard in his shirtsleeves, Molly noticed that his body was trim, without the paunch so typical of men his age. He wrung the excess water from her petticoat and cleansed the mud from her injured leg.

Ted stopped abruptly, then looked at Molly quizzically.

She blushed and answered softly, "What you see is the bottom of my Endowment garments, which I received last year in our ceremonies."

"Ceremonies?"

"The rites are secret, so I can't tell you more."

Not knowing what to say, Ted proceeded with the task. Trying to avoid touching the curious garments, he wrapped the petticoat loosely around her swelling ankle.

He looked down at Molly and explained, "In the Army, soldiers are trained to carry wounded comrades in a manner I'm afraid you'll think immodest. First, I must stand you up on your good leg. Yes, like that. Now wrap your arms around my neck while I put my arms around your waist and lift you up. Then I'll put my shoulder under your...middle, and carry you to the buggy. Then you'll prop your leg up on my jacket and away we'll go."

Ted gently lifted Molly from the ground, uncomfortably aware that her face brushed against his, and that he glimpsed the top of her breast where her dress was torn. He positioned Molly on his shoulder, holding her steady with his hand on her buttocks, and carried her the 30 yards to the buggy. He could feel her bosom, belly and thighs warm against his body. As he lifted her up into the carriage, he hoped Molly did not notice the telltale bulge in the front of his trousers. If she did, she took care to look away.

Ted drove back to town as fast as he dared with the unruly horse. Neither he nor Molly attempted conversation over the noise of the buggy.

Molly was aware that her leg was exposed by the billowing of her skirt as the buggy raced along. She felt mortified at her clumsiness and comforted by Ted's decisive action. But how to feel about his evident maleness, which she had never known she could inspire in a man? Molly felt equally disappointed and grateful that he was leaving Deseret in the morning.

When the horse and buggy reached the Carter house, Ted and the women more gracefully carried Molly to her room. Amelia, Margaret and Fawn bustled about solicitously to make her comfortable. Mercifully, John had not arrived back from his business affairs.

At the front door, Amelia thanked Ted for his visit.

"It's all my pleasure," he insisted.

Amelia handed him a thick letter. "I wrote it to Franny this afternoon."

"I'll deliver it in person," he promised. "Please convey my well-wishes to Molly. My stagecoach leaves too early in the morning to look in on her myself."

Ted drove the buggy back through town to the livery stable, shaking his head in wonder.

"Imagine," he said aloud, "becoming all aroused by carrying a modest 17-year-old Mormon girl over my shoulder! Indeed, a girl who tried to convert me! Well, it *has* been six months... since Lydia rewarded me so generously for being pleasant at her mother's Thanksgiving dinner. When I get home to New York, I'll tell Lawrence that I'm ready to meet those ladies he keeps insisting would make perfect wives."

# Chapter 5

The return stagecoach trip to Ogden was more pleasant, cooler and less crowded than Bailey had found it two days earlier. Feeling more cheerful than customary in recent years, he climbed down from the coach in Ogden and brushed the dust off his clothes. His train through Gettysburg to New York City would depart in three hours.

Eager to stretch his legs before being confined again, Ted checked his suitcase with the baggage master and headed toward a part of town he had not seen on May 10th. He walked briskly and was surprised when he found himself humming.

"I must be looking forward to going home," he said to himself.

At the corner of two broad streets near the southern edge of town, Ted glimpsed a weather-beaten sign in front of a crude wooden building near an adobe house. The sign read, "Jonathan Browning, Gunsmith."

"Why not?" he asked himself aloud.

After the brightness outdoors, the interior seemed very dark as Ted stepped into the building. His attention was drawn to a forge being worked by a tall boy, about 15 years old. Alongside the forge, a burly, barrel-chested man sat on a large anvil. The man was bearded, elderly and balding. Nearby were a foot-powered lathe and three work benches, each weighed down with a heavy vise. Tools and guns in various stages of disassembly were scattered on the benches. Three younger boys were in the back of the shop, pawing through piles of discarded metal. The air was pungent with the smells of hot coals, raw wood, oil, varnish, and acids used before soldering and brazing.

"Mr. Browning?" Ted asked.

The old man stood up stiffly and walked to the counter. He looked at Bailey coldly and said, "What can I do for you, Mister?"

Taken aback by the hostile tone, Ted replied, "Mr. Browning, my name is Edward Bailey, and I write for the

*Empire Monthly Review."*

"What can I do for you?" he asked louder, traces of his Tennessee origin still in his speech.

Ted hesitated. "I thought, as long as I was here, I'd try to learn something more about the massacre that occurred at Mountain Meadows. A dozen years have passed and no one has been punished for those murders. After all, some 120 men, women and children were killed, seemingly without sense."

Browning interrupted him. "I wasn't there and even if I was, why should I talk to you, a Yankee Gentile stranger?"

"I've heard your name spoken with respect before, when I was a reporter for the *New York Herald* back in '46. A man named George Wood and a judge named Hendricks."

Browning's expression softened and he almost smiled. "Yes, back in Quincy, some 30 years ago, before I was baptized as a Saint. Hendricks helped get me elected Justice of the Peace. He was friends with Abe Lincoln, too."

"Lincoln?" Ted asked.

Browning nodded. "My cousin Orville, a lawyer like Lincoln, came to Quincy before me, but his house was too small to put Abe up when he was circuit riding as a lawyer. So he asked me to do it, since my house was large and comfortable. I was making a good living as a gunsmith."

"Orville Browning? The former Senator from Illinois and Secretary of the Interior, who mediated the dispute over where the Union Pacific and Central Pacific tracks would meet?"

"Yes. Though we're not close anymore, I suppose it's his doing that I'm a Saint. When hard times hit Tennessee in '33, I took Orville's advice and moved to Quincy. It was there I met Joseph Smith. Eleven of my 17 living children were born in Illinois."

Ted whistled. He had considered John Carter's 16 children an astounding number.

"As of now, I have three wives, and I intend to have more children," Browning said. "What about you?"

Ted's attention was drawn to a shotgun on the counter. Engraved on the gunstock were the words, "Holiness to the

Lord--Our Preservation."

"I have two daughters. I'm a widower."

"I'm sorry to hear that, Mr. Bailey. But you're still young. I was older than you when I came to Utah and married my second and third wives. You could do the same."

The idea of it caused Ted to smile. "Only if I became a Mormon, Mr. Browning."

The gunsmith appraised Ted coolly.

"John Moses," the older man called. "Take Mr. Bailey out in the buggy and tell him a little about Utah. Then bring him to the railroad station so he can catch his train to the East."

The oldest of the boys came forward, shook Ted's hand, then showed him to the carriage house. Carefully, he drove through the wide Ogden streets.

"Did you fight in the War, Mr. Bailey?"

"I was a major in the cavalry, then lieutenant colonel," Ted replied. He was pleased that John Moses Browning did not drive as fast as Molly Carter.

"The cavalry! Did you use Henry and Spencer carbines? Those short-barreled, breech-loading repeating guns that use brass cartridges instead of powder and balls?"

"Both of them. The Henrys load 15 rounds, the Spencers seven."

"Yes, I know," the young man said excitedly. "How did they perform in combat?"

Ted told him of battles where the breech-loading carbines gave huge advantages to Union cavalry over Southern cavalry, which was armed with single-shot, muzzle-loading carbines.

"I knew it!" the boy replied. "To be able to load quickly and shoot without reloading, ready to fire again by pulling on a lever!"

Ted nodded. "The Rebs complained that we could load on Sunday and shoot all week."

"And shoot continuously from a prone position, or while riding!"

"Most serious cavalry actions were fought dismounted," Ted explained. "Horses are very easy targets for riflemen."

"Were there reliability problems?" the young man asked. He listened attentively while Ted explained them in detail.

"Of course, our loyalties were divided in the War," the boy said. "The original Browing home is near the Shenandoah Valley, burned out by Union cavalry troops."

Ted winced, reminded of his part in the devastation of the beautiful valley.

Young Browning did not seem to notice as he pointed out the features of the small city. "We settled Ogden in '47, though it's named for a trapper who located his cache here in '26. Before that, the Indians met for trade and games at the grassy meadow north of town. Pa moved us to the south of town, away from the main business streets, since he isn't what most folks call sociable, and men who want reconditioned guns or repairs know where to find him. They say the Central Pacific will buy up the track from here to Promontory, so Ogden will become the transfer point between them and the Union Pacific."

Ted was impressed by the boy's earnest intelligence.

"You must have some questions about our Church, Mr. Bailey. Can I answer them?"

"No, thank you," Ted insisted with amusement. "How'd your father become a gunsmith?"

"He hated farming and loved hunting, Pa says, like his own father hated farming and loved fiddling. I'm lucky, I guess, that I love gunsmithing. In his idle time, Pa helped the local blacksmith and learned his trade. Those old mechanisms weren't hard to get the hang of, but he didn't know how to make a gun barrel. So he apprenticed himself to a Nashville gunsmith. For his pay and a little more money, the gunsmith sold him some rifling and boring tools. That gave him his trade, first there, then in Quincy, then Nauvoo. Pa crafted a lot of the metal work for the Temple and other buildings in Nauvoo, then he blacksmithed and crafted metal fittings for wagons and equipment for moving thousands of people west."

"I arrived at Nauvoo during the final battle," Ted said. "I found his gunshop, but he'd already gone."

The boy directed the buggy toward the station. "Of course,

that was all before I was born. Pa even invented a five-shot repeating rifle in Illinois, but he lacked good machinery and skilled helpers like my brothers and me, so he couldn't make as many as people wanted to buy. Here in Utah, Pa started a tannery and sawmill, built an iron-roller molasses plant, fixed all kinds of machinery, made plows, milled irons and nails, and invested in real estate. He was elected city councilman and justice of the peace, was appointed probate judge, and served in the legislature. Plus all his work for the Church."

The boy looked up expectantly, but Ted asked no questions about the Church.

"Me, I like taking guns apart, fixing or replacing broken parts, and making them work once again. How many ways guns can be improved! Quicker loading, faster shooting, accurate at greater distances, more durable and reliable, easier to manufacture and maintain. Why not all at the very same time!"

Ted smiled at the enthusiasm of youth, and the illusion that anything was possible.

When they arrived at the station, Ted thanked young Browning for the ride and the tour. He retrieved his luggage from the clerk, then sat down to wait on a bench.

Ted found himself envying Mr. Browning. What man would not be thrilled to have a son who was so earnest, competent and responsible? And so unabashedly proud of his father. He could not imagine Martha or Lucy ever boasting so freely about him. Young Browning would do fine, Ted was certain, though he was less sure that Molly Carter would get the opportunities in life she deserved. Perhaps it was their large families or pioneer lives that brought forth such impressive youngsters. Ted wondered if it could possibly be their religion. They seemed to produce virile boys, not puerile men like the ones his daughters married.

Ted heard the piercing whistle of the train as it steamed in from the West. A surge of excitement raced through him. In six days, he would arrive in New York City. He would be home.

The shrieking whistle reverberated in his brain. He was going home to the parties and the gossip, the politics, the demands of Martha and Lucy, the arm-twisting by Lydia's brothers to invest in schemes whose honor he questioned. Lawrence would ask constantly if he was ready to be introduced to this or that woman of the proper social class. They would expect him to spend lavishly on things he did not want, and meet with people whose company gave him no pleasure. Soon it would be summer, and the New York City streets would be filled with endless noise and smoke, and stinking horse manure in the sun. His only refuge was his work, the one dimension of his life that delivered more than fleeting satisfaction.

Ted squirmed as he sat on the hard wooden bench. His piles were beginning to itch and burn, and he knew the pain would only worsen. With one day of respite in his detour to Gettysburg, he would ride five days on the train.

"My work needn't be done in New York," Ted mumbled aloud.

A lady waiting for the train looked up at him.

"Why not stay in the intermountain West, then when I've seen enough of it, head farther west to the Pacific? Why not, indeed? I can do as I damn well please."

Offended by his profanity, the lady glared at Ted. He did not notice. The enormous iron engine and seven trailing cars screeched and clanged to a lurching halt in front of Ted. The train exhaled steam and heat as if impatient to race eastward again.

Ted rose with a quickened pace and stood in line for a refund on his ticket. With a trace of a smile, he waited his turn to buy a stagecoach ticket to Salt Lake City. Cheerfully, he walked the few steps to the telegraph office and stood in line.

He handed the clerk a hastily-scrawled message to the *Empire Monthly Review*.

"LAWRENCE. STAYING HERE AWHILE. WILL SEND NEXT ARTICLE FROM UTAH. AFTERWARDS, UNCERTAIN. BAILEY."

Ted watched to be sure that his message was telegraphed to New York City. Then he went to the Ogden Post Office and dropped Amelia's letter into the mailbox. Surely, he thought, Amelia would forgive him for not delivering it himself.

# Chapter 6

At his desk in his office, John Carter looked up in surprise.

"Bailey? Shouldn't you be 500 miles toward Chicago by now? Is anything wrong with the railroad?"

"It's fine, John. But before I could get on the train, I had some curious sense that I should stay here awhile. You see, nothing compels me to return to New York."

Carter smiled broadly. "It isn't so uncommon, Ted. Many people feel themselves drawn to us in precisely this way for God's purpose. The whisperings we hear aren't restricted to only a few."

Ted suppressed a grimace. "Perhaps. But I'll only be in Utah a short while. I've promised my editor a story from here."

"There's no lack of hostile accounts," Carter said. "Amelia's father must comb every source before he sends them unsoftened by any scribbling of fatherly love. For some unknowable reason, Amelia saves every scurrilous page inside a drawer, separate from everything else."

Ted stiffened. "I assure you, John, no words I write will be more scurrilous that the truth demands."

Carter carefully appraised the reporter. "And I believe you," he said softly. "After you left the other day, Amelia showed the contents of that drawer to Molly and me. We read the pages from all those years, alternately disgusted and amused at what's been written about us. Toward the bottom, we found three yellowed clippings from the *New York Herald*, now more than two decades old. It thrilled Molly to see your name on the byline."

"What did you think?" Ted asked. He was surprised to feel more than a professional curiosity.

"Amelia and Molly both wept as I read aloud your testimony about the sacking of Nauvoo."

Ted felt a chill run through him at the thought that, 22 years later, he could still make women weep.

"I know an elderly widow who'd like to rent out a room, not

247

far from my homes," Carter said. "She'll furnish board if you want it, and her grandson will be happy to earn money as a groom for the horse you'll need. Amelia will be delighted when she hears you're staying there."

"I'd appreciate your introduction, John."

Carter hesitated. "Please bear in mind that, as a Gentile, you won't be welcome at most of our popular activities, our weekly socials with dancing, for instance. We have so many miners and railroad men in the vicinity."

"I understand."

"And when you ask questions for your report, you'll find that many of us are suspicious if not hostile to Gentiles, and hate Gentile criticism."

Ted shrugged. "Reporters are accustomed to hostility."

"As are we," John said. "But none of us is obliged to pretend we like it. I have a favor to ask of you."

"May I ask what it is before I consent?"

John smiled. "Molly needs tutoring to pass the entrance examination for the University of Deseret. Unfortunately, the subject is mathematics, which neither I nor any of my wives ever learned beyond simple sums. And Molly refuses to seek special help from the Elder who teaches arithmetic and natural history at her school. He rebuked her soundly for questioning his authority on the Biblical story of Jacob and the spotted goats."

"It would be my pleasure," Ted readily agreed. "From what I've seen of Molly, I expect she'll be an excellent student."

"Thank you, Ted. Our only other recourse is to ask Bishop Daniel Tuttle of the Episcopal Church. He teaches mathematics here, but as you can imagine, we don't wish to send Molly to him. Could you come to our home late this afternoon, then stay for supper with us?"

"Nothing would please me more," Ted replied. "Where, by the way, is the Episcopal Church?"

John drew him a small map on a corner of the *Deseret News*. "They meet at Independence Hall, since they have no church building. But I believe Bishop Tuttle is in Montana now. I suspect he gets lonesome in Utah Territory."

248

John reached into his desk and pulled out a small volume. "Please accept this from my family, Ted. Welcome to Deseret."

Ted looked at the gift that weighed heavy in his hand. It was a copy of the *Book of Mormon*.

# Chapter 7

Ted entered the adobe meetinghouse, uncertain that this was the Episcopal church. In the dim light, he saw a bearded but youthful man arranging prayerbooks at the front of the building. Ted walked through the empty meetinghouse, wondering how many seats in Independence Hall were filled on Sundays.

"Bishop Tuttle?" Ted asked. "I heard you've just arrived from Montana."

"In late August," he replied with a smile. "Are you a Latter-day Saint?"

Ted shook his head and introduced himself. He was uncertain if the clergyman was pleased or disappointed.

Bishop Tuttle was younger than Ted had expected. In his early 30s, his hair was already thinning, but his eyes showed intelligence and determination.

"Welcome to the Gentile Church in Utah Territory," he said.

"I understand the Mormon Church is monolithic," Ted said. "But surely there's more than one non-Mormon church."

"No," the Bishop replied. "At present, ours are the only non-Mormon Christian services in Utah."

"The entire Territory?"

"A Roman Catholic priest once came from Nevada, but he only bought land for a future church and went home. And a Congregationalist chaplain held services for awhile, but he left after a Gentile doctor was murdered in cold blood. We'll persist nonetheless. Next year, we plan to lay the cornerstone for a cathedral in Salt Lake City and finish building an adobe church in Corinne."

Ted nodded. "From what I overheard the Irish tracklayers saying, Corinne has strong need of a church."

"As do we all," the Bishop said. "The Walker Brothers and other Gentile businessmen are opening branch offices in Corinne. Naturally, Brigham Young is well aware of it. Already, he has half the track laid for the Utah Central Railroad from here to Ogden. Next year, when he drives that final spike, each blow of the maul will mean death for the commercial power of Corinne."

"Perhaps he'll accomplish that feat better than the men who attempted it at Promontory."

"We all have great challenges, Mr. Bailey. Tell me, are you a married man?"

"A widower," Ted replied.

"I am sorry," Bishop Tuttle said gently. "I asked because I'd hoped we might enlist your wife to penetrate the homes we cannot. Mormonism aims its fiercest shafts at womanhood, and in helping such sufferers in Utah, a woman could accomplish much more than any man."

Ted glanced around the small meetinghouse, which appeared to seat about 200 people. The size of Independence Hall stood in stark contrast to the magnificent Tabernacle that accommodated 10,000.

"What do you think allows Mormonism to hold such power over its people?" Ted asked.

The Bishop stroked his long beard and pondered the question a moment. "Their high proportion of officers to privates. The intelligent interest and loyalty and devotion of disciples are sure to be promoted by according to them some authority and devolving upon them responsibility."

"I beg your pardon?"

"The Mormons make every man a priest. Much satisfaction is thus given to the self-assertion, ambition, and desire for leadership, natural to man. Our own church would profit by taking heed."

"Then what is natural to woman?" Ted asked.

"Self-sacrifice," the Bishop stated. "Is it not natural to mothers and wives? Strange as it seems, its strenuous demands must be accounted as an element of strength to Mormonism. The glory of the sacrifice hallows the agony of suffering."

Ted shook his head in disbelief. Bishop Tuttle had evidently never met Lydia, Martha or Lucy Bailey. He wondered about Molly Carter, but he said nothing.

"And the fresh converts, constantly coming with the glow

and fervor of their religious devotion, dispel the chill that would otherwise creep over the old inhabitants of Utah. Have you been to any of their prayer meetings?"

"No," Ted replied.

Bishop Tuttle sighed. "Mormon faith impels their preachers constantly to assert, 'I *know* this doctrine is true.' This persistent iteration and reiteration of 'I know!' and 'I know!' while not very satisfying to the judgment of a reasoning man, undoubtedly has a tendency to strengthen confidence and assure conviction with the multitude."

Ted noted the clergyman's observations for his story. For a man of God, Bishop Tuttle seemed as worldly-wise as Brigham Young was reputed to be.

"How do you get on with President Young?" Ted asked him.

"He is so powerful a man in everything here, and so unscrupulous a man, I fear, in most things, that my policy is to have as little as possible to do with him."

"And what does he think of you?"

Bishop Tuttle smiled. "With his keensightedness he must know, that in will if not yet in reality, by our services and our schools, we are putting our clutches to his very throat."

Ted could not help but wonder if the Utah air contained some element that made everyone who breathed it believe life offered scant limitations.

"That seems rather optimistic, Bishop Tuttle."

"We, too, have faith," he said.

\*\*\*

Across the dining room table, Ted watched Molly solving the trigonometry problem he gave her. She seemed more mature to him than when he first saw her four months earlier. Even her newer dresses seemed more carefully fitted to her figure. As a dinner guest, he learned that Margaret had made them with her new sewing machine. And he heard John mildly rebuking Amelia for not purchasing the yard goods from Zion's Cooperative Mercantile Institution, but from a Jewish merchant,

253

who was unconcerned that Brigham Young might criticize its ostentation.

Ted knew that Molly's destiny was bearing half a dozen children before age 30 and sharing a household with several sister wives. Or this nonsense about remaining an old maid! He had not come closer to touching Molly than handing her books or papers, yet he could not forget the feeling of her body when he carried her. Ted wished he could resolve to go back to New York, resume his life there, and set about finding a proper Christian woman, hopefully one with wits as well as charm.

"Done!" Molly exclaimed. "You promised you'd show me the manuscript for your story for the *Empire Monthly Review*."

Ted handed it to her. "Here, you can read it while I check your solution."

## OBSERVATIONS OF A GENTILE NEWCOMER TO UTAH
### by
### Edward Bailey
September 1869

At the mouth of a canyon on the western slope of the Wasatch Mountains, 15 miles east of the Great Salt Lake, Brigham Young announced to his followers 22 years ago, "This is the place." It is indeed the *last* large place to be linked by rail to the rest of the continent.

Until 150 days ago, Utah remained so remote that most depictions of it could persist without regard for their truth. Angry denunciations by apostates existed side-by-side with Mormon missionary tracts and notes airily published by observers passing through.

What do the Latter-day Saints ultimately seek to accomplish? The Mormons believe that this life is but a passing stage between premortal existence, as spirit sons and daughters of God, and postmortal life as bodily-resurrected beings inheriting the glory for which each of us qualified on Earth. The spirit sojourns here to acquire a physical body so, united as body

254

and spirit, it can progress toward the perfection of God.

The Mormons believe that God will usher in His Kingdom only through the mediation of human cooperation. And in the time since their gospel was revealed some 40 years ago, the Holy Spirit has inspired men and women toward triumphs of material and moral improvement. Through their efforts, these improvements must gradually and steadily spread across the globe until the Kingdom of God is established. Only then will Christ return to the Earth.

As ambitions go, it is not a bad one, a theocratic Manifest Destiny. Perfection is an admirable goal, and after four months here in Salt Lake City, I can testify to some evident successes. Their beliefs seem to lead to less rowdyism, less profanity, less rampant and noisy wickedness among Mormon youth than among young people in any town I have ever visited. But beyond their own unique ways, they permit no latitude for our American pluralist traditions.

When one enters a Mormon home or business, he is greeted with the same affability expected from the general population. Or indeed, better. Yesterday, a Mormon developer told me about a house he has under construction. "I'm building it for some of you Gentiles," he said. "It's on one of the best sites in the city. I want you Gentiles to have fine sites and comfortable houses, for we think you are cut off from many of the sources of happiness that we enjoy." Our Episcopal Bishop, Daniel Tuttle, has assured me that, in rendering aid to his Gentile poor, he has gone more than once to the Mormon ward Bishops for assistance. "They did not refuse me," Bishop Tuttle said.

But where community interests conflict with those of individuals, discord must be expected. Last year, Brigham Young founded Zion's Cooperative Mercantile Institution, a wholesaler and retailer all in one. Independent Mormon merchants were notified they were expected to merge with the Church cooperative, taking shares in it for their shops. Those who refused were damned economically by Brigham Young, "We shall leave them out in the cold, the same as the Gentiles, and their goods shall rot upon their shelves."

Wisely, the leading Mormon merchants in Utah sold their stock and signed their businesses over to ZCMI. Within six weeks, 81 branches were established throughout most Mormon settlements. For Mormon customers, too, buying from the Gentiles signifies weakness of faith. It is indeed appropriate that the trademark of ZCMI is the Lord's all-seeing eye, painted over the portals to every branch of the store.

As a Massachusetts-born man, I am struck by how the Mormons have created an idealized likeness of an antebellum New England economy. It is not at all like the American West. *Laissez-faire* capitalism, rugged individualism, and private corporations are concepts very foreign to the Vermont-born Brigham Young. The bonanza dreams of the miners are even farther distant from his sacredly communitarian business ventures. This conflict of economic presumptions may be more to blame for the antagonism between Mormons and anti-Mormons than either their religion or polygamy.

Contrary to some popular reports, the institution of polygamy has not led, as in Siam, to women being isolated in guarded harems. Most marriages here are not plural, and most plural families have few wives. Since the progeny of men figure into their degree of "exaltation" in Heaven, procreation is the stated first purpose of marriage. But this undisguised ambition does not keep females from receiving surprisingly equal treatment with males. At the new University of Deseret, which would be a combination high school and college in the East, 307 men and 239 women have matriculated. Next year, Utah women will gain the same voting rights as men.

Not all residents of Utah are Latter-day Saints, to be sure. Within its 105,000 square miles live 85,000 inhabitants, 1,000 of whom are not Mormons. About a third of these Gentiles are soldiers at Camp Douglas, which sits on a bench in the hills three miles above Salt Lake City, its cannon hovering over the town. Perhaps 250 Gentiles can be found among the 13,000 residents of Salt Lake City. There are five Jewish merchant companies and five Gentile lawyers, and a handful of U.S. officials. Throughout the territory, the railroad and stagecoach companies each employ some 200 Gentiles, and there are scattered miners and traders. The census of Mormon apostates is unknown.

With completion of the railroad, Gentile numbers will inevitably rise. It is no secret that the mountains of Utah bear gold and silver no less than in surrounding states and territories. To date, the rigors of freighting rock out in wagons have kept these claims less than profitable. But increasingly common is the sight of prospectors with packs on their shoulders and picks in their hands. If gold and silver are discovered in abundance, there will be no keeping them out. So far, the Mormons have been content to profit by selling flour, potatoes and peaches to the Gentile-owned mines in nearby territory. Knowing the easy-money corruption of mining, Brigham Young forbids it among his flock, preaching instead the virtues of hard work.

And the hard work is evident in this virgin land. At the heart of Salt Lake City is Temple Square, where mammoth granite foundations of a new edifice of worship have begun to rise from the ground. Adjacent to it is the newly completed Tabernacle, a wonderful, elliptical building with a tortoise-shell of a roof, upheld by a complicated system of arched timbers on massive sandstone walls. The Church's public works program turns the earnest labor of thousands into roads and bridges, irrigation works and public buildings. The Church has also launched such diverse manufactures as iron, sugar, cotton and silk, plus wool and livestock cooperatives. In Utah, beliefs beget landmarks.

East of the Temple block, the square lying across Main Street is constantly bustling with activity. Here, the General Tithing Office, which has branches throughout Mormondom, operates not only as a tax office, but a bank, marketing bureau, and central exchange for bartered goods and labor. Through the tithing yard, wagons move in and out, loaded with tithes paid in kind. There are stables and storehouses and livestock to be merged into Church herds on the range. To the east is the Lion House, one of several homes for the families of Brigham Young, and the Beehive House, a handsome colonial building of yellowish adobe.

As beliefs beget landmarks, landmarks may beget curious imaginings. For the past several months, I have resided in a Mormon boarding house, initially designed as a home for five wives. It is an elongated structure, entered by several doors, each of which leads to a suite of private rooms for a wife and her children. The dining room and kitchen are one for all. My landlady, the kindly surviving widow among the five, is hostess to three gentlemen boarders and myself, each of us with a private sitting room and bedroom. I do not know how long ghosts linger in dwellings, but late at night, I have caught myself wondering. How would I feel if my landlady were more youthful and we gentlemen were her plural husbands in some even more latter-day *menage*?

\*\*\*

"Ah," Molly smiled, "do your brother husbands share your humor? Are you really going to print that, Ted?"

"I don't know. In this day and age, men can publish awfully scandalous things."

"Yes, men can," Molly said. "The rest of us must use *noms de plume*."

Ted laughed aloud, as he often did in Molly's company. "Well, your trigonometry is correct." He handed her the paper across the table and began to write an algebra problem.

Molly reached beneath the table and brought out two books. "Grandfather sent me some poetry, Ted, by Robert Browning and Elizabeth Barrett Browning. Must I solve more equations, or can we read them?"

"All right," he relented. "Which one?"

"*Sonnets From the Portuguese*," she said eagerly. "'How do I love thee, let me count the ways.'"

Molly looked away from Ted as Amelia entered the room. "That's enough studying for now, Molly. Would you clear the table for supper?"

Molly hesitated at the door, listening as Ted spoke to

Amelia.

"I plan to see Frances and Charles very soon," he said. "My older daughter has just given birth to a boy, and my younger daughter is expecting her first child. I'll be going East before Thanksgiving and wouldn't think of bypassing Gettysburg."

"You will return, won't you?" Amelia asked.

"I haven't decided that yet, and may not until after I get there. But before I go east, I plan to hire a guide and ride south to the upper Virgin River Valley. The scenery is said to be so much like Heaven that you Mormons have named it Little Zion."

"You won't need a guide if I come with you," John said, entering the dining room. "I have business not far from there, at Cedar City."

Ted smiled at the prospect, then winked at Molly. "Ah, Molly, what do you suppose are your father's designs? To wear down my defenses, then baptize me in the Virgin River?"

# Chapter 8

The two men on horseback, with a pack horse trailing, had ridden south for several days along a road that bore traces from decades of wagon wheel ruts. From time to time, they encountered other horsemen and stopped to exchange information on the conditions ahead. Most of them were Mormon elders traveling among the villages in the region or on business to Salt Lake City.

Bailey craned his neck to look at the map that Carter was reading. Ted pointed to a place on the map west of the trail.

"That's where it happened, isn't it?"

John stiffened. "Where what happened?"

"The Mountain Meadows massacre. Over a hundred victims, a dozen years ago. No one has ever stood trial for it."

John spurred his horse abruptly. "We'd better keep moving, Bailey. The days are growing shorter than you realize."

As Ted rode behind Carter across the arid plains, he pondered the question that filled his mind ever since they left Salt Lake City. When he returned East next month, should he remain there, among the people he had always known?

Bailey and Carter slowed their horses as they entered a spectacular gorge, as magnificent as Ted had been promised. Eons of flowing water had carved through beds of red and white sandstone, leaving strangely colored sheer walls 3,000 feet high. The sandstone, shale and limestone rocks contrasted with the autumn foliage of the trees near the water, bigtooth maples and box elder, cottonwood and willow. An immense red-brown mountain rose sharply from the desert floor and loomed on the near horizon. After riding through dry country for days, Ted was surprised by the sight of trickling waterfalls. They rode past balanced boulders and through gorges so narrow that they were hidden until the horses were inside them. Ted's first view of a free-standing arch, rising in red sandstone over 300 feet, left him breathless.

Late in the afternoon, Carter halted his horse and climbed

down. Ted quickly dismounted too, pleased to have reached their destination. John pitched the tent while Ted hobbled the horses where they could graze and drink their fill. As he gathered firewood, the leaves of hardwood trees turning flaming colors reminded him of New England.

Ted warmed his hands over the fire. "You've been making and striking camp quite deftly without much help from me," he said. "I never had to learn to manage during the War because an orderly took care of my needs."

John looked up from the equipment. "When I served in the Mormon Battalion, I learned Army methods, and its weaknesses. And their officers learned that the Nauvoo Legion had made us competent soldiers. That knowledge worked to our advantage in '57, when the Army came to seize Utah from Mormon control. It made their officers cautious about us because we knew about the Army's reliance on supply trains. Without having to engage in pitched battle, we could burn supply wagons, run off their livestock, and destroy shelter and forage in their path, leaving them unable to live off the land. We delayed their advance until our early, severe weather forced them to retreat to winter quarters."

Resting with their backs against their saddles, the two men watched the fire as they ate their supper. Ted would have liked a cup of coffee, but Amelia had not thought to pack any.

"Have you read the *Book of Mormon* I gave you?" John asked softly.

Ted braced himself. "Yes."

"What did you think?"

"I find I agree with Mark Twain."

"What did he say?"

"He called it 'chloroform in print.' Though perhaps it's the wholesome Deseret air that causes me to sleep so soundly."

John laughed. "Perhaps it gives you comfort."

Ted stared into the fire and said nothing.

"I'd hoped you'd feel otherwise, of course. Especially with what I'm about to say."

Ted was amazed when he saw Carter pull a bottle of

whiskey from his saddlebag.

"Have we traveled beyond reach of the Word of Wisdom?" Ted asked. "I've never seen you drink hard liquor before."

"The last time I had a drink was seven years ago," John said, "when I sent my eldest son off during war on a foreign mission. The time before that was in 1847, when I learned my youngest son had fallen to his death beneath the wagon wheels on the emigration West."

"Many men's children drive them to drink," Ted sympathized.

"I brought some shot glasses. I expect that passing a bottle back and forth isn't to your liking."

Puzzled, Ted sipped from the glass that John handed him. The whiskey was good, warming the cold night without burning. John tossed the liquor down his throat. They sat silently looking at the fire, listening to the animal sounds in the narrow canyon. After five minutes, John refilled their glasses.

"Are you an atheist, Ted?"

Ted sipped his whiskey before responding. Surely, *his* spiritual beliefs were not the reason John Carter was violating the wisdom of his faith.

"No," he replied. "I believe in a Creator, though the War has left me doubtful of the religion in which I was raised. I confess that I envy your passionate faith in your Church. But for myself, I believe I can live a moral life without the promise of Heaven or threat of Hell."

"Think you'll remarry someday?"

Ted shrugged. "It isn't good for a man to be alone. And the War left many marriageable women of an appropriate class and age."

Ted noticed that John's glass was empty and his speech had grown slurred.

"It's shame you Gentiles can't marry lots of them."

"I don't know how you do it, John."

"It's the mystery, Ted. Sealing for all of Eternity. Oh, it's pleasurable, young women in bed. For procreation, of course. And keeping Amelia, too, we've been through so much. She is my wisest wife. But when your pecker won't get up, better if it's Fawn and not Amelia. She's young enough to be my daughter. That makes a man feel young, Bailey. Not lustful, sinful like men charged up by drinking, going to whorehouses. Worse, seduce a woman and not a damn thought about her after taking their pleasure. Not immoral at all to have four wives. Margaret's a sweet soul but she doesn't want it, so I leave her alone. Couldn't do that if she was my only wife. I love her, like I love them all. Emmeline's wiles are amusing, but I must chasten her often. I am a very busy man. If our women aren't treated well, they leave us and our religion dies. Without them, how can man become like God?"

How, indeed? Ted wondered, gazing past the fire. In the darkness, the rock formations seemed even more curious than by day.

"What do you call this place, John?"

"Kolob Canyon."

"An Indian name?"

"No, ours."

"What does it mean?"

John's voice, slurred by unaccustomed drink, grew louder and deeper as he recited with the authority of God, speaking to Abraham in *The Pearl of Great Price.*

"'I saw the stars, that they were great and that one of them was nearest unto the throne of God...and the name of the great one is Kolob, because it is near unto me for I am the Lord thy God; I have set this one to govern all those which belong to the same order as that upon which thou standest.'"

"God lives on a star?" Ted asked.

"Not a star. A planet that goes round the great star Kolob. A single day there is equal to 1,000 years on Earth."

Ted looked up at the stars in the moistureless sky. "Where is it?"

"That has not yet been revealed."

John poured each of them another drink, then quickly downed his own.

"What d'you think of us?"

Lulled by liquor, fatigue and the hypnotic fire, Ted's mind was too unclear to dissemble. He did not censor his words before he answered.

"I admire you," he said, "individually as industrious people, and for all your community has accomplished. I can truly tell Frances that her sister is well cared for and loved. But your theology! It's as incredible as your father-in-law warned me. I cannot see myself ever converting out of honest conviction."

"I only met Amelia's father once. He picked me up bodily, threw me out of his house."

"That little man?" Ted asked, amazed.

John nodded. "Men will attempt astonishing things for their daughters."

Ted thought of his two daughters and sighed. It was out of duty, not pleasure, that he would see them in the coming weeks.

"What d'you think of Molly?" John asked Ted across the fire.

"She's a lovely girl," Ted answered readily. "And she has a fine character to accompany that loveliness. I wish my daughters were more like her."

"She's a contrary girl, like her mother was at 17. Molly says she opposes plural marriage, claims it likens women to brood mares! Amelia tells her she's being ridiculous. We should've burned those books her grandfather sends!"

Ted nodded sympathetically. "I suspect she comes by it naturally, John. Wasn't her father equally contrary?"

John smiled, despite himself, but he soon grew serious. He took a deep breath, then as he spoke, every sign of inebriation in his voice disappeared.

"Molly threatens to remain a spinster, Ted. And when I see the determination in her eyes, I believe her. She has offered us only one alternative. She loves you. And she knows you'd never court her, out of decency toward her mother and me. For reasons she *refuses* to divulge, Molly suspects you might be interested in her as a woman."

In the darkness, Ted felt himself blush. Molly? He felt stunned.

"But she's so young," he said weakly.

"Our girls marry young, frequently to older men."

"And I'm a Gentile."

"Naturally, we hope that will change."

"I'm a war-damaged cynic, a freethinker, almost an atheist. My life expectancy is no more than a dozen years."

"Longer if you live as we do. Four months here have changed you already."

Ted wondered if the change was so evident. "Molly won't be able to live fully in your community if she's not sealed to her husband in the Endowment House."

"She knows that."

"Is it only because I'm well-educated?" Ted asked. "And from the East?"

"Your education is attractive, she does admit. But being an Easterner is no advantage in her eyes."

Ted inhaled deeply, then exhaled. "Is it that I have an excellent tailor, and a profession that must seem terribly romantic to a young girl?"

"I asked her the identical questions," John insisted. "Molly shook her head, then said something about your wisdom and humor, gentleness and honorable conduct."

Ted held out his glass and John filled it.

"Don't you and Amelia disapprove?"

"Frankly, I do. But I trust Amelia's judgment in these matters."

John set aside the bottle without pouring another drink for himself.

"I don't need an answer tonight, Ted. Nor before you leave Utah Territory. I'd ask only one thing from you. If you don't wish to marry Molly, please do not return to Deseret. She'll recover from this passion, then recognize that marriage in the Church is best for her."

Ted sipped the smooth whiskey and reflected over the past several months. Why had he been so unable to leave, after he sent off his first article to Lawrence, then the second and third? Why did the mere thought of being banished from Utah fill his veins with icy dread? He thought of the disdain of his daughters in New York, and the empty flattery of women he could not envision with desire. Were the friendly suppers with the Carters the source of his good cheer every Tuesday and Thursday? Or was it being with Molly in their chaste tutoring sessions? Why did he feel such loneliness every Saturday night, when the Carters went to socials where men danced with Molly and single Gentile men were unwelcome?

Ted looked up again at the stars. Kolob, he thought to himself in bewilderment and disbelief.

Although he had tried, he was unable to forget the intimacy of Molly in his arms. She was right that she would be a more difficult wife than most men, entitled to many wives, would abide. Ted could not bear to think of Molly rebuked and chastened by any man who was her inferior.

Ted heard the quaking cottonwoods before he felt the shiver through his clothes. Through the silence, the whispering was undeniable.

# Chapter 9

Ted gazed affectionately at Molly as he finished his morning coffee. Her open wrapper exposed her full-breasted chest while she nursed the month-old baby girl. He smiled at his wife and daughter, then glanced over to the corner to make sure that his three-year-old son had not wandered into some mischief.

"Ted, dear, are you staring lecherously at my bosom?"

"Indeed I am, Molly. Nonetheless, I must get downtown to the courthouse for the trial. It's crowded with newspapermen from the East, San Francisco and Virginia City. They've all come to interview Ann Eliza Young about her suit against Brigham Young for divorce and alimony."

"Ah, Ann Eliza," Molly said.

"Do you know her?"

"Not well, though I've seen her at socials and the theater. She's eight years older than I am."

"Tell me, Molly, what would you have done if Brigham Young took a fancy to you?"

She pondered the question for a moment. "I expect he would've had a revelation that I'd refuse him."

"Perhaps he did," Ted replied.

Ted kissed his family, then left the house and walked briskly toward the Federal Courthouse. As he passed the railroad station, a large man wearing a wrinkled suit called out, "Bailey!"

"Polson! I haven't seen you since New York. What are you doing here?"

"Covering the trial, of course." He set down his heavy carpetbag. "So the rumors about you are true."

"I've hardly tried to hide it," Ted replied. "I expect Lawrence has told everyone."

"Lawrence thinks you're quite mad, though we all enjoy your pieces in the *Empire Monthly*. You haven't become one of them, have you?"

Ted shook his head. "But my wife is. We've been married four years."

"A lovely girl, I hear, and quite young. They say that all the girls in Utah marry young. Brigham Young!"

Polson laughed loudly, then sneezed into a large handkerchief. "Did you see what your old paper, the *New York Herald* said?"

"No."

Polson's corpulent face strained with the effort to remember. "Something like, 'If the government would send a fresh detachment of young, good-looking soldiers to Salt Lake City, the ranks of polygamists would be decimated by female deserters.' You've enlisted in that detachment, yourself."

"I don't qualify as young, I'm afraid. But I do forget my age when I'm with Molly."

"Especially in bed, I'll wager." Polson slapped Ted on the back. "I hear that's the only pleasure a man gets here."

"You'll find Mormon innkeepers happy to serve strong spirits to guests," Ted assured him. "Molly, too, indulges my coffee, pipes and moderate liquor without any looks of disapproval."

"A refreshing change from Lydia, then. Lawrence said you brought the new Mrs. Bailey to New York, and had a dreadful meeting with your daughters. They were patronizing, he said, and contemptuous toward their Mormon stepmother."

Ted looked at his pocketwatch, wondering how he could gracefully escape. "I expected little better from them. I haven't seen them since, and we exchange only occasional letters."

"Still, I'll bet Molly begged you to let her stay on in New York City."

"You'd lose that wager, Polson," Ted replied. "Molly was appalled by what she saw of New York, and the cities and mill towns in the East. To her, they seemd so crowded and dirty compared to Utah. But I enjoyed our visit. At the hotel in New York, I signed the register, 'Edward Bailey and Wife, Salt Lake City.' The next day, some mischievous wag crossed out 'Wife' and put in 'Wives.'"

Polson clapped Ted on the shoulder. "I bet you'll succumb and take a few yourself, before long. Of course, you couldn't bring them all when you come home to New York. Did you see that cartoon two years back, when the new anti-polygamy law passed?"

"No."

"Surrounded by dozens of wives and children, Brigham Young asks President Grant, 'What shall I do with all these?' 'Do as I do,' Grant replies, 'give them offices.'"

Polson grinned and glanced down at his watch. "Ah, time to go witness King Brigham stripped of his holy raiments and lashed by the scourge of decent law. Hmm, not bad." He pulled out a thick notebook and copied down the words.

Polson continued to speak loudly, scribbling while they walked to the courthouse. "'Once we peek behind the curtain of Young's harem, led inside by a 'lady' who's lain in his bed, he'll have no way of stemming his comeuppance.' Can't you just smell the blood about to flow?"

Embarrassed to acccompany his former colleague, Ted said nothing. He felt no calling to be a scandal monger, and he wished to remain in Salt Lake City.

## THE DIVORCE OF THE MUCH-MARRIED MR. YOUNG
by
**Edward Bailey**
October, 1874

One of the curious legal battles of our age is now being waged in Salt Lake City in the U.S. Territorial Courthouse. Being sued for divorce by his 27th wife is Brigham Young, not only President of the Mormon Church, but its Prophet, Seer and Revelator.

To be sure, Mr. Young does not rank as the most married Latter-day Saint. That honor is reputedly claimed by Apostle Heber Kimball, having wed 45 women and fathered 65 children. Several of Mr. Kimball's wives have divorced him, for divorce is a right of unhappy wives and not uncommon in Utah.

But this disgruntled wife of Mr. Young refuses to go away quietly. Ann Eliza Webb Young has sued him for $500 in monthly alimony and substantial legal fees.

The central legal dilemma is as follows. If the Judge rules that Brigham Young is already wed to a legitimate wife, and cannot legally be married to Ann Eliza, then the petitioner is entitled to nothing, other than generous sympathy. But if the Judge determines that Ann Eliza is indeed a wife, then all the thousands of plural marriages of Utah must likewise be deemed valid. A great victory for the Latter-day Saints would result, at a small price in alimony for Mr. Young. Such a ruling, of course, would contradict the Poland Act that bans polygamy, passed by Congress in 1872.

This much-married Mr. Young is still imposing and erect at age 71, of medium height and a somewhat corpulent build. His face and voice are pleasant, with eyes of unwavering steel gray, and lips compressed and thin. His sandy-colored whiskers and light brown hair betray just a few scattered graying strands. Outdoors in summer, President Young appears comfortably dressed in public in a white coat, white vest and linen trousers, with a black cravat, a straw hat and green goggles to shade his eyes from the glaring sunlight. He wears a watch and chain, light gaiters on his feet, and carries an umbrella. Full of blustering outdoors vigor and cheeriness, he has a keen sense of humor and irony.

From this man, Ann Eliza's escape unfolds like a popular melodrama. She was once, in fact, an actress on the Salt Lake City stage, and is well cast as a lovely, wronged heroine. Already once divorced, Ann Eliza was married to Mr. Young for three years, before fearing persecution, she fled from him in the night.

Ann Eliza, now age 30, was born in Nauvoo, Illinois and raised in a polygamous family in Utah. Her father, a well-to-do carriage maker, lost a fortune in '37 in the Mormon banking scandal in Kirtland, Ohio, although he quickly regained his financial footing. When she was 17, Ann Eliza contends, she first grew aware of Brigham Young's interest in her as a woman. Soon, he sent for her to join the troupe of actors at the newly-opened Salt Lake City Theater, which he personally owns. At this theater, Mr. Young selects the scripts and calls the tunes. He dislikes tragedy and disfavors excess romance over monogamy. Tender-hearted, he once ordered a staging of Oliver Twist withdrawn because the beating of Nancy was too violent and bloody.

Mr. Young arranged for Ann Eliza to live four days a week at his Lion House residence, since her family lived quite distant from the theater. With its three stories and 20 gables, the Lion House was home to a dozen of his wives and many daughters.

The Lion House may be imagined as an oriental harem, veiled and deep cushioned, with incense floating through thick, wicked air. Alas, I regret to disappoint my Readers, but my mother-in-law, as honest a woman as I know, is a frequent visitor there. The Lion House, she swears, resembles nothing more depraved than a strict female dormitory transplanted intact from New England, Mr. Young's native home. It is named for the shaggy, reclining lions carved in stonework above the front entrance, not for the virility of the beast. Religious duty and austerity, bountiful motherhood, industriousness, and sexuality only for procreation, are its hallmarks. Ann Eliza disliked the frugal, female atmosphere there.

Ann Eliza was not the first actress to enchant Mr. Young. A true romantic, he became enamored at age 64 of an actress named Julia Dean Hayne. He designed a huge green sled, embellished with two large wooden swan heads and drawn by six horses, and christened it, "The Julia Dean." But Miss Hayne was a Gentile and would not marry him. Years later, after she married then died in childbirth in New York, Mr. Young was reputed to have her baptized into the Church and sealed to him as his wife for all Eternity.

Ann Eliza's theatrical skills were applauded, but were more minor than those of Miss Hayne. She retired from the stage after two years, and married her first husband in the Endowment House. Three years later, after the birth of two sons, she divorced that husband. It was then that her most serious allegation against Mr. Young arose.

In 1868, she claims, her elder brother was forced into

bankruptcy due to a financial dispute with none other than Brigham Young, himself. This brother was allegedly threatened with excommunication unless Ann Eliza agreed to become Mr. Young's wife. Once married, she says, he failed to provide adequate financial and emotional support. While chaste marriages are not unknown in Mormondom, Ann Eliza swears that hers with Mr. Young was consummated.

How does a woman escape from Salt Lake City when her all-powerful husband owns the only railroad out of town? Openly, Ann Eliza bought a ticket for herself and a chaperone to Ogden, from where they could travel either east or west. Secretly, the night before they were scheduled to depart, they boarded a carriage to the first Union Pacific stop east of Ogden. For 40 miles the carriage lurched along in the darkness, the driver losing his way not once but twice. All the while, Ann Eliza wondered if her driver was a treacherous spy for Brigham Young. The carriage bumped its way to the depot at dawn, just as the train chugged in. Her confederates, meanwhile, had smuggled her belongings out of her hotel and shipped them on to Laramie as the possessions of someone else.

Financially, Ann Eliza has capitalized on her drama by joining the burgeoning lecture hall circuit. Standing-room-only crowds welcome her in many cities. Naturally, the prurient can be relied upon to attend, but the widespread interest in the plight of this one woman is more surprising. Perhaps it can best be explained by some irresistible melding of piety with forbidden passions. "Polygamy in the United States!" Ann Eliza exclaims. "Polygamy among Anglo-Saxons! Who was original enough to conceive the idea?" With such permissible fare for church-going men and genteel ladies, she has book offers from dozens of New York City publishing houses.

In her affidavit, Ann Eliza contends that her husband's personal fortune is worth $8 million, ample to afford a comfortable alimony for her. Without a doubt, Brigham Young is well-off, reputedly one of the largest depositors in the Bank of England. But that money, he insists, belongs to the Perpetual Emigration Fund of the Church, dedicated to bringing Latter-day

Saints here to Utah. He refuses to disclose the precise amount of his wealth.

With their own stake in this dispute, the monogamous Reorganized Mormons, who follow Joseph Smith III, not Brigham Young, have tried to raise the stakes for the nation. "Neither is this deemed a *local* but a *national* matter," they editorialize, "for if the Mormon hierarchy be found, on trial, the supreme power in Utah above the United States, then it is the supreme power over all the United States."

Women, too, disagree with strong passions. According to one Mormon wife, not my own, "Preaching against polygamy is like collecting money for the heathen, who would've been better off if they'd never seen a Christian."

However Ann Eliza's suit is resolved, its ambiguity gives it weak moral value. Whatever the truth about her brother's threatened excommunication, Mr. Young clearly did not coerce a young girl to relinquish her maidenhood for his pleasure. It is equally credible that he saw Ann Eliza as a wayward divorcee with two sons, all in need of his guidance on Earth and the hereafter. He did not keep her enthralled, but freely offered her religious divorce.

Two questions remain in this latest among the many strange skirmishes regularly fought out in the Salt Lake City streets. Is it merely that a few embattled Gentiles have seized upon Ann Eliza's overdramatization as a potent new weapon to wield against their perennial Nemesis? And of final and deeper significance, is there to be some check on the power by a 'Prophet' who possesses less decency than Mr. Young?

\*\*\*

Ted considered seeking Molly's impressions, but he feared she would dissuade him from using certain of his favorite words. He walked briskly to the telegraph office and forwarded his account to Lawrence.

In front of the Walker House Hotel, Polson boisterously called out to Ted. Owned by apostate Mormon brothers, the newly-built hotel had six colonnades and four stories, packed with reporters.

"Well, Bailey, what'd you think of the proceedings?"

"I think the Church will survive it."

"Not if I can help it. Want to hear a few gems from my Polson Pen column?"

Polson pulled out his thick notebook and read the scrawled words aloud. "This reporter asked Mrs. Young, 'They say your husband plans to allege adultery against you in his defense. Do you think they could manufacture that kind of evidence?' She replied, 'They could find 2,000 Mormons to swear to anything that the President told them.'

"It gets even better, Bailey," Polson smirked. "Ann Eliza rightly feared for her life from the bearded young men called the Danites. Known assassins, some of them have even dared to publish their confessions of mayhem. Understandably afraid, Ann Eliza still refuses to disclose what goes on behind the blocked-up windows of the Endowment House. One can only imagine what orgiastic black magic may be practiced there under the guise of Christianity."

Ted sighed but said nothing.

Polson licked his lips and continued. "Not for the first time has Brigham Young interfered in the romantic life of the young. One suitor of his daughter, Alice, was packed off to the Hawaiian Islands to serve as missionary. Then, after another suitor broke his engagement with Alice, the young man's party was ambushed 400 miles south of Salt Lake, barely escaping the unidentifiable attackers. Tragically, Alice later committed suicide."

Ted feared that Lawrence would be disappointed in his story. Polson and others like him made the public want to read the most salacious possible interpretation.

"Ah, then there's this," Polson said proudly. "Tearfully, Ann Eliza read me a letter from her mother. 'Your death would have been far preferable to the course you are taking,' her mother wrote. 'Flee from your present dictators, as you would from the fiends of the darkness. I was praying for your death before you had sinned past redemption.' Thus can a mother, herself a corrupted polygamous wife, have her morals tragically torn away from the normal maternal feelings of her sex."

Polson looked up again. "How do you like my headline? 'THE PROPHET OF UTAH AS A LOVER.' Well, I'll wager you could use a drink, Bailey. I know I could. I'll buy, for old times sake."

Wearier than he had felt in many years, Ted shook his head. "No, thanks, Polson. I'd like to get home to my family."

# Chapter 10

Molly entered the house carrying the mail in her hand.

"Perhaps you should become a polygamist, Ted."

Ted looked up from his newspaper and examined her face for any sign of joking. Finding none, he asked, "Ah, Molly, would you go to such lengths to get me into the waters of baptism?"

She shook her head. "If I had three sister wives, I could readily spend three weeks a month immersed in my medical studies. Then they could help attend the children while I doctored the sick."

Ted tried to envision such a household. "Remind me to ask Bishop Tuttle if I must become a Mormon first."

Molly kissed him, then handed him an envelope.

"You're going to be an excellent doctor," Ted assured her. "But tell me, Molly, do you find me so demanding?"

"Oh, no," she replied. "After all, it was your mathematics tutoring that made this possible. But when I finally become a physician, how can I take care of Carter and Joanna?"

"We can hire help. Not every woman in Salt Lake City has young children."

"Is that what people do in the East?" Molly asked.

Ted nodded, glancing at the letter. It was postmarked New York City.

"But I'd feel bad," Molly said, "being away from the children when your income is more than ample to support the family."

"Well, if it makes you feel better," Ted replied, "I have less income now than when you married me. Between the '73 Panic and the corrupt Grant Administration, business is very demoralized. I thank God that most of my money is in New York City real estate, not stocks and bonds, let alone in my bank when it failed."

Ted reluctantly opened the letter. Frowning, he read it aloud to Molly.

279

March 12, 1877

Father,

Imagine our mortification to read in the *Empire Review* of your intention to let our little brother Carter be baptized into the Mormon Church! To take this *inconceivable* step is one matter, to publish it for all New York to read is quite another. It is unfortunate enough that you *persist* in your self-imposed exile in Utah Terrritory, and embarrass us monthly with your apologistic articles. But this course will entitle our half-brother to become an *immoral* polygamist in a dozen years!

Carter is not yet seven and will not know right from wrong for *many* years. But has he even been *exposed* to proper Christianity? We read of your Bishop Tuttle in your columns, and he appears to be a wise and reverend gentlemen. Perhaps he can talk some sense into our brother, if indeed our father lies beyond hope.

Lawrence and Polson, and *all* your other friends here, concur with us in these sentiments. All of us, we promise you, are appalled. We fear that if you are not deterred, you will someday give away our dear little sister Joanna into a *harem*.

Father, you must desist from this course. God only knows *what* our Mormon "stepmother" has done to corrupt your mind and degrade your sentiments. Though you have ceased confiding in us in these matters, we read your columns monthly to reassure ourselves that you have not entered your dotage. Until this latest column, we felt comforted. Our own sainted Mother can only be recoiling in horror in Heaven.

*Please* reconsider this decision, if the wicked act is not yet done. Despite your exile among the heretics in Utah, *you*, as Carter's father, are charged with ultimate authority in spiritual affairs.

With daughterly affection and fervent prayers,

Martha and Lucy

"I should've anticipated that letter," Ted sighed. "I apologize to you, Molly, for what my daughters believe and say."

"What do you plan to do?" she asked.

"Nothing," Ted replied. "The decision is yours and Carter's, not mine. However, I won't disclose to my readers that you've invited me to marry more wives."

Distracted, Molly stroked his arm. "When must you leave to catch the Utah & Southern?"

Ted winced at the thought. "In an hour. The train won't be so bad, but I'm dreading that endless stagecoach south from Nephi."

"Do you have to go?"

"Yes. I promised Lawrence I'd serve as an eyewitness to the execution."

## THE MOUNTAIN MEADOWS MASSACRE IS LAID AT LAST TO REST
by
**Edward Bailey**
March 1877

John D. Lee shook hands and bid farewell to those around him, then called to the firing squad. "Center on my heart, boys. Don't mangle my body!" Then, without a twitch or groan, he died from the fusillade of bullets fired by five riflemen at close range.

It was cold at the scene of the Massacre, where the final victim's life so ceremoniously ended. Justice, actual and poetic, demanded that the execution occur at the same long, green valley that was irrigated in blood 20 years earlier. Lee said that his conscience was clear before God and man, and he solemnly proclaimed his belief in the Mormon gospel taught by Joseph Smith. He spoke of his love and sorrow for his family, naming three wives, not the 19 alleged in some hostile accounts. But he defiantly condemned Brigham Young and the witnesses whose statements convicted him *alone* of all the first degree murders.

Neither Lee nor I flinched as the firing squad took his life. I saw far too many men killed during the War to shudder now. Yet I still feel haunted by the message.

Like the Donner Party's plight and its recourse to cannibalism, the Mountain Meadows massacre was a tragedy of the West, where the Fates and human nature came to battle. Both shameful dramas seem simple to us in hindsight, but to the hapless actors they could have only unfolded in agonizing complexity.

Though it has taken decades to unearth them, certain facts are now beyond dispute. At dawn on a Tuesday in September 1857, the Fancher party with 137 men, women and children, some 30 wagons and a large herd of livestock, was attacked by Indians at Mountain Meadows, Utah Territory. They sustained a few casualties but managed to circle their wagons and set up good earthwork defenses. Their returning gunfire killed some Indians and wounded others, forcing the attackers to withdraw before launching another failed assault. On Wednesday, the Fancher party remained under siege but not active attack, when three riders broke out of the circle, heading for Cedar City, 35 miles away. One was killed by gunshots, and the other two were wounded as they fought their way out, then back inside the circle. But the wounded men saw a white man fire his gun against them.

On Friday, the emigrants were approached by two men, riding under a white flag of truce. One of them was Major Lee, who somehow persuaded the party to relinquish their belongings to the Indians, and commence walking toward Cedar City. As soon as the men were disarmed and separated from the women and children, the militia and Indians joined in exterminating them all, except for 18 little children too young to bear witness against them.

What evil could have seized the minds of these men? They were not vicious border ruffians, accustomed to capricious murder. Lee was a wealthy farmer and Mormon Bishop.

To make any sense at all of this tragedy demands some

history. In 1849 after statehood for Utah was denied, Brigham Young was appointed Territorial Governor. Only a handful of Gentiles lived here then, or could, because the Mormons established settlements everywhere they found reliable water. When a few Gentiles were appointed as Federal officials, they found it hard to accept the fact that, despite their own legal authority, Governor Young determined all matters of importance with the unquestioned allegiance of the populace. For reasons good and ill, the Latter-day Saints were distrustful of Gentile authority. To be sure, some officials *were* venal and incompetent, and for years, the tensions mounted. Then, in 1856, a group of Mormons broke into the Federal Court and seized some documents. The intimidated judges, other local Federal officials, and a disgruntled mail contractor complained to Washington that the Mormons had surpassed mere insubordination and were now traitorous.

President Buchanan resolved to quell this defiance. He appointed a Gentile governor and dispatched 2,500 Army troops to take control over Utah. In July '57, unofficial word reached Salt Lake City that regiments of infantry and dragoons, artillery batteries, and wagon trains with supplies for 15 months were moving west. The news arrived on the tenth anniversary, to the very day, of Brigham Young's first entrance into the Great Salt Lake valley. That day, ten years earlier, he vowed, "If our enemies give us just ten years unmolested, we would ask no odds of them; we would never be driven again."

Ten years, it is surely agreed, is a lengthy duration for any people to conduct themselves as if they are saints. In fact, the year before, Brigham Young ordained a Reformation to overcome the backsliding and apostasizing. The interrogating and preaching, the catechizing and rebaptizing further inflamed religious passions. The tinder was ready for the spark of the Army's approach.

Most of us forget the Mormon plight in Missouri, when they were disarmed by hostile militiamen. But they could not forget. Unable to tolerate the very thought of being occupied by an unfriendly army, Governor Young proclaimed martial law in

Utah Territory. Unofficial Indian agents, including John D. Lee, recruited tribes as allies of the Mormons, promising the chance to loot wagon trains as incentive for their help. It was vital for the Mormons not to anger the potentially murderous Indians, who outnumbered them four to one in southern Utah.

The Nauvoo Legion was assembled, trained and ready to fight if Utah was invaded. Orders were issued to all Saints to conserve supplies, accumulate ammunition, and prepare to resettle after burning food and shelter that could fall into the hands of the invaders. In particular, they were ordered not to sell grain to the Gentiles. Mormons in Nevada, Hawaii and California were told to sell their property and come to Utah at once, with all the arms and ammunition they could gather.

This was the setting into which the Fancher party unwarily and fatally marched. The families came from Arkansas mostly, though a small group of Missouri men joined them when they started south from Salt Lake. The Old Spanish Trail, the only passable route to California in fall and winter, is a difficult route, long and dry, with little forage and water beyond the sparse Mormon settlements in southwest Utah. The emigrants were understandably desperate to acquire extra food and supplies before venturing into the desert. They could only have been furious when the people in Cedar City refused to sell to them.

Undoubtedly, the talk was ugly on both sides. Some Missouri men were said to boast that they had taken part in the assassination of Joseph Smith. Accusations surely flew about the recent murder in Arkansas of Parley Pratt, a beloved Mormon Apostle, after he married another man's wife. Having endured the miseries in Illinois and Missouri, many settlers were angered, if not vengeful, by the prospect of being forced from their homes yet again. Some of the travelers, unable to buy, may have helped themselves to goods, or let their livestock graze on Mormon fields. And they were on the Old Spanish Trail, the obvious route for the Army to invade Utah from the southwest.

Much is known about this executed man, who has been so universally demonized. Born in 1812, John D. Lee joined the

Mormon Church in '37 in Missouri, then became a policeman and bodyguard to Joseph Smith in Nauvoo. He had been a mail carrier, stage driver, farmer, soldier and clerk. After the migration west, Lee helped found the town of Parowan and its ironworks. He served as probate judge and was elected to the territorial legislature. It is said that Lee was adopted as Brigham Young's son in a solemn Church ceremony.

What do I personally believe happened on that cruel Friday in September '57? As many of my Readers know, I am a Mason and not a Mormon. I was a Union Cavalry officer during the War, and I know the obligation to follow orders, even the dreadful "Take no prisoners." With this background, I believe the tragedy at Mountain Meadows could only have unfolded one way.

On Sunday, September 6, after church, the Cedar City Stake High Council convened to discuss what should be done with the troublesome emigrant company. After spirited and angry debate, they decided to dispatch an express rider to Salt Lake City and take no further action until directions were brought back. But the capital was 300 miles away, and communications between the settlements were slow. There was no telegraph then, and express riders were allowed 100 hours in each direction. When the letter reached Brigham Young on Thursday, his urgent and immediate answer was to help the emigrants. The order reached southern Utah two days after the massacre. To his death, Lee denied knowing that the message to Young had been sent.

Lee was under the command of Colonel Dame and Lieutenant Colonel Haight, neither of whom was present at Mountain Meadows. Haight was President of the Stake. When Lee and Haight met in Cedar City on Sunday, they agreed that the Indians be encouraged to attack the travelers, stealing their cattle and goods, but not to kill them. Then, while returning to his home, Lee encountered Indians prepared for battle. The Mormon leaders, they said, had directed them to kill the emigrants, and they wanted Lee to command them. Trying to postpone hostile action, Lee told them to camp near the emigrants and wait while he brought more Indians. But at dawn on Tuesday, the Indians attacked the Fancher party.

Lee arrived on Wednesday, along with more Indians and 14 other whites. He sent a message to Haight, requesting instructions, while over his objections, the Indians attacked again and were again repulsed with losses. That evening, the three desperate riders rode out from the wagons, and the two survivors saw that white men were part of the ambush. To the Mormons, all would be lost if word got out, with the U.S. Army camped just a few days ride away.

On Thursday, more members of the Nauvoo Legion arrived, under Major Higbee. There were now 54 white men at the scene. Lee insisted that he urged Higbee to order the Indians to withdraw and let the emigrants go. But Higbee told him that the riders' knowledge forced Dame and Haight to decide otherwise. Higbee handed Lee written orders from Haight to decoy the emigrants. Then the militia was to kill everyone old enough to talk. Lee swore he dropped the orders to the ground, exclaiming he could not obey them. That night, the troubled Mormons prayed for guidance, and strength to do what they were required as soldiers. After great anguish and counseling, Lee resolved to obey.

On Friday, Lee and another man, carrying a white flag, rode to the Fancher camp where a white flag also flew. The emigrants welcomed Lee as their deliverer. He quickly persuaded them to disarm, abandon the wagons and livestock to the Indians, and walk the 35 miles to Cedar City.

Two wagons were driven up, one to carry the small children and guns, the other a woman and three wounded men. The wagons, with Lee walking between them, moved out, followed by files of women and older children. Far behind them, the emigrant men walked in single file, each escorted by an armed Saint. "Halt! Do your duty to God!" came the signal command. Lee and the drivers killed the wounded in the wagon, while each escort slew his disarmed victim. The Indians killed the women and older children. Quickly, the massacre was accomplished. Lee was later identified as the man who drove livestock and wagons to Cedar City, some of the Fancher loot the Indians did not take.

That Friday night, Dame and Haight arrived at a nearby ranch, and they rode out to Mountain Meadows on Saturday morning. According to Lee, they were horrified when they saw more than 100 stripped bodies of the dead. They showed remorse but quarreled bitterly. Dame denied his involvement, while Haight insisted that nothing was done without Dame's orders. Dame responded that he did not know there were so many. Haight retorted that the orders were not dependent on the number of victims. Then they ordered the bodies buried in shallow graves.

For his role in the massacre, Lee was excommunicated in 1870. Still, two years later, he obeyed Brigham Young's order to move across the Colorado River to operate the ferry at the mouth of the Paria River in Arizona Territory.

Why has it taken 20 years to execute justice for its victims? California newspapers first publicized the tragedy in October '57, then the national press gave it wider notoriety. What is called here Buchanan's Blunder ended in an uneasy truce in '58, and the surviving children, well cared for by Mormon families, were located and returned East. But Federal officials found resistance when they tried to uncover the truth. Then the War intervened. Backed by 200 Army troops, a Federal judge tried to investigate after the War, but witnesses could not be found and the grand jury would not indict. Finally, in 1874, the Poland Act took criminal jurisdiction away from Mormon-dominated probate courts. Federal charges were brought against Lee, Dame, Haight and Higbee, among others, but only Lee and Dame were captured.

At Lee's first trial in 1875, no Mormon in good standing testified for either side. The jury of eight Saints and four Gentiles deliberated three days and was deadlocked. Last year, Lee was tried again in front of an all-Mormon jury. This time, the District Attorney promised that he would prosecute only Lee and no one else. Suddenly, other participants in the massacre appeared, and their testimony placed the blame entirely on Lee and the man who had carried the white flag of truce. After a quick trial and three hours of deliberation, the jury convicted Lee alone.

Singled out for disgrace and sacrifice, Lee reveals much in his confession. Still, one perplexing question remains. There must have been some reason, however desperate, for the Fancher men to disarm themselves and follow Lee. A clue to what made him worthy of their trust may lie in what Lee swore were written orders from Haight. This clue is the word "decoy," like a duck decoy placed in a lake to fool flying ducks into thinking the lake is free from danger. As a Mason myself, I can suggest an explanation. John D. Lee and Isaac Haight are known to have been members of the Nauvoo Masonic Lodge. Perhaps a man in the circled wagons gave a Masonic distress sign and Lee, expecting it and knowing he would harm and not assist them, responded nonetheless as a Mason. If so, he betrayed not only his word as a man and so-called Christian, but his military honor, and whatever moral obligation a former Mason might owe to his brothers and their widows and orphans.

The betrayal might not have mattered at all. Perhaps the Fancher party was doomed to extermination regardless of blame, like other victims of Indian wars. But after 20 years, vengeance has been satisfied, if not justice. The blood has finally dried in Mountain Meadows, a landscape that bore witness to treachery engendered by mindless fear.

***

Molly read the final lines and handed the manuscript back to Ted.

"Must you publish this?" she asked. "Most people have forgotten the massacre, if they ever knew about it. And after the War, 120 deaths seem so..." She let the sentence fade unfinished.

"Insignificant?" Ted asked.

"No," Molly said. "Treachery is never insignificant. But we were at war, and wars always lead to civilian casualties. Like the brother I never knew who died on the trail."

"I'll not make the truth a casualty, Molly."

"Then publish it, Ted. But you haven't diminished my faith in the Church. The character flaws of certain men or deceits deemed necessary for our welfare do not weaken the worth of our teachings."

Molly stood and walked to Ted's chair. She drew his head to her bosom, kissed his forehead, then quietly stepped out of the room.

# Chapter 11

In New York City, Lawrence unwrapped the neatly written manuscript from Ted Bailey. He scanned the cover letter, inviting him yet again to visit Utah. Then he weighed Ted's proposed article for the December issue, a story on Deseret Hospital.

"It was opened by the Women's Relief Society in 1882," Bailey wrote. "It's staffed entirely by female doctors, most of them mothers and wives. Molly agrees to be interviewed, but only if her comments are unedited."

Lawrence agreed that the idea had possibilities. But he would have to consider whether he could promise that Molly Bailey's views would not be edited.

Lawrence read down the letter, cordial and gracious as always. But he shook his head in amazement at Bailey's excitement over his infant son's first words. The man was 58 years old!

## THE END OF A VERY SHORT ERA
### by
### Edward Bailey
November 1884

Last week, the Liberal Institute, consecrated to freedom, equality and fraternity, closed its doors in Salt Lake City for the last time. Only 13 years old, its solid, well-designed building was sold to the Presbyterian Church for less than 14 cents on the dollar.

One might suppose that Mormon Church hostility led to the Liberal Institute's demise. Though the Saints may well have prayed for divine intervention, the corpse bears no evidence of foul play. Instead, the official Church policy was to pretend that the Institute did not exist. It was the opening this year of the sumptuous Walker Opera House that struck the death knell by competing for the Gentile theatrical and literary trade.

The Institute was founded in 1869 by disaffected and apostate Mormons known as "Godbeites." William Godbe, a successful English apothecary here, did not intend to be a schismatic when he and his followers founded the monthly *Utah Magazine*. But over time, its authors drifted from articles to arguments, then to resisting authority. To the Godbeites, the Church of Jesus Christ of Latter-day Saints was no longer the advanced and liberal institution of their conversion. They formed a rival Church of Zion, but lacking the zeal of true Mormons, soon abandoned their pallid imitation and turned instead to free-thought spiritualism. Such spiritualism believes that the scientific and intellectual currents of our century run contrary to Christianity in general, and to Mormonism in particular.

Financed in part by Eastern donations, the Liberal Institute was constructed at a cost of $50,000. Sixty feet square at its base, the building seated 1,000 people in a half-octagon shape, which facilitated hearing and seeing. The ceiling rose an impressive 30 feet. Temporary seating doubled the capacity, and a removable floor permitted dancing. Its address at Second South and Second East Streets shows its proximity to the heart of Mormondom.

At the building's dedication on July 2, 1871, Susan B. Anthony and Elizabeth Cady Stanton addressed an enthusiastic, overflowing audience. Two days later, 2,000 people celebrated July Fourth at its ceremonies beyond earshot of the orations of Brigham Young. "People are fairly flocking to the Institute," gushed the Godbeite *Salt Lake Tribune*.

The Institute was open to all denominations, and Methodists, Presbyterians, Jews and Lutherans worshipped in it. But the Reorganized Mormon Church used it most often as a staging area for preaching to their Utah cousins. The sons of Joseph Smith, David, Frederick and Joseph III, were among the "Josephite" missionaries who could be heard preaching at the Institute.

Still, Spiritualism was the predominant faith. Orson Pratt, Jr., apostate son of the Apostle, played the organ. Poetry by

Longfellow, Tennyson and Whittier comprised the hymns. A session among the Progessive Spiritualists could be equally combative and enlightening. I recall one Sunday meeting where Unitarianism, scientific materialism, orthodox Mormonism and unrepentant atheism each had a turn on the floor. Demonstrating from the Bible, one speaker "proved" that Abraham was a liar and coward, and Jacob a thief. At once, he was followed by a "lineal descendant of the House of Israel," who rose to defend not only his ancestors but his Mormonism. Then a "wandering Bohemian" shared his views on the "Origin and Evolution of the God-idea," followed by a physician who eloquently argued that the Bible was the worst book ever published, teaching the worship of a monster!

What sense can one make of all this? Perhaps only that freedom of speech was alive and well in Brigham Young's Deseret.

Educational undertakings were always welcome at the Liberal Institute. Countless lectures over the years expounded such themes as the origins of life, the progress of science, chemical and microscopic experiments, law and domestic relations matters, and popular culture. Ventriloquists, phrenologists, magnetic and hypnotic healers were always popular, and trance-speakers spoke as mediums for the dead. One medium, displaying a peculiar local twist, sought to carry posthumous messages from the spirit of Joseph Smith, said to be visiting Utah for awhile. The murderers of Dr. Robinson, a Gentile lured away at night by false emergency and assassinated, were tried in the Liberal Institute in '71 and again in '74, as the prosecutors sought the largest capacity non-Mormon hall in the city.

Temperance and female suffrage are among the few beliefs shared by both the Liberals and Mormons. The role of education is not. As the *Salt Lake Tribune* described the Children's Progressive Lyceum held in the Institute, "It is one of those Sunday Schools where children are taught to do their own thinking... The chief method relied upon is to draw out of the child what it knows and understands and develop its powers rather than to make it a little machine into which somebody else's wisdom is pumped. No creeds are taught on the strength of Authority, ancient or modern."

After President Young died in 1877, his successor, John Taylor, thrust a new mission on the Liberal Institute. When President Taylor urged that non-Mormons be excluded from teaching Mormon youth, a well-regarded teacher lost his employment and established a school for 135 students in the Institute. Of Utah's hundreds of schools, none is tax-supported. The electorate, knowing that the *Book of Mormon* cannot so readily be taught in public schools, repeatedly votes down Gentile proposals for them. But the school in the Institute was forced to close, its high ceiling leaving the room both too cold and too costly to heat.

By then, the Liberal Institute was already in decline. In 1879, its dignity had degenerated so far that it became the venue for a sparring exhibition, with ample head punching promised in the advertisements. By 1881, a billiard competition was held at the hall, enhanced by wagering enough to attract a crowd. We trust the Presbyterian Church can elevate the Institute toward nobler purposes again. But those of us who enjoyed its lively intellectual battles can only mourn the passing of its mission.

*** 

Lawrence shook his head, bewildered. Surely this was yet another reason for Bailey to return to New York. But Ted gave no indication that he would soon, or ever, come home. What could be so compelling about Utah, Lawrence wondered, that his favorite correspondent refused to end his self-imposed exile there?

# Chapter 12

"What was that?" Ted exclaimed, sitting up abruptly in bed.

Molly was already standing. In the darkness, he could see her silhouette in her robe.

"Pebbles tossed against the window, I think."

Ted followed Molly as she ran down the stairs.

"I'll get a lamp," he offered.

"No!"

Molly opened the back door. A tall figure dressed in dark clothes slipped inside.

"Father!" she whispered, throwing her arms around his chest.

"It's all right, Molly," John said, stroking her hair. "Your mother's house is being watched, but I don't think they followed me here. Have you got somewhere to hide me?"

"Of course, John," Ted answered.

Carter followed Ted and Molly up the stairs to an almost hidden closet within the attic. He cautiously inspected his small quarters.

"Even if they search the attic, they won't find you here," Ted assured him.

"There's a $50 bounty for my capture."

In the darkness of the attic, Ted could not see John's face as they listened to the noises of the Salt Lake City night. All was quiet except for the occasional barking of a dog in the distance.

"I was afraid I'd never see you again," Molly said. "It's been most of a year."

"Since spring of '85," Ted muttered, "when the Supreme Court declared open season on polygamists. Strangers are asking our children about your whereabouts, John. The regular officers aren't so bad, but the bounty hunters are common ruffians. They swagger, bluster and threaten, and they brandish revolvers to frighten the women and children."

"Are the children scared?" John asked.

"No," Molly said. "The children can tell who the deputies

are, even when they disguise themselves as tramps or peddlers or tourists."

John shook his head sadly. "What in God's name do they expect me to do? Put aside three wives and let them fend for themselves, without my help? As it is, my family is all scattered. I don't even know where Fawn and Margaret are."

"Margaret is living with friends in Arizona until all this madness passes," Molly said. "And Fawn has returned to where her tribe lives."

"How is she faring?"

Molly hesitated. "It's a mean Idaho town, Father. They treat your children as half-breeds, not as sons and daughters of a respected Utah businessman. I know nothing about Emmeline."

"That I know," John answered bitterly. "Emmeline was granted a civil divorce and given some money raised from a distress sale of my real estate."

A racking cough seized John, and he was unable to speak for a long minute.

"I detest that I can't support my family in hiding! I'm 65 years old, and should be bouncing my grandchildren on my knee. But I'm in good company. President Taylor is in hiding, and he's 76."

Molly's eyes gradually adjusted to the dim light in the attic, and she could make out her father's familiar features.

"I've stayed mostly in the south, near St. George," he said. "But I couldn't bear not seeing Amelia, and I've carried some messages for the Church. We've organized a system of guards and signals, so we can travel about. And many sheriffs have no interest in arresting their boyhood friends, so they warn us of the whereabouts of the deputies."

"Mother stayed with Aunt Franny only two weeks," Molly told her father. "She said she couldn't stay away. Her heart is here."

"You haven't broken any law," Ted insisted. "You married all four of your wives before the first Anti-Bigamy law in '62."

"Nonetheless, I'm disenfranchised, just like a common felon," John sighed.

"Did you hear what happened last Fourth of July?" Ted asked him.

"No."

"As dawn rose on Independence Day, all of Salt Lake City woke up to see every flag flying at half-mast over every building controlled by Mormons. I thought of you and silently cheered."

"Thank you, Ted."

"Around City Hall, crowds of Gentiles milled, threatening to force entrance and raise the flag high. Some even called for troops from Fort Douglas to undo the insult. As if you Mormons had burned the flag, instead of half-masting it in mourning!"

"When the crowds finally managed to raise the flag," Molly said, "there was much fretting over how the flags would fly three weeks later, on Pioneer Day. Then Ulysses Grant died and the question became moot, as all the flags stood at half-staff."

John laughed, but his laughter soon turned into another fit of coughing.

Molly looked at him with concern. "I'll bring you some medicine, Father."

In the distance, a dog howled, then a closer dog. Nearby, a gate creaked as it opened. Ted and Molly glanced at each other in the darkness. Molly kissed her father, then hurried down the stairs. Ted followed behind her.

Suddenly, the front door flew open. Three deputy marshals stood in the hallway.

"Don't worry, Ma'am. We don't want anything but the Polyg. We know he's here."

Ted stood between the deputies and the stairs. "We haven't seen my father-in-law since last spring."

"Then you won't mind if we search your home."

"Of course, I mind. Under the Fourth Amendment, you have no such right."

The men glared at Ted.

Three-year-old Ned toddled from his bedroom at the top of the stairs. "Grandpa?" he said.

"Neddy!" Molly cried, racing past Ted and the deputies and up the stairs. She embraced the boy and held him tight.

"He's up there!" a deputy said.

The men pushed past Molly and Ned and drew their guns.

John stepped out of the attic, his hands high in the air. "I won't put my family further at risk," he told the deputies. "God only knows what you're capable of doing in the name of the law."

With Ned grasped in her arms, Molly stood beside Ted as they watched her father being marched away.

# Chapter 13

Dear Ted,

For the first time I can recall, I must reject one of your manuscripts. It is, I acknowledge, a passionate expression of a viewpoint seldom seen in the East. But it is not in the now-familiar style of Edward Bailey, the respected gentle skeptic that your public awaits to read for his detached view on the happenings in the Intermountain West. That is the image I must maintain for this magazine, and the style best suited for the advancement of your eminently well-deserved reputation.

I fear you are personally too close to this matter to maintain the proper objectivity. Incredibly, I read your article as a polemic that seeks to justify the old *status quo* on polygamy, anathema to all *other* non-Mormon Americans. Frankly, I had hoped for a column expressing jubilation that a festering social infection has at last been lanced and drained. Your readers long ago lost patience with the polygamy controversy.

For God's sake, Ted, do not take this rejection as any lack of professional respect for your perception, judgment and writing. I sincerely want you to continue as our Intermountain West correspondent. As you well know, the piece is too long. I suggest you edit out the excessive apologistic passion, and I will happily publish a suitable revision. I will understand if you decline.

Warmest personal regards,

Lawrence

Ted indignantly looked up from the letter. Lawrence had, from time to time, mangled his columns with an unsympathetic editorial pen. But never in 25 years had he rejected a story outright from the *Empire Monthly Review*. Convinced that Lawrence could not possibly be right, Ted sat in his study, rereading his rejected manuscript.

## HOORAY FOR OUR SIDE—THE MORMONS SURRENDER ON POLYGAMY
by
**Edward Bailey**
October 1890

Last month, on September 24, the Latter-day Saints abandoned the practice of polygamy, a characteristic unique among American religions. The Manifesto, proclaimed by Mormon Church President Wilford Woodruff, came four months after the Supreme Court upheld the Edmunds-Tucker Act as constitutional, and while Congress was debating new laws to disenfranchise *all* Mormons in Utah.

There is, to be sure, great relief that this vexatious problem has been resolved. But before we proudly congratulate ourselves, let us weigh the decency of how this triumph was achieved, and how fitting with American guarantees in our Bill of Rights and Constitution.

In 1862, when the Southern states-rightists were elsewhere preoccupied, Congress passed its first Anti-Bigamy Law. But soon, this law was found weak. The secrecy of plural marriage rites made cases impossible to prosecute, and Mormon grand juries refused to indict the Brethren. Overzealous Gentile judges chose anti-Mormon jurors where they could find them, and in 1872, Brigham Young and other men were arrested and indicted for lascivious cohabitation. The Supreme Court did not agree, as their ruling was telegraphed back to Utah: "Jury unlawfully drawn; summons invalid; proceedings ordered dismissed; decision unanimous, all indictments quashed."

In 1874, Congress passed the Poland Act, and under it, a polygamist was fined $500 and sentenced to two years in prison. His conviction was upheld by the Supreme Court, though they reversed another verdict when a wife was forced to testify against her husband. While Federal prosecutors struggled to convict other men, the Church made plural marriages even more secret.  Lower courts held that Brigham Young's disgruntled "wife" was no wife, and not entitled to alimony.

The Government even resorted to diplomatic channels to halt the Mormon immigration of lawbreakers.  The *London Examiner* ridiculed the effort: "Finding themselves powerless to cope with the Mormon pest in the U.S., the authorities have issued a plaintive appeal to the governments of England, Germany, Norway, Sweden, and Denmark begging aid in their troubles.  The morality of this Circular is admirable; the logic is lamentable."

In 1882, Congress passed the Edmunds Act, declaring polygamy a felony punishable by up to $500 and *five years* in prison.  It banned unlawful cohabitation, the mere act of living with more than one wife, as a misdemeanor with a $300 fine and six months in prison.  The Edmunds Act legitimized children conceived prior to the law, and it granted amnesty to men who publicly recorded their marriages and agreed to cease further practice.  The unrepentant were disenfranchised from voting, holding public office and serving on juries.  The law furnished money to hire Federal marshals to track down polygamists, gather proof of cohabitation, and bring the accused to trial.

Mormon President John Taylor responded, "We shall abide all constitutional law, as we always have done; but while we are God-fearing and law-abiding and respect all honorable men and officers, we are no craven serfs, and have not learned to lick the feet of oppressors, nor to bow in base submission to unreasonable clamor."

President Taylor went into hiding five years ago and was never seen publicly again.  He should not have been expected to acquiesce without a fight.  Taylor, himself, was badly wounded by gunshots aimed at Joseph and Hyrum Smith in jail in Carthage, Illinois.

"They killed your prophets," Taylor said in a sermon in the Tabernacle, "and I saw them martyred, and was shot unmercifully myself, under the pledge of protection from the Governor, and they thought they had killed me; but I am alive yet by the grace of God... Shall I be recreant to all these noble

301

principles that ought to guide and govern men? No. Never! No. Never! NO. NEVER!..I won't do it, so help me God."

The Utah Commission, charged with enforcing this law, sought further powers. They prepared a test oath, which all citizens were made to sign before voting. Under protest, I signed this oath, myself. "I do solemnly swear or affirm that I am not a bigamist or a polygamist," it reads, "that I am not a violator of the Laws of the United States prohibiting bigamy or polygamy; that I do not live or cohabit with more than one woman in the marriage relationship."

I found it hard to keep from laughing as I signed the oath. For it gingerly excludes adulterers who keep mistresses, and men who seduce countless women without responsibility for any of them or their children. Yet this law forbade 12,000 decent men and women from voting. Soon, Idaho Territory passed its own test oath law, which essentially disenfranchised *all* Mormon Church members, most of whom have *never* been polygamous. Two thousand citizens lost the right to vote and hold office, as if they were felons. Then nine months ago, the U.S. Supreme Court *upheld* this law. Idaho leaders boast that their juries can convict any Mormon of a crime, regardless of guilt.

Meanwhile, the first polygamist was brought to "justice" under the Edmunds Act when his wife was discovered in hiding. Hauled before the Judge, she refused to be sworn as a witness, so he sentenced her to the penitentiary for contempt. But the next day, at her husband's insistence, she took the oath and admitted they were married. He was summarily convicted by an all-Gentile jury, fined $800, sentenced to four years in the Utah Penitentiary, and denied bail pending appeal. The Supreme Court upheld the verdict in 1885, and that unleashed pandemonium.

I gasped when I saw that first handbill. "**$800 REWARD!**" it proclaimed in two-inch boldface type. "To be Paid for the Arrest of John Taylor and George Q. Cannon. All Conferences or Letters kept strictly confidential." I was grateful *not* to read, "dead or alive." The bounty is, after all, a substantial sum of money. Taylor was President of the Church, and Cannon was

302

once Utah's Territorial representative in Congress and editor of the *Deseret News.*

Less prominent polygamists, such as my father-in-law, fetched $50. John Carter was in his mid-sixties, a veteran of the Mexican War, a prosperous millwright and contractor who worked on the transcontinental railroad. He employed numerous workers and was father to 19 children.

John disappeared one night in early 1885, "called on a mission on the underground," I later learned. He took refuge in the canyons of southern Utah, where rugged terrain makes pursuit difficult.

That year, throughout Utah, collecting evidence became ugly and unmerciful. There were few sources: hostile Gentiles, apostate Mormons, monogamous Saints with grudges against suspects, and the practically defenseless wives and children. Bounties were paid for finding "Cohabs," as unrepentant cohabitants were called. Soon, the entire Mormon community became victims. They were spied upon and raided, their property ransacked, their Gentile neighbors tempted with bribes. Detectives peered into bedroom windows at night and broke into the houses of suspects.

Pregnant wives, bearing proof of forbidden sexual union, were hauled up as witnesses before Judges. Confronted by a terrible choice, they could either betray their husbands, deny knowledge of paternity, or refuse to answer and be jailed for contempt of court. One hapless wife delivered her child while in prison. Most polygamists fled their farms and businesses to escape arrest. Others built ingenious hideouts in their homes, shielded behind layers of hidden panels and trap doors. But whether in hiding or imprisoned, the men could not support their families, who often had to rely on others for food and shelter. The entire Mormon community was terrorized, though most were innocent of any crime. Leaderless, demoralized and often divided, they did not forswear polygamy.

The victims of this travesty showed restraint. When one Apostle was arrested, the young men gathered around him. "Give the word, Brother Snow," they vowed, "and they'll never take you from town." "It's all right," the old gentleman replied. "Providence has ordered this matter."

But Providence was not generous to all polygamists. One Deputy Marshal nearly killed a man trying to escape arrest for unlawful cohabitation, then he shot another man in the back for this *misdemeanor* and killed him. An all-Gentile jury acquitted the Deputy of murder. "The blood of innocence stains his soul," the *Deseret News* lamented. "No sophistry or petty fogging will take it away, and no lying verdict will blot it out. It will show up red and gory through all the official and judicial whitewash that may be applied." When the Deputy sued the *Deseret News* for libel, demanding $25,000 in damages, the newspaper resigned itself to the extortion and paid him $1,000.

Lesser inanities proliferated, too. In 1886, the organizers of the Industrial Home Association of Utah sought funds from Congress to finance and build a home for repentant plural wives. They claimed that legions of such wives were desperate to escape their immoralities, if only they and their children had the means to ward off starvation. Congress appropriated $64,000, and the Women's Industrial Home was duly built. But to date, only some 20 women have ever sought shelter there, and the number, if *any*, who are castoff or escaped plural wives is unknown.

In the meantime, the Mormons scouted sites for colonies beyond the grasp of U.S. law. President Taylor visited western Mexico and urged "escape colonization" in the states of Sonora and Chihuahua. Other Mormons established a colony just north of the U.S. border in Alberta, Canada. Some Apostles fled on missions to England and Hawaii. As if at war, they used a secret "Cohab code." In code, "White Blowed Up Splendid Pockets Compass" meant, "St. George retreat discovered. Things lively. Move your quarters. Go south."

George Q. Cannon was on a train en route to Mexico when a sheriff came aboard, looking for him. All the passengers conveniently failed to identify him, even a Nevada Senator who knew Mr. Cannon well from Congress. Yet inadvertently, a friend gave him away. Fearing a Mormon uprising, 26 soldiers escorted Mr. Cannon to Salt Lake City, where his bail was set at $45,000 for this misdemeanor charge. Most members of his family were placed under heavy bonds to show up as witnesses against him. All of them appeared at his trial, but Mr. Cannon did not, forfeiting the exorbitant bail. President Taylor, still at large, had counseled him to remain free so he could serve the interests of the Church.

My own children, safe inside monogamy, taught me the words to the Cohab song:

> "All you Cohabs still dodging round
> You'd better keep in underground
> For if with number two you're found
> Then they'll pop you into limbo!"

It was not with a latter wife, but with his daughter, my wife Molly, that John Carter was captured. In a tragicomic farce, in disguise and occasionally women's clothing, he had outwitted them for eleven months. But time generally favors the hunters, not the hunted.

John refused to plead guilty, instead defending his case with all his energy and zeal. I found myself appalled throughout as Molly and I watched this trial. The prosecutors did not have to prove sexual intercourse, since the "habit and repute" of marriage to more than one woman presumed cohabitation. But I was most aghast that the courts agreed to make each latter marriage a separate crime punishable by six months in prison.

John told nothing but the truth and as little as possible of that, but he was quickly convicted, one of 1,200 Mormons jailed for polygamy. His misdemeanor summed to an 18-month sentence. The Penitentiary was crowded far beyond capacity, so his punishment was postponed several months. All that while, John worked hard on his business, hoping to secure financial support for his family. His sales and rents had plummeted, as men in jail or hiding were forced to default on their debts. When he was called, he calmly reported to prison.

My wife has a photograph of her father, posing with George

Cannon, who surrendered at last, and a dozen other men. They are dressed in striped uniforms and seated on the steps of the Utah Territorial Prison. Staring dignified into the camera, the men reflect no shadow of moral disgrace, as if their prison stripes mean nothing more degrading than a masquerade. It was the final photograph of John Carter.

John once smuggled a letter to me by way of a newly released "tough," as the Cohabs called inmates in the prison for other crimes. He implored me to take good care of my wife and all of his. "With firm conviction that plurality of wives was a law of God," John wrote, "I entered into that union honorably with a sincere purpose. My family was united with me in believing this to be of the highest, holiest, most sacred character in the sight of the Most High. I could not cast aside my wives whom I had married under these beliefs." To the end, he was utterly unrepentant.

The next week, John died of some respiratory illness, common where large numbers of poorly fed people are housed too close to one another. Each of John's wives had been blessed with one-fourth of a man of first-rate character, a far better lot in life than the whole of a man of third-rate.

In summer 1887, as he predicted, President Taylor died while in hiding. His wife Sophia had died five months earlier, but he was unable to visit her in her final hour because spies were known to be watching her house. A lonely death had also come to Phoebe Woodruff, wife of the new Church President. Words she spoke twenty years ago in the Salt Lake City Tabernacle came to my mind.

"Shall we as wives and mothers sit still and see our husbands and sons, whom we know are obeying the highest behest of heaven, suffer for their religion without exerting ourselves to the extent of our power for their deliverance? No! Verily no!!...If the rulers of our nation will so far depart from the spirit and letter of our glorious Constitution as to deprive our prophets, apostles, and elders of citizenship, and imprison them for obeying this law, let them grant us this last request, to make their prisons large enough to hold their wives for where they go we will go also."

Despite its persecutions, the Edmunds Law remained weak, so President Cleveland asked Congress, "I recommend that a law be passed to prevent the importation of Mormons into the country." Congress responded with the Edmunds-Tucker Act of 1887. This law stole the right to vote from Utah women, and now my wife, who has committed no felony, is no more enfranchised than any other woman in these United States.

But the worst outrage was committed against the Mormon Church. The 1887 law dissolved the Church as a legal corporatation and escheated its property, except for church buildings and cemeteries, to the United States Government. It stripped the Church of its bank accounts, real estate, stocks and bonds, and it abolished the Nauvoo Legion. Designed to put an end to Mormon economic power in Utah, the Edmunds-Tucker Act escheated 200 miles of railroads, a $300,000 woolen mill, a large cotton factory, a wholesale-retail merchandiser with 150 stores and $6,000,000 of yearly sales, and some 500 cooperative manufacturing and related enterprises. Hoping to stem the flow of Mormon immigrants, the Act dissolved the Perpetual Emigration Fund.

After President Taylor's death, Wilford Woodruff and Apostle Joseph F. Smith steadfastly prepared the sixth application for statehood for Utah. Their Church dissolved and its leadership scattered underground, the Mormons' last hope lay with the U.S. Supreme Court. They believed the Court would see that the Edmunds-Tucker Act could not be reconciled with the pure principle of the First Amendment, "Congress shall make no law respecting an establishment of religion, or prohibiting the free exercise thereof."

For three years, they clung to that hope, heartened by the Court's reversal of the law that made each marriage a separate crime. In population, the Saints maintained a heavy majority in Utah Territory. The 1880 census counted 120,300 Mormons, 14,100 Gentiles and 7,000 apostates. Mormon birth rates continued high, as did immigration, which despite persecution, brought in 10,000 Saints during the years '81 to '86 alone.

But by 1889, the disfranchisement of all polygamists and women had effectively whittled down the electorate. Federal judges refused to grant citizenship to Mormon immigrants on the grounds that an oath they swore in the Endowment House was treasonable. With the disarray, the notorious solidarity of Mormon votes was cracking.

Way back in 1852, when optimism about early statehood still ran high, their political unanimity was a cause for jest among the Saints:

> "For Mormons always vote one way
> And soon a voice they'll get,
> And unison will bless the day
> That shines on Deseret.
> But never mention what we've said
> For this particular reason,
> That if you do, we're good as dead,
> Because you know, IT'S TREASON!"

Until a decade ago, in fact, some of that "unanimity" was enforced by an insidious numbering scheme on Utah ballots. But with redistricting and appointments of anti-Mormon election judges, as well as voters brought in from the railroads and mines, the Mormon lead suddenly evaporated. Amazingly, Gentiles won elections in both Odgen and Salt Lake City.

At long last, my party had won! That night, I could not sleep, as many Gentiles celebrated by marching with torchlights through the Salt Lake City streets. They yelled and drummed until early morning, beat on tin pans and cow bells, blew on horns, and lit fireworks. But though my party had won, I could not celebrate, because I knew our victory was fraudulent.

By May 1890, the Church was in dire straits. Almost all its leaders were in exile, hiding or prison, and many women had been forced to leave their homes. The economy was in ruins and the Church had few resources left to perform its functions. Then the penultimate blow was struck. In a six-to-three decision, the Supreme Court upheld the Edmunds-Tucker Act as constitutional.

Then *further* legislation was proposed in Congress. A new bill sought to disfranchise *all* Mormons, most of whom have never been polygamous. The law would demand from the Saints a cruel choice, to give up their Church or their right to vote.

I was among 400 Utah Gentiles who signed a petition to Congress denouncing this bill as unrepublican, undemocratic, and unnecessary. It was also, most importantly, *immoral.* Continued denial of statehood for Utah would, with some vestige of decency, achieve the same result in time.

This, then, is the context of President Woodruff's Manifesto. He prayed to the Lord and received a revelation that polygamy must be relinquished to save the Church. As a sign of good faith, he razed to the ground the old Endowment House, the site of the secret marriage rites. But nowhere does it say that the "Prophet" has renounced plural marriage.

Since Mormon women have been likened to slaves, we must finally ask how this sect treats its women. My own wife, Molly, is a respected physician who attended the University of Deseret, one of the first colleges to admit women students. Her patients are not only women and children, but men who welcome treatment by a female doctor. In fact, Utah has the highest proportion of female doctors of any territory or state. Mormon women have built, staffed and run a hospital for years, and a school for nurses and midwives. It was Molly's innate intelligence, born of wisdom-seeking people, plus her competence nurtured by these beliefs, that first drew my admiration, then love. Though some may doubt it, the masthead on the *Women's Exponent*, an unofficial but devoutly loyal Mormon journal, reads, "For the rights of the women of Zion and the rights of women of all nations."

Could there be some causation here? Perhaps the pioneer strength of these women makes them shrink away from the world less than their sisters in the East. Perhaps the ranks of Mormon females, so enhanced by immigration, are more inclined to active pursuits. And ostracism of Mormons from normal society has demanded strength and bound them tightly together.  To be sure, a mass defection of women from Mormonism would quickly bring about its demise.

At present, the true cause is unknown, but history will inform us of the truth.  If women here continue in responsible roles, then it must be in the character of the Mormons, or indeed their faith, to value and employ female talents.  If, on the contrary, the authority of Mormon women retreats, while that of other women is advancing, then we can only conclude that their sentiments have been used in a war fought for the benefit of men.

*****

Molly stood for several minutes in the unlit room before Ted became aware of her presence.  She looked at him quizzically.

"What's so upset you, Ted?"

He handed her the manuscript and letter in silence.  Molly read them both quickly.

"Thanks for the attempted public compliment," she said.  "But I always thought it was my body that captured your attention."

With a weak smile, Ted looked up at Molly.  "Shall I put that into the revision?"

"You will revise it, then?" she asked.

Ted shook his head.  "In the clamor of triumph, Lawrence doesn't care to be bothered by the truth."

Molly reread the last sentence of his rejected column.

"That will never happen to women," she said.

# Chapter 14

Molly tried to disregard her exhaustion as she drove the buggy to the railroad station. The January afternoon was blustery and gray, and she was up all night attending to the birth of twins. Fearing that the mother would die in childbirth, the midwife sent for Molly at dusk, and the women and babies struggled for hours. Despite their efforts, one infant died at dawn, but his mother and twin brother gained strength throughout the morning.

Molly hoped the snow, which had fallen all night and day, would not delay the train for long. She tied the reins securely to a post, then stepped into the warming gas heat and bright electric lights of the station. The clerks looked unconcerned as the scheduled time of arrival came and went. Impatiently, Molly waited, wishing she had something hot to drink. The longer the train was delayed, the more hazardous the drive home would be.

Finally, the train whistle shrieked, then the train, spewing steam, chugged noisily into the station. Molly scanned the windows of the passenger cars. She barely recognized Ted when she saw his face. He looked tired and aged, wearing spectacles, and now mostly bald with fringes of white hair. Her father had appeared so much younger before he died. Molly smiled indulgently as she watched Ted step off the train, no longer spry but still trim at age 65. She had no doubt that she had married very wisely. And now that polygamy was not a threat, she must redouble her efforts to convert him.

"I am so glad to be home," Ted sighed as he embraced her. "It's been a hard couple of weeks. How are you and the children?"

"We're all fine," Molly assured him.

"Traveling to South Dakota in the dead of winter strained my aging body worse than I expected. The Union Pacific must be suffering financial troubles, if its poorly maintained roadbed and equipment are any sign."

"Look over there," Molly whispered.

She pointed to two tall, well-groomed Negro soldiers who had just stepped down from the train. The men walked briskly toward the heated waiting room.

Ted nodded as he climbed into the buggy after Molly. He wrapped the blanket tightly around them both, but left her hands free for the reins. The icy wind blew on their faces as she drove toward home.

"The Army has four colored regiments," Ted explained, "two cavalry and two infantry, commanded by white officers. Though often understaffed and badly treated, they've earned outstanding records in fighting the Indian campaigns. They act more respectable than most white enlisted men, and show better unit pride and morale, high reenlistment and low desertion."

Molly was thankful they were nearly home. The snow was deepening as they turned off the main thoroughfares.

"Were those soldiers at the Sioux reservation?" she asked. "Or Wounded Knee?"

"Perhaps at the Sioux reservation. But the Seventh Cavalry was at Wounded Knee. They were mostly inexperienced, poorly trained white recruits, unnerved because their guns were no match for the Indians' Winchesters."

"The Indians were better armed than the Seventh Cavalry?"

"The Army had old single-shot Springfields," Ted replied, "converted from muzzle-loaders after the War. The Indians had Winchester repeating rifles, an excellent gun for close action. John M. Browning invented them, Molly, and the Winchester single-shot rifle. I met him when he was a youngster in Ogden, one day after I met you."

Molly drove the buggy into the carriage house and attended to the horse. Ted greeted Ned and Joanna in the parlor, then waited for Molly to join him in his study. In the doorway, Molly felt the blissful warmth from the gas heater on her chilled hands and face, as the exhaustion from her vigil of the previous night returned.

Beneath the bright illumination from the Tiffany electric lamp, Ted was vigorously writing. He would not miss her for several hours, she knew.

# ARE THE MORMONS THE "PRIME MOVERS" IN THE GHOST DANCE?
by
**Edward Bailey**
January 1891

Gathering together in the northwestern Plains have been Indians by the thousands from many tribes. Sioux and Cheyenne, Arapaho and Ute, Bannock and Shoshone, and a dozen other nations have been joining together with common purpose. Such commingling is remarkable in itself, since tribes of the Plains are prone to warring with one another. But its peaceful mission notwithstanding, the Ghost Dance religion has now led to tragedy.

In early December of last year, General Nelson Miles, who knows the Sioux Indians well, warned his Army commander about the dangers of the Ghost Dance religion. "Many nations have gone west to Nevada and have been shown somebody disguised as the Messiah...I cannot say positively, but it is my belief the Mormons are the prime movers in all this."

A few weeks later, the Army intercepted a band of rebellious Sioux camped in the snow at Wounded Knee Creek. Believing that their Ghost Shirts would protect them with magic powers, the Indians chose to resist and fight the soldiers.

The Ghost Dance is no war dance, to be sure. It is, above all, a religion, with unmistakably Christian features, urged upon the tribes by men ceremoniously ordained as priests. White cotton Ghost Shirts, painted with the sun and moon, stars and birds, are the Ghost Dancers' attire, clothing not native to the Indians.

The Ghost Dance originated two decades ago with a mystic Paiute prophet, Wodziwob. It was carried by Bannocks and Shoshones to other Indian nations, but when the shaman disappeared and presumably died, the dance vanished quickly as well. Now revived in Nevada by another Paiute, Wovoka, the dancing has resumed in earnest.

313

An eyewitness, the wife of the postmaster and trader near Wounded Knee, South Dakota, has described the rites. "The Indians cut the tallest tree, then set it up in the ground where four head men stand. The others form a circle and begin to go around and around the tree. For three days, they do not eat or drink. They keep going around in one direction until they become so dizzy that they can scarcely stand, then they turn and go in the other direction and keep it up until they swoon from exhaustion. When they regain consciousness, they tell their experiences to the four wise men under the tree. All their tales end with the same story about the two mountains that are to belch forth and bury the white man, and the return of good old Indian times."

By November of last year, the Ghost Dancers had aroused the concern of the Indian Bureau agents. In these modern times, most Indians gather peacefully at the agencies, wanting nothing to do with challenging the Army. But the Indians still resisting authority are known to be formidable opponents. Superbly trained and indoctrinated for courage, they are excellent warriors, with stamina and strength, stealth, cunning, horsemanship and skill with weapons. Man-for-man, they are far superior to Army soldiers, as was shown against Custer at Little Big Horn in 1876.

Of particular concern were defiant, potentially hostile Sioux, 600 men and their families, who had united at a high plateau in the Pine Ridge Reservation. They owned Winchester repeating rifles and ample ammunition. To quell this disturbance and others, President Harrison ordered 3,500 Army troops to assemble in South Dakota.

By now, of course, Army forts surround Sioux country. Orders are sent by telegraph, and troops are moved around quickly by railroad. But the individual soldiers are lacking. Army life is unattractive, the pay is low and the discipline harsh, with frontier living conditions full of discomforts. The peacetime Army, more concerned with conserving ammunition, arms its soldiers with single-shot guns, not repeating rifles.

General Miles could not have been sanguine about the

314

outcome of confronting the Indians. He was especially troubled about the settlement where Chief Sitting Bull was still restive, and where the Ghost Dance was highly influential. General Miles ordered the Indian police to arrest Sitting Bull, a remarkable man who had led the Sioux at Little Big Horn and later traveled to England with Buffalo Bill. The Indian police tried to arrest Sitting Bull and Big Foot, another Sioux chief, but the Ghost Dancers attempted a rescue. In the furious fight that ensued, Sitting Bull was killed.

Wounded, Big Foot escaped and led his tribe to the Pine Ridge plateau to join the hostile Sioux already there. But on the way there, they encountered a small group of Seventh Cavalrymen and agreed to be escorted to Pine Ridge. They camped for the night near Wounded Knee Creek.

That night, the rest of the Seventh Cavalry arrived, with orders to arrest and disarm Big Foot's tribe, then march them to the railroad that would transport them to Omaha. The Indians awoke the next morning to find 500 soldiers surrounding them. Four artillery pieces were aimed at them from the hills. The Army prepared a heated tent and ordered the Indians to surrender their rifles inside it.

Boxed in, outnumbered and outgunned, the Indians should not have been tempted to fight. But they were loathe to give up their prized Winchesters, and knowing that, the soldiers searched the Indian tents. A medicine man called for resistance, and a shot was fired. The Indians grabbed their guns, concealed under blankets, and fired on the nearest group of soldiers. Soldiers and Indians fought at close quarters, shooting, stabbing and clubbing. The artillery in the hills opened fire and drove the surviving Indians into the open. When the firing stopped, 90 of the 120 Indian men lay dead, including Big Foot and the medicine man. Sixty-two of the 230 Indian women and children were killed, and 50 more Indians were wounded.

Why have the Indians left the reservations, knowing the Army will be ordered to drive them back? And what may be the truth of General Miles' accusation that the Mormons are "prime movers" in the Ghost Dance?

Indian shamans have traditionally entered into trances and received revelations concerning spirits and the return of the dead. The Mormons give credence to such visitations, indeed expect them, since the Indians are considered members of a lost tribe of Israel who have lamentably forgotten their heritage.

Sitting Bull, himself, was told the Mormon message by a half-Sioux Mormon woman named Isabel. He once described his own revelation of the Great Spirit. The Great Spirit, dressed in a beautiful robe, stood with some long-deceased warriors and told how the whites once persecuted him, so the soil would swallow them up as in quicksand. Sitting Bull designed a Ghost Shirt with the thunderbird, moon and stars, and told the Indians to wear it as protection against bullets.

Many observers have noted an uncanny likeness between the Ghost Shirts and the Mormon Endowment ritual clothing. Both are white cotton, prominently adorned with symbols, and reputed to shield their wearers from harm. I am aware of these, I confess, because my wife has worn them ever since her Endowment at age 16. I will not disclose their symbols, only that they differ from the Ghost Shirts. But I once saw images of suns and moons and stars in stonework on the Temple in Nauvoo.

As they dance, the Ghost Dancers call out the names of departed relatives and friends for their resurrection. This is not so far removed from the peculiar ideas of the Mormons concerning the salvation of their ancestors. Both the Mormons and Ghost Dancers claim that their priests can heal by their touch.

The Mormons are the most active Christian missionaries to the tribes who are the spiritual leaders of the Ghost Dance. In 1872, the Mormons organized a farm in Thistle Valley for a hundred Utes, a tribe closely related to both Ghost Dance prophets. In 1880, Mormon missionaries baptized Shoshone Chief Washakie and 422 of his followers. Some 200 Mormon Indians, Bannock or Shoshone, now live at the Fort Hall Reservation. Other Shoshone converts share the Wind River Reservation with the northern Arapaho tribe. The Arapaho have been the great apostles of the Ghost Dance, bringing it first to the Cheyenne and Sioux, then to more remote tribes.

Still, no Indian member of the Mormon Church has ever been known to be a Ghost Dancer. In fact, the Mormons have tried to calm the Ghost Dance craze, saying it engenders as many superstitions as liquor. And if their Indian converts disobey the reservation rules against the Ghost Dance, the Mormons know they will be charged with fomenting yet another insurrection.

Some Indians have sought Mormon advice concerning their own troubles with the Federal Government. In 1884, when the Government reneged on its contractual payments to the Indians, the Shoshones talked of waging war against the Army and the Indian agents. Aware of the war against polygamy, they invited the Mormons to join them. "The Lord had sent heavenly messengers," an inquiry came, "and great events are about to take place, and they believe the Great Mormon Chief will give them the very best of counsel." The Mormon leaders urged the Indians to avoid trouble.

While some influence may exist, the Mormons cannot fairly be thought the "prime movers" in the Ghost Dance. And they can certainly not be blamed for Wounded Knee. Butchery and shameful massacre are suggested by the numbers of the dead, bloody vengeance for the Seventh Cavalry's own General Custer. But the Army also lost men--25 killed and 39 wounded--heavy casualties among a 500-man unit, and a far higher loss than would occur with the deliberate intent of a massacre. On both sides, it was more likely a tragic blunder.

Far more to blame than the soldiers is the deluge of trappers, traders, farmers, miners, stockmen, merchants, railroad builders, and all their modern inventions, that continue to seize Indian resources. Some 8,500,000 whites now live where 50 million buffalo wandered only 40 years ago. The buffalo, the main source of food and clothing, shelter and trade for the Indians, have been slaughtered down to scarcely 1,000. The Indian Bureau, through incompetence and corruption, keeps the promised rations and supplies inadequate. It promotes factionalism, recruits Indian police to nullify the chiefs' authority, teaches children to disdain their own culture, and suppresses what it arbitrarily deems barbarous practices. Even poor and sparse Indian land, which was promised to remain reservation, continues to be systematically stolen away for white ranching, mining and settlement. Embittered by the breached contracts, frustrated and helpless at the destruction of their lives, the Indians cannot be blamed for seeking divine intervention.

"The water and mud will sweep the white race and all Indian skeptics away to their deaths," Wovoka promises. "Then the dead Indian ancestors will return, as will the vanished buffalo and other game, and everything on earth will once again be an Indian paradise."

Though equally millennial, the Ghost Dancers covet a far different utopia from the Saints. All of us can only hope that this latest, senseless episode draws a final shameful curtain on the Indian Wars.

# Chapter 15

In early January 1896, Ted and Molly Bailey and Amelia Carter stepped off the electric streetcar at Temple Square. As they joined the jubilant crowd, the artillery boomed above them at Fort Douglas. Factory whistles blew and church bells rang in celebration. President Cleveland had just proclaimed the admission of Utah as the 45th state of the Union.

Molly and Amelia looked up at the magnificent white Temple, completed and dedicated three years earlier. Along with 250,000 other Utah residents, overwhelmingly Mormon, they rejoiced at the proof of peace and acceptance with the Federal Government.

In the cold, Ted looked around him, composing the story for the *Empire Monthly Review.* "I'll call it, AT LONG LAST, STATEHOOD FOR UTAH," he spoke aloud to himself.

"No other territory has been forced to wait almost fifty years to become a state. But more than polygamy, the real issue of dispute was the reasonable perception that the Mormons had in fact established a working theocracy, a government controlled not by democratic, Constitutional procedures but by decisions of unelected leaders of the Church."

Molly and Amelia were far too elated to hear Ted's mumblings.

"But Mormon political parties are now dissolved, and Church leaders have declared that Church officials should not and would not run for public office. A new Utah state constitution now guarantees that no law can be passed restricting freedom of the press or the establishment of religion. Males and females enjoy equal privileges in civil, political, and religious matters. Sectarian control of public schools is forbidden, and polygamy is banned. Properties confiscated from the Mormon Church have been returned by the Federal Government."

For several hours in the chilly air, Amelia, Molly and Ted embraced friends in Temple Square before returning to the warmth of Amelia's home. Carter Bailey and his wife and daughter soon joined them for supper, then Joanna Bailey and her fiance. Ned Bailey, age 12, ran up the steps and dashed through the door just after Margaret and Fawn arrived.

"It's such a grand occasion," Amelia said. "I wish John could've lived to see it."

"As do we all," Fawn said.

"Have you heard about Emmeline?" Margaret whispered.

"No."

"She left Utah with a Gentile. They went to Nevada, I think."

"No! You don't think she'll apostasize, do you?"

"I always suspected she was weak in faith."

"Well, John was always over there, chastising her for some dereliction."

Ted smiled at Molly across the table. "This story on Statehood is going to be my final scribbling for the *Empire Monthly Review*."

"But why?" Molly asked.

Amelia rose and pulled out a drawer from the sideboard. She held up a thick file of papers. "You know I've kept all your stories, Ted. We've enjoyed them all."

"Because I'm over 70," Ted replied, "and not at all convinced I've got anything new to say. The West is settled, the Indians are on reservations, and you Saints are well behaved, at last. I'm too old to become a war reporter, though I suspect we'll go to war again soon."

Molly took his hand. "Your talents will always be needed by the Church, Dear."

Amelia nodded. "We're starting a new project to document our history, Ted. We'd be grateful to have you join us."

"Seventy isn't old for one of us, Dad."

"Even if it were, Pa, no one is too old to help."

"You know there's so much to be done," Margaret said.

"By *everyone*, Grandpa."

Ted smiled in resignation, composing aloud the last sentence of his final column. "At last abandoning the dream of establishing a theocracy in Utah, the Saints will concentrate instead on establishing a theocracy everywhere."

Around the table, his wife and children, their spouses and his grandchild, his mother-in-law and aunts, nodded and smiled at what they saw as his progress toward wisdom.

# BOOK FOUR

## BEDEVILED IN PARADISE

# 1903

Anders Erickson opened the window of the small mission house on the Tuamotu Island of Ana'a. Winter, he scoffed to himself. Winter was the incessant damp grayness of Norway, or the icy winds off Salt Lake. The South Pacific night felt unnaturally mild to a man whose knowledge of winter was so intimate. In Norway, the nights filled the winter. But here, 200 miles east of Tahiti, the tropical nights passed in a merciful thirteen hours. Across the island, in the hours before dawn, the lanterns burned in the darkness to keep ghosts away.

Anders knew it was useless to go back to his mat on the floor and try to sleep. He looked past the pandanus trees to the small Mormon meetinghouse where he would preach later that morning. Even in the humid summer, the meetinghouse was a cool and pleasant place. Like the small mission house where Anders lived, its roof was woven of coconut thatch and its floor was clean white coral pebbles. The lumber and posts of both buildings came from the trunks of breadfruit and coconut trees. Brother missionaries lived in other villages on the island, not far away. But Anders' missionary companion had left abruptly a month earlier, and his replacement had not arrived. Missionaries were supposed to stay there three years.

As he planned what he would say in his sermon, a remembrance of sorrow came over Anders. Sailors on their way to Tahiti had brought the news from the Marquesa Islands, 400 miles to the northeast. On a far Marquesa Island, just south of the equator, the painter Paul Gauguin had died.

"What was the cause of death?" Anders asked the sailors.

"Syphilis," they replied, expecting to hear warnings about the wages of sin. The sailors were surprised when Anders' face expressed only regret.

"Gauguin should've been a Mormon," said a Catholic missionary, joking with a French Protestant.

Anders stared blankly at them both.

"He was a practicing polygamist," the Catholic priest

explained. "He left a wife and five children in Paris, then unceremoniously married a 13-year-old girl in Tahiti."

"Gauguin went home to Paris for awhile," the Protestant missionary said, "but neither wife would have him when he returned from the other. So he went off to the Marquesas with a 14-year-old schoolgirl from the *Catholic* mission."

The priest glared at the Protestant missionary.

"I must inform you," Anders said coolly, "that Latter-day Saints have not practiced polygamy for 13 years."

In the small mission house, Anders gazed out from the northeast window. Only in the vastness of the Pacific would the Marquesas be considered nearby.

Anders had met Gauguin on one occasion, a night so humid he could almost drink the water in the air. He had learned that the painter's wife, Mette, the wife in Paris, came from the same district in Denmark as Anders' father.

That evening, Gauguin spoke with nothing but contempt for the missionaries.

"The missionary is no longer a man, a conscience," Gauguin said. "He is a corpse, in the hands of a confraternity, without family, without love, without any of the sentiments that are dear to us. Emasculated, in a sense, by his vow of chastity, he offers us the distressing spectacle of a man deformed and impotent or engaged in a stupid and useless struggle with the sacred needs of the flesh."

"But those are Catholic missionaries," Anders protested. "Families are dear to us too, and we likewise believe the propagation of the flesh to be sacred."

Anders tried to speak without blushing, since he had left Salt Lake City before he was able to marry. Like the French Catholic priests, he struggled to resist the willing sexuality of the young native girls.

Anders felt the air hanging thick with moisture that night, too humid to evaporate sweat. He proposed a swim to cool down, having recently learned in the welcoming south Pacific. Gauguin was an excellent swimmer, but Anders had never swum in the cold north Atlantic.

326

When they returned, cooled and bathed, Gauguin showed Anders a portfolio of small woodcut prints. There were pictures of animals and trees, and images of heathen idols set in places of honor. But other prints showed brown men and women in erotic entanglements, or nude with their genitals exposed.

Anders calmly paged through the prints. He admired the colors, then spoke plainly, as a missionary must. "It seems you violate the taboos that bind European artists."

"Oh, the old European traditions!" Gauguin scoffed. "The timidities of expression of degenerate races!"

Anders bit his tongue so he could not speak the words that came to it. *Claiming to be wise, they became fools, and exchanged the glory of the immortal God for images resembling mortal man or birds or animals or reptiles.*

"It seems you seek the right to dare anything."

Gauguin shook his head, then asked Anders if he had any absinthe.

"No," Anders replied.

Gauguin shrugged, unsurprised, then confessed an episode from a decade earlier, soon after he first arrived in Tahiti.

"I had need of rosewood for my carving, and a young handsome fellow offered to lead me into the mountains," Gauguin said. "It is a mad vegetation, growing always wilder, more entangled, denser, until, as we ascended toward the center of the island, it became an almost impenetrable thicket."

Anders nodded. He had spent several weeks on Tahiti and had also felt entranced by the lushness of the jungle.

"Why, in all this drunkenness of lights and perfumes with its enchantment of newness and unknown mystery, why was it that there arose in the soul of a member of an old civilization, a horrible thought?"

Anders shuddered at the knowledge of what this horrible thought could only be. But he said nothing as he listened.

"The fever throbbed in my temples and my knees shook," Gauguin confessed.

Biblical admonitions filled Anders' mind. *Therefore God gave them up in the lusts of their hearts to impurity, and to the*

327

*dishonoring of their bodies among themselves, because they exchanged the truth about God for a lie and worshiped and served the creature rather than the Creator, who is blessed forever. Amen.*

Gauguin spoke softly. "Then my companion showed himself full-face. His calm eyes had the limpid clearness of waters. Peace forthwith fell upon me again. I felt an infinite joy, a joy of the spirit rather than of the senses. It seemed to me a fitting conclusion to the struggle which I had just fought out within myself against the corruption of an entire civilization."

Anders, too, had rejoiced at the painter's triumph. Paradise, for once, was not violated for the self-indulgent pleasures of European men. For centuries, the whalers and slavers and merchants had dispoiled the Islands for their own gain and defiled them with old world diseases.

Syphilis, Anders thought to himself in the dark mission house. Gauguin contracted it in Paris from a dance hall prostitute, the sailors told him. The painter drank with them on countless occasions, the sailors claimed, and toward the end, he indulged in orgies of drinking with the natives. To counteract the constant pain of an ankle broken in a fight in Brittany, Gauguin took more and more laudanum and morphine. He once swallowed a large dose of arsenic, but vomited up the poison before it killed him. Anders knew that the sweltering equatorial heat, worse in the Marquesas than Ana'a, must have multiplied his suffering from the syphilitic lesions on his skin.

"It was an *artistic* mission," Gauguin had insisted.

That night, when Anders paged through the prints, he plainly recognized the face of melancholy that Gauguin had etched into the shadows. Anders knew they shared a familiar spirit. And he heard Gauguin's words, "the melancholy of bitter experience which lies at the root of all pleasure." But he could offer the painter no cure for melancholy, and Gauguin soon left for someplace else where absinthe might be found.

Anders had hoped, even started to believe, that his melancholy was left behind when he emigrated to America from Norway. But he had found, to his chagrin, that along with himself and the sea, melancholy was the sole common inhabitant between the island where he now lived and the old world where he had been raised.

Anders had been too young to remember the day when his family entered a pietistic community on the western coast of Norway. His earliest memories were of bleakness, cold and gray, as if some force had sucked the color out of the landscape. But the community had chosen its setting well, since its religion espoused the hatred and denial of the world, and the mortification of all lust. Separating from the corrupting world was the only way to assure their purity.

Anders grew accustomed to solitude, for his older brother died within a year, and his parents were not blessed with more children. With his father, he spoke Danish, and with his mother, Norwegian, and they spoke little with each other. Anders worked with his mother in the large commual garden, where they devoted their greatest efforts to cultivating medicinal herbs. The community ate only one meal a day, and then in silence, the men apart from the women. Inside the tiny church, they sang solemn hymns, but nowhere did Anders hear the sound of laughter. Only rarely was the sacrament of the Lord's Supper celebrated, to assure that no unworthy person might partake of it.

Despite its retreat from the world, the community was well-educated and owned numerous books on theology and mysticism. Among its members were mathematicians, who charted the course of comets and calculated the date when the end of the world would surely come. Anders was taught French by a Parisian mathematician, and his father carefully monitored his other schooling. Great emphasis was placed on Scandinavian and German theology, though Anders secretly indulged in more natural history than his father, if he had known, would have allowed. Candles to read by were scarce, but were not needed on the long summer days. The long winter nights were devoted to contemplation and prayer. So while Anders had little knowledge of the actual world, he had read Swedenborg and Kierkegaard. At a young age, he understood

329

Kierkegaard's confession, "My depression is the most faithful mistress I have known; no wonder, then, that I return the love."

One winter, Anders' mother walked into the sea, then he and his father moved into tiny cells that were reserved for solitary males. Every day, his father counseled him about God and the nearness of the End of Days. Anders heard the eager yearning for both in his voice, but even as a boy, he could never envision God in that way. The Christianity of his father was somber and humorless, pietistic and legalistic, and demanded complete abjection before the Throne of God. So thorough was the depravity of man that conversion was not assured even after many years of pious repentance. Sternly, his father warned Anders against the evils of his awakening sexuality. Every week, they wrote confessions on their spiritual condition, which the Superintendent read aloud at the Sabbath meetings. With his days spent in contemplation in the chill and dampness, Anders' father contracted tuberculosis. He aggravated his illness by fasting and suffered from it until he died two years later.

In the distant mission house, Anders sighed to himself, thinking of that lone and dreary world. Suddenly feeling hungry, he stepped into the kitchen and chose the ripest papaya from the fruit tray. He slit it open with a knife and scraped away the black seeds from the apricot-colored flesh. The lush fruit melted in his cheeks with a foreign sweetness.

Anders buried his father in the austere communal cemetery, and prayed that he had earned his wish and his reward. Then Anders abandoned the small community and set out for Oslo.

But within a few days, Anders found himself appalled by the capital. Over the past fifty years, its population had bloated seven-fold, and the city was suffering from the strains of growth. On Oslo's main streets, stately buildings stood side by side with hovels, among the rubbish and stinking black smoke and foul steam that rose from the sewers. Accustomed to a village on a fjord, Anders felt homesick for open, uncongested space. Even the harbor was crowded with a thousand or more ships. Inexpensive American wheat was flooding the European markets, so cast-aside farm laborers were flocking to the cities and undercutting urban wages. Anders was grateful to find a job as a laborer on the docks, though the backbreaking work paid very little. He ate fish and potatoes in his tiny, run-down tenement, and though he felt lonely, he did not feel poor.

Secure in his knowledge of the Hereafter, Anders searched for a religion that would offer him meaning in this lifetime. He returned to the Lutheran church, renounced by his parents as too lenient on man. As the Lutherans portrayed him, Jesus was far more merciful than the unrelenting God of Justice he knew. Anders basked in the comfort while he sat as close to the stove as he dared and studied to become a clergyman. As if the drama were enacted before his eyes, he watched Martin Luther expose the fallacies that underlay the universal church. If the church possessed no Treasury of Merit, earned by Jesus and the saints and bartered for forgiveness when a sinner paid for an indulgence, then what did its priesthood really own? Nothing more than dusty relics of the saints! It was surely Divine intervention that kept Martin Luther from being martyred as a dangerous heretic.

Like his father, Anders Erickson ardently desired to be a man of God. But while the Lutheran church was a comfort to his emotions, it did not reach the source of his melancholy. After his ascetic childhood, simple grace as a gift of God seemed far too generous to Anders. Was it not necessary to share in Christ's suffering? Accustomed to devoting six hours every day to worship, prayer and contemplation, Anders feared that the undemanding church would be unrewarding in Heaven.

As he carried heavy cargo on the docks, Anders pondered the nature of man. Did a man enjoy free will, or were his actions and fate all determined by a force that he could beseech but never sway? He struggled to recall the name of the German philosopher who said, "Man is a masterpiece of creation if for no other reason than that, all the weight of evidence for determinism notwithstanding, he believes he has free will." Yet without free will, Anders knew, his upbringing did not make any sense.

One day, on the Oslo docks, a well-dressed man handed

331

Anders a newspaper, the *Skandinaviens Stjerne*. That evening, Anders read it and found himself at once intrigued. The Latter-day Saints insisted on free agency, too. He turned the page and read about a concert to be sung the next day by the Oslo Branch Mormon Choir. Curious, Anders went to hear the choir, then stayed for the preaching, then perused the tracts. He read Joseph Smith's words, "The intelligence of spirits had no beginning, neither will it have an end. It is a spirit from age to age and there is no creation about it."

Anders was surprised to find that the Latter-day Saints were neither dusty nor relics. For weeks, he struggled to understand what the Church possessed that seemed so refreshing to him. But before he understood the answer, he felt it, for he realized that his melancholy had vanished.

What the priesthood possessed was knowledge of a plan that organized the meaning of his life. It pleased Anders to learn that Martin Luther had been posthumously baptized into the Mormon Church.

Half the world away, Anders licked the sticky papaya juice from his fingers, then wiped the knife clean with his handkerchief. Unlike his pietistic father, the Mormons did not prohibit such innocent delights.

The mission leader from Salt Lake City had asked him questions before he would baptize Anders into the Church.

"Do you believe that God has restored His Gospel through revelation?"

"Yes," Anders replied.

"Is it your intention to be baptized by immersion and arise and enter into a new life?"

"Yes," he answered fervently.

"Do you believe Mormon priests have full authority to baptize in the name of Christ?"

Anders inhaled deeply. Did he believe that Mormon priests had full *authority* to baptize in the name of Christ?

"Yes," he answered with more hope than full conviction. He was quickly plunged into the cold water of the fjord.

When Anders emerged, shivering, he truly felt he had

embarked on a second life. Every day, he worked eleven hours at the docks, then studied English and proselytized at night. But he had little to show for his missionary labors.

"It seems every household in Norway has already been approached by brother Mormons," Anders sighed.

"It's the gleaning after the vintage is over," the mission leader agreed.

"Then I must go to America."

The mission leader shook his head. "We need men like you here."

"You have too many immigrants in Utah?"

"That isn't it."

"Then what is it?"

The mission leader saw the ardor in the young man's face. He could not bring himself to tell Anders that there were indeed too many immigrants.

"You may go," he relented. "But before you do, you must gather as much of your genealogical history as you can."

In his Bible, Anders found his father's birthplace, but he had no money to go to Denmark to seek his grandparents' baptismal records there. He rode the train to his mother's village in western Norway, almost familiar to him from his earliest years. He entered the Lutheran church by the sea and approached the pastor. Anders carefully explained that he belonged to the Church of Jesus Christ of Latter-day Saints and sought the names and birthplaces of his ancestors. But the pastor turned Anders away with crude insults. Mormons had come from America too, asking the same questions and attempting to convert his parishoners.

On the train back to Oslo, Anders felt only more convinced that he must go to America. The faith of the Latter-day Saints seemed so thoroughly American to him. Who else but an American would receive a revelation of a religion where men may become gods? It was surely unprecedented, like America itself, and it owed almost nothing to Europe. As his ship steamed west away from Europe, Anders felt no desire to look back.

Anders listened to the sounds of the tropical night. Through the window, he heard a raspy chirping but could not tell if the noise came from an insect or bird, a mammal or amphibian. The habit of sleeping only six hours a night had remained with him after he left the cloister.

Anders enjoyed the passage across the Atlantic Ocean, but had no time to linger in New York. On the journey by train to Utah, he stared out the window every daylight moment. He spent a pleasant winter in Salt Lake City and was surprised to be called on a mission so soon.

"Of course, I will go," Anders replied. "It's a great privilege to serve on a mission. But why have you set *me* aside to send to the South Pacific?"

"It's your gift for languages," they told him. "The best-loved missionaries are often the best linguists. You speak French but aren't French, you speak English but aren't English, which may win favor with the French authorities."

Anders nodded in understanding.

"But the Tahitian language is deceptive," they warned him. "It seems to have only a few hundred words. That deceptive simplicity was in part what attracted the London Missionary Society a century ago."

The steamship voyage from San Francisco filled Anders with an eagerness that sometimes soared into euphoria. Aboard ship, he shamelessly begged other passengers for any literature they had about the islands of the Pacific. Anders studied the maps for hours, memorizing the two types of islands, which bore each other no geological resemblance. Islands like Tahiti were the exposed tips of massive undersea volcanoes, whose mountainous windward slopes grew lush vegetation and rainforests, nurtured by waterfalls and rich volcanic soil. The other island type were atolls, created by living coral over many thousands of years, and gradually capturing sparse soil and vegetation carried by the birds and scarring winds. Ana'a was such an atoll, a low-lying, oval ribbon of land encircling a shallow lagoon.

Despite his missionary enthusiasm, Anders was careful not

to offend the other passengers, and he offered Mormon tracts only to those who asked for them. It felt natural to him to be restrained. Yet as the ship approached Tahiti, Anders felt his excitement surging, for it was a majestic looking island. The lofty mountain peaks were obscured by clouds, but their steep verdant sides, laced with silvery cascades and deep ravines, seemed to him the very image of paradise. The wind and waves were welcoming and gentle as he stepped onto the dock at Pape'ete.

But it took only a few hours for Anders to learn how despoiled earthly paradise had become. Tahiti, he discovered, was a narrow-minded, provincial French colony whose peace was punctured by the jangle of honky-tonk music and the raucus liberty of drunken, fighting sailors. Its government was topheavy with petty bureaucrats, men whose presence in Tahiti only served to rid France of their meddling inferiority at home.

That first morning, Anders left the white-washed house of his host and stepped over sleeping natives, both men and women, lying in tattoo parlor doorways. Degenerate with venereal disease and weakened by absinthe and rum, their bodies smelled of sweat and vomit, and scents that Anders recalled from the prostitutes on Oslo streets. He could smell carrion and rancid cooking oil and rotting fish, and on the docks, the mingled odors of rusty iron and acrid urine. Pape'ete reminded Anders of Europe. As he walked behind them in the streets, he smelled the musky ambergris perfume of the Frenchwomen.

Near the ships, Anders heard sailors speaking Danish and Norwegian, but they wanted none of the salvation he offered them. They shoved him aside, cursing him with liquored breath, reminding him of the rough treatment he and other Mormons had received in Norway.

Anders listened to the gossip in the missionary parlors that night, and he began to understand why the Mormons had few successes there. The French Catholics and Protestants dominated the faith of the natives. On the island of Tahiti that year, the official French census counted only *eight* Mormons.

Worse, in the schism between Latter-day Saints, the

Reorganized Church was capturing the Islands. Called *Kanitos*, 'Saints' in Tahitian, these followers of Joseph Smith III had won 1,550 souls on Tahiti and other Society Islands. But on the Tuamotu Islands like Ana'a, the numbers were far more favorable. There, the French census counted 860 Utah Mormons, and another 98 were found on Austral Islands like Tubuai. Of all the natives who called themselves Christians in French Polynesia, the Latter-day Saints, together, claimed one of every eight.

It came as no surprise to Anders that many Islanders adhered to his religion. The Polynesians were the last of the Nephites, like Mormon and Moroni, and were more righteous than their Lamanite cousins in the Americas.

The first Sunday after he landed in Tahiti, Anders read the *Book of Mormon* to the eight attentive natives.

"And it came to pass that Hagoth, he being an exceedingly curious man, therefore he went forth and built him an exceedingly large ship, on the borders of the land Bountiful, by the land Desolation, and launched it forth into the west sea, by the narrow neck which led into the land northward.

"And behold, there were many of the Nephites who did enter therein and did sail forth with much provisions, and also many women and children; and they took their course northward. And thus ended the thirty and seventh year.

"And in the thirty and eighth year, this man built other ships. And the first ship did also return, and many more people did enter into it; and they also took much provisions, and set out again to the land northward.

"And it came to pass that they were never heard of more. And we suppose that they were drowned in the depths of the sea. And it came to pass that one other ship also did sail forth; and whither she did go we know not."

With their lineage established by the *Book of Mormon*, Polynesian men held full priesthood status among the Latter-day Saints. The two rival churches shared that gospel.

Anders was delighted to learn that the Polynesians shared many traditions with the Church. They told legends of a deluge and forbidden fruit, of men like Joseph and Cain and Abel, and a confusion of tongues. Surely, Hagoth was their heroic Hawaii Loa, the man who organized the settlement of Polynesia. Even their heathen past could be excused, since Hagoth and his followers departed in their ships a century before Jesus preached to the Nephites in America. Other Christians imposed monogamy and denounced the native dances as ungodly, but not the Latter-day Saints.

Anders struggled to make more natives understand why their loyalty must belong to the Salt Lake City Mormons, not the *Kanitos*. But over the weeks, he found his efforts nearly futile. They would stare blankly at him when he tried to teach them to sing "Utah We Love Thee." Finally, the mission president advised Anders to seek souls on other islands, instead of battling the *Kanitos* in their stronghold on Tahiti.

Anders left Tahiti the next day. He boarded a small and filthy inter-island boat, its spaces filled to overflowing with chickens and goats, and smells that came from being flushed out too rarely in the tropical heat. His missionary ardor undampened, Anders moved upwind from the animals and hoped the boat would cross as fast as possible the 200 miles to Ana'a.

On the morning when the atoll first came into view, Anders was standing at the bow of the boat. He shaded his eyes in the sunlight, but the intensity of its beauty was still dizzying. Unlike Tahiti, a steep mountain peak did not rise at its center, but instead, a shallow lagoon lay fringed by dense, sweeping arches of coconut palms. The water near the outer shore was so clear that Anders could see curious coral formations, handsome seashells and a variety of brilliantly colored fish. The sand glared like crystalline snow beyond the shimmering, irridescent turquoise water. The tropical colors scorched his light eyes.

As they waited, the people on the shore waved to Anders, and he cheerfully waved back. The sailors were absorbed in calculating the precise direction of the wind. If they failed to drop anchor to the lee side of the island, the boat could be broken up by the surf against the reef.

Dressed in brightly-colored but proper Christian clothes, the natives welcomed Anders as he stepped onto the island. Many of them, men and women, wore pink hibiscus flowers behind their ears. His brother missionaries greeted Anders warmly, then walked with him a short distance to a welcoming feast. As he sat among them, eating fat roasted pig and broiled eel, Anders felt sure he had embarked on the plan that organized the meaning of his life.

But how soon he came to fear that his melancholy had boarded a faster ship from Norway and was waiting to greet him on Ana'a!

Halfway between Australia and California, halfway between Japan and Chile, the oval ring of land was a minuscule fifteen miles across. Anders Erickson found himself on an inconsequential speck of coral, isolated by a vast and briny sea.

Worse, the atoll seemed possessed by an eerie presence that forced Anders to look inward. Unlike Tahiti, Ana'a had no lava caves to hide in, no mountainous ravines or dense rainforests where a man could lose himself. Its highest point stood eighteen feet above the ocean, and its soil was sparse and thin, incapable of nourishing the luxuriant crops of Tahiti.

Anders tried to find comfort in the natural beauty of the atoll. Massed in all sizes and shapes, the coral reef was full of holes that housed the tiniest fishes and largest sharks. Inside the ring of land, the lagoon was shallow, its water glassy and transparent above a bottom of pure white sand. But outside the narrow ring, the coral reefs obscured the safe passages, making sailing hazardous. When Anders stared down into their dark abysses, he could imagine them as abodes of monsters of the sea, eager to devour any man who might tumble into their depths. To him, the reefs appeared to harbor devils.

Two months after Anders arrived on Ana'a, a great typhoon struck the Tuamotus. Terrified, he watched from a flimsy shelter as mighty ships and their crews were tossed and demolished by the ocean. Out his window, through breaks in the sheets of rain, he saw his congregants' huts blown down by the fierce, unceasing wind. Rows of sturdier buildings were bashed into lumber, then swept away without a trace. The storm did not relent for two days, while 500 people drowned, a hundred Mormons among them. Unable to rejoice in his own salvation, Anders felt a deepening humility at the fragile gift of life. Memories of his mother walking into the sea returned to haunt him.

Yet as his grief receded, Anders questioned how any man, surrounded by such beauty, could stay melancholy for long. *The penalty of the Fall presses very lightly on the valley of Typee.* Even on the longest winter nights, the people needed little fuel and clothing. Fish, shellfish and eels were abundant and delicious, harbored by the reefs and lagoon. And the fish were beautiful, like the bright green parrot fish, striped red and gold around its head. Coconut trees offered up their trunks for houses and boats, and their fronds for baskets, mats, thatching and twine. Coconuts gave their milk for drinking, their meat for food and oil, and copra to be dried for feed and cash. Just a few weeks of work could bring a skilled diver a year's worth of money from the luminous black pearls and mother-of-pearl shells.

Nature offered men so many gifts, yet all of them meant little to Anders. What he sought was a gift to the spirit, not to the senses. Covetously and impatiently, he prayed every night on his knees for a physical, undeniable sign that would dispel every doubt in the authority of the words that he preached. To Anders, the sense of mystery and excitement, the certainty of great events, and omens of even greater ones, were at the core of what drew him to the faith. As Brigham Young said, "To possess an inheritance in Zion or in Jerusalem only in theory--only in imagination--would be the same as having no inheritance at all. It is necessary to get a deed of it, to make an inheritance practical, substantial and profitable." In his melancholy, Anders felt unmentioned in the will, disinherited.

The sign he craved had to be unmistakable, far beyond the lesser visions granted to him in the past. Soon after he arrived in Salt Lake City, Anders had dreamed that his mother came to him, asking him for something he had neglected to give her. At first, he was sure he saw a *ganger*, a ghost who walks after death. But in his dream, he heard his mother's half-remembered voice saying, "And judgment was given to the saints of the most High; and the time came that the saints possessed the kingdom."

With those words still in his mind, Anders awoke, alarmed and remorseful. That morning, he went to the Temple to be baptized on behalf of his father and brother. Then he asked a woman to be baptized for his mother, which surely was the purpose of her midnight visit. The spirit missionaries had come to her and counseled her in spirit prison, just as Anders was instructing the living. Missionary work for the living and Temple work for the dead were essentially one and the same. That night, Anders and his mother both slept well.

Vigorously and cheerfully by day, Anders performed his tasks on Ana'a. He taught the children in the mission school, and led prayer meetings on Monday, Wednesday and Friday evenings. He preached in Tahitian on Sundays, then in English for the foreigners and the occasional sailors who stopped by. He bought wheat from trading ships and made bread for the Lord's Supper, using coconut milk instead of wine. With satisfaction, he watched his congregants, dressed in clean white clothes, singing Mormon hymns in their native language. The *Book of Mormon* was newly translated into Tahitian, and he impatiently awaited its publication. Anders planned to build a chapel of coral rock, to be financed by the tithes of pearl-diving members of the Church.

But despite the friendliness of the Islanders, Anders often felt useless and unworthy. From the pulpit, he watched with secret envy the reflection of God's word shining brightly on the faces of the brown men and women who listened to him preach. Weak and ashamed of his envy, he knew he could not confess his doubts to any mortal man. As his prayers for a sign went unanswered, his melancholy deepened, along with his questioning of the authority that had brought him to the South Pacific.

In the darkness, Anders struck a match and lit a candle. He carried it across the room and held it close to a large map hanging on the wall. The Marquesa Island where Gauguin died was not far from the one where the first European sailors senselessly pursued and then massacred 200 curious natives. These Spanish sailors carved the date, 1595, in a tree, and left behind as a gift three large crucifixes.

Anders wondered if some spirit imbued Polynesia that made Western men unable to obey either God or the decent authority of men. From that earliest European landing, incident after bloody incident testified to depravity and disobedience.

Anders went back to the kitchen and saw the pineapple that the sailors from the Marquesas had sold him. He sliced it open, his nostrils quivering at the acidy ripeness. The fruit tasted sweet but felt sharp on the edges of his tongue. He blew out the candle to conserve it.

Anders had read the journal of the first French explorer, Louis de Bougainville, who arrived in 1768. Bougainville had confessed the nature of his welcoming gifts. "They pressed us to choose a woman and come on shore with her, and their gestures, which were not ambiguous, denoted in what manner we should form an acquaintance with her."

Bougainville described his voyage as like sailing into the Garden of Eden. Could that explain the disobedience spawned by the Islands? Anders wondered. His father's faith never questioned that man was born in original sin, and that man was, beyond doubt, depraved. But to Mormons, Adam's sin was nothing more damning than a transgression. Yet, without the depravity of man, how could we even glimpse the unimaginable holiness of God?

Anders sighed deeply. In the Islands, man certainly appeared to be depraved. Far deadlier sins than fornication were quickly committed by Europeans. Slave ships sailed to the Marquesas seeking labor for South American plantations, and for mining bird dung deposits used as fertilizer. The slavers enticed their native victims with promises of adventure and material goods, then sailed away with them aboard and bartered them for cash or rum.

The early Spanish missionaries, in exchange, offered the

natives the gift of salvation. But on Tahiti, the Islanders so terrified two Catholic priests that they turned their mission house into a fortress, then abandoned it and sailed back to Peru.

Anders wondered about his own missionary ardor if the natives on Ana'a were still occasional cannibals, instead of being generous and kind.

He recalled watching from the steamship the day the islands first came into view. A Scottish merchant, Silas MacGregor, was standing next to him on the deck.

"That's Tubuai," the Scotsman said.

"Tubuai," Anders repeated softly, for he knew a piece of its history. Remote and small, the island was the unlikely setting for the first Mormon Church ever founded outside America and England.

"We won't be landing there," MacGregor said. "But the mutineers from the *Bounty* sailed there twice."

Anders watched the mountainous island in the distance. "Mutineers?" he asked.

"Don't you know the story, Lad? I thought all seafaring men would've heard it. It was back in 1788, almost a century and a quarter ago, that the *H.M.S. Bounty* sailed to Tahiti on a mission to gather breadfruit trees."

"Why?" Anders asked.

"The Englishmen sought to transplant breadfruit in the West Indies," MacGregor said. "It was to be a cheap food for their slaves. So the *Bounty* remained in these waters six months, then set sail to the east. Captain William Bligh was a fine navigator and helmsman, and though demanding of his men, surely no crueler than the common ship captain of his day."

Anders ignored the salt spray in his face as he listened.

"Alas, the Captain's second-in-command was Fletcher Christian, a deranged, disobedient man, who beguiled the lesser men into believing that they could stay in paradise with impunity. It was surely the animal lure of the Islands and the heathenish belief that life is short. Cruelly, they set Captain Bligh and eighteen loyalists adrift in an open boat, with only scant food and water. Then the mutineers sailed the *Bounty* to

342

the island you see there before you, Tubuai.  But the savages here saw their true nature and repelled them."

Anders gazed at the island.  "Did any of the loyalists survive?"

"Aye, that's the miracle," MacGregor said.  "Shipwrecks are common and the ocean is vast, so Fletcher Christian and his mob of mutineers never imagined they'd be found out.  But Captain Bligh had to sail a mere 41 days before the loyalists reached a Dutch-owned island in Indonesia.  They'd come 3,000 miles.  It was surely a sign from God for all men to see, as His hand is always seen in men's choice between obedience and mutiny."

"What became of the sailors?" Anders asked.

The Scotsman smiled, enjoying the tale.  "Captain Bligh lived almost 20 years more, and became an Admiral, then Governor in Australia.  The mutineers sailed on to Tahiti, where a few men stayed to await their destiny."

MacGregor pointed to the now-receding island.  "But Mr. Christian and most others set sail again and landed once more here at Tubuai.  They built themselves a fort, but after a few months, they were driven out again by the natives.  So they sailed the *Bounty* south to Pitcairn Island.  There, within months, the mutineers were massacred almost to a man by the natives.  Their half-breed great-grandchildren are still living on that island, Lad."

Anders looked out across the mute, unchanging ocean that witnessed these events long ago.  He could not help but wonder what Mr. Christian had done to merit such a fate from the natives.

"What happened to the mutineers who stayed in Tahiti?"

"Aye, they had a hand in the destiny and dynasty of Tahiti. A native warlord promptly hired the mutineers, armed with their muskets, in a war to vanquish his enemies.  Victorious, these European sailors were there to witness the coronation of King Pomare I and the sacrifice of three human beings in his honor."

Anders swallowed hard.  "Human sacrifice?"  He wondered what traces of the ancient religion persisted across the generations.

"It's true, Lad," MacGregor said. "Then the mutineers, too, suffered a fate no less ignoble. When word of their treachery reached the authorities, they were seized in Tahiti, then shipped back to England in irons. They faced a proper trial and punishment. The mutineers were hanged on a sailing ship as a sign for all sailors to see."

Disobedience, Anders sighed to himself in the dark mission house. Could it have been a noble impulse that brought men like the mutineers and Gauguin back to the Islands after they left? Yearning to be cleansed by uncorrupted nature, they could not escape the ills that they had carried with them from Europe. Without a sign of hope, they grew ever more dissipated instead.

In distraction, Anders cut into the pineapple again, but the knife nicked his finger when it caught in the core. He mumbled a Danish curse he had learned on the docks but tried not to say anymore. A drop of blood widened across the yellow pulp as the acidy liquid stung his finger. He put his finger to his mouth and tasted the salty blood and sweet juice.

Anders tugged at the undergarments he was given during his Endowments in the Salt Lake City Temple. He was grateful that the sultry rainy season was past. Even in winter, the garments stuck to his body in the humidity. But in summer, when the sweat poured from his skin, the rash beneath his garments was almost unbearable. He saw the native men wearing the colorful long loincloths they wore like skirts, but he resisted the temptation to try them at home. Not a superstitious man, Anders was unafraid that God would fault him for wearing a *pareu.* But his upbringing had conditioned him to discomfort for the cause of religion.

Uneasily, Anders recalled his Endowment ceremony in the Temple. At first, he had enjoyed it, learning the handshakes and tokens, and the penalties for revealing them to outsiders. As instructed, he gestured with his thumb, sliding it below his chin from his left ear to his right, as if slashing his throat. He liked the certainty and drama of the ritual, and the warmth of participating with the others in the room. Anders gestured as he was shown, with a low slash across his abdomen.

He did not hesitate to swear the oath of sacrifice. "And as Jesus Christ has laid down his life for the redemption of mankind, so we should covenant to sacrifice all that we possess, even our own lives if necessary, in sustaining and defending the Kingdom of God."

Nothing on Earth or in Hell, he believed, would keep him from honoring that covenant. To Anders, the Endowments were a gift of wisdom and power and blessing from the Heavenly Father.

He listened to the words the leader spoke.

"You and each of you do covenant and promise that you will pray, and never cease to pray, Almighty God to avenge the blood of the prophets upon this nation, and that you will teach the same to your children and your children's children until the third and fourth generation."

Anders was startled by the venomous words. *Avenge the blood of the prophets upon this nation.*

Anders stood in numb silence. Sudden tears stung his eyes, and his mouth grew dry. How could he, a man who piously desired to become an American, swear an oath of such vengeance? How could he vow to teach it to his great-grandchildren?

Bewildered, Anders listened as the other white-clothed people complaisantly mouthed the vow. Then he stole a glance around the Temple room. He was grateful to see that he was not the only one stunned into speechlessness.

The moment soon passed, and the ceremony progressed to other, simpler matters of faith. Anders swore more innocent oaths, then crossed through the veil to the Celestial Room, where a crowd of jubilant people surrounded him. But he left the Temple shaken, unable to confess how horrified he was to any man.

As he lay awake in Salt Lake City that night, Anders pondered the oath of vengeance. Joseph Smith, of course, had not received that revelation. Comforted, Anders saw that it *must* be an error, an incorrect translation, whose truth would one day be revealed. But in the dark mission house, he was less sure.

How crucial it was to be sure! He thought back to the sureness of his father's ascetic cloister, who *knew* that Christ's Second Coming and the End of Days were near, and struggled only to predict the exact date.

The Mormons did not try to predict the precise date, but they were certain of the place, which was Zion. And Zion was no longer only the American West. It was the Kingdom of God, found wherever His people gathered in the Americas and Europe, Asia and the Islands of the Pacific.

Anders had learned how quickly the Pacific Islanders were drawn to Christianity. A few years after the *Bounty* sailed away, thirty Protestant members of the London Missionary Society landed in Tahiti. In a dusty government office in Pape'ete, Anders read their earliest depictions of the natives.

"Their manners are affable and engaging; their step easy and firm, and graceful; their behavior free and unguarded; always boundless in generosity toward each other, and to strangers; their tempers mild, gentle and unaffected; slow to take offense, easily pacified, and seldom retaining resentment or revenge, whatever the provocation they may have received."

The natives had received deadly provocations. Influenza and tuberculosis, veneral disease and measles conspired with the ubiquitous liquor to deplete the native population by some 70 percent.

By 1812, King Pomare II had become a Christian. By force when necessary, he persuaded many of his subjects to be baptized, until he died of alcoholism at age 40. The last of his dynasty, King Pomare V, died from the ravages of alcoholism a decade before Anders arrived.

It pleased Anders that most natives sincerely practiced their Christianity, rigorously keeping the Sabbath and wearing modest clothes. Yet the Catholics and Protestants seemed tireless to him in their dissipation. He was appalled by the drunkenness of the Bastille Day celebrations, which lasted most of a month. Anders solemnly believed that, for their own survival, the Islanders should all become Mormons.

Anders wondered, as his father never doubted, if depravity

was natural to man. On the ship from America, he had read the *Voyage of the Beagle* by Charles Darwin, who spent a month on Tahiti in 1835. As the ship crossed the equator, Anders read with excitement about the *Beagle's* westward course, the same route sailed by the Nephites whose descendants populated the Islands. Indeed, who else could have brought to Polynesia a type of sweet potato known to grow only in South America?

MacGregor sat down next to Anders as he was reading the natural history.

"Darwin writes that the natives seem genuinely Christian," Anders said. "Even when the missionaries aren't watching."

"Aye," MacGregor nodded. "But his *Descent of Man* and *Origin of the Species*! How could anyone believe that men might be descended from anything lesser than God?"

Anders wondered if such blasphemous ideas were just further evidence of how the Islands spawn disobedience in men's minds. Darwin had been Anders' age, 22, when he embarked on that journey.

In the mission house, Anders lit the whale-oil lamp on the desk. A week had elapsed since he had written in the journal that all missionaries were instructed to keep daily. He dipped his pen into the ink and recorded the events of the previous Sabbath.

"After morning service, I invited all who felt it their duty to be baptized to present themselves at a place on the beach, where I waited for them. I baptized two men, Tuhoi and Temapu, and in the afternoon, I confirmed them. We were much blessed with the spirit of the Lord, and union and fellowship abounded among us as brethren. That night, I found that no consecrated oil remained, so I blessed some coconut oil, then anointed and blessed a sick girl, who has now recovered."

Anders knew he should write more, but the words sounded hollow as he read them back. He wondered if it was proper to record his thoughts about the death of Gauguin. Even half the globe away, authority was less distant than it seemed. He feared a stern rebuke, such as he had heard given to other men. "You have my love and respect," the European mission president had

347

written, "but I have felt for many months that you were taking things altogether too easy."

Anders picked up a book from the desk, an old dog-eared copy of *Typee*. It was a gift from MacGregor, who had warned him that, in it, Herman Melville slandered the missionaries. Anders read those pages again.

"Heaven help the Isles of the Sea! The sympathy which Christendom feels for them has, alas! in too many instances proved their bane. Among the islands of Polynesia, no sooner are the images overturned, the temples demolished, and the idolators converted into nominal Christians, then disease, vice, and premature death make their appearance. The depopulated land is then recruited for the rapacious hordes of enlightened individuals who settle themselves within its borders, and clamorously announce the progress of the Truth. Neat villas, trim gardens, shaven lawns, spires, and cupolas arise, while the poor savage soon finds himself an interloper in the country of his fathers."

On shipboard, Anders borrowed MacGregor's copy of *Moby Dick*, then perused page after page on the natural history of whales. When a school of whales swam so near the ship that they darkened the sea, Anders was struck with such breathtaken awe that he forgot to be afraid of their stampeding. As they spouted briny spray that blew in his face, he came to understand that to Melville, whales were far nobler creatures than their human hunters.

Anders fingered the old copy of *Typee*. He was unsure if the story Melville told was true, how at age 22, he jumped from a whale ship in the Marquesas. His leg burning with infection, he escaped into the forest, where the natives kindly nursed him back to health. But they were cannibals and refused to let him go. Not knowing if their healing was a gift or a ritual prelude to a feast, he escaped from the cannibals, too. Then, in Tahiti, Melville joined a mutinous refusal to set sail and was jailed for six weeks in Pape'ete.

Cannibalism! Anders shuddered at the depravity of it. A month after he arrived in Ana'a, when he had earned their trust,

Anders asked his congregants to tell him about the old cannibalism. Reluctantly, with much coaxing, they brought him to the site of an ancient stone temple, tumbled-down and overgrown with ferns. This temple, they confessed, had once been used for human sacrifices. His brethren explained that a war of extermination was fought among these Islands a hundred years earlier. The people of Ana'a won this war, so the victors ate the bodies of the slain. The heads were brought to this temple as trophies of honor for the gods, and a sign for all people to see.

His legs trembling, Anders paced off the length of the temple, eighteen paces. Then he noticed how the stones were set just wide enough apart to display a row of human skulls. The people on Ana'a never ate one another, they quickly explained, though the vanquished women and children, brought as slaves, might be eaten if they became unruly. From the pulpit that Sunday, Anders warily regarded his congregants. Were they savages or descendants of worthy Nephites? The people in the Islands seemed so generous and kind.

Anders wondered what would make him jump ship. The Tubuai mission of the Mormon Church was organized by a man who had once jumped ship in Polynesia.

Anders learned the story from an old, one-legged missionary, James S. Brown. Anders was sent to meet him before leaving Utah.

"Being called to the Islands of the Sea," Elder Brown told Anders, "you should know the events that happened there.

"I did not arrive at the beginning," the old missionary explained. "I was called instead to march with the Mormon Battalion in the Mexican War. Then I found myself in California in '48, when we discovered gold at Sutter's Mill. It was the following year that I went to the Pacific, an illiterate youth not yet 22 when we landed."

Well into his seventies, Elder Brown was sound of mind but frail. His voice was strong and his countenance fierce.

"Addison Pratt was the man who first conceived of the mission, back in 1843. No, he was no relation to Apostles Orson and Parley Pratt, just a man who disobeyed his father in his youth and went to sea."

Anders nodded as he listened. He was well aware of what his own father would say about his choices.

"Addison worked hard but hated tyranny," Elder Brown said. "And the ship captain's injustice outraged him. He said the captain once ordered a sailor stripped to his pants and flogged with a cat-o'-nine-tails until his blood ran into his shoes. The sailor's crime? Merely stealing a small salt cod and dividing it among the hungry men. 'The skipper supposed himself out of reach of law,' Brother Addison said, 'going from bad to worse till we hardly dared to say our souls were our own.'

"For such cruelty more than all else, Addison jumped ship in Hawaii. He learned some Hawaiian on Oahu, and often went to the missionary house to grind coffee for his employer. He was very dissatisfied with the missionaries. 'Never at any time,' Addison said, 'would any of the missionaries, either male or female, speak to me, no more than if I had been a dog.' After half a year, he worked his way home on a whale ship, and later sailed on merchant ships, coast guard cutters and a steamboat, facing gales and pirates and smugglers. Then he landed and got married, and was baptized a Latter-day Saint. With his wife and four daughters, he went to Nauvoo and set to work building the Temple."

Nauvoo, Anders silently thought. It seemed to him almost a mythical city. He once saw an old photograph of the newly finished, then abandoned Nauvoo Temple.

The old missionary sipped some water. "Our Prophet Joseph Smith agreed with Addison's idea, and sent him with Benjamin Grouard and two others on a mission to the Hawaiian Islands. Brother Grouard had left home as an unruly boy of age 14, then sailed the greater part of the world, learning nautical, mechanical and shipbuilding skills. But when the four Elders reached New Bedford, they found no ship that would soon sail west to Hawaii. So they booked passage instead on a whaler bound east to Tahiti. Our missionaries did not learn for a year that the Prophet was martyred two months after they landed."

350

"This was 1844?" Anders asked. "Seven years *before* the missions to Scandinavia, Germany and France?"

Elder Brown nodded. "Their first landfall was the island of Tubuai, where some Americans lived, but no missionaries, 400 miles south of Tahiti. Tubuai is a beautifully pleasant and mountainous island, and Brother Addison resolved to establish a mission there. A good jolly soul, he lived among the natives as they lived, faring as they fared by hunting and fishing. Other Christian missionaries landed in Tubuai and proposed to stay, but the natives treated them coolly, knowing they would demand houses and hogs, hens and people to work for them."

Anders smiled at the story, eager to see Polynesia for himself.

"They say 3,000 people once lived on Tubuai," Elder Brown said. "But then a canoe adrift with starved corpses was blown there, carrying a plague that spread throughout the island. By the time Addison landed, only 200 natives survived. It's a sad fact that the Pacific islands that hold intercourse with whites are less populous than those that refuse. Graveyards and villages overgrown with vegetation silently testify to this truth."

Anders nodded solemnly, then asked, "What happened to the other Elders?"

"One died at sea the first month, and another, discouraged, sailed home in 1845, only to die as he ventured west from Nauvoo. Elder Grouard sailed on to Tahiti. But the French and English missions had been active for decades, and he was able to make only a few converts. Some Tahitians seemed to believe, but they would not obey, fearing they would lose favors from the English and French. So Grouard left the next year for Ana'a, where he was the only white missionary. Within five months, he'd baptized 620 islanders, including some who'd been cannibals just a few decades earlier."

Cannibals, Anders thought, appalled.

"Grouard and Pratt baptized thousands of Polynesians before Brigham Young ever saw the Salt Lake Valley," Elder Brown said. "For nine unbroken years, despite slanders by the French authorities and other missionaries, and with almost no help from the Church, Brother Grouard labored to strengthen our mission. He built three boats for inter-island mission travel, which brought the mission money from trade. Grouard persisted, even after all the other white brethren but one went off to California to mine gold."

"But how did *you* come to Tahiti?" Anders asked.

The old missionary smiled at the younger man. "After five years of lonely effort, Brother Addison set sail for America. He sought to bring his family and a new crop of missionaries like me. I first met Addison in the goldfields of California, and together we went east to Deseret. There, in the winter of '49, he taught lessons for many weeks on the language and customs of the Islands."

"Tahitian was the first language taught in Utah?" Anders asked, amazed.

"Perhaps even the entire West. But I did not attend, since I was called to the mission just a few days before we set out across the desert, the mountains, then the ocean. We sailed for 33 days, and I was seasick every one of them. At night, I would lay in my berth and imagine that my flesh had worked loose from my bones, and the calves of my legs were rolling about my shinbones without control. Of course, I had both my legs then. My left leg was shot up only years later when a camp-mate mistook me for a bear."

"What was it like when you arrived?"

"When we landed at Pape'ete in 1850," Elder Brown explained, "the French authorities were not pleased to see us. They, and the Catholic priests, feared we were gaining too much influence, so they restricted our preaching and travel. They forbade us from getting any of our support from the natives, as was our custom, because we got none from the Church. Still, we preached and healed when we were asked, and I spent my days learning to read and write, and speak Tahitian. We had to learn many curious things, like how the Polynesians greet each other by rubbing noses.

"Brother Grouard was in Tubuai at that time, building the schooner *Ravaai*. It was a fine mahogany vessel of 80 tons burthen, with 12 double bunks in a spacious cabin. But news reached us in Tahiti that Grouard had been arrested. It seems that some native Mormons held governmental offices on Ana'a, and left the authority of those offices to their sons when they went on missions to nearby islands. Grouard had taken away those offices, the French authorities were told. But at his trial in Pape'ete, he was acquitted of all charges.

"With other missionary families, Addison's wife and daughters landed some months later in Tubuai. The French authorities allowed Addison to go there but not to preach, so he worked stitching canvas for the foresail and jib of the *Ravaai*. The wives taught school in Tubuai, while other missionaries were dispatched among the Islands. I was sent to Ana'a."

Anders leaned in closer as Elder Brown's aging voice began to falter.

"By 1851, many Mormons on Ana'a had fallen away from the Church. Worse, they joined a new native religion, with rites of masqueraded, fervored dancing that climaxed in sexual promiscuities. At once, I rebaptized as many lapsed Saints as I could, all in full view of four envious Catholic priests. Only thirty natives gave allegiance to the Catholics, while 900 were loyal to me. My school was full of exuberant children, while theirs stood empty. I was nonetheless astonished when a French man-of-war landed in Ana'a. Soldiers and *gendarmes* had come to arrest me for sedition."

"Sedition?" Anders asked. "Was it true?"

The old missionary shook his head. "Perhaps I listened sympathetically to the natives who complained about living under the French yoke of bondage. And I did encourage them to gather in America. But I never established my own government, run by Mormons on Ana'a, as I was charged. And when I hoisted the American flag, I didn't mean it as a sign of resistance to French authority.

"Still, I was brought in chains to Pape'ete. They fed me only bread and water for eighteen days, then convicted me at trial, and deported me on the first outbound ship. Brother Grouard made sure the first vessel leaving port was the *Ravaai*.

"Within months, all Mormon missionaries were banished from French Polynesia. Yet our influence persisted in the Church and economy we created and left behind. We also left a legacy of hostility to the Catholic missionaries."

"Hostility?" Anders asked.

Elder Brown nodded. "The Catholic priests soon obtained civil office on Ana'a, and they forbade all Mormon meetings, in public or private. So the native Saints held clandestine meetings. But the authorities found out, and a policeman and two Catholic priests tried to disperse the people. A bloody fight ensued. The *gendarme* was run through with a fishing spear, and a Catholic priest was killed with the *gendarme's* sword. The other priest narrowly escaped with his life, but managed to send word to the authorities. They dispatched French troops from Pape'ete."

Elder Brown sighed deeply. "When it was over, five Mormon priests, my brethren and friends, were hanging from a beam tied between two coconut trees. Some 30 or 40 others, some of them women, were sentenced to hard labor on Tahiti. From a distant island, I could do nothing but mourn and prepare to go home. The first Catholic church in the Tuamotu Islands was built upon the ruins of our Mormon chapel in Ana'a."

Anders visited that usurping Catholic church a few months later when he reached Ana'a. He stood outside it, pondering all the labors his forebears had abandoned when they left. Yet they established a foundation more sure than rock. One of every five people on the Tuamotu Islands remained Mormon.

It was commonplace, Anders knew, to build upon the ruins of vanquished temples. But every time he passed it, the traces only added to his melancholy.

As Anders blew out the whale oil lamp, he recalled another temple he had seen. While still on Tahiti, he had ventured away from Pape'ete to escape the drunken depravity around Bastille Day. At the southern end of the island stood the ruins of an ancient and enormous Nephite temple. Anders stared at it in wonder.

Not far from the temple was a shop, whose window bore a

sign in Chinese. Anders stepped inside and inhaled the mingled odors of cinnamon, incense and dried fish.

Anders had never met anyone Chinese before. He greeted the shopkeeper in French, then asked, "What happened to the temple?"

The shopkeeper answered him in French. "It was dismantled in the 1860s, when the stones were rebuilt into a villa for a European."

Anders looked around the dusty shop. "What was he doing in Tahiti?"

"He was importing liquor here, until he thought of a new way to get rich. Cotton prices were high in Europe, due to the American Civil War, so he started a plantation in Tahiti. When he couldn't buy slaves, he brought workers from China instead."

"What happened to him?"

The shopkeeper shrugged. "The plantation went bankrupt when the Civil War ended. The European died young, but we're still here."

Anders decided to buy a few of the raw vanilla beans that grow as pods of climbing orchids on Tahiti. The Chinese shopkeeper carefully weighed the long brown beans, then showed Anders how to crush the vanilla seeds with a mortar and pestle.

"You should steep it in rum to extract its full flavor," he said.

"Yes," Anders replied. He inhaled the delicate insistent fragrance, knowing he could only crush it and mix it with sugar.

How small the Earth had grown in these latter days! The entire world had become like an island, where one man with inspiration could leave a legacy that endured for good or ill. By the time Anders reached the Islands, the descendants of those Chinese workers had become the merchant class. Their shops had everything for sale, medicines and vegetables and meat, weapons and absinthe, women and men.

Anders felt his own mission was to elevate the paradise around him. He would be like those early missionaries who brought gifts of beneficial plants, sugar cane, pineapples and pamplemousse, eucalyptus, rubber and gum trees. He would build on what the civilized world had offered for a century, the charming white-washed houses, the structures of painted wood with large verandahs, the markets where buyers paid cash for the radiant black pearls and dried coconut meat. The gift of precious innocence was lost, so he, himself, must uproot the moral and physical corruptions planted by ill-intentioned Europeans. Anders would tirelessly work to save souls, and much more. If only his melancholy would permit him. If only he would be granted a sign!

Sadly, Anders thought back to his final interview with the mission authorities, shortly after he met with Elder Brown. Hoping to hear his last instructions, he had walked briskly to the meeting. But the authorities watched Anders across the desk as they interrogated him with an intensity that left him feeling sullied and insulted.

Hesitantly, Anders asked them, "Did I say something improper to Elder Brown?"

"No, Elder Erickson, not at all."

"But if you doubt my intentions," Anders asked, "why send me to an outpost so far removed from authority?"

The two men looked at one another, then one replied, "Several early missionaries to the Islands have been boldly disobedient."

"Who?" Anders asked.

"Hiram Clark," the man said. "Walter Murray Gibson, Benjamin Grouard and Addison Pratt."

In astonishment, Anders asked, "Grouard and Pratt?" Elder Brown had testified of loyalty and dedication, not disobedience.

The authorities nodded solemnly.

"But how?"

"Hiram Clark was a zealous missionary in England," the man explained, "so in 1850, he was named the first mission president in Hawaii. But within ten weeks, he abandoned his mission and boarded a ship for the Marquesas. He claimed a testimony from the Lord told him to go there. Clark wrote to Brigham Young about the natives, 'They are guilty of all kinds

356

of whoredoms and abominations, and the more men the women can accommodate the greater they consider the honor.'"

The authorities watched as Anders shuddered involuntarily.

"Clark wrote of admonishing his brother missionaries, 'lest they should be overtaken by the tempter; feeling ever desirous of taking the same caution myself.'"

Anders shook his head. "What happened to him?"

"Clark never reached the Marquesas. When he landed in Tubuai at Pratt's mission, he started taking improper liberties with native ladies. Fearing that Clark would undo all his labors on the island, Pratt had him quickly disfellowshipped. Clark sailed home to America, where he slashed his own throat two years later."

Anders thought of the oaths and dire penalties at his Endowment, two weeks earlier. "Was Hawaii such a difficult mission?" he stammered.

"Not at all, Elder Erickson. Some men boldly succeed while others are weak and disobedient. Within three days of landing in Hawaii, two Elders had baptized 130 natives. By 1855, we had 4,000 native Saints, despite losing many in a smallpox epidemic. The *Book of Mormon* was printed in Hawaiian that year."

Anders did not know what this interrogation meant. But Elder Brown's depiction of Polynesia had given him a deep desire to be sent there by the Church.

"I was raised in a *celibate* faith," Anders insisted on his own behalf. "I was taught ways to conquer sinful urges."

The authorities nodded in approval. "Perhaps. But sexual sin was not Benjamin Grouard's disobedience."

Anders felt bewildered by this news. "The same missionary who devoted nine years of his life, baptizing thousands of natives and tirelessly building vessels for the Church?"

"Yes, Elder Erickson, the same man. When our missionaries were expelled from Polynesia, Grouard went to San Bernardino, California. It was our way station between the Pacific Islands and Salt Lake City. But from its beginning, that settlement suffered far worse dissention than any community in Utah.

357

Land disputes and apostasies were common, and the judgments of our leaders were disregarded. Grouard was one of the dissenters."

"What did he do?"

"In 1855, Grouard and two other men ran for public office, against candidates named by the Church for confirmation by the voters. They were overwhelmingly defeated, of course. But Grouard was called before the Church court to explain his unauthorized behavior. Grouard said simply that he intended no harm, wishing only to serve the community if the people chose to elect him. Naturally, his explanation was judged unsatisfactory. He was ordered to apologize for what he'd done, but he stubbornly refused to say he was sorry. So Grouard was disfellowshipped from the Church."

Anders bit his tongue hard. In his studies to become an American citizen, he had come to understand that a citizen had the right to run for office. But he did not want to be rejected from this mission.

The authorities observed Anders' face, then continued. "Addison Pratt also lived in San Bernardino with his family. But soon, troubles with the U.S. Government caused Brigham Young to summon home all loyal Saints from California, Nevada and Hawaii. Nearly all obeyed counsel, at the sacrifice of their land and improvements. One who disobeyed was Addison Pratt."

Anders was too curious to bite his tongue. Pratt had so willingly sacrificed so much before.

"Why?" he asked.

"Utah was too cold for him, Pratt claimed. He stayed in California and continued to attend church and administer to the sick. But Pratt was considered weak in faith and not alive to his obligations."

Anders doubted that could be the whole truth. Elder Brown had told him that, despite encouragement by Mrs. Pratt, Pratt had refused to take a second wife. He had devoted seven years to battling promiscuity in Polynesia, and perhaps the Utah War had seemed mutinous.

Anders shrugged, relieved that Utah was now a state and polygamy no longer a concern. "I am alive to my obligations," he said.

"We're here to assure that you are," the authorities replied.

Anders hoped he could distract them from more probing questions. "Who was the fourth missionary you named?"

"Walter Murray Gibson," one answered, "a new convert who persuaded Brigham Young to reopen our mission in Hawaii in 1861. Gibson brought excellent credentials. He'd been a Government representative in Guatemala and Costa Rica, and master of a cargo ship to the East Indies. But unknown to the Church, he'd been jailed for fomenting a native revolt in the East Indies. Gibson aspired to be an oriental potentate."

Warily, the authorities watched Anders' face, but they learned nothing.

"Once ensconced in Hawaii, Gibson's delusions of grandeur bloomed. By corrupting the local taboos and superstitions, he was able to awe the Hawaiians with his power. Gibson placed the *Book of Mormon* inside a hollow stone and warned the natives that if they touched it, they would suffer instant death."

Anders shook his head in disgust.

"Gibson demanded cash for anointing the Hawaiians as priests and elders, bishops, apostles, and an archbishop. Even as *priestesses* of temples! He used this money to buy land on the island of Lanai in his own name, and he ordered Church lands and chapels on other islands to be sold. Gibson told the native Saints to sell their livestock, houses and land, often at very low prices, and dedicate all proceeds and labor to buying and improving Church property on Lanai. The natives paid him tributes in foodstuffs, goatskins and fish. They worshipped him and served him virtually as a god."

Anders tried to comprehend the depth of this depravity. Could any man possibly believe that God existed to lavish on him all the gifts that he desired?

"In 1864, two Apostles came from Utah to investigate. They saw his corruptions and excommunicated Gibson at once. But he owned half the island of Lanai, and refused to sign over to the

Church any of the property held in his name. It took the Apostles and proper missionaries many months to convince the Hawaiian Mormons that they'd been bled and defrauded."

"What became of him?" Anders asked.

"Gibson was elected to the Hawaiian legislature, then was made Prime Minister by the King. Twenty years elapsed before he was finally unmasked as a fraud, and tossed out of Hawaii. Gibson died in penniless exile in San Francisco."

Anders smiled at the vindication.

"The Church Gibson helped to build is still thriving," the authorities said. "We have 83 branches in Hawaii, 43 meeting houses, and 5,000 members. That's perhaps one of every six Hawaiians."

Anders felt grateful when the authorities shook his hand and approved him for his mission to Polynesia. For as he, himself, had discovered in an equidistant quadrant of the globe, the world was eager to acquire this new American religion. Even in faraway New Zealand, one of every twelve natives had become a Latter-day Saint.

Anders went to tell Elder Brown the good news.

"Did you ever want to go back to French Polynesia?" Anders asked.

"Yes, and we did go back," Elder Brown replied. "For two decades, the Church abandoned our missions in French Polynesia. No news arrived from Salt Lake City, let alone any help. But left on their own for a generation, the natives practiced a religion faithful to the visions of Joseph Smith."

"Didn't you find that amazing?" Anders said.

The old missionary smiled. "Even more astonished were two Josephite missionaries on their way to Australia in 1873. By chance, they landed in Pape'ete and discovered that Polynesians were accurately teaching Church doctrines. Some 2,000 Saints were scattered on twenty islands across 1,000 miles of the Pacific. Then, for two more decades, the Reorganized Church, the *Kanitos,* quietly harvested what we had sown.

"In 1892, after 40 years, and despite a leg amputated nearly up to my hip, I was called back to missionary service. My son and I remained more than a year on Ana'a. But we refused to make any alliance with the *Kanitos*, an organization by persons who had been excommunicated, and had not divine authority."

Elder Brown and other Utah Mormons had made inroads in French Polynesia in the decade before Anders arrived. But the *Kanitos* still outnumbered them nearly two to one.

A week before he left Utah, Anders was brought to a curious settlement, Iosepa, fifty miles west of Salt Lake City. The town looked similar to most Mormon villages, familiar now to Anders, with its several dozen houses, a chapel and school. But while other Utah towns were filled with blue-eyed New Englanders and northern Europeans like himself, Iosepa was populated by brown-skinned Hawaiians.

"Iosepa?" Anders had asked.

"It means 'Joseph' in the Hawaiian and Tahitian language," his host told him. "Fifty years ago, Addison Pratt proposed that a gathering place be organized for Polynesian Saints."

"Here?"

"No, in Southern California, in a climate congenial to their own."

Anders stood in the dry, alkaline wind and imagined how foreign Iosepa must feel to the Hawaiians. The settlement lay in the desert, in Skull Valley. It appeared, nonetheless, to be a prospering plantation, and Anders saw fish being raised in ponds. Hundreds of carefully watered fruit and walnut trees had been planted a few years earlier in the arid soil.

"What's that building?" Anders asked, pointing to a shanty of raw wood. A crude flagpole stood in front and smoke rose from the chimney.

"The pest house," the host replied. "Our lepers are quarantined there, so we can care for them."

"Lepers? Here in Utah?"

"We've never had more than three," the man explained. "But we aren't gathering in any more Saints from the Pacific Islands. Our winters are too cold for them here, and they can't make good *poi* from our wheat."

Anders stared in silence at the pest house.

"But they have nowhere else to obtain their Endowments, or baptize their ancestors. So we've planned to build a Temple on the island of Oahu, the first in the world outside Utah. When it's finished, these Hawaiians will go home."

Leprosy! Anders thought, shuddering alone in the small mission house. It was endemic in Polynesia, he knew. In Tahiti, the French Protestants took care of the lepers, but other than isolating the victims, they could do little more than in Biblical times. In Hawaii, the lepers were cared for by the Catholics. The Catholic priest was said to smoke a pipe to mask the foul smell of infected flesh, before he died of the disease. He is the one who is a saint, thought Anders grimly.

In his melancholy, Anders prayed once again that he would never be called to treat leprosy on Ana'a. He feared he would not have the faith to lay his hands on a leper's head and anoint him with consecrated oil.

Anders went to the window and saw his image reflected in the glass. Perhaps healing a person who was deathly sick would soon be the sign he was awaiting. The natives were so eager for his healing. And the Gentiles would often ask to be baptized if they or their children got well. As he spoke the blessings, he took comfort in knowing it could do no harm. Preaching came easily to Anders because the words belonged to other men, but healing demanded his own authority.

Anders looked at his reflection in the window. His hair and skin were pale, almost white, common enough in Scandinavia. But the contrast with the natives sometimes made him feel ghostly, as if their color was correct and his mistaken.

Far more readily than Anders himself, the Polynesians understood why they must baptize their ancestors. They could chant their genealogies back many generations, and they carefully taught their children the vital details of their ancestors' lives. The grandparents of some congregants had been baptized by Elders Pratt, Grouard and Brown, while others seemed to have believing blood, as if their spirits had been waiting all their lives to hear the gospel. A Polynesian could as readily have traveled to Norway and baptized him.

Anders knew almost nothing of his own genealogy, and had no living family to enlighten him. At the pietistic cloister, neither ancestry nor progeny mattered. Perhaps a member of a tribe of Israel had wandered into his own Nordic lineage. It might explain his own believing blood, how he knew from that first *Skandinaviens Stjerne* that he belonged to this American religion. His genealogy might explain his own abject failure to disbelieve in the depravity of man. Yet every sign around him pointed to that depravity!

Restlessly, Anders stepped out the door and walked a few paces from the mission house. The moon had long since set in the purple night. Anders scanned the unfamiliar stars of the southern hemisphere. As far south of the equator as he once lived from the arctic circle, he felt lost without the North Star. Even the Milky Way was foreign. It formed a brighter, wider arc in the tropics than the stars he knew from the latitudes far north. The path of ghosts, his father had called it, or the winter street leading to Heaven.

Anders took a few steps to a fragrant *tiare* tree that stood beside the window. He cupped his hands behind some leaves and drew a pungent flower toward his nose. He inhaled the strong scent, then pinched the flower from the tree and slid it behind his ear, as native men and women often wore them. Reflected in the window, he smiled at how it looked so misplaced in his thin blond hair. Unlike the ascetic sect of his father, the Church did not forbid such folly.

Anders remembered the last summer he spent in Norway. The Mormons had organized midnight flower-picking excursions and field trips that set out just before dawn, at four o'clock. Anders was accustomed to such hours, since the pietistic brethren met every midnight for worship. On one excursion, he met a pretty Mormon girl and found himself tempted to marry her. But when he prayed for guidance, Anders recognized that he must wait and marry an American. So many converts in Norway were poor servant girls, or widowed, divorced or unmarried mothers.

Anders plucked the *tiare* flower from his hair and threw it onto the ground. It reminded him of a peculiar native depravity. For months, he had tried without success to convert the *mahus* on the island. A *mahu,* he had learned to his amazement, was a man who willingly dressed as a woman and performed all the feminine tasks. Worse, they performed erotic dances without shame and had sexual relations with other men. But far from being scorned for what they were, the *mahus* were honored members of their villages. "Perhaps no place in the world are they so common or extraordinary," Captain Bligh had lamented. Anders and other missionaries tried in vain to turn the *mahus* away from their aberrations.

Anders had seen the *mahus,* and real women too, dancing the *tamure*, gyrating their hips with breathtaking speed and violent eroticism. Depravity, thought Anders as he watched them. *For this reason God gave them up to dishonorable passions. Their women exchanged natural relations for unnatural, and the men likewise gave up natural relations with women and were consumed with passion for one another, men committing shameless acts with men and receiving in their own persons the due penalty for their error.*

The fevered drumbeats set his heart racing, but only the willing native girls tempted Anders. They seemed so unnaturally sincere when they intentionally caught his eye. As Eve must have been to Adam, Anders sighed, forcing his gaze away. He watched the glistening sweat beneath their breasts, and thought of Brother Clark slashing his own throat.

"The defects in the native character were given to them by Europeans," Grouard had written, "except licentiousness, that is an abomination as natural to them as for them to breathe, an old heathen practice."

Twice, Grouard had married native girls, Anders knew, but that was under polygamy and unthinkable now. But with his missionary companion gone, who would know if he stopped struggling against the needs of the flesh? And a woman might alleviate his melancholy. If only he would be granted a sign! But by what right did he dare demand a blessing from God?

Anders picked a ripe banana from a tree beside the house,

and pulled a strip of peel from the fruit. But he suddenly felt undeserving of it, and set it down on the ground. Anders stepped back into the warm mission house. He could smell the fragrance of *tiare* where it penetrated the cut on his finger.

His brother missionaries on Ana'a had told Anders the rumor that plural marriages were still performed in Mexico. And they whispered that the President of the Church had fathered children by all five of his wives after polygamy was forbidden in 1890.

Anders tried to imagine what it was like to have multiple wives. He tried to envision his mother and father in a plural family. Could his father have silenced the redoubled chatter? Would his mother have walked into the sea? Though no one spoke the words, Anders knew why his mother had no more children. He wondered if celibacy was such a struggle for his father. His father dedicated his life to scrutinizing the smallest sin, while the depravity of most men went unrepented.

With a surge of revulsion, Anders recalled the tales Gauguin had told him about the old native religion.

"The Areois were men of learning," Gauguin told Anders, "more enlightened than the other men of their race. They soon seized hold of the religious and political government of the island. They established a powerful feudal state which was the most glorious period in the history of the archipelago."

Anders listened and nodded, but was unprepared for the painter's next words.

"The Areois taught that human sacrifices are pleasing to the gods, and they themselves sacrificed in the temples all their children save the first-born. To avoid the murder of men, they resigned themselves to the killing of children."

"Infanticide?" Anders gasped. "It's too depraved to be believed."

"Is there any other worthy change the missionaries have brought about?" Gauguin asked.

"There have been many worthy changes," Anders argued.

Gauguin shrugged. "In the society of the Areois, prostitution was a sacred duty. We have changed that.

Prostitution has not ceased, it is simply inexcusable and without grandeur."

With melancholy fatigue, Anders recalled the saying of a President of the Church. "God will hold us responsible for the people we might have saved, had we done our duty." Anders wondered if Americans were ever shackled by the humility that hobbled him in his work.

Anders stared out the window at the sea and strained to conceive of his destiny. He tried to envision his children and grandchildren, but every image he saw of a woman was Polynesian. He struggled to imagine a more distant fate. But despite all his efforts, Anders could not see himself enthroned as a god on some nameless planet, surrounded by a wife and countless progeny. The leap was too far from his pietistic childhood in Norway. His brain cramped with the strain of imagining, and his field of vision narrowed to a likelier fate. Anders saw himself, in willful disobedience, hanging from the yardarm of a sailing ship as a mutineer. He clutched his throat in horror and forced the image from his mind.

"Was I to have made this far journey," Gauguin asked, "only to find the very thing which I had fled?"

As the morning star rose over the horizon, Anders dressed in black clothes and planned what he would say in his sermon. He would tell of a missionary, Elder Smoot, who drowned in the sea but was miraculously restored to life by fellow Elders, then went on to establish the Mormon Church in Tonga. He would say that even such a scoundrel as Walter Murray Gibson sent "intelligent native brethren" to organize the Church in Samoa, where it has thrived. He would impress them with the rewards of hard work. Carefully, Anders translated Brigham Young's words into Tahitian, "Whoever wastes his life in idleness, either because he need not work in order to live, or because he will not live to work, will be a wretched creature, and at the close of a listless existence, will regret the loss of precious gifts and the neglect of great opportunities."

Distracted by the sounds of fishing boats, Anders left the house and walked a few paces toward the beach. The humid air hung still, the trade winds not yet awakened. The coconut palms arched in silhouette across the clouds, so unlike the place where he was raised.

*Holiness to the Lord.*

Anders heard the words, as if spoken aloud in the dawn. With longing, he searched the eastern sky for a sign. The low-lying atoll was so tiny, and the ocean surrounding it so immense.

Anders watched the sky transform as if by magic. The plum-colored night receded to the west and was supplanted by a shade of blackberries mixed with cream. Over the lagoon, the yolk of sun ascended, illuminating the layers of papaya clouds. The color of the clouds intensified to salmon, then quickly paled again to shrimp. Sunrise does not linger in the tropics. The clouds lightened to peppermint, more white than pink, then drifted across the buttercream sky.

From the east, the foreign, sweet smell of crushed guava filled the wakening breeze and left a coating of fragrance on Anders' skin. The sun layered gold between the turquoise bands of ocean over the sand and the lapis lazuli ribbons above the reefs. Blessed to witness the splendor of such gifts, Anders bowed his head humbly at the endowment. The tropical glare felt harsh to his pale blue eyes.

*Holiness to the Lord.*

The words struck Anders with a startling awareness. The tropical dawn was no more a gift than was the rainbow. Like the rainbow, it was a sign of the Celestial covenant. Anders Erickson, like the Earth, was not made to face his own shadow.

His legs felt weak from the presence of the Lord, and he fell to his knees in the sugary sand, at long last. It was triumph as much as obeisance. What came to Anders in the dawn was not a gift, but an unassailable sense of entitlement. It was his birthright as a spirit no less eternal than God, Himself. Despite depravity and disobedience, all souls receive the gift of immortality. But through the Church, he could know his own unique place in this life, and in Celestial glory.

Anders had envied the stories of signs, the visions of Jesus or angels in white garments, the words of joy testified from heaven. But he felt only a burning. It started with warmth in his fingers and toes and radiated inward to his bosom. The burning ascended his spine, then settled and glowed in his brain. He shivered as the final trace of melancholy burned away.

Anders lingered in the sand a few moments, then he rose without reluctance from the ground. The time for humility was past. There were souls to be saved for the Kingdom of God, as it rolled forth to fill the whole earth.

# BOOK FIVE

# ORGANIZATIONS AT WAR

# Chapter 1

Frank Bailey and Peter Hall pulled their bicycles to the side of the narrow Colorado road. They brushed the dust off their pants and sat down on a log, then opened the sack that held their meager lunches. The kind housewife had apologized that she could not offer them anything more than a small withered apple and bread thinly spread with peach sauce. As they thanked her and offered another blessing for her family, Frank hoped she did not see their disappointment. In the summer of 1934, Frank and Peter were 18 years old and still growing.

"Who would've thought this Depression would last five years," Frank grumbled.

"Five years!" Peter said. "That's only since the stock market crash. Even the Roaring Twenties passed us by, while Utah was stuck in a mining depression. Our entire youth! Who knows when we'll ever get jobs or go to college, let alone hope to get married."

Frank shifted his tall, husky frame on the log. "The money I'd saved for my mission quickly went to feed my family. It wasn't much, but I was grateful I had it to give my father."

Peter licked some of the peach sauce off his thumb. It was delicious but made him wish there was more. "I couldn't believe it when I heard about your family."

Frank stared away to the Rocky Mountains in the distance. "Our hardware and building supply business was in that location 20 years," he said. "Dad once employed 23 people. But a year ago, it all went bust. With construction work dried up, contractors weren't buying, and customers with any money were so tight that they'd buy their tools and paint at Sears to save a few cents. Dad couldn't make the mortgage payments on the big house he'd bought in '28, so he just mailed the keys to the bank. We moved into a small rented house in an old shabby neighborhood in the wrong part of town. Dad was grateful when he got a crummy assistant manager job at Montgomery Ward."

Pete nodded sympathetically. "My father is scraping by, but

there's no extra money for anything. Back when I was 12, Dad promised he'd give me a Ford Model A roadster when I was 16 if I ranked in the top five of my high school class. I was so excited, I came in third. But all the while, I knew in the back of my mind that Dad couldn't keep his promise."

"I had to drop out of football in my junior year," Frank said. "My father explained he couldn't pay the doctor or dentist bill if I broke a leg or got a tooth knocked out. Golly, I loved playing football! Setting someone on his ass when I was blocking. I gave up Scouting too, so I could earn extra money, even though I'd almost made Eagle Scout. I know it hurt my father, having to take money at age 50 from his son. I'd hoped to go to Europe on my mission, like Dad did. I guess I'll never get there now."

Frank smiled wanly, remembering the small pleasures he had taken for granted at the time.

Peter chewed his sandwich slowly, savoring each bite. His wiry body seemed always to be hungry. "We might as well be serving our missions here and now," he said. "Family men need those scarce paying jobs more than we do."

Frank threw a rock across the empty road. "I hate not being able to help the families we proselytize, Pete! Not in *this* life, at any rate. So many children, and public relief pays so little. That little girl yesterday made me want to cry. She was so thin, and that cough! Those enormous blue eyes staring up at me. She needed medicine, and all I could do was lay my hands on her head and pray. I felt almost unkind as I whispered to her mother and explained how children who die before age eight go directly to celestial glory."

"Her mother took our tract," Pete said hopefully. "She promised to read it."

"Let's go back there this afternoon," Frank suggested. "Then to the Post Office. I'm expecting a letter from my father."

"Gracie said she'd write me in Denver, too."

"Gracie really looked beautiful at the Senior Prom."

Peter grinned at the compliment and the memory of that night. "I was surprised to see you there, Frank. You told me you weren't going."

"I thought I couldn't afford it," Frank explained. "Then Dad and Ma each handed me five $1 bills. Neither one of them told the other, but both told me the same story. It seems that Grandmother Molly had given them some money before she died, and said it must be spent on something worthy but unessential. Ma said she hadn't understood exactly what Grandma Molly meant at the time. Dad said I could take the Buick if I was careful. I would've asked the Erickson girl, but I figured she already had a date."

"Which one of the Erickson girls? There are so many."

"Any of them!" Frank laughed. "They're all beautiful and smart. But it was so late, I asked Ellie, who I'd met at Mutual Improvement Association dances. She isn't as pretty or as clever, but she has a nice figure."

"That she does," Peter sighed.

"Ellie sounded very pleased when I asked her, though I'm sure she guessed the situation. And she looked prettier than I expected when I came to her house and pinned the corsage on her dress."

"That dress revealed more of her than the General Authorities would approve," Pete said, smiling. "And the band played all the sentimental new songs that gave me lots of excuses to hold Gracie tight. 'You and the Night and the Music,' 'Isle of Capri,' 'Deep Purple,' 'Blue Moon,' 'I Only Have Eyes for You.'"

Frank nodded. "Ellie looked so great in her daring dress that a lot of fellows, even football players, kept cutting in on me to dance with her. Her eyes were all bright with excitement when she sang into my ear, 'The Object of My Affections' and 'I Wanna Be Loved By You.' Ellie has a very pleasant voice. Then it was over. No one knew we were going to the Prom, so we weren't invited to any of the after-the-ball parties. But the night was lovely, moonlit and warm. Ellie didn't object when I drove to the heights above the city where Gentile kids with cars go to neck."

Pete raised his eyebrows as he looked at Frank.

Frank was uncertain whether he was boasting, or confessing to a fellow priest.

"I kissed her with affection," Frank said. "But Ellie folded herself into my arms and responded to my kiss with more enthusiasm than I imagined. She said, 'Thank you, Frank, for the most enjoyable night of my life.' She opened her mouth wider as we kissed some more. Ellie didn't object when my fingers touched the soft skin her dress revealed. Or when they touched her breast, first over her dress and then under her dress, then inside her brassiere. Her bare skin, her nipple hard in my hand, felt so wonderful. Pete, I was really aroused. Ellie raised her arms over her head and let me unhook her brassiere so I could caress her breasts and kiss them. I put my other hand on her knee, then moved it slowly over the silk stocking, and pushed it higher, past the top to the bare tender skin of her thigh. No other girl had let me put my hand so high. We kissed some more, and I reached farther up her thigh and touched the stocking strap of her garter belt. Then I reached even farther, between her legs, past the hem and inside her panties, and touched her mound before she pulled my hand down to the stocking top."

Pete whistled. "That's farther than Gracie *ever* lets me go."

Frank looked away at the mountains. "Of course, I remembered that intercourse is forbidden outside marriage, but I couldn't resist kissing and caressing her. Ellie whispered, 'Frank, I know what you want to do, and I'm very tempted to let you. You're likely the handsomest fellow who'll ever want to do this with me. And I confess that I'm very excited, myself. But I can't offer my virginity to someone, attractive to me as you are, who doesn't even *pretend* to love me. Let alone risk getting pregnant! We can neck some more, if you want, but you'll have to take your hand away from between my legs.' I was tempted to pretend that I loved her, so Ellie would let me go farther. But before I could say anything, I realized in disbelief that she'd unbuttoned my pants and was stroking *me*. Well, it didn't take long."

Pete exhaled, then inhaled again. "You know that's a

serious sin," he said softly. "It's good for you to confess it."

Frank nodded, relieved to have told someone. "When I brought Ellie home, we could see in the window that her parents were waiting up for her. We kissed goodnight at her door, and I thanked her for a grand evening. Tears filled her eyes when she thanked me and said that it might be the nicest night she'd ever have in her life. As I drove away, I realized I didn't know what Ellie meant."

Pete watched a vulture circling over the remains of a possum killed on the road.

"It's this damned Depression, Frank. Among all the things it's stolen is hope for magic in this lifetime. Everywhere but in Hollywood, of course. Did you call Ellie again?"

"I called her the next morning," Frank said. "But I didn't ask her out again."

"Why not?"

"Because I'll never want to marry Ellie. Not like you want to marry Gracie."

Peter smiled broadly. "I've written Gracie a dozen letters since we left Utah. I hope she's feeling half as lonely for me. Let's go to the Post Office first thing."

The two missionaries climbed back on their bicycles and raced toward town. Pete arrived first at the General Delivery window, and came away with two thick envelopes. He had finished the first page when Frank rode up, out of breath.

"Anything for Frank Bailey?" he asked the man behind the counter.

"Just this," the clerk replied, handing Frank a thin envelope. It was labeled in his father's neat script, with the return address, "Ned Bailey, Salt Lake City."

Frank stepped outside under the trees and read the letter. "Son, come home at once," it read. "I've arranged a job for you, working at Boulder Dam near Las Vegas."

"Pete!" Frank called. "How much money do you have? I've got to catch the next train for Salt Lake City."

Pete looked up from his letters. They counted their money, but even pooled together it was not enough.

375

"I could sell my bicycle," Frank suggested.

Pete shook his head. "You won't get near what it's worth. Why not just ride the rails? I'll give your bike to the next missionary they send out here."

Frank looked up with concern at his missionary companion. "Don't you think I should wait until I can be officially released?"

"That job won't wait," Peter warned him. "And you have your whole life to fulfill your mission."

That night, Frank and Peter waited in the shadows of the rail yard for the guards to step away from the boxcars. They could hear muffled human noises in nearby shadows and knew they were not the only ones who waited. Hours earlier, Pete had inquired when the westbound freight train was scheduled to depart. "At midnight," he was told by a suspicious but puzzled clerk. The clerk had never seen a hobo dressed in a clean white shirt and tie.

The guards crossed to the far side of the train. "It's safe," Pete whispered.

Frank hesitated. From the shadows, five men leaped forward and raced to a closed boxcar. But before they could force the doors open, the railroad guards ran back and collared them. In their lights, as they dragged the men to a distant shed, Frank saw that the door of another boxcar was ajar.

"Good luck, Brother Hall," Frank whispered as he sprinted toward the car. From the shadows, a dozen figures quickly followed.

Frank was uncertain if he should be pleased or dismayed when two hobos hoisted themselves into his boxcar. Warily, he regarded them before they noticed him. They did not shut the door as tightly as he had.

In the feeble moonlight of the rail yard, he could see that they were both unkempt. The taller one was sinewy and gaunt, as if eating was less than common for him. Frank gasped aloud when he recognized that the other hobo was a woman. She was attractive but thin and rawboned, wearing overalls and a boy's heavy sweater.

The woman heard his gasp and saw him staring at her. "All my life I wanted to travel," she explained. "This sure beats the fate I escaped at home."

The train lurched forward as the engineer released the brakes. The whistle blew and the train pushed forward.

Through the gap in the door, Frank saw a shadow moving toward the ladder. Then he heard footsteps crossing the boxcar roof. The tall hobo slid open the door and Frank saw a pair of legs swing down over the edge. The train gathered speed, jerking all of them backward, as the hobo grabbed the legs and pulled the other man into the boxcar.

The new hobo nodded silently to the others, then offered a bottle of homemade whiskey as a gesture of thanks. Above his unshaven cheeks was a faraway look in his eyes.

"Where're you going, Kid?" the woman asked.

"Salt Lake City."

"Why the hell go there?" the tall hobo said. "Town's crawling with Mormons."

"You aren't one of 'em, are you?"

"Yes."

"Haven't met many Mormons riding the rails. Think it's beneath them, I guess."

"You think it's beneath you, Kid?"

"No."

"You got a girlfriend there?" the tall hobo asked. "Does she have a sister?"

"No," Frank replied.

"Why not? Don't ya have to get yerself a lot of wives?"

The hobos laughed among themselves and at Frank. They offered him a drink of whiskey and were pleased when he refused.

"You're okay, Kid," the woman said.

In a deep deliberate voice, the new hobo said, "You got one of them *Book of Mormon* books on you?"

Frank nodded.

"Can I have it?"

"What're you going to do with it?"

"I dunno. Read it. Sell it. Swap it for something else."

Frank could not read the man's face in the darkness, but he had seen the questioning eyes. He reached into his knapsack and handed the well-worn book to the hobo. The man wordlessly slipped it in with his belongings.

"It's too dark to read it," Frank said, "so I'll tell you what it says."

The three hobos moaned in unison.

Frank recited a passage from memory. "'Now this great loss of the Nephites, and the great slaughter which was among them, would not have happened had it not been for their wickedness and their abomination which was among them; yea, and it was among those also who professed to belong to the church of God.'"

The ride was bumpy, punctuated by frequent stopping and the squealing of wheels scraping against the rails. Frank was unsure if he was speaking to the hobos or to himself.

"'And it was because of the pride of their hearts, because of their exceeding riches, yea, it was because of their oppression to the poor, withholding their food from the hungry, withholding their clothing from the naked, and smiting their humble brethren upon the cheek, making a mock of that which was sacred, denying the spirit of prophecy and revelation...'"

From the snoring, Frank realized that all three hobos had fallen fast asleep. He sighed and curled up on the boxcar floor, listening to the rhythmic clanking of the wheels on the rails.

Frank awoke when a hand shook him gently. The train was slowing for its approach to Salt Lake City.

"You're lucky we came along," the woman said. "Otherwise, you might've had to find an eastbound train."

In a deep voice, the hobo explained. "When the train slows to about 20, you can jump and get away before the brakies and railroad dicks can pick you up. But you'll kill yourself if you don't jump right. Watch how we do it."

"My mother will fix you all a meal if you come by our house," Frank offered.

"And listen to more preaching?" the tall hobo said. "No

thanks, Kid."

Deftly, the first man jumped from the train, waved and ran from the tracks. The woman followed next, then the other man, all of them rapidly disappearing. Mumbling a prayer, Frank leaped off the train. He hit the ground hard, running so fast his legs hurt, then he dodged away from the tracks.

***

Frank Bailey looked up from his *Saturday Evening Post* and glanced again out the window of the speeding Union Pacific Salt Lake City-Los Angeles Express. The desert terrain was still desolate, like the last fifty times he had looked. Well, he thought to himself, the scenery is more pleasant than what he had seen from the boxcar.

Through the coach car, an elderly conductor walked toward Frank. "How much longer until we get to Las Vegas?" Frank asked.

The conductor pulled his railroad watch from his vest pocket, looked at it thoughtfully, and replied, "At the rate we're going, about an hour and three-quarters."

"Thank you," Frank said.

"Got a job waiting for you, son?" the conductor asked. "Young men like you from Salt Lake City don't go to Las Vegas much, unless it's to work on the dam."

"That's correct, Sir."

"Yes, they say the Six Company people like to hire Mormon kids as laborers. They do as they're told, don't get drunk, and work without soldiering on the job. Well, good luck, son."

The conductor smiled kindly as he walked through the car into the next one. He reminded Frank of his Bishop, an old family friend of the Baileys.

Troubled about leaving his mission without authority, Frank had called on the Bishop the previous day.

"In times like these, you shouldn't feel bad about leaving," the Bishop had instructed Frank. "Aim your missionary zeal instead toward the men working with you at the dam. God

379

knows they need it. But don't be too discouraged if you fail. After laboring all day in that terrible heat, the Gentiles may be too mindful of liquor, gambling and fornication to pay much attention to your message."

"Yes, Sir."

"Are there any confessions you'd like to make before you leave?"

"No, Sir," Frank said abruptly.

The Bishop smiled at the solemn decorum of the young man. "What's it been, Frank, six months since your Grandmother Molly died? How I miss that old girl! She must've been well over 80 and widowed for 35 years. I couldn't understood why Molly never got married again, and to a proper Saint."

"Grandma Molly used to say that Grandfather Ted had spoiled her too much to be a wife of any other man. I wish I'd known him."

"He was one of our better Gentiles," the Bishop admitted. "Of course, his corpse was barely cold before Molly had him baptized and sealed. He always knew she'd do it, she insisted. Ted Bailey wrote some amusing things about us in that *Empire* magazine of his."

Frank nodded to the older man. "They say that Grandfather Ted not only never converted, but was practically an *atheist*. I was surprised when Grandma Molly willed to me, of all her grandchildren, all those now-yellowed pages of his articles. But I've been far too busy to read them. Now that you mention it, I even forget where I put them."

"Your father once complained that he might've succeeded me as Bishop except for Church misgivings about his father's influence over him. Ned seemed almost embarrassed by both his parents. Molly was so outspoken with Church teachers, even the General Authorities. She'd insist that women were losing power in Utah, just as women were advancing in influence in the other 47 states. Of course, I told Molly it was all in her mind."

"Why'd she think that?"

The Bishop shrugged. "Oh, she said women on their own had raised building funds and collected grain stores, but the priesthood took them out of women's control. And their magazine, the *Women's Exponent*, fully loyal but independent since 1870, was shut down in 1915. 'But it was soon replaced by the *Relief Society Magazine*,' I argued with her. Yes, she admitted, but the Society owned it, so it was under the control of the Church. Molly said it was monogamy that changed things."

"How could that be true?" Frank asked.

"I asked her the same question. 'Under polygamy,' she insisted, 'the priesthood needed women *powerfully* behind the Church.' Well, it made no sense to me, but no one could think Molly was senile."

"I surely couldn't," Frank agreed. "Thanks to Grandma Molly's nagging, I learned to play the piano, at least popular music, fairly well. How she and Dad would argue about politics! If Senator Smoot hadn't lost his re-election, I might've gotten an appointment to West Point or Annapolis. But Dad is such a staunch Republican that it was useless to apply to our two Democratic Senators. So I'll work a few years, then study engineering at the University of Utah. Not that many engineering graduates can find proper jobs these days."

The Bishop shook his head in mild reproach. "Have faith, Frank, that prayer, hard work and clean living will carry you through to success. Keep yourself fit and healthy, and when you pray for guidance, listen closely to the whispered answers."

Frank watched the scenery speeding past the train. Whispered answers, he pondered. Will I recognize them?

Frank glanced at his inexpensive brass wristwatch. His father had instructed him not to bring anything of value, since he would be helpless against theft in the workers' dormitory. His inexpensive suitcase held only his toilet articles, some stationery, two extra changes of clothes, and his work shoes. His parents would send his winter clothing in October.

He finished reading the *Saturday Evening Post*, then browsed through *Collier's*. A full-page advertisement caught his eye, and he stopped to examine the picture and read the details at the bottom of the page. The new Chevrolet roadster, with a six-cylinder engine and hydraulic brakes, had a list price of $490.

He turned the page to another ad. A new, fast Ford V-8 cost $585.

Frank performed the mental calculations. By forgoing new clothes and entertainment, he could buy a new Chevy in six months, after paying for his keep and his tithing. His starting pay would be 40 cents an hour for regular time, and more for overtime, maybe $32 in a busy week. It was far better than the $15 he might earn as a clerk or soda jerk in a drug store, if a job that paid so well could be found in Salt Lake City. And a man with cash could find bargains if he shopped carefully. Modest restaurant meals could be had for two bits, work pants for $1, less on sale.

Frank knew he would have to save money for college, so he put the new car out of his mind. But maybe someone hard up would sell him a Ford Model A. For a car in good condition, I would go 50 bucks, he thought to himself.

As the train slowed near Las Vegas, Frank stood up to retrieve his meager luggage. When he stepped down from the train, he felt the blast of early afternoon summer heat.

Las Vegas! Who would have imagined there would be a prosperous town at the oasis on the trail from the Great Salt Lake to San Bernardino? But Nevada had forged an unholy alliance between Federal funding and state-blessed sin. Water and power would gush forth from Boulder Dam, and a new Federal highway would pipe in a steady stream of gamblers. In the smoky darkness of a gambling casino, who could doubt that God loved a man or a woman who struck it rich?

Frank studied the bus schedule to Boulder City, 23 miles to the southeast. The bus would not leave for three hours, so he decided to look around the town. He checked his suitcase, then walked across Main Street to the head of Fremont Street, where the two largest casinos, the Las Vegas and the Pioneer, stood on opposite corners. An array of other gambling clubs, small hotels, nightclubs, bars, restaurants, stores and pawnshops trailed down Fremont Street for several blocks. The Bishop had warned him about what he would see in Las Vegas.

Frank walked along Fremont Street until he came to a

drugstore with a soda fountain. He sat down at the marble counter and wiped the sweat from his brow with a napkin. Across from him was a Coca-Cola poster with a beautiful, smiling girl.

"Coke?" the soda jerk asked.

Frank forced his gaze away from the poster. Both the girl and the caffeine were prohibited. "No, cherry phosphate please."

The soda jerk squirted the syrups in the glass and added the icy charged water. He deftly slid the glass in front of Frank.

"You here with the railroad or the dam?"

Frank looked at the soda jerk, a tall, skinny youth about his own age. "The dam," Frank said. "How'd you know?"

"You're too well dressed to be a miner or cowboy. Those guys come to Vegas to buy what they need, gamble, get drunk or get laid. It's the liveliest town anywhere around, real honky-tonk if you know what I mean. You'll find it lots more fun than Boulder City, which the Federal government controls. Lot of cribs here, if you want to fuck. I can personally recommend a few of them."

Frank grimaced at the candor of the young man. He could think of nothing to say.

"I grew up here," the soda jerk explained. "Our big artesian wells have always made Las Vegas a watering stop for anyone crossing the desert anywhere nearby. We've grown to 7,000 people since 1905 when the town was chartered. Of course, the Mormons were here long before that."

"They were?" Though Frank was thirsty, he drank the cherry phosphate slowly as he listened.

"Yeah, but they didn't stay. Back in 1855, the Mormons sent 30 men out here to build a trading post and fort to protect travelers and mail going west. They hauled logs from the mountains and built a stockade 14 feet high and 150 feet long on each side. They built cabins and a school, a dam and bridges, and planted crops, orchards and vines."

"Is any of that still here?" Frank asked.

"Sure, at Fifth and Washington," the soda jerk replied. "The

Mormons set up a mission and tried to teach the Indians to farm like white men. But the Mormons weren't very smart miners. They found lead deposits southwest of here, but when they smelted it and cast it in molds, the ore was no good for making bullets. They didn't guess it was too rich in silver. That'll be five cents for the drink."

Frank took a nickel from his pocket and laid it down on the counter.

The soda jerk dropped the nickel into a slot machine near the door, pulled the arm, then shrugged as if it did not matter.

"I don't know why the Mormons left, but they ditched the settlement in '58. In '05, the railroad organized a townsite here and ran an auction for lots. That's when my folks came. Hell, I'd better get to work before Pop gets on my back. You want the address of that crib? I know you won't be disappointed."

Frank smiled in spite of himself, shook his head and finished his drink.

Frank was glad to be wearing a visored cap as he stepped back into the hot sun. He passed a movie theater and paused in the shade to read the posters behind the plate glass. One poster displayed Ginger Roger's dress flying up as she was being twirled by Fred Astaire. Frank felt himself flush and the back of his neck growing hot. Even the windows of the drugstores were not safe. He glanced away from the Spicy Stories pulps he knew he should not read.

As Frank turned north on Fifth Street, he grew aware of some very small houses. Those must be the cribs, he thought grimly. Prostitution was fully legal in Nevada, and adultery was less than shameful for its married clientele. Frank had vowed to keep himself chaste, but he knew he had not conquered the lust of the Senior Prom night. He prayed he could wait for sexual satisfaction until he could be safely married. But here in Las Vegas, only God and he would know if he did not.

Frank could not force his eyes away from the cribs as he passed them on his way to the ruins. A few guys on the football team had bragged about their adventures in the cheap hotels on Main Street when they were only sixteen. Frank had not known

384

then whether or not to believe them. He felt the sweat dripping down his neck. It looked like marriage would be impossible for many years.

The ruins of the Mormon fort saddened Frank as he remembered how the Utah War had led to its hasty evacuation. He did not linger but walked quickly back to the station to catch the bus that would take him to Boulder City.

# Chapter 2

Frank felt pleased with himself on a Sunday afternoon, late in September 1934. In an hour, fifty guys would be crowding into the dormitory recreation room to listen to the Eddie Cantor Hour on the big Philco radio. But for now, no one else was around while he sat at the dilapidated upright piano, trying to play music by ear.

Things had been going well for Frank. Even after tithing, he had $254 in the bank, saving most of his paycheck and making even more playing poker. Frank had quickly understood his advantage, playing sober against drunken opponents. When he played poker, he drank ginger ale and acted like he was swacked too, and they quickly forgot he was not. He bought a Ford 1930 Model A in good shape from a guy who gambled away his whole paycheck and needed that $40 more than he needed the car. Frank planned to drive home on Thanksgiving to show the Model A Coupe to his folks.

Frank had found himself well enough liked by the other men, even though they could see he was smarter and harder working than most of them. He deferred to his elders, as was his custom, and found the old-timers pleased to teach him the skills of manual labor. He learned how to use a pick and shovel to best effect, how to pace himself to endure the full shift in the heat, and how fast he could work without making the other men look lazy. His large frame grew leaner and his muscles hardened into rock. Other men fought at the workers' dormitory, but nobody picked fights with Frank. Even men inclined to harass a Mormon were hesitant to challenge a youth six feet tall, hard and fit at 185 pounds. Nor was Frank eager to defend himself among men who might be streetfighters and adept with knives. To fit in, he occasionally and purposely used profane language, though certain words still stumbled over his tongue. He tried to conceal his revulsion at the crude and constant boasting of some men about their exploits with women.

Frank was always invited along on their excursions to Las

Vegas. "You queer, Kid?" they taunted him when he refused. One of them grabbed his *Book of Mormon* out of his hand and tossed it around the dormitory room among the other willing conspirators. "You keep it," Frank said calmly. "And read it, if you can read. I'll get another." The man whose hands it landed in tossed it back quickly to Frank. "Thanks," he replied, "but the offer stands."

Frank suspected that when they offered him liquor, they had a bet on who could get him to succumb. Though he had never tasted liquor in his life, and did not intend to start, he was glad that Prohibition was repealed. Prohibition politics were wild cards, and Frank disliked games with wild cards. The Republican governor of Utah once vetoed a statewide Prohibition bill, then lost the statehouse to Simon Bamberger, a Jewish Gentile Democrat. Frank's dislike of Prohibition was also practical. It had fostered organized crime.

Frank sat at the piano trying to play some new songs he had heard on the radio and the juke box. He tried "All I Do Is Dream of You," then "June in January." They sounded good to him, his right hand capturing the melody and his left hand guessing at the chords. At the end of the tune, he looked up and noticed that a sandy-haired, older fellow had entered the recreation room. Jack McDonald was his name, Frank recalled. He looked to be about 35 and sounded like he came from New York.

"You play pretty well without sheet music, Kid. Do you know 'The Ballad of Joe Hill?'"

"Sorry, Jack. I don't know it."

"What about 'The Preacher and the Slave?'"

Frank shook his head.

"How about 'Casey Jones?' Joe Hill wrote both of those."

Frank looked closely at McDonald. The New Yorker was well groomed and sturdy, about five-foot-eight and 160 pounds. He looked like a welterweight boxer, his lopsided nose revealing that it had been broken a few times. From the way he talked, he seemed not to be a mere working stiff, but one of those smart and educated fellows who were not too proud to work as laborers these days.

"I don't know it, Jack."

"Then how about 'The Union Scab?'" he asked belligerently.

"What are you getting at, McDonald?"

"What do you know about the man, Joe Hill?"

"Who?" Frank asked, perplexed.

"Aren't you from Salt Lake City?"

Frank nodded.

"Then you've got to know the story," Jack said coolly.

"Maybe I should," Frank replied, not looking for a fight. The name was familiar from something peculiar that his Grandmother Molly had told him.

"I guess it happened before you were born," McDonald said. "Joe Hill was a Swedish immigrant who worked in the Utah copper mines. He also wrote songs for the International Workers of the World. That is, until a winter night in 1914 in Salt Lake City. That night, a grocery store was robbed and the grocer and his son were both killed. But before he died, the boy shot at and wounded the gunman, who left behind a long trail of blood. That same night, way across town, a doctor treated Joe Hill for a gunshot wound. Without any more proof or motive than that, Joe Hill was convicted of the murders. The Utah authorities ignored the pleas of President Woodrow Wilson and the Swedish Ambassador for a new trial. Joe was executed by a firing squad."

Damn New York know-it-all, Frank thought to himself. What was it that Grandma Molly had said about Joe Hill?

"The night before his execution," Jack said, "Joe sent a telegram to the IWW leaders. 'Don't waste any time in mourning. Organize.'"

"Didn't Hill explain how he was shot?" Frank asked.

"The gunfight was over a woman, he said. But to protect her reputation, Joe refused to identify her."

Frank scoffed, "IWW means 'I won't work,' not 'I won't talk.' Any woman who'd let herself be screwed by a Wobbly couldn't be *kept* from coming forward to save her lover's life."

Jack shook his head sadly. "That's what the judges thought, too."

Frank suddenly remembered what his Grandmother Molly had told him.

"Whatever happened that night was entirely between the Gentiles," he said. "My grandmother was astonished that in a drama taking place in Salt Lake City, none of the actors were Latter-day Saints. Not the grocer and his son, not Joe Hill, not the presiding judge nor the Utah Supreme Court judges who denied Hill a new trial. Even the jury was only half Mormon, well below the random odds."

"That doesn't mean Joe wasn't framed, then railroaded by an unjust system."

"Perhaps," Frank said, "but not by us. Besides, isn't Joe Hill more dangerous as a martyr than he ever was as a songwriter?"

Jack whispered, "One can only hope, Kid."

"I've seen you reading that thick book by Karl Marx. Are you a Communist or just a Wobbly?" Frank had never, to his knowledge, met either.

"I'd be stupid to tell you if I were," McDonald said. "I'll just say that I'm dismayed at the lousy condition of our country and world, and I admire the efforts of some radicals, including Communists, to try to change things. And I don't appreciate how our U.S. Department of Injustice used political trials to try to crush the International Workers of the World in 1918. They made simultaneous sweeps against every IWW headquarters in the nation, indicted all the leaders and got over 100 sentenced to long prison terms."

Frank shrugged. "We were at war."

"As we will be again," Jack insisted. "I don't think you people are aware of how dangerous conditions really are. In Europe, democracy is held in contempt, with all its demogoguery and ineptitude. Many influential and educated people, even in Britain and France, are advocating more authoritarian, centralized government, not far from Fascism, to control labor and vital businesses. Fascism in Italy, where it

390

started, is vicious toward its opposition, such as Communists. Fascists brutally torture their political prisoners, but they're credited with making trains run on time, and most Italians find them tolerable. Other Europeans don't feel threatened by their militaristic spectacles and nationalistic propaganda. They find it ridiculous for a poor country like Italy to display such glorification of Mussolini and his strong, centralized police."

"What about Germany?" Frank asked.

McDonald glanced toward the door, then continued. "Germany is another matter. Despite losing the World War, Germany is strong, and Hitler is demanding that the peace treaty be drastically revised. His brand of Fascism threatens renewed war in a Europe so sick of war that it's loath to fight again for *any* reason. And the Nazis abuse their political prisoners even more harshly than the Italians. They've sworn to get rid of their Jews, who've not only been patriotic, but some can trace their ancestry in Germany back to the invasion by Julius Caesar. Do you know what trait Karl Marx hated in a man above all others?"

"I have no idea," Frank said.

"Servility," McDonald answered. "Marxists won't be servile, so they're often the first victims of Fascist and colonial brutality."

Frank felt like he was being proselytized. Was this how the Communists recruited new blood? He listened, dismayed, wondering why McDonald had targeted him.

McDonald paused and lit a cigarette. "Like America, the entire world is suffering a disastrous Depression. Bad as it is here, it's far worse overseas, where few places have yet recovered from the War. Russia has made great strides since the Revolution, but it is chaotic internally. In Africa and Asia, the British, French, Dutch and other colonialists are immorally exploiting the native people, their natural resources, cheap labor and lives. In some colonies, patriots are demanding independence, but meanwhile, the Japanese have learned from Europe. Japanese imperialists forcibly took over Korea, and now its army is trying to make China its colony."

"Aren't the Russian Communists just as harsh to their

opponents as the Fascists?" Frank argued. "What about Trotsky, and those stubborn Russian peasants who've been starved to death?"

"Well, that's true," Jack admitted. "But the Russian Communists intend to stop those measures when their terrible military, economic, and social difficulties are resolved. Unlike Fascism, Communism *wants* to become democratic and benevolent to its ordinary people."

"Yeah? How about those bombs delivered to the homes of prominent politicians after the War? And that bomb that killed 33 innocent people on Wall Street."

McDonald's face reddened as he cautiously regarded Frank. "Those bombs were set by rightist provocateurs. They hoped to discredit us and provoke violence against us."

"How do you know that?" Frank challenged.

"J. Edgar Hoover couldn't find any of the bomb-throwers to indict," McDonald said. "Even after the Bureau of Intelligence gathered dossiers on hundreds of thousands of leftist radicals and deported many of them."

"That doesn't prove anything."

"Do you know your own history, Frank? Utah has been colonized too, by the Eastern financial interests. When the Federal Government persecuted polygamists in the 1880s and confiscated the assets of your Church, your leaders went to Wall Street to borrow money. All they had to mortgage was Utah Power and Light, and Utah-Idaho Sugar, and other companies you Mormons built from *nothing* by your labor. The financial nets tightened around you and left you beholden to the moneyed interests. You should join us, Frank. Marxists, whether Socialists or Communists, are the most effective fighters against exploitive colonialists and Fascists."

Jack took a few draws from his cigarette, then continued in a quiet voice. "America has made progress since Roosevelt took office 18 months ago. But our democracy is a sham and our economy is frail, exploiting workers for the benefit of capitalists. Too many states are only economic colonies, whose resources and manufactures go almost wholly to enrich capitalists elsewhere. States like Utah and other Western mining states, and Southern cotton and tobacco states."

McDonald looked around the room to make sure that no one had entered and overheard. Well-paying jobs were so scarce that such ideas were grounds for quick replacement by men who were more grateful. Some employees were spies for the contractors, they had heard.

"Men and women in those states have little real political power," McDonald said. "The outside business interests buy the politicians with contributions, own or co-opt the newspapers and radio stations, restrict their local patronage to companies that cooperate, and offer lucrative jobs to professionals who comply with their requests. The local politicians do exactly what the capitalists want. Labor unions are non-existent or in retreat. If the public gets restless, they can be distracted by scapegoating immigrants, beating or lynching some Negroes, appealing to old-time religion, or displaying meaningless gestures of populism. The system works to re-elect and give Congressional seniority to the factotums in both parties. Take your Senator Reed Smoot, re-elected for 30 solid years."

Frank stiffened. Reed Smoot was not only a Senator, but an Apostle of the Church.

McDonald snuffed out his cigarette. "Was it the Sugar Trust who demanded that Smoot ram through his Smoot-Hawley Tariff? It raised import taxes on 1,000 products. A thousand economists denounced the tariff as a delusion and fraud, and they warned it would export the Depression worldwide. Just as they warned, other countries retaliated, and our foreign trade fell by 70 percent within two years. Was it the banking interests who urged Smoot to set harsh terms for European countries to repay their War debt to us? How could they pay if tariffs kept us from buying their goods! Was it the Mormon Church that made Smoot fight against the League of Nations?"

"You've got that wrong," Frank protested. "The Church endorsed the League of Nations. The President of the Church rebuked Smoot for implying that our theology was contrary to it. And even though men like my father supported it, Smoot fought the Boulder Dam bill from the start."

Jack lit another cigarette. "Let's take this enormous dam you and I are building, Frank. It's colonialism of Nevada by California. A public utility could've built a small dam for local power, water and flood control. But our recent Republican President, the Californian Herbert Hoover, authorized this huge Federal dam, even though he'd normally call it *abominable* socialism. At Federal expense, this dam will generate cheap power, helping Southern California industries outcompete other regions. The water from the dam will flow to farms and subdivisions in desert areas that could never grow without it. Even the flood control benefit is for California, keeping another Salton Sea from forming in the Imperial Valley."

Frank listened to the older man. "If it makes you feel any better, Jack, this Depression has wiped out Smoot's substantial assets."

"It's no consolation for the terrible unemployment," Jack said. "At least Roosevelt has some new ideas. Do you know who convinced him that spending might cure the Depression?"

"Who?"

"Marriner Eccles, a Mormon banker and Governor of the Federal Reserve. Eccles also wants to restrict the power of the New York bankers. Some of Roosevelt's ideas, though, grant centralized authority to the Federal Government and take it from local control. I've got misgivings about that."

Frank nodded. "It wasn't so long ago that we had a few scrapes with the Federal Government, ourselves."

Jack laughed, then continued soberly. "Roosevelt has granted even *more* jurisdiction to the Bureau of Investigation than it had before. It seems they've reassured the public by seeming better and less corruptible than many local police. Still, I wonder why Roosevelt kept J. Edgar Hoover as Director, even though the Republicans appointed him. Maybe Hoover's investigations turned up something embarrassing to the President or his family."

"Like what?"

"Who knows?" Jack shrugged. "Hoover can be very

thorough. He wanted to deport Emma Goldman as an anarchist, so he proved that her American naturalization was flawed. Have you read anything by Emma Goldman?"

"No," Frank replied.

"Well, of course not," Jack said, "not in Utah. Emma Goldman wrote, 'Religion is a superstition that originated in man's mental inability to solve natural phenomena. The church is an organized institution that...has turned religion into a nightmare that oppresses the human soul and holds the mind in bondage.'"

The anarchist's words made little sense to Frank. Of course, men were unable to *solve* natural phenomena, since such truths were unknowable until they were revealed. And the Church had to be an organized institution, for how else could authority be transmitted? The opposite of a nightmare, his religion *freed* the human soul by recognizing the eternity of its existence. But Frank said nothing, knowing that McDonald would be unsympathetic to these truths.

Jack was disappointed to get no argument to seize and vanquish. "The powerful Department of Injustice," he continued, "exiled and excommunicated the immigrant critics of America. And though the War was over, the Federal Government used the Army to break the steelworkers' strike. The coal workers' strike was broken, then the railroad workers' strike, labeled as Communist-inspired. One night in 1920, Federal agents raided every Communist organization in the country, dragging many suspects from their beds on trumped-up charges. But finally, J. Edgar Hoover had gone too far, and the anti-Red crusade and dragnet were called a 'gigantic and cruel hoax.'"

McDonald crushed his cigarette in an ashtray. "Remember this, Frank. Just because there are Communists in a union doesn't prove that labor's struggles aren't legitimate.

"A few months ago in San Francisco, the longshoremen went on strike against their own union leaders. Corrupt union dispatchers, in the pockets of the shippers, were extorting kickbacks from the men they assigned to work crews. Frisco is a strong union city, though its unions care more about money than social good. But this abuse was so blatant that they stood behind the rebel union leader, a young Australian Marxist, and shut down the city in a general strike. Then the showdown turned ugly. National guard troops were called to the waterfront, and there was violence, even a couple of deaths. I was there on the picket line when the cops charged, swinging their billy clubs."

"You told us you got beat up in a bar fight over a woman," Frank interrupted.

"Why give the bosses a reason to fire me?" Jack said. "It seems the Frisco strike reminds people of the Seattle shipyard strike in '19. 'REDS DIRECTING SEATTLE STRIKE--TO TEST CHANCE FOR REVOLUTION,' screamed the reactionary press. Back then, the IWW wound up in pitched battle with the American Legion. One IWW man, a World War veteran like me, was castrated, hanged and shot to death by a mob of Legionnaires."

Jack paused when he heard several men joking outside the door. "Well, Bailey, I don't expect I've changed your mind. But I'd be grateful if you don't say anything about our little talk."

"No more than I'd hope to change your mind about religion as the opiate of the masses."

Though he heard that Frank had promised nothing, Jack grinned. "Hey, it was worth a shot. Anyway, I'm leaving after payday. News of my fight with the Frisco cops will get to Personnel soon, if they don't know it already. Well, good luck, Kid."

McDonald turned to leave but Frank stopped him.

"Why'd you target me, Jack?"

McDonald regarded him cautiously. "Because you aren't servile, Bailey. At least not yet."

# Chapter 3

Frank hopped off the Bamberger interurban train and walked down the tree-shaded street. He stopped at a sturdy brick and timber factory building, then checked the address and opened the door. The sweet smells of cooking fruit permeated the air as two men in overalls lumbered past him. The men were weighed down with heaping crates of potatoes, apples and onions. Frank watched them pour the produce from the boxes and return to the loading dock for more.

Cheerfully, Frank followed the aroma to the kitchens at the rear of the factory. Kettles of pears and peaches were bubbling as they thickened, stirred by women in white aprons, their hair covered. He looked up at the filled jars and cans already piled to the ceiling, and guessed there must be tens of thousands. Frank searched for a particular face among the women. Astrid looked flushed and overheated when he found her.

"Frank!" Astrid called.

"So this is the Church Welfare Plan," he shouted over the factory noise.

Astrid nodded, pointing to a sign that hung nearby:

> "It ain't the guns or armaments
> Or tunes the band can play,
> But the close cooperation
> That makes us win the day."

"You look beautiful, Astrid," he yelled.

Several women turned to see who was calling.

Frank had heard that there were 700 Mormon projects like this one, growing sugar beets, mining coal, and manufacturing Temple clothing. At storehouses, gardens, farms, dairies and meat-packing plants, the Church was trying to take its members off Government relief.

Astrid smiled, brushing back her blond hair with her forearm. She spoke a few words to a supervisor, then motioned for Frank to follow her out a back door.    After the steamy, bustling factory, the air felt cool and still.

"I started out here sewing quilts and clothing," she said, "but they decided I was better at cooking jelly.  Father wanted me to stay in school, but with six younger children to feed, I knew they needed what I can earn here.  Two of my brothers are in Los Angeles, building the new Temple.  One of my sisters is sewing upstairs, and the two older ones are helping Father in his bakery."

Frank gently touched her name plate that read "Sister Erickson."

"How is he doing?"

"A little better," Astrid said.  "With the bakery, we've never lacked for bread, but there's little money left over.   Father always bakes too much on purpose, so he can give the poor what isn't sold.  And he lets people pay him on credit.  Some of them owe him so much money that when they get cash, they go to some other store where they only have to pay for that day's bread.  Don't they realize that Father wouldn't ask for anything more than they can give?  He only laughs when my brothers calls him a Communist."

Small drops of sweat clung to Astrid's forehead.  Frank dried them softly with his fingers.  Peach-colored spots stained her apron.

Frank shook his head.  "Here it is, eight years since the stock market crash.  Three years ago, a man tried to recruit me as a Communist, and how many men have since weakened and succumbed to their appeal?  Last year, Roosevelt won 69 percent of the Utah vote.  But despite the National Recovery Act and all the other New Deal give-aways, the Depression persists.  At least I got to build something real, Boulder Dam, not humiliating make-work for the Works Progress Administration.   One of every four families in Utah is on the dole.  We're doing worse than the national rate of one in seven!"

Astrid motioned toward the factory.  "Don't you see, Frank? *This* is the answer to both Communism and the New Deal.  The Church organized these programs to free us from the burden of public relief."

Astrid's eyes were bright as she spoke. "As long as we have idle land, then we needn't have idle people. When crop prices fell after the War, many people abandoned their farms. But the Church is bringing them back into production. It's like my mother told me about, where she was born. It was a commune in a remote place in southern Utah. But it wasn't like Communism today, which is based on force and intolerance. In Orderville, the people lived by the Prophet Joseph's revelation of the United Order of Enoch. Everything we have belongs to the Lord, so He can call upon us for any and all the property we possess."

"I love listening to your voice," Frank said. "It's pretty and sweet, not too high like some girls."

"Thank you," Astrid said, blushing. "It was the 1870s, Mother said, when my grandparents deeded all their property to the Church. They got a stewardship over all of it they needed, and the United Order owned everything else. They grew cotton that they processed in their mill, and sugar cane they made into molasses. The orchard, just outside the square, grew peaches, apricots, gooseberries and grapes. They mined their own coal nearby, and had a tannery, sawmill and gristmill. And they made the commune work, as it never would've worked in the cities. In the cities, the richest men would never donate all their wealth to the Church, to be used in any way the Church saw fit. Orderville was poor, but all were equally poor, and my grandparents freely shared whatever little they had."

Frank touched her arm, then took her hand. "What became of it?" he asked.

"Well, my mother was just a little girl then," Astrid said, "but she saw what was happening to her brothers. The leaders of the Church and the commune had forgotten to make provision for their best young men. They had no shares for expansion, and all work was paid the same wages. Their boys couldn't compete with young city men, who earned good money, dressed well and turned the heads of Orderville girls. The commune was in decline by 1885, and a relic when my family left four years later. Communism must be impossible indeed if such dedicated Saints couldn't make it work."

"I wish I could marry you, Astrid."

"You haven't been listening to what I'm saying."

"Well, no. I confess I was distracted by your lips and wishing I could kiss them, and then marry you."

"Frank, I'm not yet 17," Astrid insisted softly. "I told you Father's rule, how he won't let his daughters marry until we're 20. Besides, my family needs my help. When a man and woman marry, they have all of time and Eternity."

"If I didn't go to college," Frank said, "we'd have enough money to get married next year."

"You must get an education, Frank. And I trust you pay your tithing promptly, especially in these times. And your contributions from fast days."

"Of course," Frank sighed in resignation. "But I've thought of you every day since last April. I'm so glad to be back in Salt Lake City."

"Don't you think it's time you met my father?" Astrid said.

"I've met your father," Frank protested.

"You know what I mean. Not just at priesthood meetings. He's not so stern when you get to know him. He laughs and plays with the younger children."

"All right," Frank resolved. "I'll come to visit him tonight, if you'll go with me to the movies."

"I'd love to, Frank. What's showing?"

"*You Can't Get Away With It*, featuring J. Edgar Hoover, himself. Would you rather go tomorrow night?"

Frank watched her purse her pink lips. "No, tonight," Astrid decided. "But don't think he'll change his mind and let me get married any sooner."

"Not when I'm only a student at the University of Utah," Frank grumbled. "He'll stare into me with those piercing blue eyes and imagine I'm pressing you for sinful favors. He'll say that if I can afford college, I can afford to go on a mission."

"Father won't say that."

"He'll think it. Everyone at priesthood meetings knows what Anders Erickson thinks."

400

"Well, he isn't always right. I'll bet Father thinks you want to marry my older sister."

"Which one?"

"Any of them," Astrid laughed. "You're so eager to get married, and they'll be old enough *years* before I will. Why wait for me?"

Frank stroked her hand and answered seriously. "Well, your sisters are all beautiful, of course. But you're the one I want for all Eternity. I knew it last spring, when I held you that first time at the dance. I couldn't bear it when I had to watch you dancing and smiling with those other fellows."

"You could've asked some other girl to dance."

"I didn't want to dance with some other girl. I was almost glad to be away in Las Vegas, so I didn't have to envy everyone who was close to you when I wasn't."

"Envy isn't a feeling to be proud of," Astrid reminded him with a pretty smile.

"Oh, I know. It's just that, now that I'm in Salt Lake City again, I don't want you to date other guys."

"No one has much money for dating."

"You know what I mean. I don't want anyone touching you."

Astrid laughed softly. "You sound like my father."

"A girl must obey her father," Frank sighed.

"And then her husband," she teased him. "Besides, you'll be so busy with college that you won't ever think of me. Not surrounded by those beautiful co-eds."

Frank took her other hand in his own. "That isn't true," he whispered, almost insulted. "My engineering classes will be tough, and to earn some extra money, I've joined the Utah National Guard. And of course, I have my Church responsibilities. But the rest of the time, I want to be with you. Somehow, Astrid, I know you were made for me. Promise you'll marry me when you turn 20."

Astrid reached up and brushed back a lock of his brown hair. As she looked into his handsome, earnest face, she knew beyond doubt that he loved her.

"I will, Frank.  We'll plan our honeymoon for Christmastime 1941."

# Chapter 4

First Lieutenant Frank Bailey apprehensively approached the officers' table in the far corner of the large mess tent. He wore his steel helmet and holstered Colt .45 pistol, his prescribed uniform as Officer of the Day.

For six months, since the Germans retreated in October 1943, Frank had been stationed in Naples. His unit, the Headquarters and Service Company of an Army Engineer Regiment, was one of four providing logistical support for the Allied military forces in Italy.

He had delayed eating breakfast, hoping that the Colonel would already be finished and gone. Under his breath, he cursed his lack of luck. He had seldom seen the "old man" look so angry. The "old man" was 34, young to be a full colonel not in combat command.

Frank stood at attention while being reprimanded. He was grateful that the Colonel spoke quietly so the enlisted men in the mess tent and kitchen could not overhear.

The Colonel let him have it with both barrels. "Lieutenant Bailey, as Officer of the Day, you were in charge of the guard detail last night?"

"Yes, Sir."

"And at ten o'clock last night, when the third shift came on duty, didn't one of the guards fire one round with his rifle, a Springfield '03, and isn't one rifle shot our designated alarm that enemy aircraft have been observed?"

"Yes, Sir, to both questions."

"And wasn't it a false alarm, the shot being fired by a private of the guard who mishandled his rifle while loading it?"

"Yes, Sir."

"Lieutenant, is there any doubt in the minds of you company officers and the men you command that I meant what I said a month ago, after *five* incidents of careless discharge of rifles on guard duty within two months, that the next occurrence would be punished by a court martial, either of the private of the guard or the sergeant of the guard for inadequate supervision?"

"No, Sir."

"Tell me, Lieutenant, why I am so angry about false alarms, especially at night, or do you think I'm only petulant because my orders are disobeyed and my sleep disturbed?"

"No, Sir. Alarms, especially at night, require that some men go to special duty stations for damage control here, or at the airport down the road, while the other men take cover in fox holes after putting on warm clothing and steel helmets, to protect themselves from falling shrapnel from anti-aircraft guns firing at planes from the airport and harbor."

"At ease, rest, sit down, and eat your breakfast, Frank. I shouldn't take out my frustration on you. You and four or five other Mormons are among the best company grade officers in the regiment. This matter should be too petty for my attention except that I must personally play the domination game to show that I'm firmly in command. You've heard me expound my own theory of how best to command wartime draftee Engineer soldiers to get our projects done properly and on time. That's by making my 54 officers and 1,254 enlisted men feel pride in belonging to the regiment and hesitant to do anything to disgrace it. The privileges of rank for my officers are modest, reflecting my belief that their management isn't so much more valuable than the sustained, conscientious technical work of the enlisted men. By and large, I'm satisfied with the results."

Although ordered to do so, Frank did not sit down and eat his breakfast.

The Colonel sighed. "But don't think I'm not criticized by my superiors for my decision to allow relaxed military courtesy and discipline in my regiment. And some of the men are starting to take advantage of it. My ultimatum *must* be enforced if I'm to have credibility in what I *do* demand. I presume you've written up charges already against the private of the guard."

"Yes, Sir. The company commander has scheduled a summary court martial at 11:00, and his verdict will be on your desk for review by tomorrow."

"Good. Now eat your breakfast. I hope I haven't spoiled

404

your appetite."

Frank remained standing. "Before you go, Sir, I think you should be aware that the private of the guard could be found innocent due to mitigating circumstances. He's the replacement we received only yesterday, fully qualified as a rifleman with the M-1 but not at all qualified with the '03. When he reported in, the first sergeant asked if he'd volunteer for guard duty last night, and if he could handle an '03. The private agreed to do it, saying he'd drilled with an '03, though never with live ammunition, in ROTC at Berkeley a couple years ago. He was shown how to load the clip under the bolt and said it looked easy. The guy acted like a soldier, so the sergeant of the guard never even questioned if he was qualified. And it was pretty dim moonlight last night. That's the new guy, eating breakfast over there, the tall fellow with thick glasses being watched by the corporal of the guard."

The Colonel took a deep breath and exhaled slowly. "Dammit, Frank, tell me I'm wrong. The new man volunteered for guard duty his first day here, as a favor to the first sergeant, without being carefully drilled with an '03. I'd guess that when he inserted the clip in the '03, he released his finger pressure on the top bullet too soon, and it was caught by the bolt and loaded in the chamber when he closed the bolt. Being used to an M-1, he pulled the trigger to release tension on the spring. Kaboom! Well, I guess we'll have to ding the sergeant of the guard instead, and take his stripes away for awhile. Who is he?"

"Staff Sergeant Baxter, Sir. He's in the Operations Section, one of the senior draftsmen."

"My God, Frank," the Colonel groaned. "We can't take away *his* stripes. We're working the draftsmen overtime, and all the younger draftsmen respect Baxter. If we demote him for *this*, he'll be angry and sluff off, which could make *all* the draftsmen drag their heels. Dammit! Are you a chess player, Frank? This situation is like being forked in chess. If he pleads innocent, the private of the guard will escape punishment in any honest trial, and my authority will be weakened. But we dare not charge Sergeant Baxter. Well, I suppose I've forked myself."

Frank smiled wanly. "You said forked, Sir?"

The Colonel grimaced. "I should not and will not tell the company commander that I want a guilty verdict. But maybe we can figure a way out. Tell me what you know about the new man."

"The first sergeant and I interviewed him, Sir. He's an Enlisted Reserve Corps volunteer, not a draftee, one of 50,000 ERC men the Army recruited in college with the inducement of being trained as specialists when called up. But the Army sent them to Infantry Basic Training instead, and trained them all as riflemen. He came ashore to the replacement depot at Salerno a couple of days after the 36th Division almost lost the beachhead to the German counterattack."

"Those glasses look awfully thick for a rifleman."

Frank nodded. "Before boarding a 36th Division truck as a replacement, he asked a medical officer if they wanted a rifleman with 20/200 vision without glasses. 'Yesterday yes, today no,' he was told. He's been with the replacement depot for six months. They found him to be a very useful general duty soldier, so they hid his service file like it was lost. Since he was a casual, nobody gave much of a damn about him. An ERC buddy in the Assignment Section found out their game and made him a substitute file. We picked him up from our requisition. We asked for a man with a high IQ score, and he's it."

The Colonel looked across the mess tent at the private. "Well, perhaps he's a chess player, too. You see, my dilemma is resolved if he pleads guilty. Maybe I can get him to do it, although it isn't trivial for him. He'll know the conviction is a black mark on his Army record, and possibly in future employment. But my credibility is more important than justice to him. Frank, I want to talk to the man in my tent now, before the court martial."

"But, Sir, if you're the reviewing officer after the court martial, isn't that…"

"Irregular. Yes, very. And it's shameful to induce any man to say he's an incompetent soldier when he isn't. Take charge of

406

him from the corporal of the guard, and sneak him into my tent so the exec and adjutant don't see it. Both of them are too by-the-numbers officers to understand. Then come back for him in 15 minutes."

Later that morning, the private admitted guilt at the court martial. He was fined two-thirds of a month's pay, $40, and made ineligible for promotion to private-first-class for six months.

When Frank heard the outcome, he was consumed with curiosity how the Colonel had achieved his aim. But he dared not ask, knowing the Colonel would be displeased by the question. Suddenly, Frank thought of a way to find out. That night, he volunteered for a duty most officers detested, censoring enlisted men's outgoing mail. With the razor knife in his hand, he examined letter after boring letter, some embarrassing and others full of information harmful to the Army. Finally, Frank uncovered the letter he hoped to read.

Somewhere in Italy
April 2, 1944

Dear Sam:

I have good news and bad news to report. The good news is that I've finally escaped from the goddamn replacement depot, thanks to my buddy in the Assignment section, and gotten into what's said to be the best outfit in the base section, very well run and seldom chickenshit. We live remarkably well. We have a hot shower unit, and our latrine is made of mahogany. (The wood is from dunnage for shipments from Africa, and our drivers are very enterprising at salvaging useful things when they're near the port.) Italian civilians do the kitchen work, mostly teenage kids who weighed about 80 pounds six months ago and must weigh 150 now after eating our food. They bring home what they want from our slop, so they and their families are well fed. They also bring our laundry to their mommas, who do it better and faster than the Army laundry and ask for nothing more than to keep the big bars of soap we get from our supply room.

The mess sergeant is adept at trading Spam to the farmers around here for vegetables, so our mess is very good. The regimental support is here--the chaplain, the medics, dentist, special service, but our line companies are scattered all around. After morning formation and breakfast, the men are busy working almost as if they were civilians, except the guys on guard duty or doing occasional military drill to make sure we can be used as rifle soldiers. Most of the other enlisted men are clerks, drivers, messengers, or technicians like surveyors, draftsmen, heavy equipment operators, mechanics, carpenters, welders and electricians. We have a very good regimental softball team, far too good to invite me to join. I expect to find some friends in the company, but I'm a stranger coming into a group that's been together for almost two years.

Which brings me to the bad news. Today, I pleaded guilty in a court martial for careless discharge of firearms. I mishandled a rifle like we used at ROTC, the '03, the first time I was posted on guard duty. Being me, I had no doubts about handling the '03 with live ammunition. But a strange thing happened. Before the court martial, the regimental commander himself called me into his tent for a little talk. He's young for a full Colonel, and a West Point man, no less. He started off by telling me the best year he had in the Army was the year he got his MS degree at Cal, then he rattled off the names of guys on the Cal team that went to the Rose Bowl. Then he told me why my accident on guard duty gave him a problem. He'd issued an ultimatum he had to enforce, and somebody had to be punished by a summary court martial. Was it my carelessness? the Colonel asked. Or the sergeant of the guard, who'd lose his stripes if he was guilty? He said mitigating circumstances would excuse me if I pled innocent, so it was *my* choice of who'd be punished. There'd be no rewards in it for me.

Well, I'm our father's son, not usually dumb, though I was to volunteer for guard duty with that rifle. I immediately saw his point, that using my normal rights to military justice would harm the regiment. And if I'd taken away a sergeant's stripes, my life in the regiment would be shit, and this war won't be over anytime soon. So I bit the bullet, and for the benefit of the regiment, I agreed to plead guilty.

It's ironic. You, the pacifist, were drafted and are serving reluctantly, but you're in Japanese language school. I, the patriot, who enlisted to get into some specialist school, was trained as a rifleman despite lousy vision. Well, I'm now fully trained in the Springfield '03 rifle, and I'm licensed as a driver of small and medium sized vehicles. I'll do my guard duty, drive, carry messages or whatever, mostly bored to death except when German airplanes fly over. It could be worse. If I'd gone to the 36th Division six months ago, I suspect I'd be wounded or dead.

Cioao..sayonara...etc.

Joe

Frank smiled as he read the soldier's letter. He thought about the Colonel's game of chess. Within 15 minutes and without promising him anything, the Colonel had convinced the private to act against his own self-interest. The Colonel escaped his own dilemma by forking someone else. But he had disregarded rigid rules against fraternizing between officers and enlisted men.

Frank attacked the letter with the razor knife, but abruptly, he stopped when a word caught his eye. The regimental commander *himself.* Frank reread the letter and saw a new interpretation. The private did not feel bitter, forked by the Colonel and manipulated. The Colonel had made the man feel valued, not despite but because of his sacrifice.

When Frank finished censoring the letter, the cutout places made it look like lace. Pleased not only with the answer, he felt a surprising satisfaction in the means he had found to uncover it.

Frank set aside the razor and letters, then sat down on his bunk. He debated writing another letter to Astrid, but decided against it. He had not heard from her in a week.

409

Frank lay back on his bunk and considered the nature of knowledge. Could a man ever possess too much of it? He inhaled deeply. Italy offered opportunities for knowledge that would be foreclosed forever in Utah.

\*\*\*

The next week, Frank sat in the San Carlo Opera, watching a third-rate performance of *Madama Butterfly*. An enormous Italian soprano played the tiny, tragic Japanese wife of an American naval officer who marries another woman when his duties send him home. The world is fascinated by polygamy, Frank sighed. He glanced around the antique, decaying opera house, wondering how many new Madama Butterflies would arise from this War. Surrounding him were 2,000 military personnel, Americans and British, New Zealanders, Indians, Poles and French, all eager for any fresh diversion from the regimentation and boredom, and from the prospect of an endless war with no victory in sight.

Frank was grateful to have a 24-hour pass. For the first time since the regiment disembarked in Italy, he would be on his own, away overnight from his unit. Most of his plans were conventional, but one differed markedly from anything Frank had done in his life.

When the opera ended, Frank rode the funicular railway up to the fashionable Vomero heights above the scruffy, war-battered old city of Naples. At the Army Officers Club there, he ate an early dinner, listening to the stories of the brutal, bloody combat at the Anzio and Cassino fronts. At Anzio, the Germans held the high ground and shot downward at the Allied troops whose backs were to the sea. They were lucky that Anzio was a stalemate, not a catastrophe. And at Cassino, the Allies were sustaining terrible losses attacking the Germans' seemingly impregnable defenses.

Frank felt fortunate that his regiment had suffered few casualties, unlike the combat engineers supporting the Infantry. Aside from clearing mines and booby traps, his regiment was seldom in danger, just occasional Luftwaffe bombing attacks and a few strafings.

Frank left the Officers Club and headed downhill toward the funicular terminal. With each step, the fluttering in his stomach multiplied. He was going to meet his date for the night.

The liaison had been arranged by the Assistant Regimental Surgeon, a New Yorker who laughingly called himself an experienced "swordsman." Naples was so densely populated with Allied military forces that desirable female company was in very short supply. The sympathies of American and British women officers, mostly nurses, went out to Air Corps and combat officers more than to rear echelon junior officers like Frank. Some rear echelon men resolved that problem by regularly attending parties at the Officers Club, but Frank was too busy and too little inclined. Some officers had Italian lady friends but he had no idea how they acquired them.

Frank had met his date a month earlier at a dance at the Officers Club. They had danced only once. Vaguely, he remembered that Elsa Molinari was a pretty brunette of medium height, although not young, perhaps 35. Her "gift," negotiated by the medical officer, was two cartons of Lucky Strike cigarettes. Italians preferred packs of brand-name U.S. cigarettes to the Allied Military Government paper currency. Combat soldiers received cigarettes free with their PX rations, while those in the rear paid a nickel a pack, supplies limited.

Most military personnel smoked their entire tobacco ration, but not Mormons like Frank. The cigarettes that cost Frank $1 were worth $40 American on the black market. If Elsa were younger and prettier, she could undoubtedly get more, or serve higher ranking officers, or non-comms with access to valuable supplies. Frank was aware that two cartons of cigarettes were worth ten days pay at her job at the public utility.

In his musette bag, Frank carried his toilet articles and a change of underwear and socks. As the medical officer suggested, he also brought ten candy bars and three cakes of face soap from his PX rations. From his C-rations and K-rations, he brought 20 packets of instant coffee he never used. In his wallet,

Frank carried two condoms.

In his judgment, the Army was obsessed with sex, and particularly with venereal disease. The Army VD films, melodramas on the loathsome consequences of neglect, seemed almost comical to him. But they were compulsory viewing for all personnel twice a year. Even the Colonel, the most sensible officer he ever met, was as proud of the regiment's low VD rate as he was of its outstanding engineering achievements. The "old man" made it clear that any officer in his regiment who contracted VD had better request a transfer out at the first opportunity. Before an enlisted man could get a pass, he had to show two condoms in his wallet and be reminded that Naples had many prophylactic stations for use after careless intercourse. Standard Army regulations required company officers to inspect the penises of the four lowest grades of enlisted men every month in what was delicately called "short arm inspection."

Frank paused at a balustrade and looked down at the spectacular 3,000-year-old city below him. A few miles to the southeast, Mount Vesuvius rose 4,000 feet above the Mediterranean Sea. The sparkling Bay of Naples was full of ships waiting their turn to be unloaded. On the heights behind Frank was a restaurant named "Belvedere," and he agreed that the sight was indeed beautiful.

Six months earlier, Frank would not have considered the same view beautiful. Between the Allied air attacks and the methodical German demolition, the utilities and port facilities had been devastated. His regiment repaired or leveled damaged buildings near the port, clearing the roads and rail lines so supplies could be landed and moved forward. They rebuilt the water supply and sewage systems that were deliberately shattered by the Germans. Then they sprayed DDT to prevent deadly insect-borne diseases like the disastrous typhus epidemic in Trieste in 1919. His regiment upgraded the Italian hospitals to prepare for outbreaks of malaria and combat casualties. They cleared mines and the skillfully concealed booby traps left by the German engineers. It was a terrifying assignment in a big city, particularly with the frequent harassment by the Luftwaffe.

Frank looked at his watch, then he walked toward the funicular station. At the entrance to the terminal, he recognized Elsa Molinari. Frank took a deep breath, appraising her. She looked tired but more dignified than he anticipated. She wore a dark gray suit, well tailored but shiny and worn, a hat and gloves. Elsa's face and figure were pleasing, he thought. She was well groomed and her makeup was carefully applied.

Frank stood alongside her and stammered out, "Signora Molinari?"

The woman nodded.

"*Buona sera. Io sonno Tenente Frank Bailey, amico del Capitan Taylor...*"

The Italian woman interrupted, smiling and speaking in heavily accented but precise English. "*Buona sera, Tenente.* Thank you for the courtesy of speaking to me in my language, but I am sure that my English is better than your Italian. Before I was married, I taught English at a girls' school. Also, I learned American English from listening to the dialogue in the cinema. I have always been a fanatic for American films. My given name is Elsa, and I prefer you call me that rather than Signora Molinari. Do you prefer that I call you Lieutenant or your Christian name?"

Frank winced involuntarily. "Frank would be fine."

"Franco, then, okay?"

Frank felt relieved that Elsa was making their encounter so informal. He carefully saluted a major who passed them in a crosswalk. Elsa guided him to a substantial four-story building that looked like it was built just before World War I. Hers was one of sixteen apartments.

The building superintendent waved at Elsa when she and Frank entered the foyer. Frank followed Elsa up the stairs and waited while she unlocked the door. He was surprised to be feeling no shame.

In the apartment, the furniture appeared of good quality to Frank, but nothing else of value was in sight. The wallpaper and pictures were unremarkable, the bulbs in the light fixtures were dim. A musty smell arose from the draperies and curtains,

413

infrequently aired during the cold, wet winter just past. Frank noticed two photographs on a table. One portrayed an Italian major in his forties, the other showed two girls, about ages twelve and ten.

Elsa followed Frank's gaze. "The man is my husband, Gino, now a prisoner of war in your Arizona. I am grateful he was fighting you and not the Russians when his artillery battalion surrendered in Sicily. The girls are our daughters, now living with Gino's parents in Calabria, far to the south behind the war zone. Their grandfather is a pasta manufacturer, so they can eat and barter for other needs. I was raised here in Napoli and could not live there. It's a poor life in Calabria, but I send money for the girls to attend a convent school. There aren't many foreign soldiers there to corrupt them, as I fear would happen here. And they don't see their mother renting out her pussy, as you Americans like to call it, to survive and try to hold on to my family's home."

Disturbed by her candor, Frank looked up at Elsa. He did not know what to say.

"As you can see from our apartment, my family lived comfortably until a short time ago, until your invasion of Sicily last July and the terrible inflation began. Gino had been called to duty in a large mobilization a few months earlier. We could afford to live here because he was earning a good salary as a manager at the utility company. After the mobilization, male workers were not available, so the utility company asked me to work, as I do now. If it were not for the enormous inflation, my salary would be enough, but now it is too small to buy food, keep up the apartment and clothe myself to my status. So I give companionship to Allied officers, with luck several times a week.

"Ah, Franco, you look at me with curiosity when I speak of status. Am I truly any better than those young girls in the slums below whose even younger brothers procure for them your lowest rank of soldiers? Yet it is true that I feel I do have a status to maintain. I am the wife of Major Gino Molinari and the assistant personnel manager of the utility company. What is

414

more, I have my own pride."

Not knowing what to say, Frank was relieved to simply listen to Elsa.

"To uphold my pride, I make believe I am a mistress and not a whore. Here, because Italians cannot divorce, mistresses, even if they are married women, are quietly accepted as accommodations to dissatisfying marriages. I sometimes make believe that I'm an actress in your cinema like Myrna Loy, playing the role of a worldly married woman in my circumstances, freely giving myself out with compassion to comfort a young, lonesome soldier like... Ronald Reagan comes to my mind. But in truth, I do it to survive. *Allora*, I will be your mistress for tonight, but first you must pass my physical examination. Please sit down on the edge of the bathtub in the toilet, across the hall. After I take off my jacket, I will wash your--whatever you call it--and examine it to make sure that you show no diseases."

Her forthrightness disarmed Frank, and he silently complied with her inspection. When she was satisfied that he was safe, Elsa handed him a towel. He was glad to be wearing olive drab underwear and not his garments.

"Tell me, Franco, are you a Catholic or a Protestant? Evidently you are not Jewish. And I notice that your breath does not have the smell of liquor or tobacco like most officers have when they come to me from the Officers Club."

"Not smoking or drinking is part of my religion, Elsa. I'm what you might know as a Mormon."

"Ah, a new kind of Protestant."

"Well, not exactly. You see, the Latter-day Saints are no commonplace Protestants, but a new Christian religion. I'm a member of the priesthood."

Elsa smiled, amused by his words. "I've never before given my body to a priest. Do not feel bad. Before you are a priest, you are a man."

Frank did not know what to feel. He walked across the room to where he had left his musette bag. Ceremoniously, Frank gave Elsa the two cartons of cigarettes, the powdered

415

coffee, the candy and soap. "A small gift for my mistress for the night."

"My lover for the night has been quite thoughtful," Elsa said. "So many packets of coffee! *Molte grazie, amante mio.* Now, come with me."

Elsa led Frank into the bedroom, then slipped off her worn shoes. He noticed good furniture in the bedroom too, a double bed covered by a white bedspread, a dresser with a mirror, an armoire, a ceramic crucifix, and two night stands with a radio on one of them.

"Franco, have you ever had a mistress, or are you married?"

"I'm engaged to be married. We were supposed to be married at Christmastime, 1941."

"Why did you not marry her? Surely, you were still in America then."

"She was willing, but I felt it was unfair to her."

"Unfair to marry her? But why?"

Frank tried to explain. "You see, if Astrid and I were sealed in the Temple, she'd be my wife for time and all Eternity. But if I'm destined to die in this war, I'd want her to remarry and be married to her husband a long time and have many children with him. But even if she did, she'd still be my wife for all Eternity. Somehow, it didn't seem right."

Elsa smiled at him gently. "A peculiar religion you have."

"I suppose we seem peculiar," Frank shrugged. "But if I were married, I certainly wouldn't be here tonight. Not that my Church approves of *this*."

"Why would you not be here, Franco?"

"My Church hates adultery almost more than any other sin. Last year, an Apostle, one of the 15 highest men in the Church, was excommunicated for violating the Christian law of chastity. His wife was the most powerful woman in Utah, once a legislator, then president of the Women's Relief Society. Maybe her independence drove him into an affair."

"Perhaps it was just desire," Elsa said. "Is it desire with you, or is it knowledge?"

Disturbed by Elsa's question, Frank pretended not to

understand her English. "I don't exactly know what you mean," he stammered.

"It doesn't matter. I will satisfy your need for both. I suggest you put your clothes on the chair over there and your protection on the night stand."

Blushing, Frank complied with Elsa's directions. In his underwear, he shivered in the unheated room.

"Would you find it stimulating to undress me, Franco? Or to watch me undress myself in what your colleagues call a striptease, or are you in a hurry to…"

Feeling his face flush again, Frank quickly interrupted. "I've never undressed a woman. Well, not completely."

Elsa's nod and smile told Frank that she understood. Standing with her back to the mirror, she took off her earrings and necklace and stood in front of Frank. With growing excitement, he eagerly but clumsily removed her blouse, her skirt and slip. Like her suit, her lingerie appeared expensive, but it too, showed the wear of years. Elsa pointed to the stocking straps below her corset. Frank unfastened and slid down her coarse cotton stockings, then he cautiously removed her corset. The feel of the delicate skin of her thighs aroused him further.

Elsa joked, "Since I have lost weight and flesh in my hips, I look trim enough wearing only a light girdle. But this heavy corset protects part of me from the pinches on my buttocks and groping of my breasts when I am riding the *funiculare*. Your soldiers are well behaved most of the time, but some of my countrymen are not, and the worst are the men who suspect I go out with you American officers. After the War, there will be much anti-American feeling, because you invaders are now so favored over Italian men."

Frank enjoyed the sound of Elsa's softly accented voice, but his excitement kept him from listening to her words. He cupped her generous breasts, unbound from their corset, and touched her nipples with trembling hands. Gently, Elsa swept his hands aside, then moved to the bed to pull back the cover and quilt. The linen was gray from too infrequent laundering. Elsa gestured that Frank should remove his shorts and put on the condom. Then he gently pulled down her panties, trying not to think how the lace had grown so torn. Gracefully, Elsa slid them down her thighs and legs and lay supine on the bed, her arms and legs open to him. Through his excitement, Frank noticed that her arms and legs were thin and her ribs showed through the flesh. His eyes traveled to the dark hair of her groin. He mounted her and climaxed quickly.

Physically and emotionally satiated, feeling warm and relaxed in the soft, unfamiliar bed, Frank dropped off to sleep for several minutes. The experience for him was far better than he had imagined. He grinned sleepily when he awoke to see Elsa standing at the armoire, wrapping herself inside a robe.

"Thank you, Elsa," he called.

Thinking he was asleep, Elsa turned in surprise at his words of gratitude. She gestured for him to come into the kitchen while she prepared her evening meal. Frank declined when she invited him to share it, since Allied soldiers were ordered not to eat from the scarce civilian food. But he accepted a cup of her Italian coffee substitute without caffeine, while she gratefully nursed a cup of his coffee. They split and shared a candy bar Frank had brought.

"I expect you will want to try copulating again in an hour or two," Elsa said. "I suggest we try some different ways I can show you. Remember, there is no need to hurry. I am your mistress until seven o'clock tomorrow morning."

Frank nodded, finding it hard to answer Elsa's candor in words.

"But before then, let us talk about you. Have you been a soldier a long time?"

"Since 1940," Frank said. "Before that, I studied engineering at the University of Utah. It isn't far from Arizona, where your husband is. To earn some money, I enlisted as an ordinary soldier in the Utah National Guard. Then, when Germany defeated France and threatened England, the National Guard was mobilized into the U.S. Army. They sent me to school to become an Engineer officer, and afterwards, to North Africa, then here to Naples. But if this War ever ends and I survive it, I'll find some other work than engineering."

"Why?" Elsa asked.

"I'm more curious about people than things."

Elsa stroked his arm and said softly, "When I asked about your religion, Franco, I did not understand your answer."

Frank tried to explain for a few minutes, but the setting felt all wrong to be undertaking missionary labors. There were few Italian Mormons, he knew. But there were 15,000 German Mormons, some who had served in foreign missions, and others who had hosted Utah missionaries in their homes. Sharing a gospel and belief about the future, their men were German soldiers for the same reason Frank was an American soldier. Instructed by the Church to serve their country, they would kill their nation's enemies. But Frank was convinced that no man could be a devout Nazi and Latter-day Saint at the same time. Still, the European Mormons were too few to speak out against the Nazis without becoming targets themselves. Only the Lutherans and Catholics held and withheld that power.

Elsa interrupted his thoughts. "This sounds a little familiar to me. A movie, a few years ago, about your Brigham Young. Dean Jagger is a most attractive man, and Mary Astor was one of his wives. Strange to have so many wives. Now that you have conquered us, we are seeing American movies again."

"Don't you feel danger, Elsa, inviting strange men to..."

"Rent my pussy, Franco? Some, of course, yes. But I cannot exist if I am paralyzed with fear. What else do I have that is valued by men besides my body and my company? The building superintendent watches out for me, he roams around the building and he has keys to the apartments. It would not surprise me if he is somehow able to observe us in the boudoir. I pay him money to keep him satisfied and I am sure he is rewarded by your Army Intelligence Division. Do not doubt that there are dossiers on women like me who are friendly with your officers. The Germans and Fascist *Polizia* must have dossiers, too. But I have confidence that your Army will punish officers who might abuse me too much."

Frank had not considered the possibility. "Have you had

bad experiences with American officers?"

"A few," Elsa shrugged. "Some seem to despise all Italians. Others are merely cruel men who enjoy humiliating me by demanding sodomy not for their pleasure but to make themselves believe they are superior to women or Italians, I don't know which. As if their own women would not do the same if it was necessary."

Frank shuddered, thinking of his mother and sisters and Astrid. He prayed they would never be forced to prove Elsa wrong. Frank felt awkward in the silence. Although she was a prostitute, there was nothing servile about Elsa.

Frank pointed to the crucifix on the wall. "Your family is Catholic?" he asked.

"Naturally," Elsa smiled. "Babies must be baptized and children confirmed, marriages must occur in churches after a mass, and last rites given to the dying. Colorful ceremonies are part of our society. But too often, our Church is an insult to reason and knowledge. As a modern, educated woman, I am embarrassed by the new superstitions our recent Popes tell us we must believe to be good Catholics and avoid damnation. Is it not outrageous that a Pope forced Galileo to recant scientific truths that contradicted teachings having little to do with religion?"

"Yes, but that was 300 years ago."

"What about the dogma of Papal Infallibility, where God does not allow the Pope to be wrong on any matters of faith? Was that Pope infallible when he made Galileo swear that the sun revolves around the earth? The Church hasn't yet corrected its mistake. Then there was the dogma of Immaculate Conception and another one is pending now, the Bodily Assumption of Mary into Heaven.

"It's kept Italy provincial," Elsa said. "Northern Italians despise us in the south, calling us ignorant and priest-ridden. The Church has been terrible for Italian patriots, perhaps the largest reason why Italy was not unified until 1870. When Italy at last became a nation and the army of the King took over Rome, the Pope declared himself a prisoner and refused to recognize the government. In the last war, the Church would not

420

furnish priests as chaplains, and young conscripted priests often served as nothing more than medical orderlies. Is that infallible? Men fighting and dying need the comfort of priests. When the Church finally made peace with the government, it was 1929 and with the Fascists. They crawled into bed together while Italy was led into disaster. Is that infallible? What benefit to Italians was the glory of Mussolini and his alliance with an evil anti-Italian like Hitler? The only ones who help are the Italian partisans, who sabotage the Germans in northern cities and behind the fronts, and they are mostly Communists who brave Mussolini's torture and prison, exile and death."

Communists again, Frank thought. "Haven't we Americans helped at all?"

Elsa smiled warmly. "Considering how we fought you as our enemy in North Africa and Sicily, you have been very easy on us. Your military police are annoying, but so much less than the Germans were. So we behave well, knowing that your Engineers control the water and your Negro stevedore soldiers unload the ships that carry food. Come, let us lie down intimately in bed, and listen to the radio. I like to hear Bing Crosby on your Armed Forces Radio, and the lady singer Dinah Shore. After that, we can tune to German radio, where Axis Sally will tell us more bad news about the battles on the front than your Army does.

"Ah, Franco, I can see that you are ready to make love again. Good. I don't know why, but you have made me lonesome for my Gino. Please do like he does to make copulation more enjoyable for me, with me on top. If you will lie on your back. Yes, Franco, like that. I am sure it will give you much pleasure, too. The woman you will marry should thank me for teaching you this way."

Through the rest of the night, Frank slept fitfully, feeling strange in the oversoft bed beside a woman for whom he felt affection but not love. He was troubled by the fact that he felt no shame. He weighed the idea of waking her for another try, but he did not. Elsa must be tired, he knew, and he was no longer so eager.

Elsa woke him at seven o'clock. As she bathed and dressed, Frank watched her, feeling compassion for the grave uncertainties of her life. Without speaking, they smiled at one another while she ate her breakfast, a piece of stale bread moistened with olive oil.

When they walked through the foyer together, Elsa waved without shame to the superintendent. Frank watched her leave for the funicular terminal, then he turned to the heights to the Officers Club. He felt like kissing her goodbye, but a man did not do that with a whore.

As he ate a large breakfast, Frank pondered the question Elsa asked him. "Is it desire with you, or is it knowledge?"

# Chapter 5

Across the desk, Frank appraised the Special Agent in Charge of the Southern California office. R. Emmett Driscoll was in his late forties and looked like a proper FBI man. Classically Irish, about five-foot-nine and 165 pounds, he wore a well-pressed oxford gray suit, a white shirt, a conservative striped tie, and well-shined black wing-tip shoes. A snap-brim hat hung on a hook behind the door. Driscoll was taking his time paging through Frank's personnel file.

"I notice that you're wearing a Purple Heart lapel pin," Frank said.

"Yeah," Driscoll said, "I was wounded on Guadalcanal as a Marine major. I was shot up worse in 1918 at Belleau Wood, but they didn't give Purple Hearts then. I wear the pin to remind me that I've survived very tough battles alongside some excellent men. And I still measure men against Marine standards of competence, responsibility, self-discipline and loyalty to the organization."

Driscoll finished reading the file. "I'm pleased to have a man with your record from the FBI Academy join my office, Frank. Welcome aboard."

"I'm pleased to be here," Frank said. "The instructors say you're one of the best SAC's."

"Yeah."

A small item in the file had caught Driscoll's eye. He looked at Frank.

"As an Irish kid from Queens and then at Fordham, I never knew any Mormons until I joined the Marines. I've learned a lot of respect in the Corps and here. I've heard the guy who invented the Browning automatic rifle and machine guns, and the Colt pistol, was one of you."

Frank nodded. "And the old Winchester rifles, too."

"But I wouldn't use a Mormon for undercover work," Driscoll said. "Few of you guys have much street smarts, and men who don't booze and smoke can't blend into the woodwork for that kind of job. Take you, Bailey. With your posture and grooming, they'd know you were a G-man naked in a nudist colony."

"Is that a problem?" Frank asked. "I'd hoped for my share of undercover work."

"Nah," Driscoll said. "We use informers when we can't disappear among the people we investigate. And Hoover wants us to look sharp, like him, so we never forget just who we are."

Driscoll looked down at the file again. "You were an Army Engineer officer, Bailey? It's odd that you'd leave engineering to become an FBI agent."

"You aren't the first to think it's odd," Frank said. "An old man in my family back in Utah, a son of my great-grandfather and his Indian wife, one of four, grilled me when he heard I'd joined the FBI. 'Is that a suitable job for a Latter-day Saint?' the old man asked me. 'Your great-grandfather died in jail because Federal policemen put him there.'"

"Four wives, huh? What'd you say?"

Frank shrugged. "I told my uncle that times had changed. Just three years ago, I reminded him, Church authorities approved surveillance on polygamous, fundamentalist Mormons. Heavily-armed FBI agents and Salt Lake City policemen arrested 15 polygamists and searched their homes for records. They served six months in prison and were paroled only after they agreed to cease cohabitation and new marriages."

Driscoll regarded Frank coolly. "Yeah, but why'd you want to join the FBI?"

Frank did not hesitate before he answered. "Well, it sounds ridiculous, I know, but I felt inspired toward it after an unusual night with an Italian lady. She told me about the vicious deeds of Mussolini's Fascist central government police. I was attracted by the opposite image of incorruptible, non-political and organized teams of college-educated FBI men who use modern science to defend the American public from crime."

Driscoll was pleased that Bailey was not as straightlaced as he appeared. "Yeah, the movies make G-men look good. Here, I need you to sign this."

Frank carefully read the loyalty oath, then he signed it. It was a trivial negative affidavit, insignificant when compared with the oaths Frank had sworn at the Temple. By the time of his Endowments, the oath of vengeance was removed from the ritual.

"Let's step out and get some fresh air," Driscoll said.

Frank followed him out the door of the office building. They walked a few dozen paces, then Driscoll lit a cigarette.

"I'm not convinced that Hoover doesn't have my office bugged," he said.

Frank could not tell if the Special Agent in Charge was joking.

Driscoll took a draw on his cigarette. "At the Academy, you were extensively trained on how to do what's legal and proper. But I'm telling you now that some of our assignments may seem improper or unethical, even illegal, including wiretap and microphone surveillance and surreptitious entry that might be masked as burglary. Some of these assignments originate in Hoover's Office, or even the White House. And Special Agents risk being disavowed if the operation is bungled and the local police can't be persuaded to look the other way."

"Aren't they always willing to co-operate?" Frank asked.

"The local police sometimes resent it when the FBI claims credit and publicity for their accomplishments in fighting crime. And for them, it's a one-way street. We rigidly observe the rules against disclosing information, while we expect them to give us information freely. Of course, we often disregard disclosure rules when we're asked to co-operate with anti-Communist Congressmen or Senators."

Driscoll inhaled the smoke deeply, then flicked a long ash as he exhaled.

"J. Edgar Hoover isn't the sort of leader you and I respected in the Army or Marines. But don't underestimate his genius at public relations and handling a bureaucracy essentially beyond control by either Congress or the Justice Department. By hook or by crook, and undoubtedly by hoarding a lot of embarrassing information about prominent people, he's held on to his job since 1924. And that's despite strong political differences with most administrations. The infallible image cultivated for Hoover and the FBI is enormously valuable to us. It's won us money and freedom of action from Congress, which usually hates the idea of a strong Federal police force."

"I'd like to investigate white collar crime," Frank said.

"Sorry, Bailey. White-collar criminals aren't our top priority. Not when disloyal people hide in offices in the Government, where they engage in espionage, steer policies to the benefit of foreign powers, and cloak enemy propaganda with seemingly official sanction. Under the guise of academic freedom, they sabotage our schools and colleges. When a man insists there's inequality of wealth or discrimination against Negroes in this country, we must wonder whether he is a Communist. And behind the Communists are their sympathizers, fellow travelers, and Communist stooges. But for some reason we've been unable to uncover, Truman doesn't believe there's a loyalty problem. So Hoover is working with Congress instead."

Emmett dropped his cigarette butt to the ground, then crushed it under a well-shined shoe.

"You see, Frank, the FBI must work *in secret* to develop evidence that'll hold up at trial. But the House Un-American Activities Committee can work *in public* to unmask suspects and Red Menace schemes that we can't prove in courts of law. Like cases where the evidence is tainted or inadequate. Joseph McCarthy is leading the loyalty crusade in the Senate, and HUAC is gathering lists of suspect names. Unfortunately, lists of Communists have grown so commonplace and worthless that even Hoover rarely pays them much attention. Like before the War, when HUAC sent him names of 1,124 alleged subversives, all of them Federal employees, and Hoover found grounds to fire only three. Our focus has got to be tighter. We need the names and files of all who could be dangerous in a crisis with Russia, and broader authority to detain them."

"Not just immigrants?" Frank asked. "American citizens?"

"Yeah. And not just Communists in government. We're

426

going to arrest a dozen Communist Party leaders and test the Smith Act of 1940. That law made it illegal to belong to a group that advocates overthrow of the U.S. Government. Hoover is disappointed, since he wants to go after all the top 55 Reds. But unfortunately, our exposure in Congress is drying up some of our sources. So in addition to informants, wiretaps, bugs and surveillance, we disorganize the Reds by planting disinformation, like false evidence that a guy is a snitch."

Frank nodded at the concept of disinformation. Though she had little to do with his decision, he had been careful to mention Elsa to his new boss.

Driscoll regarded the younger man. "You may feel, now or later, that such work is too far out of line for your scruples, Frank. And you've been warned that Congress has exempted the FBI from Civil Service rules that protect employees from arbitrary dismissal. That means you must do as you're told, resign or be fired. But don't even think of going public about our work. If you incur the wrath of the Director, he can force you out and blacken your reputation so you'll never get a comparable job in the Government or even outside it."

Driscoll shook Frank's hand before he stepped back into the building. "Enjoy your Christmas vacation. I'll show you the ropes when you get back."

The next morning, Frank and Astrid boarded the train to Utah to spend Christmas 1947 with her family. Astrid was just beginning to show her pregnancy.

They took a cab from the station in Salt Lake City, and climbed out in front of a two-story stone house set back from the street behind shade trees. Frank was pleased to know that Anders' bakery must be prospering.

Frank stepped into the warm house behind Astrid. Surrounded by his children and grandchildren, Anders Erickson was beaming with delight.

Anders was holding a magazine page. "Did you see this?"

Frank glanced at the black-and-white photographs. Beneath palm trees on a beach stood a strange looking raft.

"Norwegians," Anders said, his speech revealing a lingering

trace of an accent. He smiled with as much pride as if the men in the photograph were some of his own dozen children.

"Norwegians set sail in a tiny hand-made raft from South America," Anders said. "They landed in the Tuamotu Islands, where I once was, and proved that the Polynesians could've come west from the Americas, precisely as the *Book of Mormon* says. Ah, I knew it all along. The Polynesians are so much like ourselves."

Frank had heard that the Army was preparing to test nuclear weapons on islands in the Pacific. Atomic bombs would be tested in Nevada, too. The prevailing winds in Nevada were from the west, and the Salt Lake Valley was the nearest populated area east of the site. The Federal government assured them there was no danger, but after the devastation at Hiroshima and Nagasaki, Frank was unconvinced. Yet in a mission vital to America, someone had to bear the risk.

In the back of his mind, Frank feared that nuclear war would be the instrument of the coming Armageddon. The Church had always urged the Saints to keep a two-year store of food on hand, ready for an ultimate day of need. But now the vast stockpiles of food and fuel and water, stored for the millennial war, had an immediacy that could be triggered by a single human finger.

Frank looked at the peaceful photographs in Anders' magazine. The islands appeared so far away, on a different and less dangerous planet.

# Chapter 6

The telephone rang on Emmett Driscoll's desk. He answered it, listened without speaking, then hung up.

Driscoll looked up at Frank Bailey, recently promoted to Senior Special Agent.

"Have you ever heard of a guy named Jack McDonald?"

"The name is common," Frank said, "but I knew a Jack McDonald who was a Communist."

"How'd you know him?" Emmett asked.

"McDonald tried to recruit me back in '34, at the workers' dormitory at Hoover Dam. He'd read an old dog-eared copy of *Capital* and preach the gospel of Karl Marx like it was something of value. Jack was IWW back then. Last I heard, he was bloodied in a Longshoremen's strike."

"Yeah, like the Wobblies say, 'Every strike is a small revolution and a dress rehearsal for the big one.'"

"Right," Frank scoffed. "What's McDonald been doing all these 20 years?"

"He's been in Hollywood," Emmett said. "We think McDonald might know something about Communist influence in the motion picture industry. We're bringing him in for interrogation."

"Communists!" Frank said contemptuously. "They're doomed to fail."

"Yeah? What makes you think that?"

"If Mormons can't keep up a commune, no one can. It's one of our failed experiments, Emmett. Like Brook Farm and the Shakers, we came out of a communitarian tradition. Some of our communes survived for a decade, and my mother-in-law was even born on one of them. But they failed, as all communistic systems must."

"Yeah?" Emmett asked. "Why?"

"Because it's natural for men to make comparisons among themselves. And men who find themselves disadvantaged will naturally abandon or overthrow or sabotage whatever is holding them back. Ambitious, smart and healthy men can *always* do better for themselves when they aren't bound to the forced equality of a commune."

Emmett looked incredulously at Frank. "Well, that's not what Hoover thinks. He calls Communists 'masters of deceit.' 'As common criminals seek the cover of darkness, Communists, behind the protection of false fronts, carry on their sinister and vicious program, intent on swindling and robbing Americans of their heritage of freedom.'"

"If you want a sinister and vicious program," Frank said, "take a look at organized crime. It's invading legitimate businesses and has the money to fight back."

"Still spoiling to tackle white-collar crime even after all these years, Bailey? Well, Hoover doesn't think organized crime is a mortal threat. By the way, Frank, congratulations. I hear your wife just delivered a baby girl. What's that, three kids in five years? You're putting us Irishmen to shame."

A call from the receptionist informed them that the agents had brought in Jack McDonald. Frank wondered how McDonald had escaped the dragnet, after the Hollywood blacklist went into effect in '47. Ten directors and writers had served several months in prison for refusing to testify before the House Un-American Activities Committee.

Frank followed Driscoll into the interrogation room, then waited as two agents escorted McDonald inside. A flicker of recognition crossed McDonald's face as his aging eyes met Frank's. He appeared no less defiant than he had been twenty years earlier. The dossier on McDonald was several inches thick.

"Mr. McDonald, are you a Communist?" one of the two interrogators asked.

"I'm a Marxist," McDonald replied.

"Do you advocate the overthrow of the U.S. Government by force or violence?"

"No."

"Have you ever been a member of a subversive group?"

"No."

"Have you been a member of the International Workers of the World?"

"Yes."

"Are they not a subversive group?"

"They are not."

"Where have you been living during the past ten years?"

"Ten years ago, I was a gunner's mate on a battleship in the Pacific, after I enlisted at age 42. Since then, I've mostly lived in Hollywood, though I've spent months at a time in Mexico."

"What have you been doing in Hollywood?"

"Trying to keep the motion picture unions free of corruption."

"Weren't you trying to organize them into Communist cells?"

"No."

"What are the names of the people you were working with in Hollywood?"

"I worked alone."

"You worked alone?"

"I worked alone."

Frank leaned against a wall and listened with dispassion to the standard questions and unflinching answers. McDonald disavowed conspiracy, so he could not be easily convicted of subversion. But McDonald refused to divulge the names of comrades. Frank knew that the naming of others was the only proof of repentance Hoover trusted.

Latter-day witchmongering, Frank sighed. It had been years since the FBI caught anyone important, like Alger Hiss and the Rosenbergs. And even those victories were incomplete. They convicted Hiss only of perjury, and though the Rosenbergs were executed for treason, they could never make Julius denounce his comrades, even by sending his wife to her death. It saddened Frank that the Rosenberg children would grow up as orphans.

Frank felt certain that American Communism was no mortal threat, yet he did not dare express his doubts. He could not afford to be branded soft on Communism, himself. And after all, the Hiss and Rosenberg cases proved that the Communists

431

were out there.

Frank wondered how long this inquisition would persist. He held little hope that it would end soon. Between the Catholics and Protestants, the Inquisition and its counterparts survived two centuries, from 1492 until 1692. In 1692, in New England, Joseph Smith's great-great-grandfather and his great-great-great-grandfather each testified against a woman on trial for witchcraft. Both women were convicted and duly hanged. But if Joseph's visions of the Angel Maroni had come 150 years earlier, could they have been deemed anything but witchcraft? Before the civil authorities could let him be assassinated by gunshot, the religious authorities would have had the Prophet hanged.

What ended that Inquisition? Frank wondered. The Age of Reason? Galileo was caught in its dragnet, but Newton was allowed to dabble in alchemy. No, Frank thought, the answer could not be that rational. More likely, it was some bored and embarrassed alliance of disciplined clergymen and educated laymen. As he listened to the droning of the questions, Frank was aware that he was both.

# Chapter 7

Frank closed the door behind him as he stepped out of the office of the new Special Agent in Charge of Southern California. The new SAC was a Texan, John Henry Koenig, a Korean War veteran.

For years, Frank had turned down management positions in the FBI. He had gotten his fill of management during the War, and he preferred investigation.

Koenig had handed Frank a file of papers.

"Well, you got what you wanted," Koenig drawled. "You're finally off Communist detail."

Frank had not been surprised. It was 1961, and a new Attorney General, Robert Kennedy, had just become their boss at the Department of Justice.

"The mob?" Frank said hopefully, opening the file.

"Kennedy gave those assignments to non-FBI units, the Organized Crime and Racketeering Section, and a unit formed to investigate Jimmy Hoffa and the Teamsters Union."

"Why not the FBI?" Frank asked.

Koenig shrugged. "He thinks Hoover isn't interested in going after organized crime."

Disappointed, Frank turned to the file in his hand. He was assigned to investigate bank and bankruptcy fraud, money laundering, and extortion. Frank detested white-collar crime, and he had been trained to investigate it. But why had Hoover abdicated his authority to disorganize the most widespread and organized white-collar crime of them all?

Three years had now elapsed since the Apalachin raid, when New York state policemen broke up a conference of 60 Mafia leaders in an upstate New York town. Yet the FBI was still officially denying that any national problem existed from organized crime. Frank did not know the numbers nationwide, but in the FBI office in New York, four agents were assigned to organized crime. Four hundred were investigating Communists.

Frank looked out the window at the gray February drizzle.

433

To him, the deployment of men made little sense. By the mid-1950s, the destruction of the American Communist Party was all but complete. Based on FBI investigations, the Justice Department had indicted 126 Communist leaders, convicted 93 and sent them to jail. Only ten of those rounded up were acquitted, while the remainder died or saw their cases dismissed for hung juries. Some of their lawyers even served time in jail for disorderly conduct. In America, the remaining party leaders had grown old and ineffective, and the membership had diminished to an insignificant few thousand.

Still, the FBI persisted in its propaganda campaign against the Communist Party of the United States. In 1958, special agents in the Crime Records Division wrote *Masters of Deceit*, though Hoover was credited as author. Frank was pressed into giving speeches that hustled the book into a best seller, on his own time, away from Astrid and the children. He could not complain for fear of being transferred to some remote office across the country.

Hoover persevered in his contention that only weak local police allowed nationally prominent crime figures to thrive. Congress and the presidential administrations seemed blind, too. But for years, Frank had known that organized crime was corrupting American labor, wealth and morality. If nothing else, the mob was running gambling and other vice in Las Vegas.

How could he influence the priorities of the Director? Independent initiative was interpreted as disloyalty. Even if he was allowed to proceed, Frank knew he would be granted few resources. And surveillance on the Mafia was far tougher than the normal caseload. Wrapped inside their legitimate businesses, Mafia transactions were difficult to track, and they hired skilled lawyers to resist justice. The syndicate was politically entrenched in some states, so cooperation by local police was uncertain. And as under Prohibition, some agents were almost sure to be corrupted by the easy money. There would be more physical risks and fewer politically crucial successes.

Frank did his best to cheer up. The FBI faced challenges

enough without declaring war on the mob. Perhaps Hoover's advanced age had simply made him overly cautious. Was it unreasonable for an old man to become so set in his ways? And the Mafia did not directly confront the FBI, so Hoover could stand by and watch as state and local authorities tried their best.

Then a more disturbing thought occurred to Frank. Could the mob possess some secret knowledge about J. Edgar Hoover, himself? Frank weighed the possibility. He had heard whispers about Hoover's curiously close relationship to Clyde Tolson, the FBI's second in command. Hoover and Tolson ate lunch and dinner together most days, and they vacationed together twice a year. Neither man had ever been married. And Hoover let it be known that on social occasions, Tolson should also be invited. Hoover collected antiques and always dressed more nattily than his colleagues.

Frank shook his head in disbelief. Surely, it could not be. As a moralist, Hoover was unsurpassed even by Latter-day Saints. Yet what else could explain his persistent deployment of agents away from rich and thriving organized crime, to chase instead a tired coterie of old men?

# Chapter 8

"I'm sick of mucking in the fraud files, John Henry. I'd like to see some action before I get too old or lose my nerve."

Koenig looked up at Frank. "I can't do it," he drawled. "You're the best fraud examiner we've got, and we need your solid investigations to win the tough trials. Hoover is aware of your record, Frank. You've earned those fast promotions you've gotten."

"And I'm grateful for the opportunities," Frank said. "But that isn't all I can do. Here it is 1964, and I've been chasing Communists and bank fraud since '47. I'm still in excellent physical shape and I get top scores on the pistol range."

"It's not that you can't do it, but we need you where you are, especially now that we're tackling organized crime. Face it, Frank, you aren't the best choice for undercover work. You look like the G-man you are and wouldn't last an hour around the mob."

Frank had expected this objection. "Then place me among men who look like me."

"Who?"

"The Ku Klux Klan. I hear we're aiming a Counter-intelligence Program against them."

Koenig laughed at the idea, but soon relented. "All right, Frank, I'm a Texan, and I'll give you an audition. Let me hear some racist talk from you that doesn't make me laugh again."

Frank looked at Koenig in dead seriousness. He had not rehearsed, but the words he had heard and detested all his adult life flowed convincingly. His acting capability surprised him less than how passionately he wanted the assignment.

Koenig nodded in satisfaction. "Okay, Frank, I'll put you on the anti-Klan team. But why does it matter so much to you?"

Frank stiffened to his normal posture. "The Klan is the same sort of mob that forced my ancestors out of Missouri and Illinois. They aren't just criminals, but despicable thugs who terrorize defenseless people."

"You'll be in no less danger," Koenig warned him. "Especially if they see those skivvies you wear. You'd better kiss your wife and kids goodbye like you mean it."

Frank knew the difficulties of civil rights investigations in the South. Southern juries were infamous for refusing to convict whites who committed crimes against blacks. During the '30s and '40s, the FBI investigated 1,500 such cases and won only 27 convictions. Too often, local policemen conspired in the cover-ups, sometimes in the crimes themselves. Even under cover of darkness, blacks were frequently too afraid to talk. Morale was low for such work among FBI agents in the South. Until the '60s, when the neglect became politically embarrassing, Hoover all but abandoned civil rights investigations. It was not that Hoover approved of the Klan, far from it. Klansmen, like black protestors, willfully and insubordinately defied proper authority.

Frank put on his work clothes and boots and boarded an airplane south and east. He was met at the airport by a young FBI agent named Nick.

They climbed into an old pickup truck with a gun rack in the back window.

"You're my wife's brother," Nick informed him of the plan. "You got fired by a Jewish tire dealer in Milwaukee, and you're pissed. There's a meeting tonight and you'll get to tell them all about it. Don't feel like you have to hold back."

Frank's fingers trembled when he put on the Klan robe that Nick gave him. He was on a mission, he reminded himself. The symbols on the robe were so foreign to those he knew.

"You've got to be careful about one thing," Nick said.

"Just one?" Frank asked with a grimace. "What is it?"

"Maybe one in five Klansmen are FBI informers. I don't know who they all are, and they don't know about me. If you use your gun, you're likely to shoot one of us."

Frank nodded.

Nick introduced Frank at the meeting. In the moonlight, eyes appraised him from the holes in white hoods. Frank tried not to stand ramrod straight.

"Bloodsucking bastard son of Satan fired me, gave *my* job to a no-good lazy coon. I didn't even steal nothing, but I should've. Taken back by *right* what belongs to *us* as white Christians. And what was his so-called beef against me? Only taking what was mine by *right*, and *chastening* the bloodsucking whore I used to call my wife. Oh, it wasn't like I killed her or nothing, not that she didn't *deserve* it. But she won't forget anytime soon how she *begged* me for it. Well, the Jew boss didn't *like* it, it made him *feel* bad. As if it's any of *his* business. Now I got no place to live but with my sister and Nick. Nick's a good man, he's one of us."

Murmurs of approval circulated among the robed men in the field.

Another man rose to speak, and all grew quiet. "Our mission for tonight is teaching a few lessons," he said. "One of our darky churches is getting a tad uppity lately. They had some troublemaking civil rights nigger as a guest preacher last Sunday. It's our job to take them down a few pegs and remind them what happens to rabblerousers around here."

Eager shouts reverberated in the darkness. The mob piled into pickup trucks and old cars, in a caravan following their leader. Frank rode with Nick. They did not speak.

They drove a few miles to a dirt road almost hidden by a thick stand of oak trees. Through the dust kicked up by the pickup trucks in front of them, Frank could see a small lighted building. In front of it, there was a gathering that seemed to him no more uppity than a church social. Black women, old men, small boys and girls were dancing in the clearing while lively but ancient musicians played an accordion and fiddle. Plates of food lay half-consumed and abandoned on the tables.

The caravan screeched to a stop in the gravel and the hooded men leaped out of their trucks. They sloshed gasoline from greasy cans onto their torches, then they lit them. Every one of the black people froze.

Behind his hood, Frank quickly realized that something had gone very wrong with the plan. Not a single able-bodied black adult male was in sight. Frank felt for his gun in its shoulder holster. He thought he felt dark eyes watching from behind the trees.

The Klan leader seemed oblivious to the danger. He grabbed the fiddle from an elderly musician and smashed it against the man's head.

"Torch the church!" he called.

Half a dozen hooded men ran past the terrified people to the church. By the light of the torches, Frank could see the rickety wood, the tarpaper and peeling paint. In an instant, the building was engulfed in a fiery explosion fed by gasoline. The old black men cried out and the women wept to see their church consumed by flames.

Suddenly, Frank heard a single gunshot ring out from the oak trees. A Klansman dropped his torch as he slumped to the ground.

"Run to the pickup," Nick called to Frank. "We're getting out of here."

As they ran, they saw with alarm that 100 yards away, two Klansmen had grabbed a teenage girl. One of them held a torch up to her face, threatening to burn her with it. She screamed and fought as they forced open the door of a truck and pushed her inside.

Nick quickly turned and ran toward the girl.

"Nick!" Frank yelled, running hard to catch up with him. Frank could hear screams coming from the truck. He could hear that the truck would not start.

Halfway to the girl, Frank caught up with Nick. He grabbed Nick's arm and held it tightly.

Nick glared with resentment at Frank.

"You know what our mission is, Nick."

"But the girl!" Nick said. "Those rotten sons of bitches will…"

"Our job is to observe, so we can testify in court that the Klan unquestionably committed crimes."

The screams were more subdued, but the truck still did not move.

"We can't risk disclosing our mission," Frank said calmly. "We'd endanger our informants, and policemen here won't hide the fact that we're FBI. Besides, if we have to fire our guns, someone could get killed."

Nick bitterly pulled his arm away. "The girl could get killed."

"Just as if we weren't here. You know the rules."

They stared at the truck, which had finally managed to start. Just before it sped away, Frank saw the door open and a body fall to the ground.

"Let's see if she's okay," Nick said.

"You know we can't."

Nick spat in disgust. "Let's get out of here."

On the couch in Nick's apartment that night, Frank did not sleep. His mind played and replayed the appalling events of a few hours earlier. Was there anything else he could have done?

As he flew back to California, Frank shuddered at his undercover experience. At the airport, he hugged Astrid and Susan, Joshua and Rachel more passionately than they ever recalled.

The next morning, Frank reported the details to the Special Agent in Charge.

"Don't feel bad about it," Koenig said.

"I don't feel bad about it," Frank answered. "Our hands were tied."

"Now that you've tasted undercover work, Frank, I wish I could place you with the Black Panthers or the Nation of Islam. Or the Reverend Martin Luther King."

"Don't we have some black agents for that?"

Koenig scoffed. "Until a couple years ago, there were only five black FBI agents. And all of them were guards and drivers and waiters, glorified servants for the Director. Hoover made them Special Agents so they wouldn't get drafted during the War. Of course, we've had paid informants inside black organizations for years. Hoover says that, in Communism, 'we see the cause of much of the racial trouble in the United States at the present time.'"

The Ku Klux Klan confrontation was fresh in Frank's mind. "Do you believe that, John Henry?"

441

"No," Koenig said. "But 50 years ago, the Communist Party Manifesto proclaimed it would agitate among Negro workers to unite them with all class-conscious labor. Hoover used that as a reason to investigate Marcus Garvey."

Frank did not recognize the name. "Marcus Garvey?"

"Garvey led the Universal Negro Improvement Association. By 1920, he had so many followers that 25,000 people from 25 countries attended his convention in Harlem. All U.S. cities with sizable black populations had branches. That is, until Hoover had Garvey deported to Jamaica for mail fraud. Of course, we've had the National Association for the Advancement of Colored People under surveillance for more than 20 years."

"I investigated Communists for years at the FBI," Frank said. "No one ever found a link between the Communists and the NAACP. If anything, it's anti-Communist."

"Well, Hoover thinks blacks are easy prey for Communists," Koenig said. "So the country is safer without *any* organized movement or black leaders. We've got wiretaps on the Congress of Racial Equality and the Student Non-Violent Coordinating Committee. But Hoover thinks Martin Luther King is the most dangerous."

"Why him?"

"King can motivate great masses of people and he's got a few Communist friends. We've had wiretaps and bugs on him for years. So far, there's no evidence that his Southern Christian Leadership Conference is a Communist front. But we've got some entertaining stuff on King's sex life."

"Like what?" Frank asked.

"Sounds of drinking and partying and sexual activities," Koenig said. "Telling raunchy jokes and tales of the sexual accomplishments of friends. A few months ago, I saw a memo that Hoover had scribbled across, 'King is a tom cat with obsessive degenerate sexual urges.'"

Frank shook his head. "Fine things for a man of the cloth. And a married man, too."

With a grin, Koenig drawled, "How many wives did your

442

founder have, Frank? I heard four dozen."

Frank shrugged and said nothing.

"Hoover is an equal-opportunity moralist," Koenig said. "In the '20s, when Southern grand juries refused to indict Ku Klux Klan leaders for murder, he gathered information on their sexual habits instead. He finally convicted an Imperial Kleagle of transporting a woman across state lines for immoral purposes."

"What're we doing about King?" Frank asked.

"We've launched a counterintelligence program against him, like we've got against the Klan. We're working undercover to disrupt and disorganize his movement, discredit him with the Government, and destroy him professionally and personally. FBI technicians made a composite tape of the sexual words and sounds we picked up, and we're going to mail a copy to King."

Frank grimaced. "King won the Nobel Peace Prize, John Henry. Do you personally believe he's a Communist?"

"No," Koenig said. "Neither do a lot of Special Agents, but everyone's afraid to tell Hoover. You've heard that old legend about the Bureau, Frank."

"What legend?"

"There was once a gunfight, and Hoover told the press that an FBI agent was killed. But he was wrong, and the agent was only wounded and in the hospital. So the other agents all drew straws to decide which of them had to go finish him off. Personally, I believe that the American Communist Party no longer wields any influence or control, not over black activists or even the New Left."

"Then why doesn't Hoover see that?"

"Because guys who don't believe it say it's true. And Hoover thought he'd eradicated the Communist Party once before. His efforts drove its members down to 5,000 by the early 1920s. But Hoover watched those numbers creep up again to 80,000 over the next 20 years."

"That didn't come from nowhere," Frank argued. "I seem to recall a Great Depression in the meantime."

"Sure," Koenig said. "And what do you think it would take this time?"

# Chapter 9

Frank Bailey mulled over the file he was examining. FBI investigations yielded so many facts, more facts than any other institution. And while many facts spoke clearly for themselves, the dossier in front of Frank was uncommon. Unlike the usual subversives, the subject of the file was a world-famous businessman, whose facts must be interpreted with caution. It was May 1968, and Howard Hughes, the reclusive billionaire, was buying up casinos in Las Vegas. Frank's job was to discover if there were any racketeering violations.

Frank opened the file to the beginning, to a technical patent drawing of an oil drilling bit. Hughes' father had bought the patent and built it into a prosperous manufacturing company, which Howard Hughes inherited at age 20. Hughes used this wealth in the '20s and '30s to produce Hollywood movies, such as *Scarface*, based on the story of Al Capone and his Chicago mob. During those years, Hughes became famous as a pilot who set a speed record flying around the world. His innovations to early airplanes led to establishing Hughes Aircraft, an engineering and manufacturing company. Frank examined the technical drawings of a huge plywood cargo plane, called by Hughes the Hercules flying boat, though nicknamed the Spruce Goose by others. As a contractor in World War II, Hughes tried to develop the plane, but it flew only once. When the war ended, Hughes acquired controlling interests in Trans World Airlines and RKO Pictures.

The range of Hughes' accomplishments impressed Frank. By 1950, when the Korean War started, Hughes Aircraft was developing electronic weapons systems for missiles and military planes. In the '60s, the company manufactured the Early Bird, the world's first commerical communications satellite, and an unmanned Hughes Surveyor spacecraft made the first soft landing on the moon. Many hundreds of Hughes helicopters were now flying in Vietnam.

Frank flipped through more pages until he recognized the

old nemesis, Communism. In 1952, RKO Pictures produced *Las Vegas Story*, a melodrama about a buxom nightclub singer. The screenwriter, a member of the Screen Writers Guild, was subpoenaed to testify before the House Un-American Activities Committee about Communist infiltration into Hollywood. Within his legal rights, Hughes immediately fired the man, even before he refused to testify whether or not he was a Communist. But the screenplay was unfinished, and the writers hired to complete it also belonged to the Screen Writers Guild. They insisted he receive on-screen credit for his work, and the studio agreed in writing. But when the movie appeared without the credit, the Guild threatened to strike against the breach of contract. Hughes responded by firing 100 employees. "It is my determination," he said, "to make RKO one studio where the work of Communist sympathizers will be impossible." In a clipping in the file, three members of HUAC commended Hughes.

Hughes made other controversial movies. Frank glanced at an ad for *The Outlaw*, featuring a buxom cowgirl filmed in three dimensions. "*IT'LL KNOCK BOTH YOUR EYES OUT!*" The film earned a "condemned" rating from the Catholic Legion of Decency.

A wave of nostalgia carried Frank back to an April night in Naples decades earlier. He hoped Elsa could still enjoy American movies after the War.

Frank forced his thoughts back to the file before him. By 1953, other shareholders were filing lawsuits because Hughes was running RKO Pictures into the ground.

Another thick sheaf of papers described the founding of the Howard Hughes Medical Institute in 1953. In the numbers, Frank found evidence of brilliant financial manipulation. As assets were swapped between Hughes Tool, Hughes Aircraft and HHMI, Hughes Aircraft could now add lease costs in its charges to the Government for military equipment. And if the Internal Revenue Service granted tax-exemption to HHMI, Hughes could save millions of dollars in taxes without expending any cash. But in 1956, the IRS disallowed the deal as artificial. Frank turned the next page in the file. In 1957, the IRS reversed its stance. A few pages later, Frank saw a memo about a $200,000 loan made by Hughes to Vice President Nixon's brother.

Frank found the next item even more troubling. As a pilot, Howard Hughes crashed his airplanes four times, and the last crash in '46 nearly killed him. For the pain from his injuries, he started taking codeine, prescribed by his doctor, and was still taking it. Frank shook his head in amazement, wondering how any man could endure 22 years on such a powerful narcotic.

The file did not answer that question. It said only that the billionaire never left his room anymore. Without cause for electronic surveillance, the FBI investigators did not know precisely how incapacitated Howard Hughes might be. But rumors were reported in the file. It was said that Hughes was so thoroughly obsessed with germs that he allowed just a handful of men to approach him. Through doctors' prescriptions in various names, these five men procured his drugs. And four of these five personal aides were Mormons.

Frank had seen the job openings in the Hughes organization advertised on the bulletin board of his church, and in other Mormon churches throughout Los Angeles. A few words in the file explained that in 1947, a Mormon named Bill Gay had become Hughes' assistant. Ever since then, Mormons were hired as his guards and secretaries, his aides, drivers and medical attendants. But for a decade, even Gay was not allowed to see Hughes because the billionaire feared that Gay might be carrying germs from his family.

Frank scratched his head and wondered if he knew any of these young men. The Mormon aides were surely blameless for procuring drugs when Gentile doctors wrote the prescriptions. He returned to the financial information. Hughes Aircraft was producing almost 800 helicopters for the Army. But to Frank, the numbers made no sense. Hughes could only be losing tens of millions of dollars at the contract price. Frank flipped to another page. A few years earlier, Hughes feuded with the management and other shareholders of Trans World Airlines. He sold his stock for $550 million, but now a bitter lawsuit was threatening to take much of it away. And while the suit was pending, Hughes was using the cash to acquire Las Vegas casinos.

Frank recalled his youthful years building Boulder Dam, now renamed Hoover Dam. The dam had made the explosive growth of Las Vegas possible.

A new picture in the file looked familiar to Frank. It was Robert Maheu, a former FBI agent, now chief of Hughes' operations in Nevada. A memo outlined the details Frank had forgotten. Maheu left the Bureau after the War but came to its attention again in '61, in a failed CIA-concocted scheme to assassinate Fidel Castro with poison capsules. Involved with Maheu in the plot was John Rosselli, once the Chicago crime syndicate's labor relations specialist in Los Angeles. In 1943, Rosselli, other members of the old Capone gang, and a union business manager were convicted in a multimillion dollar motion picture industry extortion scheme. Rosselli and five others were now under indictment for rigging high-stakes gin-rummy games that targeted Hollywood celebrities.

With Rosselli and Maheu in the CIA plot was Sam Giancana, a member of the Chicago syndicate. In 1963, when the FBI belatedly wiretapped calls from Las Vegas hotels and casinos, they found skimming of millions of dollars of untaxed revenues. These millions, Hoover said, were thought to be invested in a "multitude of nefarious purposes" by organized crime. A newspaper reported that Giancana shared in the skim.

With disbelief, Frank stared at the file. In March 1962, J. Edgar Hoover personally warned President Kennedy that a woman who was making regular visits to the White House was the mistress of Giancana and Rosselli. Through his disgust, Frank felt proud of the Bureau's thoroughness.

Frank flipped the page and was surprised to see another familiar name. Edward Morgan, a former FBI inspector, was now an attorney for Howard Hughes. Morgan also represented Jimmy Hoffa, president of the Teamsters' Union, in prison for jury tampering and fraud.

Frank paged through the file. The year before, with Maheu

as his agent and Morgan as his lawyer, Hughes acquired the operating rights to the Desert Inn and Casino in Las Vegas. But the buildings and grounds were still owned by investors, led by a Prohibition rum-runner and boyhood friend of Jimmy Hoffa, Moe Dalitz. Advising Hughes in the deal was Parry Thomas, chief executive of the Bank of Las Vegas, the bank for many casinos and hotels. The Bank of Las Vegas held large deposits from the Teamsters' Pension Fund, which it used to finance the acquisition and construction of gambling casinos.

With curiosity, Frank turned to the dossier on Parry Thomas. A Mormon by birth, Thomas maintained strong ties to Mormon business and political leaders in Las Vegas. In a newspaper clipping he was quoted, "I've got to see that this community stays healthy. I'll take dollars from the devil himself if it's legal--and I don't mean anything disparaging toward the Teamsters by that." Moe Dalitz, who was Jewish, helped Thomas be named "Man of the Year 1965" by the Las Vegas chapter of the Anti-Defamation League.

Frank returned to the main report. In the summer of '67, Hughes bought the Sands Hotel and Casino, again with the assistance of Maheu, Morgan and Thomas. Frank felt an uneasy link with all three men. Maheu and Morgan had been FBI, and Thomas had been LDS. Though active in all the deals by telephone, Hughes remained behind the scenes, catered to and insulated by his Mormon aides. A few months later, Hughes acquired the Castaways Hotel and Casino, the Frontier Hotel and Casino, Alamo Airways, the North Las Vegas Airport, and a motel.

To Frank, the file was becoming increasingly bizarre. Hughes bought a Las Vegas television station from a newspaper publisher who was once indicted for sending vicious editorials through the mails in order to incite the murder of Senator Joseph McCarthy. The lawyer who won his acquittal was Edward Morgan, who was now representing Hughes in his licensing at the Federal Communications Commission. Morgan was also helping Maheu and Bill Gay get a radio station license in Southern California. And the file reported that Morgan was an attorney for Adnan Khashoggi, a Saudi Arabian arms broker and high stakes gambler at the Sands Casino.

With his newest acquisition, the Silver Slipper Casino, Howard Hughes now controlled 23 percent of all gambling revenues in Las Vegas. And he was spending huge sums to buy up gold and silver mining claims in Nevada. A memo said that Hughes was being advised in these deals by a man with no known credentials or background in mining. He had been hired by Bill Gay to work in Hughes Dynamics, a subsidiary Gay formed without Hughes' knowledge, which the billionaire ordered closed when he learned it lost $10 million.

To Frank, it was clear that Hughes' companies were hemorrhaging cash. He was losing tens of millions of dollars a year on underpriced Army helicopter sales. He was facing a potentially disastrous judgment in a lawsuit over TWA. Still, he was negotiating to acquire Air West. He had poured $100 million into Las Vegas real estate, plus accelerating sums into questionable gold and silver mining stakes. And it was rumored that Hughes was making large political contributions in cash from the cashier's cage at the Silver Slipper.

Frank sighed. The facts were bizarre but not illegal.

Frank reached the final few pages in the file. Hughes was lobbying the Atomic Energy Commission to stop nuclear testing in the Nevada desert. Six weeks earlier, a bomb was detonated that was 50 times more powerful than the one that devastated Hiroshima. Though underground, the tests were only 150 miles from Las Vegas. They were 150 miles southwest of Temple Square in Salt Lake City.

Frank was disappointed to find no evidence of racketeering. Yet something in the file was alarming. While Hughes was distracted by his war against germs, who was in control of his empire?

The telephone jarred Frank from his wandering thoughts.

"Frank, this is John Henry. Our guys in London just arrested the man who assassinated Martin Luther King."

"I'm impressed," Frank said. "The investigation took only two months."

450

"Yes. We're holding back the press release a few hours. We'll announce it at the funeral of Robert F. Kennedy this afternoon."

Frank hung up the phone. He was proud of the FBI, yet disturbed. In all the world, J. Edgar Hoover hated three men the most, and two of them were assassinated that spring. Frank harbored no suspicion that Hoover was a conspirator, or even that he intentionally failed to protect either man. All assassinations were blots against the Bureau's prestige, yet they happened.

Frank weighed the words that Hoover had used a month before King was assassinated. His counterintelligence goals, Hoover said, were to prevent the coalition of black nationalist groups. He feared it might lead to a real "Mau Mau" in America and the beginning of a true black revolution. He sought to prevent the rise of a "messiah" who could unify and electrify blacks. Hoover thought King could be a real contender if he ever abandoned his "obedience to white liberal doctrines."

Frank inhaled deeply and stared out the window. To him, it seemed akin to Howard Hughes' war against germs. Obsessions with harmless threats allow mortal dangers to multiply in the dark. Why do we cater so reverently to demanding old men? he wondered. And what must a man do when he becomes aware that the inmate is in command of the asylum? Uneasily, Frank pondered the questions. He found himself thinking of Mountain Meadows and men who always and earnestly obey orders.

*** 

Frank emptied his desk and set his personal belongings aside to take home. He put his manuals, badge and gun into a box, to be returned to the supply room. It was his last day with the Bureau after 22 years. Including credit for his Army service time, he would retire at age 52 with a pension of more than half pay.

Koenig stopped by Frank's office to say goodbye.

"Dammit, Frank, I wish you'd reconsider. You've done a lot

451

of outstanding work for us, and you're still in excellent shape. But I guess you've held your nose a few too many times when the greater good has required us to do amoral things."

"That isn't it, John Henry."

"Then why are you leaving?" Koenig asked.

Frank sat down on top of his empty desk. "Because Hoover can't tell who we're fighting anymore. But I *know* who our enemies are."

"Who?"

"People who behave like God doesn't exist. Look around us, John Henry. All around us are drugs and promiscuity, pornography, disobedience and sloth. But in here, Hoover has created a time capsule. The world in here is disciplined and proud, dedicated, hardworking and moral, and no longer exists outside the walls of the FBI. Outside of here, our traditions and values have become inconvenient and irrelevant. I want to help the world *out there* build organizations like this one, and even better, so the values *inside here* can survive."

Koenig looked skeptically at Frank. "Just how do you intend to do that?"

"By working with the only organization that seeks to do it, worldwide."

"What's that?"

"The Church of Jesus Christ of Latter-day Saints."

Koenig was taken aback by the answer. "You Mormons are like J. Edgar Hoover, himself. Damned straightlaced morality and a thorough lack of self-doubt. There's something I've always wanted to ask you, Frank."

"What is it?"

"Has your Church ever asked you to acquire FBI information for its own purposes? Nothing secret or confidential, just information."

Frank stared straight into Koenig's eyes. "No," he replied.

Koenig smiled. "That's what I figured."

# Chapter 10

The Chevrolet sedan sped east through Little Cottonwood Canyon. From the passenger seat, Frank marveled at the beauty of the tree-lined canyon, which he had not seen for many years.

"It's great to be working with you again, Peter. It's been a long time since I abandoned our mission in Denver when we were kids."

Peter steered the car through the curves on the canyon road. "We're glad to have you back in Utah, Frank."

"Thanks," he replied. "I'm hoping that my three teenage kids can finish growing up a little farther away from all the hedonism of the Gentile world."

"Exciting things are waiting for men like you to accomplish," Peter said. "The Church is in the business of expanding the Church. Don't think this is unseemly, Frank. Of Joseph Smith's 112 revelations, 88 involved economic matters. The Church these days doesn't claim that our plans are revelations, but that doesn't make them less worthy."

"What are the plans?" Frank asked cheerfully.

Peter reached to the back seat behind Frank and handed him a long listing. Frank took a few minutes to scan the pages.

"We've certainly entered broadcasting in a big way."

Peter nodded. "Broadcasting, as I see it, is ordained in the *Book of Mormon*. 'For the multitude being so great that King Benjamin could not teach them all within the walls of the temple, therefore he caused a tower to be erected, that thereby his people might hear the words which he should speak unto them.' I took it as a compliment when one of the Federal Communications Commissioners called the Mormon Church 'a media baron of substantial proportions.'"

Frank read down the listing. "The Church owns television stations in Salt Lake City, Provo and Seattle. Radio stations in New York, Los Angeles, Chicago, San Francisco, Kansas City and Seattle, Salt Lake City and Provo, of course. Some both AM and FM. We've got an international shortwave station with five transmitters near Boston."

"The ideological war of freedom versus collectivism is raging through the airwaves, Frank. That's why we have as much broadcasting power as the Voice of America. Every day, we broadcast in five languages, English, Spanish, Portuguese, French and German, though 95 percent of it isn't Church-related. We must be able to deliver messages not necessarily welcomed by governments."

"That reminds me of a story I heard on the ship back home from Italy," Frank said. "It's about a German Mormon soldier named Huebner, who brought a shortwave radio back from his duty in France in '41. Do you know it?"

"No, what happened?" Peter asked.

"His teenage brother Helmut and two Mormon friends started listening to forbidden broadcasts from London. It seems the boys were forced to become Hitler Youth when they only wanted to join the Boy Scouts. The BBC reports from London gave news completely opposite from the news they heard on German radio. Realizing they were hearing the truth, they printed it on a mimeograph press in the Church meeting hall in their town, where Helmut was a deacon and branch clerk. They printed flyers like 'Hitler the Murderer,' then placed them in mail boxes, telephone booths and apartment entryways. Soon, the boys were arrested while sitting at their desks at school, and charged with high treason."

"High treason?" Peter said. "They were schoolboys."

Frank nodded. "They were taken to Berlin for trial, to Germany's highest court, called the 'blood tribunal.' The judges wore blood-red robes emblazoned with emblems of the German Reich. Helmut's friends were sentenced to ten years in prison."

"What about Helmut?"

"He was beheaded with an axe by the Gestapo. In fear for themselves, the Church leaders publicly excommunicated Helmut after his death. He was reinstated after the War."

Pete whistled as he glanced at Frank, then he quickly looked back at the road.

"Broadcasting is a powerful tool," Frank said.

454

Pete nodded proudly. "The Church has been broadcasting since 1922, just one year after the first commercial radio broadcast in the world. We began broadcasting the Tabernacle Choir in '29, then *Music and the Spoken Word* a few years later. It's the longest continuously broadcast program in America, carried by 50 television and 525 radio stations in the U.S. and Canada. We formed the Bonneville International Corporation a few years ago to centralize our media holdings. Then we paid the highest price ever paid to acquire an FM radio station. It's in New York, which gives us the largest concentration of listeners anywhere within earshot in America."

Pete steered the car onto a narrow road leading up a steep incline toward Granite Mountain.

"The Church is the second largest shareholder in the Times-Mirror Corporation," Pete said. "It owns the *Los Angeles Times,* several other newspapers, and seven television stations. We plan to acquire a cable television system and invest in satellite technology and receiver antennas. But we don't proselytize through our media holdings, at least not directly. And as long as we're restrained by the fairness doctrine, we've got to broadcast other views too, when we present the Church's stance on social and political issues."

Peter stopped the car at the entrance to the Granite Mountain Records Vault. The vault was built inside a cavern that was a natural fortress, where the stone had been quarried for the Salt Lake City Temple.

Frank eagerly stepped out of the car. Ever since it opened in '64, he had been curious to see the vault that stored the fruits of countless millions of hours of genealogical research.

"It can hold the equivalent of 25 million 300-page books," Peter said.

They entered the cavern through a bunker monitored continuously by a closed-circuit television camera. Their authorizations were checked, and Frank and Peter stepped through the access door. Immense steel doors of a dozen tons with blast locks kept out the contaminating air. Inside were the vaults, semicircles lined with white-coated corrugated steel stretching some 200 feet. Three tunnels were for storing records, and the fourth was an office and laboratory. Each was 25 feet wide and 15 feet high.

"We plan to acquire and store six *billion* names," Peter said.

Frank stood in the entryway, breathing in the cool, dry air, 58 degrees year-round. All his ancestors, back as far as the records would allow it, were meticulously documented somewhere inside. The FBI could learn some methods from the Mormons, he thought to himself.

"We estimate that some 80 billion people have *ever* inhabited Earth," Peter said. "So we're amassing a sizable percentage of them. Unfortunately, we can do little for the others, at least on Earth. We hope to posthumously baptize hundreds of thousands of Holocaust victims."

As he stared into the vault, Frank was awed by the ambitiousness of the Church's labors.

Peter stood close beside him. "Under 700 feet of granite, these vaults will withstand earthquakes and floods, fires and even nuclear war. And our investment program must likewise be consistent with our theology. Our assets must be readily convertible into cash in case of widespread social upheaval."

The men left the vault and climbed back into the car. They headed to Salt Lake City, 20 miles away.

Frank again picked up the listing Pete had given him. "The Church owns 316,000 acres near Orlando, Florida?"

"Yes. We think something big might develop there soon."

"What?"

"I'm not at liberty to say. We own 500,000 other acres too, making us the largest single agribusiness landholder in the United States."

"But what about our tax-exempt status?" Frank asked.

"We rigorously pay income tax on all our commercial activities," Pete insisted.

"Of course. But when does a religious enterprise become more business than religion?"

Pete shrugged. "So far, that hasn't been a problem. We've centralized control of all our income-producing properties,

456

Bonneville International, Hotel Utah, Deseret Book Company, ZCMI department stores, Zions Securities, Beneficial Development Corporation, and the others. By itself, each entity had too few checks and balances, allowing too much chance for embezzlement. We've centralized the Church funds, gathered at the ward and stake levels, and invested them for the benefit of all. Computers and centralized security give us far more control. Church financial records have not been made public since 1958. We must ensure that they're never made public again."

Peter turned for a moment to look at Frank. "You've been away from Utah for many years, Frank. Are you aware of the work of the Correlation Committee?"

"Of course, Pete. They're evaluating all Church programs for doctrinal purity and consistency."

Peter smiled indulgently. "Yes, orthodoxy and all that. But it's far more than theology. The Church is suffering from too much diversity. We've granted too much freedom to our backsliding liberals and academics, who've been seduced by the Gentile world. They foster skepticism, rebellion, even apostasy. Like President McKay's niece, Fawn McKay Brodie, who we've had to excommunicate for her blasphemous biography of Joseph Smith. And Juanita Brooks, who was admonished for her history of the Mountain Meadows Massacre."

Frank nodded in understanding. He had found both books unsettling.

"Diversity follows naturally from growth," Peter said. "A growing organization grants authority to untested people, who might then overstep it and conspire to advance their own agenda. That's what we're in a struggle against. We need able men like you to help correct these wrongs."

"How can I help?"

"The strategy is to simplify, economize and centralize, Frank. We've been tolerating too much influence from the outside world. The priesthood must be strengthened, since it's the center of the family and the source of revelation. The father, as priesthood-holder, is the channel of authority to return the Church to its rightful place inside the home. A man who's

457

uninvolved, with no office or calling or opportunity to serve, only diminishes in his own strength. Have you been participating in Family Home Evenings?"

"Not every week. The kids are busy with outside interests, you know."

"We'll send a home teacher around to explain why it's so vital to your family."

"We'll look forward to that," Frank said.

They left the mouth of Little Cottonwood Canyon and headed north toward Salt Lake City.

Peter smiled. "The Correlation Committee has been making great strides. The Division of Internal Communications is producing and reviewing all instructional materials. Already, we've stopped printing the Women's Relief Society magazine and replaced it with magazines the priesthood controls. The Relief Society had actually prevented the priesthood from determining what tasks the women would perform! So we've eliminated the financial autonomy of women's organizations, and the priesthood now determines how their funds are spent."

Frank wondered what Grandmother Molly would say, but he put the thought out of his mind.

"And we've developed new Relief Society courses," Peter said. "Like 'Ideals of Womanhood in Relation to Home and Family.' Of course you know that women are no longer allowed to lead prayers at sacrament meetings. All these things had gotten out of hand before the Correlation Committee reined them in. Now we've set up a Department of External Communications to handle our public relations."

"Who's been handling our public relations?" Frank asked.

"The Robert R. Mullen Company in Washington," Peter said. "It's just been purchased by Robert Bennett, our Senator's son. But they've got some loose cannons on board.

"The image we must project is affluent, corporate and polished, low profile in all matters except morality, in which we must be visible and impeccable. Like when Senator Smoot battled against the importation of obscene books. Of *Lady Chatterley's Lover*, he said, 'It is written by a man with a diseased mind and a soul so black that he would even obscure the darkness of hell.'

"You see, Frank, as paragons of America at its best, we expect to reshape the country in our image. We've shaped our immigrants into loyal and productive Americans, while other institutions let immigrants and minorities steer *them*. Over time, true Americans will beg us to lead them homeward, and they'll join us for the sake of their families. It will be a crusade."

"I've certainly seen the value of public relations to the FBI," Frank said. "All those movies that made Hoover and his G-men look like heroes!"

"And that's why we must avoid negative publicity at any cost. Like in 1921, when Senator Smoot made a deal with Fox Studios. He agreed to quash a bill in Congress that would've put a 30 percent tax on movie tickets. In return, Fox agreed to suppress the release of two anti-Mormon movies based on Zane Grey novels. Those films were released, but only after all the slurs against us wound up as trash on the cutting room floor."

"They *were* trash," Frank said. "As a boy, I read *Riders of the Purple Sage*. It was virulently anti-Mormon, full of hits below the belt about events Grey made up. Whatever Smoot's ethics were, the tax was a bad one and the movie deserved to be censored."

"That's just the point, Frank. The value of a favorable public image can't be overestimated. In 1937, for instance, the *Reader's Digest* reported that the Mormon Church had gotten *every one* of its 84,000 welfare recipients off the Government dole."

Frank shook his head in amazement. "Was that true?"

"No. And since we didn't bother to correct the error, the myth persists. Our actual results were far more modest, perhaps 4,000 people off the dole. And we didn't let our members with WPA jobs give them up to work for the Church. In fact, only six states had a higher average load on the Emergency Works Program. Utah's Federal Old Age Pensions and Aid to Dependent Children were among the highest in the nation."

"How can that be?" Frank asked. "We're surely not lazier

or less productive than other Americans."

"Tithes and missionary costs weighed heavily on our poorest members," Pete explained. "So they had little saved up for bad times. Some people even accused the Church of setting up sugar beet farms to break a farmers' strike against the low prices paid by the Church's sugar refinery. You know, sugar production in Utah has always been at high cost, and it would've failed entirely without Smoot's tariffs."

Peter steered the car past the old railroad yards west of downtown Salt Lake City. Frank was troubled by the admissions, but he said nothing. He was dismayed to see decrepit warehouses and boarded-up taverns so close to Temple Square.

Peter parked the car near the Church office building and turned to his old missionary companion. "I know you'll feel right at home, Frank. The head of Church Security is a retired FBI man too, along with several others."

The men stepped out of the car and walked toward the office building.

"Why do you hire so many ex-FBI agents, Pete?"

"Because you guys have learned at least two things from J. Edgar Hoover."

"What two things?" Frank asked.

"The first is his definition of democracy and justice," Peter said. "Hoover called it 'the dictatorship of the collective conscience of our people.'"

Frank regarded him dubiously. "I'm not sure I agree with that, Peter. It contradicts our Constitutional limits on the power of the majority."

"Perhaps," Peter shrugged. "But once we establish a majority, we can steer national events in concordance with our theological beliefs. We believe this can best be accomplished through existing American institutions."

"What's the second thing?" Frank asked.

"Hoover understood that the normal state of bureaucracy is lethargy. Only intense, *personal* caring about the details of its mission will keep bureaucracy from drifting into sloth."

# Chapter 11

Peter appeared at the door of Frank's office in the Church Office Building.

"We're talking to a guy who says he's your cousin," Peter said.

Frank looked up from a financial plan. "Who?"

"Kevin Carter."

Frank nodded. "We have the same great-grandfather, John Carter, but his great-grandmother was Fawn, the Indian wife. I haven't seen Kevin in years. What's he here for?"

"He wrote an article in *Dialogue* that we wanted to ask him about."

Frank took his coat from the rack and followed Peter into a small room.

Kevin Carter was about 50 and looked no more Indian than Frank. Peter observed them carefully as they shook hands.

"We wanted to ask you a few question, Elder Carter."

"I'd like to ask a few, too," Kevin said. "For instance, why was I visited at home by two plainclothed Church Security Officers, demanding entrance?"

"No loyal Church member should have any reason to refuse," Peter said.

"I didn't refuse," Kevin replied.

"They wanted to find out if you'd used unauthorized records from the Church to write your article."

"Was that why my Bishop called me in the next day, to ask about my sex life and tithing, and whether I might be straying? Where would I get unauthorized records?"

"That's what we're trying to find out," Peter told him. "The Office of Church Security is investigating breaches of information security. This isn't frivolous, Elder Carter. Jack Anderson, the popular columnist who happens to be one of us, revealed publicly that funds from a Church-owned corporation have been funneled to a right-wing organization. We must ensure that anyone who's tempted to leak documents and information is aware of our internal intelligence system."

"But my article was respectful of the Church," Kevin protested. "It wasn't radical."

"The General Authorities want to know whether you might need disciplinary action."

Frank looked across the desk at his cousin. "What was your article about?"

"Our Indian Placement Program," Kevin said. "I'd participated in it for years. Educating Indian kids in white schools, and the gospel, seemed a good way to make them leaders among their people. And help fulfill the prophecies in the *Book of Mormon*. Altogether, some 70,000 Indian kids have been brought to live in Mormon homes since the '40s."

"But now you question it, Elder Carter?"

Without defiance, Kevin tried to explain. "I only wrote that we need to examine what we're doing. You see, one of my foster kids came back to see me. Roy left the Navajo reservation at age eight, when a missionary promised him the worldly benefits of life in Salt Lake City. His parents disapproved when he was baptized, so he rarely went home to see them. Now, through no fault of his, Roy has lost his third job in the Anglo world, and he's ashamed to go back to his parents. Roy is a talented youth who could've been a real leader if he hadn't left the reservation. But he's taken up drinking and become spiritually homeless, too."

"He could've become a drunkard on the reservation," Frank said.

Kevin sighed. "At least Roy wouldn't be an outcast."

"There must be some successes among your other foster kids," Peter said.

"Yes," Kevin said proudly. "One of them went to Brigham Young University and is fighting with the Government for Indian water rights. Isn't that what this inquisition is really about?"

Frank and Peter exchanged glances.

"We're inquiring about your weakness in faith, Elder Carter."

"I have no weakness in faith. In my article, I merely raised the question of whether Ernest Wilkinson, president of BYU, had been a friend to the Indians when he served as their lawyer."

"Of course, he was," Frank answered. "Wilkinson helped write the Indian Claims Act."

"The Indian Claims Act set the value of Indian property at what it was worth when the land was seized by whites. It was a tiny fraction of its later value, and even that amount could be claimed only in cash, not the land itself. And when the Indians settled a claim, they abandoned all future claim to it. Wilkinson cleared the titles to many Mormon ranches in the West. His law firm later lobbied Congress and exempted the Mormon Indian Placement Service from some provisions in the Indian Child Welfare Act."

"Mormon Indian children have been extremely well cared for," Peter protested.

"Of course they have!" Kevin said. "But our theology tells us that the Lamanites were a degenerate tribe, so what remains of their culture has little value. I'm 1/32 Shoshone and I refuse to believe that."

Frank listened to his cousin, whose experiences were so different from his own.

"The Church can't seem to tell its loyal and deceitful historians apart," Kevin said. "We're not afraid of the consequences of examining all the documents. We *know* that the records, fully and honestly explored, can prove nothing truly damning to the Church. But disloyal historians want to rifle through the documents in hopes of detonating unexploded mines."

"Have you uncovered mines, Elder Carter?"

"I know that Wilkinson recruited a squad of students from the local John Birch Society to spy on suspected liberal professors."

Frank shrugged. "That's nothing worse than the FBI is doing at more radical universities. Infiltrating student groups, disrupting demonstrations, and investigating professors who might be aiding and abetting the antiwar movement. Don't you think that BYU would rank dead last on Hoover's priority list?"

Kevin laughed. "I once heard that President McKay offered Hoover an honorary doctorate from BYU, but he was too busy to accept it."

Frank found it unsettling that Kevin seemed to be enjoying the interview.

"Did you know Cleon Skousen when he was with the FBI, Frank?"

"Yes."

"He's now a professor of religion at BYU. Skousen says that President McKay urged him to establish the Freemen Institute, a mostly Mormon spinoff of the John Birch Society. Skousen said, 'The world hierarchy of the dynastic super-rich is out to take over the entire planet, doing it with socialistic legislation where possible, but having no reluctance to use Communistic revolution where necessary.' What does that *mean*?"

Frank and Peter looked at one another.

"And Apostle Ezra Taft Benson seems unrelenting in his efforts to imply, if not get, Church endorsement for the John Birch Society. He's not officially a member, but his wife is, and his son is the national director for public relations."

Peter could think of no more questions for Kevin Carter.

"We'll inform you of the Church's decision," he said.

\*\*\*

St. George, Utah
February 26, 1973

Elder Joshua Bailey
Latter-day Saints Mission
Sao Paulo, Brazil

Dear Joshua,

I cannot begin to express how proud I am to know that you

464

will soon fulfill your missionary calling. It is but the first of the grave responsibilities of manhood, and if well satisfied, it can propel a man onward to his unlimited potential. I pray that one day you will have a son (or half a dozen sons like your Grandpa Anders) and will experience both sides of this mysterious bond with which men have been blessed.

Brazil is rather far from here, so I do not know if the Watergate news has made its way down there. As an old G-man, I find myself intrigued by the revelations of this past year. I can only guess what secrets have yet to surface (and what the fallout in Washington will be).

At BYU, did you ever cross paths with a student named Thomas Gregory? (He would be a little older than you, I suppose.) For three months, Gregory masqueraded as a Democratic volunteer in the Muskie and McGovern campaigns. He obtained policy papers, working papers, bank statements and contributor lists, and he wrote summaries of discussions he overheard. He handed these over to the Committee to Re-elect President Nixon, in exchange for $175 a week. Gregory gave them a detailed floor plan of McGovern headquarters (not the same place as the Democratic National Committee office at the Watergate, but the same idea), which he knew would help prepare for electronic penetration and surveillance. He resigned his job the day before the Watergate break-in.

Gregory was introduced to the Watergate burglars by none other than Robert Bennett, the son of Utah Senator Wallace Bennett. (The Senator and his son are LDS, needless to say, and Gregory is a friend of his nephew.) A year before the break-in, Robert Bennett bought a Washington public relations firm, the Robert R. Mullen Company. For the previous decade, the Mullen Company's offices in Europe and Asia were covers for CIA operatives. The Mullen Company also had legitimate public relations clients. Among its clients in recent years were Howard Hughes and the Mormon Church!

On Bennett's payroll at the time of the Watergate break-in was E. Howard Hunt, a former CIA agent and one of the Watergate conspirators. Hunt and six other men (two of them ex-FBI) were recently convicted of burglary and wiretapping, then sentenced to prison. The columnist Jack Anderson (also LDS), reported that Bennett knew three days before Watergate that a burglary-bugging team was on the prowl.

When asked about his involvement, Bennett said he gave Gregory some ethical guidelines. "If you take any money from McGovern, if you apply for, or hold any position of trust in the McGovern campaign, if you allow yourself to be put in a position where McGovern is depending upon you for anything significant, that you cannot morally discuss what you are doing with Howard Hunt and take money from him. On the other hand, if you make it clear to the McGovern people that you are simply a college student wanting the chance to watch a Presidential campaign and you are willing to stuff envelopes and lick stamps in return for that privilege, the question who you talk to about experiences and who pays the expenses is your own business; that you are not doing anything all that wrong."

To this, Thomas Gregory replied, "Brother Bennett, I have gone way beyond that."

It seems that Bennett revealed what he knew to the press because he knew the White House was involved. He denies that he is Deep Throat, but I am not so sure. If he is, then it is largely our morality that could bring about an enduring change in politics. (And this despite the fact that Bennett hopes to be Senator someday!)

How did I learn all of this? Let me just say I still have sources. It all reminds me of a distinction Brigham Young once drew between the Constitution and the "damned rascals who administer the government." I can divulge a few more details when I see you.

You can be sure that your mother and sisters and I will be waiting for you at the Salt Lake City airport to welcome you home from Brazil. I have missed you, Son.

With admiration and love,
Dad

# Chapter 12

His reading glasses perched on his nose, Frank examined the fine print of the 1982 Garn-St. Germain Banking bill. He heard a faint knock on the door of the office he kept at home.

"Come in," he called absently. The matter was deeper than simple curiosity to Frank. The Church owned a substantial amount of bank stock.

A tall young man of 30, blond and robust, entered the room.

"What's wrong, Dad?" he asked.

"It's this damned banking bill that's about to become law. Jake Garn is going to wish he never put his name on this disaster. What is it about Mormons that makes us believe the financial fantasies of others?"

"Perhaps it has something to do with golden plates."

Frank read the last words of a paragraph. "I'll forget you said that, Son. Wouldn't you think our Senator would know that real estate developers shouldn't own banks?"

"True," Joshua said. "If it weren't for such a bank, we might still be in Kirtland, Ohio."

Frank looked up and motioned for his son to sit down. He would recommend that the Church sell its bank stock.

"It seems that Utah has earned the reputation of being the scam capital of America and the national test market for fraud. Eighteen FBI investigations are underway in Utah this year, one involving 8,000 investors in a $125 million fraud."

"Among *us*?" Joshua asked.

"Some of the perpetrators are, and some aren't," Frank replied. "I hear rumors that the U.S. Attorney will indict 21 people in a $32 million scam, where Mormons are both the targets and con men. Then there's a particularly sacrilegious fraud where the perpetrators insisted on beginning and ending each negotiating session with a prayer."

Joshua sighed. "I'd hate to think it's either stupidity or greed."

"It isn't," Frank said. "But maybe some deficiency of

cynicism makes some of us easy prey. Or an awe of leadership suspends disbelief. One scam targeted a Bishop early, then paid him as promised so he'd endorse the scheme to other victims. Maybe there's some mistaken idea that gaining wealth is a kind of sacred obligation."

"And we've got money," Joshua said. "You can't have fraud without that."

Frank nodded. "In Las Vegas, a group of prominent LDS businessmen set up a credit union for Mormons and ended up channeling funds to a fictitious corporation controlled by one of its managers. And Utah dominates the nation in penny stocks and blind pools, since our state government refuses to regulate them. Salt Lake City has been called 'the sewer of the securities industry.'"

"Well, our legislature is awfully busy passing laws to safeguard morality and ban pornography."

Frank regarded his son, then remembered something he had forgotten. He reached across his desk and picked up a slim book.

"I thought this would interest you, Joshua. *Come Back America,* just published by Evan Mecham, an LDS Arizona politician. If you ask me, he's a loose cannon, though he's a disciple of my old FBI colleague and your old professor, Cleon Skousen. Mecham wants to get rid of the income tax, all government borrowing and the Federal Reserve, then impeach any legislator who won't pass laws that support his ideas."

Joshua took the book without enthusiasm. "Thanks, Dad."

"Is there something wrong, Joshua? Is everything all right with your wife and kids?"

"They're fine, Dad."

"How about you?"

Joshua hesitated a long moment. "Well, there's..."

"Damn!" Frank said. "Did you see this?"

Joshua had rarely heard his father use profanity, let alone twice, even in the privacy of their home. "What is it?"

Frank pointed to a picture in the newspaper. "Senator Garn is helping to get Federal funds for the new Triad Center development in Salt Lake City. Just because a tiny piece of it has some historical value."

"How much Federal money?" Joshua asked.

"Not much, just $1.5 million. Nonetheless, it's the principle of the thing."

"Have you seen the plans, Dad? My firm is in the running to do some of the architectural work."

Frank looked proudly at his son. "What are the plans?"

"Near the Temple and Tabernacle, where old warehouses and run-down taverns are now, there'll be a $400 million development. It'll have twin office towers, a large hotel and three high-rise condominium buildings. Of course, Triad built the International Center for $450 million a few years ago near the Salt Lake City airport. They've also pledged $1 million for a medical education center at the LDS Hospital."

"I guess I can't stop being an old FBI man," Frank sighed. "Triad is owned by the Khashoggi family of Saudi Arabia, and their money came from international arms brokering. They got commissions in the hundreds of millions of dollars."

"Well, were the arms deals illegal?"

"No, not at the time. But Khashoggi has been implicated in foreign bribes and illegal U.S. political contributions. He's put his Salt Lake City assets into a Cayman Islands trust."

"How'd we meet him?" Joshua asked.

Frank recalled an FBI file he had examined long ago. "Through Bill Gay, Howard Hughes' Mormon chief of staff. Hughes owned the Sands Casino, where Khashoggi was said to occasionally run up seven-figure gambling tabs. He and Hughes also had the same lawyer, a former FBI agent I once knew."

Joshua settled into the chair. "Remember those jobs for Hughes that were posted on the Church bulletin board? A friend of mine took one of those jobs. He wasn't one of the personal aides, but a second-level employee who saw Hughes only when he was called. My friend was ridiculously well-paid, but he told me some amazing stories before he quit."

"Like what?" Frank asked.

"He said that Hughes was so terrified of germs that he

469

demanded they use fifteen tissues just to open up a cabinet. And he never left his room, which was always kept dark and never cleaned. Hughes spent all day naked in bed, watching movies, and for months, wouldn't let his bedsheets be changed. At his orders, they kept a daily log of the movies he saw, what he ate, and how long he spent in the bathroom. Part of my friend's job was administering enemas to Hughes."

"That's what codeine does to a man," Frank said, stiffening.

"The record-keeping was absurdly out of proportion," Joshua said. "There were memos and reports, checks and cross-checks, and constant filing. It was a bureaucracy gone mad. Yet his aides treated Hughes as if he were a rational man."

Frank shrugged. "What else can you expect from 30 years of narcotics abuse?"

"Finally, my friend couldn't take it any longer. It was all the doctors' fault, he insisted. Hughes had four doctors, two of them Mormons in those last years, who kept him supplied with drugs. But when Hughes died in '76, my friend broke down and told me the truth. He'd had a conflict of interest in pandering to Hughes' obsession with the irrelevant. Where else could he, with his modest skills, earn so much money and wield such power?"

"Then why did he leave?" Frank asked.

"I asked him that," Joshua said. "He said he couldn't overcome his awareness of the consequences to Hughes. A man who'd been a pilot was now a prisoner. My friend knew the financial consequences, too. The aides consolidated their own power when they urged Hughes to sell his company too soon. And in the decade before Hughes died, the value of his estate shrank by half a billion dollars. Part of that came from his own disastrous decisions, but the rest was mismanagement by men whose only talent was for bureaucracy."

Frank smiled with pleasure at the company of his son. "I was working in a Church office building when Hughes' so-called Mormon Will miraculously appeared."

"No kidding? What did it look like?"

"It was a handwritten will," Frank recalled, "dated 1968, and

470

addressed to David O. McKay, then President of the Church. It listed a few predictable beneficiaries, then bequeathed 1/16 of Hughes' estate to the LDS Church and another 1/16 to a Mormon gas station operator in rural Nevada. It was a naked hoax, of course."

"How did you know?"

"Hughes detested the nickname 'Spruce Goose' for his cargo plane, and never would've called it that in his will. But no better will appeared, and by the time the FBI looked for fingerprints, it was too late to identify the perpetrator. Still, Howard Hughes was not entirely mad about a few things."

"What?" Joshua asked.

"Hughes objected when nuclear bombs were exploded in the Nevada desert," Frank said. "We've now learned that above-ground nuclear tests, which began in '51, have caused higher cancer rates in Utah. Secret autopsies of sheep showed dangerous radiation levels in '54. But the U.S. Government covered up the data and tested bombs above ground until 1962. Now, two decades later, 1,200 cancer victims, or their survivors, are suing the Federal Government over the consequences."

Frank looked somberly across the desk at Joshua. "I hope you'll *always* weigh the consequences of *any* actions you take."

He remembered something else.

"I'm sorry, Son, I interrupted you when you came in. What was it you wanted to see me about?"

Joshua hesitated for a long moment.

"I wondered, Dad, could you join me in prayer?"

# BOOK SIX

# AN EXCOMMUNICATE'S STORY

Joshua and Rachel waited at the curb as the cab let Susan out at the Latter-day Saints Hospital. Susan was surprised at how long and tightly Joshua embraced her.

"How is he?" Susan asked.

"He could survive this stroke," Rachel answered, hugging her sister. "Dad is sleeping now, so you can't go in to see him just yet."

"Will you let me know when it's time?"

"Yes, of course."

The three of them walked up the stairs to the waiting area for the Intensive Care Unit. No one else was waiting in the chairs nearby.

Joshua looked fondly at his sisters. Susan, just over fifty, and Rachel, five years younger, were still both attractive women. They both had blue eyes and straight brown hair, though Susan's was long and streaked with gray. Rachel's face usually had a livelier look, Joshua noticed, but the stresses of the past two days had left her with lines of fatigue. She kept her hair shorter and more stylish than her sister, and wore slightly more makeup and jewelry.

Halfway between them in age, Joshua had inherited the Nordic coloration of his mother. But his hair had gone gray and his eyes had lost their boyishness years ago. He knew he looked less youthful than even his older sister. As he took Susan's hand, Joshua noticed that she showed no signs of weariness from her flight.

"How are the kids?" he asked Susan. "I know the five of them must make it hard for you to get away from Washington, D.C. to Salt Lake City."

"Fine," Susan said, looking intently at her brother. "I'm so glad to see you both."

Joshua smiled with gratitude and relief. Until that moment, he was not completely sure.

"I knew it," he whispered. "The bonds between you and me

are mightier than excommunication."

"Dad is still refusing to see Joshua," Rachel explained.

"Still, after all these years?" Susan asked.

"You know how the Church is the center of his life. Mom tries to lie with conviction, saying it's his health that keeps them away."

"But his stroke..."

"Until his stroke, he was strong as a workhorse at 83. Dad was out every day in his dark suit and tie, proselytizing visitors to the Tabernacle in St. George."

"It's all those good genes and clean living," Joshua said. "That should've been my destiny, too."

Rachel smiled. "I sure didn't think you might outlast Dad."

"It's truly a miracle, Joshua."

"Well, I take a lot of drugs every day."

"Yes, but you look a hundred times better than the last time I saw you, three years ago."

"I remember once back then," Rachel said. "Joshua saw himself in a mirror and looked so ghastly that he smashed it with his fist."

Joshua winced at the memory of those days. "I was hoping for seven years of bad luck."

"What are Father's chances, Rachel?" Susan asked.

"I can only say fifty-fifty. But I'm a neonatal pediatrician, not a neurologist or cardio-vascular specialist. You'll see how he is when he wakes up."

"I'm going in with you," Joshua said.

Susan and Rachel looked at one another.

"What, you think I can't control myself, seeing Dad at the LDS Hospital? That I'll flirt with the doctors and embarrass you all?"

"We have to respect Father's wishes," Susan replied.

"That I'm not his son!"

"Dad doesn't wish that," Rachel said.

"No, he doesn't. He thinks that through prayer and repentance, you can change."

"You think I haven't *prayed*?" Joshua asked. "Hell, I've

476

prayed to be like Lloyd."

"How is Lloyd?" Rachel asked as she turned toward Susan. "Mom showed us that picture of him from the *Washington Post*. You must be proud of him."

"And his ever-expanding authority in the CIA," Joshua said.

"It's hard not to be proud," Susan smiled. "And it's more than simply hard work. So many men who aren't Mormons seem to be corrupted in scandals over money or power or women."

"Of course, Joshua wouldn't know about that," Rachel teased him.

Joshua shook his head. "Not even close. I never was tempted by money or power, and I actually could keep it in my pants. You don't believe that, do you, Rachel?"

"Well, no."

"Have I ever told you about the first time?"

Susan paled as she glanced around the empty waiting room.

"No, I don't believe so," Rachel answered.

"It was a surfeit of missionary zeal," Joshua explained, smiling weakly. "I'd just returned from my mission, two years in Brazil, empassioned with the power of the gospel and all the virility of being 20. I liked girls as much as I imagined I should, but was wholly inexperienced with sexual practices of any kind."

Joshua paused, as if he had sworn to tell the whole truth.

"Well, not quite, I suppose. In our missionary training, the power of wicked impulses over normal teenage boys was understood. So we were given a pamphlet with twenty steps on how to avoid masturbation. Did they teach you girls the same things?"

"No! What things?" Rachel whispered.

"Oh, like avoiding spicy foods, or tying our hands to the bedframe so we couldn't touch ourselves in our sleep. 'Don't pray about this problem,' the teachers advised us, 'for that will tend to keep it in your mind more than ever.' As I struggled to suppress my own impure thoughts, I believed them no more shameful than those of other boys.

"When I returned home that summer, I got a job at the hotel, earning extra money for college. Do you remember those uniforms we wore at the hotel?"

"They were khaki, weren't they?" Susan recalled. "Tailored and sharp."

"Yes, and I was still growing, so by the end of summer, my muscles bulged beneath my clothes.

"One sultry night in August, the telephone rang at the registration desk. From an upper room of the hotel, a guest was asking for Joshua Bailey. I remembered him from when he checked in. Youthful and well-dressed in a dark business suit, he'd smiled at me and memorized my name plate. In a halting voice on the phone, he said he'd found the *Book of Mormon* in his bedside table, and he wanted to learn more. Could I come up and teach him what it meant to belong to the Church?

"'Of course,' I quickly assured him. After all, it was my calling to be a missionary. In the elevator, I wished I'd already taken the *Book of Mormon* class at BYU.

"The door was ajar when I arrived at his room, so I peeked inside. He was sitting up on the bed, his necktie loosened, with the *Book of Mormon* in the lap of his suit pants. He looked up at me and motioned me inside, so I entered and closed the door. I explained to him I was an Elder, then began the speech I'd given so many times in Brazil. He put his finger to his lips and pointed to a passage he told me he didn't understand. I leaned in closer to read the passage, but he took my hand and placed it on his starched white shirt. His chest and belly felt so flat and firm. All of a sudden, I knew this man was out-missionarying me. I wanted it so badly. He only fumbled with my garments for a moment, then enveloped me inside his lips.

*"Babylon is fallen, is fallen, that great city, because she made all nations drink of the wine of the wrath of her fornication.* Oh, don't look so shocked. Surely, *one* of you has done that to your husband.

"Ten minutes later, I left his room, trembling and mortified and thrilled. He just smiled when I explained that I had to get back to work."

"My God, Joshua," Susan said.

"Did you see him again?" Rachel asked.

"I looked up his address in the register, not knowing what I wanted from him. Numbly, I went home at the end of my shift, then lay in bed awake all night. But in the morning, I learned that he'd checked out of the hotel without even scribbling me a note. Then I began to comprehend what had happened. And I knew I'd be damned if I ever let it happen again."

"Did you confess it to the Bishop?" Susan asked.

Joshua inhaled deeply, then shook his head. "That afternoon, when my shock diminished at last, I realized I must go to the Bishop. Back then, he would ask me once a year about my sexual activities. Until that day, I'd never had anything to confess or be ashamed to admit or deny. I was an Eagle Scout and I'd earned my Duty to God Award. But now I was tainted, and I feared I'd never again enjoy the same confidence the Bishop always had in me."

"But he could've helped you."

"It was a month before your wedding, Susan, and if he suspended my Temple Recommend, I'd have to confess why to Dad."

Rachel nodded in understanding.

"So I rationalized my silence," Joshua said. "After all, the Bishop had no power to absolve me, to dissolve the sin as if it never happened. His only power was to forgive me in the eyes of the Church if I repented. And I was sincerely repentant. *Repentance falls into five steps. Sorrow for sin. Abandonment of sin. Confession of sin. Restitution for sin. Doing the will of the Lord.*

"Fervently, I did the will of the Lord, praying every day on my knees for the strength. Sorrow and abandonment came easily, and restitution through extra fasts and contributions. Still, I couldn't bring myself to confess."

"It might be easier if it weren't face-to-face," Rachel said. "But through a screen, like the Catholics."

"At least the Catholics grant equal opportunity," Joshua sighed. "Straight or gay, their priesthood holders all share the

479

same right to be celibate. But celibacy is one peculiarity we've never embraced.

"You see, what terrified me wasn't the sin I'd committed, but the knowledge I'd always managed to deny. Do you remember how you used to tease me, when I was small, as I stared at the handsome, televised face of the master of ceremonies on the Sunday morning broadcasts from the Tabernacle?"

"Yes," Susan said. "On trips to Salt Lake City, you'd push to the front of the Tabernacle to be close to him."

"Charisma was what I later thought it was, or desire to grow up to be like him. But suddenly, I'd find myself reliving a mortifying moment of eye contact in the men's locker room at those hot springs we'd go to near Pocatello."

"I never wondered about you," Rachel said. "At the dances, you always danced with so many different girls."

"Because they were all so interchangeable to me! Girls were always willing when I asked them to dance, but all the while, I'd be watching a particular boy out of the corner of my eye. I was never afraid to ask a girl to dance because I cared so little if she would.

"But I cared what men thought. In Brazil, I believed that my affection for my missionary companion was admiration, or comradeship on lonely nights, or working close beside him for something we both loved. I was horrified when I realized that what I'd felt toward him was desire. We'd both laughed when some Brazilians seemed to assume we were fags."

"You must've felt tormented," Susan said.

"Every day," Joshua admitted. "But I also felt rare moments when the irony was almost as amusing as it was bitter. From nearly its beginning, the Mormon Church has immersed in outlaw sexuality. But *why*? In my desperation, I imagined the old patriarchs being painfully tempted like me, so they soothed forbidden lusts by taking a multitude of wives. After all, Brigham Young's final words were 'Joseph, Joseph, Joseph.'"

"Joshua!" Susan said. "Evil-speaking about the Lord's anointed!"

"Well, we'll never know. Perhaps our patriarch John Carter passed along some gay gene when he found a way for himself to make do. But the option was foreclosed to his natural great-great-grandson, and unlike Gentile boys, I couldn't dissipate my desires with a variety of girls."

"Not at Brigham Young University," Rachel smiled.

"At BYU that year, I was one of 7,500 returned missionaries. Do you remember why I left on my mission after only one year of college?"

"Your lottery number for the Vietnam War draft was in the single digits," Rachel said.

"But you supported the war absolutely," Susan argued.

"Yes," Joshua answered. "I was nonetheless entitled to deferments both as a clergyman and as a student. The Bishop counseled me to take the missionary deferment first. The war was winding down when I returned from Brazil, then it ended as I finished college.

"Every day at BYU, two passions battled inside me. One was the fierce, testimonial loyalty of a successful returned missionary. The other was panic that I would be unmasked.

"How could I keep the shower door slightly ajar, as that anti-masturbation pamphlet suggested? Something might inspire an impromptu erection and give me away. Admitting to being a homosexual leads to automatic dismissal from BYU!"

"Wasn't BYU trying aversion therapy in those years?" Rachel recalled.

"What's that?" Susan asked.

"Wiring a man's genitals," Rachel explained, "then showing him a film of naked men and applying electric shocks if he's aroused."

Joshua shuddered. "The psychologists promised that aversion therapy works. Of course it works, so does torture."

"Couldn't you honorably be celibate?" Susan asked.

"That's precisely the dilemma, Susan! Yes, I could be celibate, but only as a second-class Latter-day Saint. And I could not be second-class."

"So you married Trudy?"

"Yes. I met her at a devotional assembly at the Smith Fieldhouse. There were many pretty girls at BYU, but Trudy stood out, noninterchangeable among them. It was her eyes, I think, so bright and green, with a strength that I wanted sealed to me."

"Girls always liked you," Rachel said.

"I suppose," Joshua admitted. "And returned missionaries like me enjoyed a status that few societies ever grant to boys our age. Trudy was moved by my earnestness when I led the prayer meetings. But she never guessed the reason for the fervor of my prayers."

"Did you pray to know if Trudy was the one for you?" Susan asked.

"I prayed, and I listened for an answer. But all I felt or heard was negation. Still, my need to get married was urgent. So I lied to Trudy and told her about a blessing I'd felt for us from our Heavenly Father. *That* was blasphemy, Susan. At our wedding in the Temple, Trudy and I were both virgins, except for that isolated encounter in that upper room of the hotel."

Anxiously, Susan glanced around the waiting room again.

"Well, you know most of the story," Joshua said. "Trudy has been a blessing to me, and if, indeed, she's sealed to me for all Eternity, it's surely her loss and my gain. Our kids seem happy, though they're embarrassed and sad at my excommunication and illness. As if they, sealed to me, bear some of the guilt and responsibility. So I remind them, *We believe that men will be punished for their own sins, and not for Adam's transgression.*

"I was a proper husband and father for as long as I could be, fifteen years. I exhausted my energies on my family and work, the Church, and avoiding men's eyes. How I coveted the sins of ordinary men! Sneaking a little coffee or skipping church on vacation to play golf. It surprised me to discover a warm intimacy with my family, and for those years, it was enough. Trudy and I found a relaxed, respectful enjoyment of each other, more than most people are blessed with, I suppose."

"What was so lacking?" Susan asked him.

482

Joshua stared toward the window. "Fifty percent of my soul."

Joshua abruptly stood up and walked toward his father's hospital room. "Rachel, is it time to go in?"

Rachel glanced at her watch. "It's only been an hour. Dad needs to rest."

Joshua sat down next to his sisters again. "Well, enough about me. How are you, Susan? Do you get lonely being so far away in Washington, D.C.? It's been almost ten years since you left."

"Of course, I miss my family in Utah," Susan answered. "But the Washington area has more Mormons than anywhere else east of the Mississippi, so I'm not lonely that way."

"Mom tells us you've been proselytizing for the Church in suburban Washington," Rachel said.

"'Every member a missionary,'" Susan replied with a smile.

"How about down in the District of Columbia?" Rachel asked.

"That isn't my calling. And it's not a safe place for a mother of five."

"No, I guess not," Joshua agreed. "Do you remember what BYU was like in 1970, Susan? Before President Kimball announced his revelation that black men can become priests."

"That year, I was a senior," Susan recalled, "studying Child Development and Family Relations."

"Like half the women students," Rachel said.

"And you'd tease me about planning my life up to the names of my first four children."

"Well, you didn't deny it," Joshua said. "That year, on the Provo campus, of the 25,000 students, *fifteen* were black."

Rachel shrugged. "What else would you expect? Ninety-nine percent of the faculty must've been Mormon, and 97 percent of the students."

"Don't you remember it, Susan?" Joshua asked. "At every major athletic event away from home, demonstrations were held against racism, and us. At Colorado State, eggs were thrown, and molotov cocktails that didn't explode. Stanford severed all relations with BYU, and nine people were arrested at the University of Arizona. A riot broke out at the University of Wyoming, after black athletes were dismissed for wearing black armbands protesting the presence of Brigham Young University. The *Deseret News* editorialized that these protests showed 'what can happen when you are granting minority groups special concessions.'"

"I always felt comforted by 2 Nephi 26:33," Susan said. "'He denieth none that come unto him, black and white.'"

"Maybe it comforted you," Rachel argued, "but we still deemed black men unworthy to become priests."

"Of course, that's all in the past," Susan said.

Restlessly, Joshua stood up again. "Yes. Blacks are welcome in the Church, but not homosexuals like me. Consider, if you will, the nature of sin. Believing as we do in free agency, sin can arise only from choice. And what madman would *choose* to be a queer Mormon!"

"If it isn't a choice, where does it *come* from?" Susan asked.

"Personally, I like the story in Plato's *Symposium*."

"What story?"

"Eons ago," Joshua began, "in the primitive, uncorrupted world, each human soul had two halves. Some of these souls were male-female, while others were male-male, or female-female. But these humans grew wicked, and the gods punished them by severing them into two. And so, forever after, each half has been doomed to seek its other half to be complete. A nice story, isn't it, Susan? And not so different from our belief that pre-existing spirits wistfully await tabernacles of flesh."

Rachel smiled at the story. "It could actually be partly true. Ultrasound tests reveal that far more twins are conceived than born alive. And for months, the surviving twin is steeped in hormonal soup. If so, then it's nature, not a crime against it."

Joshua turned to his older sister. "I know what you're thinking, Susan, and what you'd say out loud if you didn't love me so much. 'Resist temptation and Satan will flee from you.' That it's just a cross to bear, no weightier than crosses borne with less noise by better Saints.

"Well, perhaps. But when Joseph Smith discovered his own polygamous nature, could he *not* have wondered if it was sin? Through prayer and revelation, he came to understand that what had been forbidden must be sanctified. There must be no sex between persons except in a proper marriage relationship. *This is positively prohibited by our Creator in all places, at all times, and we reaffirm it.*"

"Yes, without proper marriage," Susan said, "disease runs rampant, and prostitution and despair."

"Fine then, let us marry," Joshua agreed, "and not just legally, in some dreary courthouse. As Utah said about statehood during the Civil War, 'We show our loyalty by trying to get in while others are trying to get out.'

"By all rights, Utah should be the *first* state in the nation to sanctify same-sex marriage. Instead, we're the first to specifically *deny* recognition if such marriages are ever legal in another state. And Mormons are busily lobbying for laws like ours in other states."

"Even if properly married, transsexuals are treated even more harshly by the Church," Rachel said. "Transsexuals and doctors who perform sex change surgery face mandatory and immediate excommunication."

Joshua stood with his back against the window. "Excommunication! Can you imagine what that means to me, Susan? Some ancient, distant relative who lived and died in Denmark, never having even *heard* of Joseph Smith, but captured in our genealogy and posthumously baptized in the Temple, has better odds of salvation than I do. All the signers of the Declaration of Independence, all the Presidents but a few who were our enemies, all of them were baptized after death into the Church. While the name of Joshua Bailey is stricken from the records. I have to go in to see Dad!"

"Joshua, he's in intensive care," Rachel said. "We can't disturb him."

Joshua sighed deeply and sat down. "Do you remember the first time you were baptized for one of our ancestors? I do. 'For and on behalf of Isak Erickson, who is dead.'"

"I remember that," Susan recalled. "His name was discovered in a dusty basement in Denmark in a barely legible baptismal record. When we found Isak, we learned where other ancestors might be. I was immersed for some of the women."

"Did you ever read Grandpa Anders' missionary journal from Tahiti?" Joshua asked.

"It was many years ago," Susan said.

"I'll show it to you, if you'd like. Anders wrote about meeting Gauguin."

"What did he say?"

"Gauguin told Anders an ancient legend of a god-man visible in the rugged rock of a dreaded, sacred mountain."

Joshua struggled to recall the words. "'A soft clinging woman touched the hair of the god and implored, 'Let man rise up again after he has died...'

"'The angry but not cruel lips of the god opened to reply. 'Man shall die.'"

Joshua smiled. "It makes the hair on the back of your neck stand up, doesn't it?"

"No wonder the Polynesians took to Christianity so well," Rachel said.

"Anders also wrote about the earliest missionaries in Tahiti, who would tattoo signs of infamy into the cheeks of fallen women. Not their sin, but the blazon of judgment they wore, brought them shame."

"Our missionaries?" Susan asked.

"No, not ours," Joshua replied.

Rachel shook her head. "And it's some other 'Christian' ministers, not ours, who'd gladly brand Joshua, too. To them, AIDS isn't a disease, but a proper scourge."

"Before the new drugs, I suspected that, myself," Joshua sighed. "The disease seemed none other than the buffetings of Satan, or the chastening rod of the Lord. In that mirror I smashed, I'd seen my ravaged body as the book of my life, where God could read my obedience and disobedience in every thought, word and deed. On the darkest nights, I was afraid that we're wrong about our Heavenly Father being friendly, an

486

exalted man. God seemed Calvinistically and unpredictably stern, as our Puritan and Pietistic forebears never doubted."

"Grandpa Anders certainly traveled far from his ascetic childhood," Susan said.

"Do you remember that old piggybank Dad gave me for Christmas when I was three?" Joshua asked.

"That pink, ceramic piggybank?" Rachel said. "It stood in front of the fireplace for years."

"It was almost as big as you were then," Susan smiled. "You could only carry it with both your arms wrapped tight around its belly."

"Dad labeled it in black letters, *MY MISSION*, and I'd drop in it all the nickels and dimes that you girls and our relatives and friends would give me. I anticipated my mission with such joy."

"How do you feel about it now?" Rachel asked.

Joshua thought before he spoke. "I remember those years with the fondness of youth and unquestioned faith. Before I left for the Language Training Mission in Provo, the patriarch laid his hands on my head and spoke his blessing. 'Your life mission will be to build Zion,' he said, 'for as long as you stay faithful to the gospel of our Lord.' Then he reminded me, 'The gospel is to save, not to condemn men.'"

"I remember that haircut they gave you," Rachel said. "It was so *short*."

Joshua laughed at the memory of it. "Every morning, we'd get up at 5:45, then spend seven hours in classroom lessons, five hours in memorization, and an hour in physical exercise. With meals, inspirational films and proclamations of our faith, we were kept constantly busy. After six weeks, I could say in fluent Portuguese, 'Our Church leaders are all good, honest men who perform their responsibilities in the Church as representatives of the Prophet and the Apostles, providing necessary assistance to each individual member. Because they represent God's Prophet, it is necessary that we listen to their advice and follow it. I testify that your happiness depends on the extent to which you follow their direction.' I bet I could still say it in Portuguese."

Rachel and Susan smiled at their brother.

"Then they assigned me my missionary companion, and counseled us to never separate from one another. We were told story after story of missionaries who left their companions for mere minutes, and came back to find them either fornicating or dead. Then I was told to tell him that I loved him. I found that easier than most."

"And you didn't suspect why?" Rachel asked.

"No," Joshua said. "As we flew on that airplane to Sao Paulo, both of us were so excited. Like fighting a war, serving in a foreign mission is a grave responsibility of manhood. The mission president greeted us warmly when we landed. 'Do you fully understand the Church teachings on blacks?' he asked each of us intently. Remember, this was 1971.

"'Of course,' I replied. I was proud that I'd memorized the words of President Joseph Fielding Smith. 'There were no neutrals in the war in heaven. All took sides with either Christ or with Satan. Every man had his agency there, and men receive rewards here based upon their actions there, just as they will receive rewards hereafter for deeds done in the body. The Negro, evidently, is receiving the rewards he merits.'

"'Good!' the mission president exclaimed, clapping me on the shoulder. 'We've been successful here among the German community, who'll like you both well, I have no doubt. You might tell them about your Nordic ancestors, Joshua, as if they couldn't see it in your features. And the Portuguese Catholics will sometimes listen. But identification is the real problem here. Brazil abolished slavery only in 1888, and tens of millions of people, about 30 percent of the population, are some combination of white, Indian and black.'"

Joshua stood up and glanced toward his father's room. He got a drink of water from the fountain.

"I'd never known anyone of African descent before, but in my years in Brazil, I met hundreds. And many of them would've otherwise been outstanding Mormons. My companion and I carried the *Book of Mormon* in English, German and Portuguese translations, and we engaged in zealous competition with other missionaries, both our own and other Christians. I'd often

488

receive hunches and whisperings about who might be a willing convert, or what might inspire a reluctant one. I felt that God was watching over me and helping me know what I should do, even in minor decisions.

"Not long after I arrived, I felt honored when I was introduced to one of the 56 General Authorities. He was traveling among our missions in South America, and he reminded me again not to baptize blacks. But I wasn't prepared for all that meant.

"The following week, I was sitting in church among the congregation, all European and Indian. A handsome boy of 14, with green eyes and light brown hair, arose to be ordained as a deacon. The branch president enthusiastically recommended the boy for the Aaronic priesthood, praising his earnestness for the Church in spite of his family's aloofness. I watched, as I had many times, recalling my own pride at earning that rank and responsibility. The branch president asked the congregation to show our approval, and the boy beamed in delight from the front of the church when we raised our right hands. Then the obligatory question was asked about negative votes. Three American missionaries, including my companion, stood up as one. The congregation gasped, and so did I."

"I've never seen a boy rejected," Susan said.

"Nor had I," said Joshua sadly. "You see, his brothers had appeared somewhat Negroid to the American missionaries who'd visited their home. The boy was devastated. He could still be a Mormon, but no one tainted by black lineage could become a priest.

"I soon learned that identifying racial background was a large part of my missionary calling. As we proselytized, we had to take note of the precise shade of the person's skin, hair and eyes, the shape of his nose and texture of his hair, and the color lines on his hands and feet. If we discovered Negroid features, we'd invent some excuse to walk away. But people frequently look different from their families. So when we visited a man or woman at home, we had to ask them for family photos. With genealogy as a pretext, we'd probe discreetly into their racial history, using a 12-page booklet we were given as a guide."

"How'd that make you *feel*?" Rachel asked.

"Like a Nazi," Joshua sighed. "And this was before I ever imagined that I was tainted more darkly than they. When we'd unearth evidence of black lineage, we'd haltingly explain what our prophets said. If they still wanted to be baptized, their membership records were marked."

"Was the Temple in Sao Paulo finished by then?" Susan asked.

"No, and I was grateful we didn't have to explain that blacks couldn't enter it to baptize their ancestors. Don't get me wrong, I loved my mission and Brazil. Once, on a Sao Paulo street, I even cast a demon out of a girl. I wish you'd had that opportunity, both of you."

Rachel looked at her brother in silence.

"By age 20," Joshua said, "I'd experienced more of the world, and more intimately, than all but a fraction of men ever get to know in a lifetime. Throughout six continents, a million Latter-day Saints have gained that depth and diversity and cross-pollinated knowledge. Even if a man goes home to a village, he doesn't return to precisely what he'd been. I felt that in myself as I stepped off the airplane in Salt Lake City. The parochial was tempered with the cosmopolitan, and I was ready for ever-expanding responsibility. I could feel Dad's admiration as he shook my hand at the airport.

"But within a few months, all of that confidence crumbled. Suddenly, I was like a baptized Brazilian Mormon who dutifully researches his genealogy and exhumes evidence of African blood. Should he confess it and become scarcely tolerated in the Church he loves, no more eligible than a woman to hold the priesthood? Or should he stay in the closet and pray that no one ever finds out?"

"You could've chosen to stay faithful to Trudy," Susan said.

Joshua smiled with resignation. "For me, the only choice was how long I'd live a lie. I might've risen to the ranks of the General Authorities of the Church. I might've been not only President, but Prophet, Seer and Revelator! And why not? I'm a fifth-generation Latter-day Saint, and a true believer in the gospel. Deacon at 12, preacher at 14, priest at 16, elder and missionary at 18, Sunday-school teacher at 21, second counselor on my ward bishopric at 27, stake high councilman at 32. Sealed to my wife in the Temple. An honors graduate of Brigham Young University, a prosperous architect and businessman. A loving father of three, and faithful husband of two. It's my one and tragic flaw."

"I wish you'd introduced me to him," Rachel said.

Susan nodded and asked, "Was he Mormon?"

"Yes," Joshua replied. "Unlike Rachel, I don't think I could ever really love someone who isn't. His name was Adam, and of course, he didn't know he was sick. His recent test had come back negative."

"How'd you meet him?" Susan asked.

"Adam was a carpenter on a project of mine. Just another of our clean-cut young men, I supposed, hardworking, upright and honest. But when I praised his fine finish work, I had to struggle even harder to avoid his eyes."

"Why?"

"You know how uncommon it is for Mormon men to be unmarried in their thirties. And Adam would tell unusual jokes."

"Like what?" Rachel asked.

"Like how Utah is the beehive state," Joshua smiled, "while most states don't even *have* an official hairdo. When he named his dogs Urim and Thummin, after Joseph Smith's seer stones, I began to suspect some weakness of faith. First in Adam, then in me.

"I suspected, but I didn't succumb. I worked and prayed, went to church, spent time with my family, and tithed. But one day, I neglected to avoid his eyes. And though not a single word was spoken, Adam witnessed the truth. That night, when I prayed on my knees, I heard no whisperings but only the beating of my living heart. So I redoubled my efforts to deny what I knew. Trudy noticed the change in me, but she said nothing, not even after I stopped making love to her."

491

"Why did you stop?" Susan asked.

"Because it felt like fornication."

Joshua stared toward the door of his father's hospital room. "Is it time for us to go in yet?" he asked Rachel.

"No," she answered.

"I was desperate to talk to someone," Joshua said. "I couldn't go to the Bishop, confessing my desires and seeking his counsel in overcoming them. His reproachful words, full of pity, would lay waste to all my years of good works. In all the world, I could turn to just one person. Do you remember what you said to me, Rachel?"

Rachel nodded. "I asked you why you couldn't just be friends with Adam. After all, no one ever died from lack of sex. Your answer surprised us both."

"What did you say?" Susan asked.

Joshua took a deep breath. "I said, 'Because sanctified, passionate sexual union is the closest a human being can come to another in this lifetime.' I knew I must go forward with free and open eyes, and never let myself be seduced again as I'd been seduced in the hotel.

"One day, about a year after I met Adam, I had to go to St. George to inspect one of my construction projects. It was raining hard in Salt Lake City that morning, and the crews here couldn't work. So I asked Adam to come along with me. We weren't in any hurry, so I drove down the back roads through the desert, not the freeway full of noisy trucks. We turned west at Cedar City, then south again, until we passed the sign for the memorial at Mountain Meadows. I asked Adam if he'd ever seen it, and he hadn't.

"A light rain was falling as we drove into the empty parking lot. We walked up the winding pathway with its pink granite walls, where the names of the massacred are carved. The chains on the flagpoles clanged in the wind where the firing squad once stood. As Adam looked out across the peaceful pastureland, I took his hand, then I kissed him."

"Were you afraid?" Susan asked.

"I wasn't afraid, because I knew the present wrongness of

my life. We walked back to my car, with its bumper sticker that read, 'Happiness is Family Home Evening.' We inspected that building in St. George, then went on to the lodge at Zion National Park. As I drove, I felt an eerie certainty that some event of enduring meaning had occurred nearby."

"What kind of event?" Rachel asked.

Joshua shook his head. "Some accidental pact of history that's diminished to a ripple but lives on. I don't imagine I'll ever learn what it was."

Joshua looked at Rachel, then at Susan. "By the time we reached the lodge, the sky in Zion Canyon was dark. I could feel my hands trembling as I registered under a false name. Adam quietly offered me a final chance to turn back. Then in a room beneath the towering cliffs, we made love, and I knew beyond knowing that this was what was meant for me.

*Blessed be the name of God, for because of my transgression my eyes are opened, and in this life I shall have joy, and again in the flesh I shall see God.*

"'You aren't wearing your garments,' I teased Adam in the morning. 'Don't you feel vulnerable and unprotected?'

"'Have you forgotten what freedom feels like?' he asked me.

"'Yes,' I whispered, 'what does it feel like?'

"'Like this.' Adam took my hand in his and ran it slowly across his muscular, nude body. 'I tossed my garments aside the night I got baptized as a son of Perdition,' he said. 'Besides, they were ripped in the process.'

"Oh, stop squirming, Susan. I'm not going to tell you what gay boys do with one another."

Relieved, Susan smiled, despite herself.

"You can tell me," Rachel offered. "I'm a doctor."

"I'd rather tell you about Adam."

"Did he come from Utah?" Susan asked.

"Adam came from Arizona," Joshua said, "and his parents, like ours, insisted he go to BYU. But instead of Provo, he talked them into sending him to the Laie campus in Hawaii. Dutifully, he studied engineering, and surfing, and got a job at the Polynesian Cultural Center next door to campus. That's where

Adam learned to work with wood, building sets, since his skin was too fair to convince the tourists that he was Polynesian. The Polynesian Cultural Center, he told me, draws more tourists than anything else in Hawaii."

"I know the Church owns it," Rachel said. "But how did it get started?"

"I asked Adam that, too," Joshua said. "In 1919, the Temple on Oahu was finished and Laie became the gathering place for Mormons from all the Islands--Hawaii, Tonga, Samoa, Fiji, Tahiti, and the Tuamotus. On Saturdays, they'd meet to trade crafts and sell food, swap stories and perform dances, which varied from island to island. Tourists came from Honolulu to watch, and over time, the Church organized the programs and charged admission. It's all because our missionaries let people dance. God, could Adam dance a wicked hula!

"After two years in Hawaii, Adam took his Endowments in the Laie Temple and set off on his mission to England. He stayed his two years, but whatever happened there, he wouldn't tell me, and he refused to return to BYU."

"Did he leave the Church?" Susan asked.

"No," Joshua said. "Adam never ventured very far from his roots as a Latter-day Saint. To him, the Church was like the epicenter of some earthquake, where all intensity is measured in reference to it."

"Like what?" Rachel asked.

"Adam would wear a white shirt, a necktie and his nameplate as an Elder, and march along with his bicycle in the West Coast gay parades. Our cosmology is so peculiar, he used to say, that it leaves Mormons with little appetite for oddness anywhere else in our lives. But Adam wouldn't let his oddness be crowded out."

Joshua smiled weakly at the memories. "One Halloween, he dressed from head to toe in gold and looked for all the world as if the Angel Moroni had just stepped off the spire of the Temple and into the Salt Lake City night. As thoroughly as he was anything else, Adam was a product of our culture. He used to laugh that, if he couldn't go to Heaven, at least no one ever told him not to dance.

"Years ago, on a business trip to New York, Adam brought me to a dance club called, of all things, the Saint. I was gripped by the sensuous feel of the place as soon as we walked through the door. The ceiling was majestic, high as a cathedral, hung with theatrical, pulsating lights. The floor was crowded with handsome men, graceful and athletic, some sweating as they danced to the powerful, virile beat. Adam and I loved to dance, and I loved to watch him as he danced. Yet the scene felt palpably dreary to me, and made me sad."

"Why?" Rachel asked.

"I didn't understand it at first," Joshua said. "But then, as I watched through the noise and strobing lights, I started to recognize why. I was a man who had money and power, and all around us, men like me were appraising men like Adam as if their bodies were their greatest worth. As I soberly watched the scene, I knew that I, for better or for worse, would gratefully have shared all I ever owned with Adam. And then I noticed something else just as disturbing. Unless they were very rich, the aging men were swept aside like refuse. And I thought to myself, this isn't a community that a man would want to grow old in. Could that be why so many of us never will?"

Joshua paused, then stood up. "Do you think Dad might be awake?" he asked Rachel.

"Susan can see him in a little while," Rachel answered.

"Can I?"

"Joshua, it might not be wise for you to go in there."

"I've got to see him, Rachel, before one of us dies."

"We'll see how he is," she promised.

Joshua sat down again.

"Did Adam go to church?" Susan asked.

"Only rarely," Joshua said, "and only to listen to the hymns. Adam would say that he should hear them while he could, for if Brigham Young was right, 'There is no music in Hell.' One Sunday, Adam slipped into the back of the church, while I sat in front with Trudy and the kids. Without turning around, I felt the fullness and the warmth of his presence. But in the back of my mind, I no longer knew what God expected from a man."

Susan took Joshua's hand. "How did the Church find out?" she asked.

"Adam and I kept it as quiet as we could for two years," Joshua said. "But people like to talk, and I was well-known in our community. Word leaked out, then a picture of us appeared in the Utah gay press. I guess Mother didn't send you a clipping."

"No," Susan smiled.

"Soon, the Bishop called me in to inquire whether or not it was true. As I faced him across his desk, I felt dozens of warring emotions. At last, I could confess it in words, but I couldn't begin to repent. I felt as sealed to Adam as I'd ever felt sealed to my wife.

"Grasping at any straw I could, I answered the Bishop, 'Our first parents in the Garden of Eden were commanded, 'But of the tree of the knowledge of good and evil, thou shalt not eat of it, nevertheless, thou mayest choose for thyself.' Like theirs, my act is nothing worse than a transgression, since 'it is not always a sin to transgress a law.'

"Then the Bishop summarily withdrew my Temple Recommend. I angrily tore the card in two and handed the pieces to him."

"Were you surprised?" Susan asked.

"Of course, I wasn't surprised," Joshua said. "From age eight, I'd known the price of an unpardonable sin. I'm willing to roll the dice in the hereafter, but whatever the cost, I've always tried to live my faith. I'd paid my tithing to the Church every year, 10 percent of my income, year after year after year. Then a wholly new emotion set in, a cynicism I'd never felt before. After all, after taxes, tithing cost me only 7 percent."

"Did you think about voluntarily leaving the Church?" Rachel asked.

Joshua shook his head. "The answer is so simple, yet bound so inextricably with what I am. I liked being a Mormon.

"Late one evening, a week after I met with the Bishop, two somber Elders appeared at my home. When I saw the official-looking envelope they brought, I was grateful that Trudy and the children were at a meeting. With trembling hands, I opened the letter, then read the cold words of a summons. 'For investigation of conduct in violation of the law and order of the Church.' I was told to present myself for trial in three days.

"I was distraught, of course, but that faded into nothingness the next day, when I found a purple spot on Adam's leg. The lesion wasn't there a few days earlier.

"Adam once vowed to me that I'd be his last lover, and he was true to his word. He'd finally caught up with Joseph Smith, he said, and what man deserved to have any more lovers than the Prophet?"

"Why wasn't Adam summoned to Church court, too?" Susan asked.

"Formal excommunication isn't mandatory for all homosexuals," Joshua explained. "Church policemen, after all, don't peer into windows at night, like the Government once did to find polygamists. But an ecclesiastical court becomes mandatory when a transgression becomes widely known. And thanks to that picture, it was known. Even without that, I held high enough rank in the priesthood to capture the attention of the Church.

"I don't suppose either one of you has been to Church court. I'd been there only once, myself, on the other side of judgment, to excommunicate a man for repeated cruelty to his wife and his son."

"Did Adam or Trudy ask to come with you?" Rachel said.

"Both of them," Joshua replied. "But as in some ceremonial drama, I knew I had to face it alone. It wasn't a simple Bishop's court. As a member of the Melchizedek priesthood, I was summoned to appear in front of the Stake President and twelve High Councilmen. All of them were men I knew well.

"The Stake President read the charges, then he reminded me, 'It is the Church member, not the Church that is on trial.' The ward clerk took down every word.

"With more honesty than defiance, I pled guilty.

"'Can you give it up?' the Stake President asked me with

pity in his eyes.

"'I *can* give it up, but *will* not.'

"'Elder Bailey, will you give it up?'

"I looked him in the eyes, with tears in my own and whispered, 'No, never. *No*, never. *No, never.*'

"Mine wasn't a difficult case. They didn't ask me to explain, so there was little to be said. The Stake President gave his verdict, then called on the Councilmen to sanction it by their vote. Among the twelve men, there were no dissenting votes.

"The notice of my excommunication came the next week in a letter delivered by the same two solemn Elders. I expected some virulent and damning denunciation, but the words were modest and somber, 'the Court's obligation to protect the Church.'"

"How did you *feel*?" Susan asked.

"I felt nothing but numbness," Joshua said. "After they left, I ceremoniously stripped off my clothes, then stepped out of my garments. I had no right to wear them anymore. I stood naked, paralyzed with uncertainty about what I should do with the garments. Part of me wanted to mail them, still warm, back to the General Authorities. Part of me wanted to toss them in the trash. But I was too disciplined, or superstitious. By the time I decided what to do, it was the longest I'd spent naked since I was 18 years old. I properly cut out the stitched images of the compass, square and rule from the breasts, navel and knee, then ritually burned the symbols in the fireplace. My clothes felt oddly unfitting when I put them back on."

"What did Trudy say?" Rachel asked.

"Her strength astonishes me," Joshua said. "That night, I apologized to Trudy and the children for all the pain I'd caused them. Then I told her about Adam's lesion. She knew what that meant, and she cried. Then I asked Trudy if she wanted to cancel our sealing in the Temple. She didn't hesitate before she said, 'No.' A divorce for all Eternity is a complex procedure, and only the President of the Church has the authority to grant it.

"Then Trudy looked at me and asked, 'Have you been tested for the virus?'

"I shook my head, unable to tell her that I couldn't face the truth the test wouldn't let me deny. I said only, 'I'm thankful I haven't spread it to you.'

"'What about anyone else?' she asked softly.

"Finally, something exploded in my brain. I cried out, 'I don't smoke or drink, Trudy, nor do I screw boys in bathhouses!'

"Trudy asked me to stay, but I moved into a tiny apartment with Adam. I didn't want to come between my family and their Church. I tried to ask Dad about the doctrine, but he wouldn't come to the phone, so I looked it up myself. If either spouse commits serious sin and does not repent, the worthy spouse and children will be given to another person in Celestial glory."

"Did Adam live long?" Susan asked gently.

"He suffered terribly, but not for long," Joshua said. "Six months after we found the purple lesion, Adam suffocated to death in the hospital, gasping for breath behind an oxygen mask. I sat by his bed, stroking his still warm hand and cheek. I felt so speechless at Adam's funeral in the Gentile cemetery. Afterward, liquor would've loosened our tongues, but I couldn't bring myself to hold a wake. I still can't believe that he's gone."

Joshua choked back the tears. "I was healthy then, but I was severed and not entitled to participate in the Church. An excommunicate isn't banished or persecuted, you know, or even actively avoided. The Church treats us kindly and prayerfully, in hopes that we may turn from our mistake and be rebaptized. But they wouldn't even accept my offerings or tithes. All my life, the Church was so demanding, that when it demanded from me precisely *nothing*, my life imploded toward nothingness. *By the rivers of Babylon, we sat down and wept, we wept when we remembered Zion.*

"When the Church sent back my tithe, I gave the money instead to the Log Cabin Club, a conservative gay group named for Lincoln. Adam was still alive then, in the hospital, and he teased me, calling it the Uncle Tom's Cabin Club. But when the Republican candidate refused the Log Cabin donation, I had to wonder if Adam was right. Until then, I'd never questioned that *my* values coincided with the official morality of our nation. I only wanted to sidestep one rule, not open the floodgates of immorality. But soon, that official morality seemed like a weapon, wielded by the powerful to justify and expand their authority. I saw it when I was excommunicated as a scout master, too, though I would die before I'd touch a boy."

Rachel looked at her brother, then at her watch. She nodded to Susan.

"You can go in to see Dad," Rachel said. "But only stay ten minutes."

"Can I go with Susan?" Joshua asked.

"We can't risk disturbing him," Rachel said. "Besides, only two visitors are allowed at a time, and Mom won't leave his side for a moment."

"When Susan comes out, then?"

"What do you *want* from him, Joshua?"

Joshua hesitated. "I want his blessing."

Rachel spoke gently, "I don't believe he can give you that."

"When you go in, will you ask Dad if he'll see me?"

"I'll ask."

Joshua and Rachel watched their sister walk down the hall and go into their father's hospital room.

"Do you remember, Rachel, how you asked me to pray with you the first time you questioned your faith? It was April 1969, and you must've been all of fifteen."

Rachel nodded. "Already, I passionately wanted to be a doctor, but President McKay had just proclaimed, 'Where husband and wife enjoy health and vigor and are free from impurities that would be entailed upon their posterity, it is contrary to the teachings of the Church artificially to curtail or prevent the birth of children.'"

"Your voice was shaky when you asked me, 'Can you imagine trying to be a doctor if you must bear a child every time you're called to it?'"

"Yes," Rachel recalled. "And you reminded me that President McKay was Prophet, Seer and Revelator, and that I should follow counsel."

500

Joshua smiled apologetically at Rachel. "Then eight years later, you came to me again and showed me something hidden in your hands. The way you hid it, I thought it had to be some vile pornography. I was surprised to see nothing worse than a button that read *Mormons For ERA*."

"Ah, the Equal Rights Amendment," Rachel sighed. "Mom had just been elected an alternate delegate to the International Women's Year Conference in Houston. I was so proud of her until I learned how it happened."

"How *did* it happen? It was a long time ago."

Rachel stretched her legs out from the chair. "The Church organized the Women's Relief Society to spread the word by telephone that they should go to the Utah state meeting, where delegates would be elected to go to Houston. The next week, 13,000 women packed the Utah meeting."

"Yes, Mother said she just talked to a few of her friends."

"The ladies were instructed how to vote on the issues," Rachel said. "Of the Utah delegation, all but one were Mormon, all but one were Republican, all but one were over 40. All of them voted against endorsing the ERA. I was so disappointed. Then later, I was shocked when we sat in front of the television set, watching the Senate Subcommittee testimony about it."

"What was the name of that woman again?" Joshua asked.

"Sonia Johnson," Rachel said. "She was a married Mormon mother of four, who'd served in missions in Samoa and Korea, lived in Africa with her family, and earned a Ph.D. But you and I listened as our Senator Orrin Hatch, a former Bishop, reproached her in his priesthood voice. You said, 'The General Authorities call such women 'Pied Pipers of sin who have led women away from the divine role of womanhood down the pathway of error.'"

"Yes," Joshua recalled. "And you said, 'If the Church enters politics, it deserves to be treated like any other political entity.'"

Rachel smiled fondly at her brother. "Two years later, Sonia Johnson was facing a court of excommunication. Unlike *you*, she offered to repent, saying she only sought the ERA, not the priesthood for women. But at her trial, her Bishop cut off the testimony after an hour and a half. Then he excommunicated her."

"Ninety minutes to obliterate a lifetime of commitment! Did she appeal the Bishop's ruling?"

"Yes, but the High Council denied her appeal. Then the First Presidency ruled that no further action was needed."

Joshua looked toward the hospital room door. "I was astonished when you whispered that you'd joined a group seeking priesthood-holder status for women."

"Why were you so surprised?" Rachel asked.

"Well, my old professor, Cleon Skousen, always said, 'The reason we have priesthood only for men is the division of labor that exists to make men equal with women. Men need to have this leadership capability in order to balance their existing inequality with women who have historically determined the development of society because of their influence over children.'"

Rachel shook her head and sighed. "I *tried* to explain to you how some of the young women from the Mutual Improvement Association were beginning to talk openly about the General Authorities' treatment of women. But when someone reported our gatherings to the Authorities, they terminated the sessions at once."

"I believe I replied, 'When the Prophet speaks, the debate is over.' And you retorted, 'Patriarchy *isn't* central to the gospel.'"

"Yes," Rachel smiled, "and you said, 'Apostasy lies under your use of the word *patriarchy*, itself.' So I asked, 'Are only men to have revelations from God?'"

Joshua laughed at the intensity of youth. "I counseled you against taking this path, but I always kept your secret. By then, I felt powerless to do anything else. I couldn't even cast out my own demons."

Rachel looked up at the sound of footsteps clicking across the vinyl floor. She watched a man and woman walk through the waiting area and go into a room down the hall.

"When you asked me to reconsider, I answered you by quoting Joseph Smith. 'He who waits to be commanded in all

502

things is a slothful servant.'"

"I thought of you at the next April Conference," Joshua said. "As I was walking across Temple Square, I heard the buzz of a small airplane flying overhead. I looked up and was surprised to see the banner it towed, MOTHER IN HEAVEN SUPPORTS THE ERA. But I was late so I hurried into the Tabernacle. Inside, one of the Apostles was intoning, "Our onward course will not be easy. The Way ahead will be blocked by landslides of lasciviousness; an avalanche of evil will bury the trail. Liars and thieves and adulterers and homosexuals and murderers scarcely seek to hide their abominations from our view.'"

Rachel smiled sympathetically at her brother. "I knew I had a problem the first time I heard what women swore in our Endowments. 'You and each of you solemnly covenant and promise before God, angels and these witnesses at this altar that you will each observe and keep the law of your husband, and abide by his council in righteousness.'"

"I guess you weren't the only woman to choke on that vow," Joshua said. "It was changed a few years back."

Rachel tried to explain. "By the time of my Endowments, I hoped to be a doctor, specializing in premature infants. And I knew that women *used to have* authority to heal by laying hands on the sick and anointing with oil. But by 1946, that authority was reserved for Elders of the Church. Boys as young as age 18 can lay hands on the sick, but not women, regardless of their skills. Women don't even have the right to bless babies they've borne from their bodies!"

Abruptly, Joshua stood up. "Come on, Rachel, let's commit a transgression. Surely we can find some consecrated oil around here. Then you pour a few drops on the crown of my head and anoint me to heal this disease. How about it, Rachel? Even doctors are free to believe in the not-yet-understood healing powers of the mind. And no one else would do it for me."

Rachel glanced around the waiting area to make sure that the man and woman had not returned. "I don't think so, Joshua," she stammered.

"Susan tells me I look so much better," Joshua said. "But

still, I don't feel strong, and some days, the nausea can be awful. And no one knows how long these drugs will keep working. I'll talk you through it. 'In the name of Jesus Christ and by authority of the priesthood…'"

Rachel looked at her brother and said nothing.

"Ah, Rachel, have I called your bluff? About women laying on hands, didn't Joseph Smith say, 'There could be no evil in it if God gave his sanction by healing'? But even though you think it's voodoo, you're superstitious enough not to challenge the Church."

"I'm sorry, Joshua," Rachel said. She could think of nothing else to say.

Joshua sighed and sat down again. "So you rebelled like Great-grandmother Molly, and like her, you married a Gentile. Everyone knew it when they read the newspaper announcement, 'Marriage to be performed in the home of the parents of the bride.' I stood in my tuxedo next to Dad and watched you nearly choke on the words, 'Until death do us part.'"

Though no one else was in the room, Rachel spoke in a whisper. "No matter how many babies a woman raises from the dead, she has no access to God but through men. And she can earn no higher glory in Heaven than her husband!"

Joshua, too, lowered his voice. "You're more apostate than I'll *ever* be, Rachel. You think the priesthood has become the chief idol of the Church, demanding your allegiance above Christ himself. But they don't bother purging private heresies like yours, and you haven't asked the Church to remove your name. You're a neonatal specialist, known and respected throughout Utah, the state with the highest birthrate in the nation. It wouldn't do to have it known that the lives of Mormon babies are lying in the hands of an apostate."

Rachel shrugged. "Rob and I like living here in Salt Lake City."

"Yes, the medical center is excellent," Joshua said, "and so is the skiing in the mountains. But when I saw Rob last week, he whispered that you've stopped giving money to BYU. He said you were protesting their written policy that expels and permanently bars Mormon students who join other faiths."

Susan opened the door and stepped out of their father's hospital room. Rachel and Joshua left their chairs and went to meet her in the hallway.

"How is he?" Joshua asked.

"As well as can be expected, I suppose. The drugs have left him exhausted, and he didn't speak. But still, he seems strong."

Joshua watched as Rachel opened the door.

"I'll ask him," she said.

Susan and Joshua went back to the waiting room. He could feel himself growing tired, but Susan still looked fresh.

"Tell me, Susan," he asked, "do you miss the Daughters of the Utah Pioneers out there in Washington? I think of you when I pass all their monuments and markers, or read the *Deseret News* about some relic they've acquired for the Church Museum."

"I miss them," Susan said, "but I stay busy."

"Is it ever a struggle to be the perfect Mother-of-Zion? The five kids always studious and neatly groomed, the husband cheerful as he heads off to work. The cookies baked, the house immaculate, the meetings always attended with high spirits. I remember when you'd shine my shoes to help me get ready for my priesthood meetings."

"Well," Susan smiled, "my daughter doesn't do that for her brothers."

Joshua thought back to those days. "When I was a boy, I read Dad's old G-Men novels. The heroes were so manly and brave. The crusading anger of J. Edgar Hoover seemed to me like the righteous wrath of the prophets as they thundered out against Babylon and Gomorrah."

"I liked to watch those old FBI movies, too," Susan said.

"Do you think Hoover and Tolson were lovers?" Joshua asked. "They were together for over forty years."

"Joshua!" Susan protested. "Of course not."

"J. Edgar took hundreds of photographs of Clyde, pictures that were supposed to be destroyed at his death, yet they survived."

"Do they show anything improper?"

"Nothing more than affection," Joshua replied. "Hoover took the pictures at their vacation resorts or while Tolson was asleep. Other photos showed them together, both in bathrobes or bare-chested at the beach, though never touching. But they ate lunch and dinner together every day, and the morning Hoover died, his servants called Tolson first."

"Well, it can't be," Susan said.

Joshua sighed. "I wish Adam and I could've lived unabashedly like that. Whether Hoover was a *poufter* is beside the point. I could be intimate friends with a man for forty years and resist the temptation to touch him lewdly. Not that I wouldn't want to! But even that evidence of sainthood doesn't advance *us* toward Celestial glory. No, we must marry and procreate."

"And you have, Joshua. Two boys and a girl. You can't wish you hadn't given them life."

"No, of course not," Joshua said. "'Even as the infant son of an earthly father and mother is capable in due time of becoming a man, so the undeveloped offspring of celestial parentage is capable, by experience through ages and aeons, of evolving into a God…' Ah, Susan, what could be a more Romantic quest?"

"Romantic?" she asked.

"The Romantic Era of the 1800s," Joshua said. "Our roots are firmly in it, and the romance lives on to this day. A secret brotherhood of worthy men, tested by adventures in far-off lands. Battles unto death against conspiracies of evil that vainly seek to hold us back. Miracles and revelations and the magic of human struggles to bring about the Kingdom of God! Love sealed to endure beyond the grave."

Susan smiled at the whimsy of her brother.

"Forward-looking romance is fresh and daring, a zealous quest for imaginative new realities. But when romance looks backward, it grows decadent. Its trappings are enticing but dispassionate, and it grows fearful of the magic at its core. A magic world view is central to our theology. A narrow world view is not.

506

"When I was a young man, I prayed for a sure testimony, some manifestation of God that would release me from doubt. *I believe in the gift of tongues, prophecy, revelation, visions, healing, interpretation of tongues, and so forth.* But never since age eight when I was baptized, did I feel truly called by the Lord, or that my salvation was complete. I'd learned it all by rote but I never really knew it by heart."

"Did that testimony ever come?" Susan asked.

Joshua hesitated for a moment, then answered softly. "Yes, that first night, as Adam slept, when the moon rose full above the steep sandstone cliffs of Zion. It was as if the messenger of the Almighty was diffusing His love through all His works. With the shock of pure knowledge, I realized that God does not hate me, but wants me to know the other half of my soul. In that solitary, undiluted moment, the oldest and best of my being was called back to God. Whatever other unpardonable sin I may commit, I can never blaspheme against the Holy Ghost.

"Ah, Susan, your eyes say, '*That is blasphemy.*' 'Such is the way of an adulterous woman; she eateth, and wipeth her mouth, and saith, I have done no wickedness.' And I haven't."

Susan took her brother's hand. She knew no words of comfort to offer him.

"I'm no apostate," Joshua cried, "excommunicate though I may be. I want to solemnly bear you *my* testimony that God lives, that Jesus is the Christ, that this is God's true church on the earth today. I *know* that Joseph Smith is a true prophet of God, that Gordon Hinckley is a prophet of God, that the *Book of Mormon* is true. That I've tried with all my power to raise my sons and daughter to be faithful Latter-day Saints. And that, for time and all Eternity, I will love Trudy and Adam with all the strength of my soul. In Jesus' name. Amen."

Joshua took a deep breath. "I used to enjoy our testimony meetings, when the microphone was passed among the congregation. I felt such certainty that I *belonged*. But after I met Adam, I began to see the meetings as odd little rituals. The repetition of '*I know*' and '*I know*' bolsters the bonds of orthodoxy in everyone, so no one wanders toward heretical fringes. I would sit in the meetings and wonder to myself, if a man was known to violate a taboo, would three-fourths of Utah want to tear him apart?"

"Of course not, Joshua," Susan reassured him.

Joshua stood up and walked to the far window. "Look out this window, Susan, to the left, at those buildings on the horizon. I designed three of them, plus many others here and in St. George. What if I'd never gotten the chance to build them? An architect can't work alone."

Susan joined him at the window and looked to where Joshua was pointing.

"Through gritted teeth, my clients let me finish the projects I was building when the news of my excommunication was announced at the priesthood meeting. Though no reasons were divulged, they'd all heard the rumors and they knew. But when those projects were finished, the clients wouldn't read my bids for new work. In a year, my business failed and I was barely able to pay my debts. All at once, I knew how those Gentile merchants must've felt when Brigham Young excluded them from his monopoly.

"Before my excommunication, I never saw it, but suddenly, the institutions offered no place where I fit. I had no church, no political party, no fraternal club, not even an alumni association. My banker and broker stopped returning my calls. Even my family was torn. When I was sick and I needed the Church and community most, I found I was doubly damned. All I could count on was a cemetery plot next to Adam."

Susan took Joshua's hand again.

"Then a new, entrapping cynicism began to clamp itself around my soul. It was a cynicism so fresh that I could taste its metallic flavor lying at the base of my tongue. Our lack of cynicism accounts for so much of our strength.

"For the first time in my life, I felt powerless and treated unjustly. I had no work, so I was rapidly depleting what I'd saved. I couldn't even sell my life insurance because I knew my family will need it. I thought to myself, 'Dad has invested well, and he'll surely give me an advance on the inheritance my kids will get someday.' So I drove down Highway 15 to St. George. But as I neared the exit, I remembered how Dad wouldn't even come to the phone. And I resolved, 'I'll be damned if I ask to borrow money from him.'

"So I didn't turn off the freeway at St. George. Instead, I kept driving southwest, toward Las Vegas. For the first time, I thought of gambling, and how winning had to be a sign that God has not forgotten me. Adrift on the freeway, I felt no permanence of community or family, no spiritual or economic guidance that the Church has always given us from *before* the cradle to *beyond* the grave. So I drove fast to get there, thinking about Elvis as the impersonation of Las Vegas, his bloated image the flip side of youthful desires. But then, somewhere in the Arizona desert, an extraordinary thing happened."

"What was it?" Susan asked.

Joshua slowly shook his head. "Halfway between the Utah and Nevada state lines, the fuel pump of my car broke down, and the engine began to sputter and die. As I steered the car to the side of the road, I *knew* it could only be a sign. Gambling was no answer for me. In awe, I fell to my knees at the mystery of God's ways.

"I stayed only a few minutes, knowing I should get out of there quickly. There was no shade, and the heatwaves, 110 degrees, were radiating up from the asphalt. I waited for an opening in the traffic, then darted across the freeway to the northeast-bound side. Waves of heat invaded my skull as I ran, and gusts of alkali dust scorched my eyes. I felt dizzy as I stuck out my thumb to hitch a ride.

"Dusk was approaching, and the intense yellow light of the sun was fading into slanting red rays. But no one would stop to pick me up. As they raced by without slowing, the heavy trucks kicked alkali grit in my face. I tasted the bitter dust on my tongue and began to worry. Life is fragile in the alkali desert, and not much daylight was left.

"Finally, in the twilight, a Winnebago with Utah plates pulled over a dozen yards ahead of me. I couldn't see who was in it, and I didn't care as I ran toward it. I gratefully climbed inside and nodded to my rescuers, a woman and two men, all elderly and dressed in white. As the driver sped back toward Utah, the other man gave me a jug of cold water, which I drank thirstily. Then the woman handed me a soft, damp cloth for my face. They were smiling and gentle, as if blessed with their choices in life. Though I was dizzy from the heat and the dust, I knew they were none other than the Three Nephites."

"From that storybook we had when we were kids?" Susan asked.

"Yes. Do you remember it?"

"I think so," Susan said. "After Jesus ascended from the Holy Sepulchre, he went to South America and gathered twelve disciples around him. He taught them the gospel, raised a dead man and cured the sick, then he prepared to return to his Father. But before he left, he asked what each disciple desired most. Nine of them asked to be reunited with him immediately after they died."

Joshua nodded. "But the other three Nephites requested a different destiny. They asked to wander the world, beholding the doings of the Father unto the children of men, until Jesus returned to them again. I never imagined them as three retirees speeding up Highway 15 in a Winnebago, one of them a woman, no less. But I recognized the Nephites at once. And if I knew who *they* were, they must know who *I* am, too.

"And so I saw that there was hope. And there *was* hope. The next week, a contractor I knew from BYU, hired me, with a wink, on a job."

"There's always hope," Susan said. "Like how those new drugs have made you almost like yourself again."

Joshua crossed the fingers of both hands.

"I was away so much of that time," Susan said. "How long was it before you got sick?"

"I took extravagantly good care of myself," Joshua replied. "And for three years, I didn't show symptoms. Each day, I'd examine my body for purple lesions, my tongue for thrush, and my armpits for lumps. It was almost ceremonial, like some ritual to ward off leprosy. I poured the energy into my body that

510

I'd always expended on the Church. But it felt unnatural. Our rituals were so thoroughly ingrained that I had to force myself to eat on our fast days.

"One morning, I awoke and found my sheets soaked through with perspiration. For two years, I grew thinner by the day and more weakened by infection after infection. In those worst days, I'd feel surreal and split off, as if I were already dead and freed of time. But I also felt a poignancy and clarity that let me laugh and cry with more intensity than my soul had ever known. Without the drugs, I would have died. But do you know what gives me just as much hope?"

"What?" Susan asked.

"*We believe all that God has revealed, all that He does now reveal, and we believe that He will yet reveal many great and important things pertaining to the Kingdom of God.*"

Susan nodded. "Yes, of course."

"I was in my car that day in 1978, when the radio announced the news of President Kimball's revelation. Men of African descent could now become priests! Tears of joy filled my eyes as I thought of the Brazilians I had known. Some of them had Negro blood but raised money nonetheless to build the Temple. I honked my horn and flashed my lights, and felt the thrill of kinship when people in other cars did the same. So what if the *Church News* quickly warned us against interracial marriage? It's a sign of hope for future revelations! Same-sex marriage could even be a sacrament in the Mormon Church someday."

Susan smiled indulgently. "I hope you aren't counting on that, Joshua."

Joshua laughed out loud. "The sin isn't in sexual relations but in *abandonment*," he argued. "The answer is commitment, as it's always been, and sanctification of that commitment. How I would've loved being sealed to Adam in the sealing room of the Temple! In those long mirrored walls that face each other, his reflection would reflect mine to infinity. We even have precedent for sanctifying the relationships of notoriously non-monogamous men."

Susan looked at her brother in disbelief.

511

"No, Susan, I'm not holding my breath. President Kimball no doubt heard whisperings from the IRS back then, concerning our tax-deductible tithes. Still, we could be blessed with a revelation about our Heavenly Mother."

Susan sighed. "I'm not counting on that, either."

"But doesn't the *possibility* gives you hope?" Joshua asked. "An Apostle said, 'The Church is bold enough to go so far as to declare that man has an Eternal Mother in the Heavens as well as an Eternal Father.' And President Hinckley says, 'The fact that we do not pray to our Mother in Heaven in no way belittles or denigrates her. None of us knows anything about her.' I suppose She must reveal Herself, or remain unrevealed.

"Do you remember the Branch Davidians a few years back? They were, like us, a charismatic, millenarian sect, whose leader was a polygamist, and who armed themselves to the teeth. They refused to surrender after killing four Federal agents, until the Government lost patience and stormed their fortress. Seventy-five men, women and children were killed or committed suicide. In vengeance, two years later, a bomb in a Federal building killed 168 people, many of them women and children. As you watched these tragedies unfold on television, didn't you see *us* 150 years earlier?"

"Well, yes," Susan said. "Blood was shed in Missouri, in Carthage and Nauvoo, on the exodus West, then Mountain Meadows."

"Why were *we* different?" Joshua asked. "We had someplace to go, to be sure, and thousands of skilled converts, eager to build Zion. Yet we are different. The year Joseph Smith was killed, 10,000 Millerites were praying for the End of Days. The year he prophesized he would see God, Indians by the thousands were dancing the Ghost Dance to usher in the resurrection. But not us. Joseph Smith may have invited assassination, but he had no death wish. Ours has always been a *life* wish. That was the wisdom I disregarded when I didn't ask Adam to be tested again."

Joshua turned and pointed out the window. "Look at those mountains, Susan. Aren't they beautiful, still capped with

512

snow? Who can doubt that Utah is indeed the Promised Land? Even the Government has recognized it and set aside more National Parks per mile of territory than in any other state. Who can stand at the rim of Bryce Canyon, above the orange, eroded rocks that seem to glow from inside, and not be stirred to the soul? Or not be charmed by the whimsically-balanced red rock magic of Arches."

"Utah is a colorful place," Susan agreed. "The salmon-colored cliffs at Zion, the Green River through Canyonlands, the white domes of Capitol Reef."

"Do you remember that place we used to go near Capitol Reef?" Joshua asked.

"Yes, I loved our picnics there," Susan said. "Cohab Canyon, it was called. I never thought of it back then, but Cohab Canyon must've been a place where the old polygamists hid out."

Joshua smiled at the old memories. "I'd never thought about it, either. But we're the only organized community in America that's actually been in the closet!"

"I wouldn't put it that way," Susan said.

"How would you put it? Our great-great-grandfather hid out, and President John Taylor, who died in hiding at age 78. President Joseph F. Smith fathered eleven children by five wives *after* we swore we'd give it up. The old polygamists couldn't abandon the wives they loved, just because of an irreligious law. And I'm no less unrepentant than they were."

"It's hard to imagine sharing Lloyd with other women," Susan said. "I'm glad the Government made us stop."

"We must *cherish* our history of standing up to Government persecution and mobs. Our history is a grand experiment in making our revelations come to pass."

"Most of it is grand," Susan agreed. "But some of it makes us sound so peculiar."

"And there've been failures," Joshua said. "But as well as trumpeting our many triumphs, we must understand our few failures. Yet we unabashedly continue to excommunicate our best historians and authors who write anything critical of the

513

Church."

"Well, they make us sound extreme."

"If we'd been less extreme, we'd be a footnote to the history of Ohio! The extremity of our ancestors was their passion. What could be more passionate than Joseph's belief that 'God himself was once as we are now, and is an exalted man, and sits enthroned in yonder heavens! That is the great secret!'"

"Those ideas seem strange to most Christians," Susan said. "We should stress what we have in common with them."

"But if we grow much less extreme, we might someday be a footnote to the history of Utah."

Susan shook her head. "I hardly think so, Joshua."

"Don't scoff, Susan. Who thinks these days of the Baptists of Rhode Island or the Quakers of Pennsylvania? We demand a high price to be Latter-day Saints. Time and tithes, and less certainty of salvation than the Fundamentalist Christians can guarantee. In America, we can't compete as just another Protestant faith."

"Our prophets are *still* seers," Susan argued. "We're approaching ten million Latter-day Saints around the world, and our numbers grow nearly five percent each year."

"Even while obliterating the names of excommunicates like me."

"That can change," Susan said.

"How can I rejoin the Church?" Joshua asked. "We've joined forces with the same sort of people who persecuted us in the past, and now vote as a block for *traditional family* values."

"But that's where morality lies," Susan said.

"Actually having *read* the Bible should disqualify us from brandishing it as a weapon! We mustn't abdicate to a simplistic Fundamentalism."

"If scriptures are too hard to understand," Susan said, "people will miss the moral lessons."

"But we're *different*," Joshua argued. "We mustn't let our converts, who covet what we've created, back us away from the testimonies that created it."

"The Authorities have warned that too personal a religion

can lead to faith-destroying activities."

"Their overriding ambition is to *not offend the Brethren,*" Joshua said. "An arrogant and overweening bureaucracy can too readily eclipse the individual and spiritual insights that gave rise to the Church."

"Revelation to our Prophets gave rise to the Church."

"I agree!" Joshua cried. "How can *we* be leading the charge to limit freedoms to express ideas that might be socially or religiously *unpopular*!"

"Some ideas are dangerous to a decent society," Susan said.

"How can free agency exist without free thought? Dissention has a price, but not as high a price as suppression. Smashing the *Nauvoo Expositor* cost the lives of Joseph and Hyrum Smith."

"Perhaps, but things have gone well for us after we stopped fighting the Government."

"We *twice* took on the U.S. Government," Joshua said. "And now we're trying to make the flag sacrosanct."

Susan looked intently at her younger brother, then she whispered, "Joshua, are you having sex with men?"

He sighed. "Only abstinence is perfectly safe."

"But Joshua, if you aren't having sex with men, why can't you quietly rejoin the Church?"

Joshua hesitated, then shook his head. "Because denying love, once you've been blessed with it, is forsaking faith. It's apostasy, and the fruits of apostasy are bitter indeed."

"You don't have to deny your love for Adam. You can say nothing about it."

"How can I say nothing when everything I've felt is its opposite? Do you know what it is to feel nothing? The Know-Nothings who filled the mobs in Illinois and Missouri, what did they feel? Anxiety, to be sure, and their own authority. But most of what they felt was negation. Incapable of imagining God in themselves, they denied that holiness is possible in anyone."

The door to the hospital room opened gently and Rachel stepped into the hallway. Susan and Joshua walked over to her.

"Is he any better?" Susan asked.

"Well, he's alert," Rachel said. "But the stroke, at least for now, has left him unable to speak."

"Will he see me?" Joshua asked.

"Dad didn't shake his head, 'No,' when I asked him."

Joshua could feel his heart beating in his chest. His mouth felt dry.

"What should I say to him, Rachel? We haven't been in the same room for years."

"Don't upset him, Joshua. For God's sake, don't tell him what you think of Boyd Packer."

"But Packer may become the next President of the Church. Twenty years ago, he encouraged physical assaults against gay men!"

"Don't tell him that," Rachel insisted. "And no politics. Don't talk about Orrin Hatch running for President."

"But Orrin Hatch is the first Mormon to run for President since Joseph Smith."

"Can you talk about it calmly with Dad?"

Joshua thought for a moment. "Hatch is excellent on AIDS and hate crimes legislation. But he's signed a pledge, promulgated by the Fundamentalists, against gay rights."

"Don't tell Dad that, either," Rachel sighed. "Just talk to him. You can only stay a few minutes."

"Tell him about the time you took Trudy and your kids to Nauvoo," Susan said.

"Why that?"

"Because it's safe."

Joshua opened the door and went inside. His heart raced as he saw the elderly man he was no longer sure that he knew. Joshua smiled weakly at his mother, then kissed her cheek.

"Hello, Dad," he said.

Frank Bailey did not smile, but Joshua was uncertain if the stroke had damaged the muscles in his face. The clock on the wall loudly ticked away the scant minutes he was allowed. Joshua took a deep breath.

"Did I ever tell you about the time that Trudy and I brought

516

the children on a pilgrimage to Nauvoo?"

Astrid smiled gently. "I always wanted to go there, Joshua. What did you see?"

Joshua sat down in a chair close to his parents. "Trudy and the kids and I took a horse-drawn wagon ride through the old, wide streets of Nauvoo. We toured the houses lived in long ago by Joseph Smith and Brigham Young, and some others, maybe even the house of John and Amelia Carter. We saw the gunshop of Jonathan Browning, and the printshop for the *Times and Seasons*. Beneath the masthead of the newspaper were the words, 'Truth will prevail.' We climbed the bluff to where the Temple once stood, witnessed now by just a few foundation stones. A different city squats there now, but old Nauvoo is not a ghost town. Its spirit is equally alive as ours.

"My wife and kids were eating cookies at an old bakeshop, so I walked alone down the bluff to the Mississippi River and stood facing west across it. I tried to imagine how it looked, 150 years ago, through the eyes of Great-great grandmother Amelia. She knew the river was just the next of a thousand more obstacles to freedom. What made her cross it? Amelia could've retreated to her father in Pennsylvania, to a comfortable home in a well-established place. I thought about the many letters I'd read to and from her sister, and I understood what Amelia must have felt. *Correctness is not measured by acceptability.*

"Then I recognized how much I have in common with our ancestors, and how blessed we are by their deeds. Amelia, who braved dangers for the passions of her spirit, and John, who died in prison, never renouncing the love sealed to him by faith. Ted, whose soul was seized by a hopeful new society, but wouldn't shield his eyes from its flaws. Molly, who bent the rules to fit herself in, and Anders, who found his world burst into color when the truth of his life was revealed."

Joshua took his parents' hands into his own. "I stayed there awhile, gazing out across the river, until the children were clamoring to leave. And as I looked west one last time, I knew that I, like Amelia and John, would have had the faith to cross it.

"There are dams downstream on the Mississippi now, and

the river is wider now than then. And I know that my children will have even wider rivers to cross. I pray they'll have the faith to forge ahead, and not be afraid and retreat. Because free will is being guided by the whisperings. And if we're afraid to listen, then revelation will cease."

# SOURCES

Arrington, Leonard J. and Davis Bitton, *The Mormon Experience* (New York: Knopf, 1979).

Arrington, Leonard J. and Wayne K. Hinton, "Origin of the Welfare Plan," in *Brigham Young University Studies* (Vol. 5-2, pp. 67-85, Winter 1964).

Bancroft, Hubert Howe, *The History of Utah* (San Francisco: History Company, 1889).

Barlett, Donald L. and James B. Steele, *Empire: The Life, Legend, and Madness of Howard Hughes* (New York: W.W. Norton & Company, 1979).

Beardsley, Harry M., *Joseph Smith and His Mormon Empire* (Boston: Houghton Mifflin, 1931).

Beecher, Maureen Ursenbach, "Priestess Among the Patriarchs," in Guarneri, Carl and David Alvarez, eds., *Religion and Society in the American West* (Lanham, Maryland: University Press of America, 1987).

Bishop, M. Guy, "The Mormon Colony at San Bernardino, California," in Guarneri, Carl and David Alvarez, eds., *Religion and Society in the American West* (Lanham, Maryland: University Press of America, 1987).

Bloom, Harold, *The American Religion* (New York: Simon & Schuster, 1992).

Bradford, Mary L., "The Odyssey of Sonia Johnson" and "All on Fire: An Interview with Sonia Johnson," in *Dialogue: A Journal of Mormon Thought* (Vol. 14-2, pp. 14-47, Summer 1981).

Britsch, R. Lanier, *Unto the Islands of the Sea* (Salt Lake City: Deseret Book Company, 1986).

Brodie, Fawn M., *No Man Knows My History* (New York: Alfred A. Knopf, 1946).

Brooks, Juanita, *Mountain Meadows Massacre* (Stanford: Stanford University Press, 1950).

Brooks, Juanita, *Quicksand and Cactus* (Salt Lake City: Howe Brothers, 1982).

Brown, James S., *Life of a Pioneer* (Salt Lake City: George Q. Cannon & Sons, 1900).

Browning, John and Curt Gentry, *John M. Browning, American Gunmaker* (New York: Doubleday & Co., 1964).

Buerger, David John, "The Development of the Mormon Temple Endowment Ceremony," in *Dialogue* (Vol. 20-4, pp. 33-76, Winter 1987).

Bush, Lester E., Jr., "Excommunication and Church Courts," in *Dialogue* (Vol. 14-2, pp. 74-98, Summer 1981).

Carpenter, Delburn, *The Radical Pietists* (New York: AMS Press, 1975).

Carr, Robin L., *Freemasonry and Nauvoo* (Bloomington: Illinois Lodge of Research, 1989).

Church of Jesus Christ of Latter-day Saints, *My Kingdom Shall Roll Forth* (Salt Lake City: The Church of Jesus Christ of Latter-day Saints, 1980).

Coates, James, *In Mormon Circles: Gentiles, Jack Mormons and Latter Day Saints* (Reading, Mass.: Addison-Wesley, 1991).

Coates, Lawrence G., "The Mormons and the Ghost Dance," in *Dialogue* (Vol. 18-4, pp. 89-111, Winter 1985).

Coates, Lawrence G., "The Spalding-Whitman and Lemhi Missions: A Comparison," in *Idaho Yesterdays* (Vol. 31-1, pp. 38-46, Spring-Summer 1987).

Cross, Whitney R., *The Burned-Over District* (Ithaca: Cornell University Press, 1950).

Decker, Ed, *Decker's Complete Handbook on Mormonism* (Eugene, Oregon: Harvest House Publishers, 1995).

Demson, William R., *10,000 Famous Freemasons* (St. Louis: Missouri Lodge of Research, 1957).

DeVoto, Bernard, *The Year of Decision: 1846* (Boston: Little, Brown & Co., 1943).

Ellsworth, S. George, ed., *The Journals of Addison Pratt* (Salt Lake City: University of Utah Press, 1990).

Ellsworth, S. George, *Zion in Paradise* (Logan: Utah State University Press, 1959).

Esplin, Fred C., "The Church as Broadcaster," in *Dialogue* (Vol. 10-3, pp. 25-45, Spring 1977).

Foster, Lawrence, *Religion and Sexuality: Three American Communal Experiments of the Nineteenth Century* (New York: Oxford University Press, 1981).

Foster, Lawrence, "Reluctant Polygamists," in Guarneri, Carl and David Alvarez, eds., *Religion and Society in the American West* (Lanham, Maryland: University Press of America, 1987).

Gauguin, Paul, *Noa Noa* (San Francisco: Chronicle Books, 1994).

Goodwin, S. H., *Mormonism and Masonry: A Utah Point of View* (Salt Lake City, 1934).

Gottlieb, Robert and Peter Wiley, *America's Saints* (New York: G.P. Putnam's Sons, 1984).

Grover, Mark L., "Religious Accommodation in a Land of Racial Democracy: Mormon Priesthood and Black Brazilians," in *Dialogue* (Vol. 17-3, pp. 22-34, Autumn 1984).

Haslam, Gerald M., *Clash of Cultures: The Norwegian Experience with Mormonism, 1842-1920* (New York: Peter Lang, 1984).

Heinerman, John and Anson Shupe, *The Mormon Corporate Empire* (Boston: Beacon Press, 1985). Updated in Shupe, Anson, *Wealth and Power in American Zion* (Lewiston, New York: Edwin Mellen Press, 1992).

Hogan, Mervin B., *The Vital Statistics of Nauvoo Lodge* (Des Moines, 1976); *The Origin and Growth of Utah Masonry and Its Conflict with Mormonism* (Salt Lake City, 1978); and *Freemasonry and Civil Confrontation on the Illinois Frontier* (Salt Lake City, 1981).

Hunter, Rodello, *A Daughter of Zion* (New York: Knopf, 1972).

Jensen, Vernon H., "The 'Legend' and the 'Case' of Joe Hill," in *Dialogue* (Vol. 2-1, pp. 97-109, Spring 1967).

Jorgensen, Joseph G., *The Sun Dance Religion* (Chicago: University of Chicago Press, 1972).

Kay, Robert F., *Tahiti & French Polynesia* (Hawthorn, Victoria, Australia: Lonely Planet Publications, 1992).

Kessler, Ronald, *The Richest Man in the World: The Story of*

*Adnan Khashoggi* (New York: Warner Books, 1986).

Klein, Maury, *Union Pacific: The Birth of a Railroad, 1862-1893* (New York: Doubleday, 1987).

Laake, Deborah, *Secret Ceremonies* (New York: William Morrow and Co., 1993).

Larson, Gustive O., *The "Americanization" of Utah for Statehood* (San Marino: The Huntington Library, 1971).

Launius, Roger D. and Linda Thatcher, eds., *Differing Visions: Dissenters in Mormon History* (Urbana: University of Illinois Press, 1994).

Loveland, Jerry K., "Hagoth and the Polynesian Tradition," in *Brigham Young University Studies* (Vol. 17-1, pp. 59-73, Autumn 1976).

Melville, Herman, *Typee* (New York: Penguin Books, 1964).

Merrill, Milton R., *Reed Smoot: Apostle in Politics* (Logan: Utah State University Press, 1990).

Myres, Sandra L., *Westering Women and the Frontier Experience, 1800-1915* (Albuquerque: University of New Mexico Press, 1982).

Neff, Andrew Love, *History of Utah, 1847-1869* (Salt Lake City: Deseret News Press, 1940).

Newbury, Colin W., *Tahiti Nui: Change and Survival in French Polynesia, 1767-1945* (Honolulu: University Press of Hawaii, 1980).

Parrington, Vernon Louis, *The Romantic Revolution in America, 1800-1860* (Norman: University of Oklahoma Press, 1987).

Peterson, Scott, *Native American Prophecies* (New York: Paragon House, 1990).

Powers, Richard Gid, *Secrecy and Power: The Life of J. Edgar Hoover* (New York: The Free Press, 1987).

Quinn, D. Michael, *Early Mormonism and the Magic World View* (Salt Lake City: Signature Books, 1987).

Quinn, D. Michael, "Ezra Taft Benson and Mormon Political Conflicts," in *Dialogue* (Vol. 26-2, pp. 1-87, Summer 1993).

Quinn, D. Michael, ed., *The New Mormon History* (Salt

Lake City: Signature Books, 1992).

Quinn, D. Michael, *Same-Sex Dynamics among Nineteenth-Century Americans: A Mormon Example* (Urbana: University of Illinois Press, 1996).

Rae, William Fraser, *Westward By Rail* (New York: Indian Head Books, 1993).

Scharffs, Gilbert, *Mormonism in Germany* (Salt Lake City: Deseret Book Company, 1970).

Scott, Anne Firor, "Mormon Women, Other Women: Paradoxes and Challenges," in *Journal of Mormon History* (Vol. 13, pp. 2-19, 1986).

Shaffer, Donald R., "Hiram Clark and the First LDS Hawaiian Mission," in *Journal of Mormon History* (Vol. 17, pp. 94-109, 1991).

Skousen, W. Cleon, *The Naked Communist* (Salt Lake City: Ensign Publishing Company, 1958).

Smith, Joseph, Jr., *The Book of Mormon* (Salt Lake City: The Church of Jesus Christ of Latter-day Saints, 1990).

Smith, Joseph Fielding, *Essentials in Church History* (Salt Lake City: Deseret Book Company, 1950).

Stegner, Wallace, *The Gathering of Zion* (Lincoln: University of Nebraska Press, 1992).

Stegner, Wallace, *Mormon Country* (New York: Duell, Sloan and Pearce, 1942).

Stone, Irving, *Men to Match My Mountains* (New York: Berkley Books, 1982).

Taylor, Samuel W., *Nightfall at Nauvoo* (New York: Macmillan Company, 1971).

Tuttle, Daniel S., *Missionary to the Mountain West* (Salt Lake City: University of Utah Press, 1987).

U.S. House of Representatives, Subcommittee on Armed Services, Special Subcommittee on Intelligence (Washington, D.C., July 2, 1974).

Utley, Robert M., *Frontier Regulars: The United States Army and the Indians, 1865-1890* (New York: Macmillan Company, 1973).

Walker, Ronald W., "The Liberal Institute," in *Dialogue*

(Vol. 10-4, pp. 75-85, Autumn 1977).

Wallace, Irving, *The Twenty-Seventh Wife* (New York: Simon & Schuster, 1961).

Walton, Brian, "A University's Dilemma: BYU and Blacks," in *Dialogue* (Vol. 6-1, pp. 31-36, Spring 1971).

Watkins, Ronald J., *High Crimes and Misdemeanors: The Term and Trials of Former Governor Evan Mecham* (New York: William Morrow and Co., 1990).

Whalen, William J., *The Latter-Day Saints in the Modern Day World* (New York: John Day Co., 1964).

# About the Authors

Carol T.F. Bennett and Joseph Friedman are neither Mormons nor ex-Mormons. Having known and liked many Latter-day Saints, they found themselves intrigued by this thoroughly and uniquely American story, from its founding by a poor but ingenious young man, to its theocratic Manifest Destiny. And the story continues into the controversies of today: the conflicts between individual passions and entrenched authority, and how communities deal with nonconformity.

Carol Bennett has a Ph.D. in Economics and lives in Austin, Texas. She has worked for a bank and a large accounting firm, and has been an independent consultant. Joseph Friedman completed a second B.A. in History at the University of California after his retirement from the Federal Government. He is a veteran of World War II and a Mason, and lives outside San Francisco. They are father and daughter.

Printed in the United States
4051

9 781585 009947